Agnes M Stewart

The Life and Letters of Sir Thomas More

Agnes M Stewart

The Life and Letters of Sir Thomas More

ISBN/EAN: 9783744688871

Printed in Europe, USA, Canada, Australia, Japan

Cover: Foto ©Raphael Reischuk / pixelio.de

More available books at **www.hansebooks.com**

THE
LIFE AND LETTERS

OF

SIR THOMAS MORE

BY

AGNES M. STEWART,

Authoress of "Margaret Roper," "Florence O'Neill," "General Questions,"
"Biographical Readings," &c., &c.

CROMWELL. Sir Thomas More is chosen Chancellor in your place.
WOLSEY.   That's somewhat sudden.
But *he's a learned man*, may he continue
Long in his Highness's favor, and do justice
For truth's sake and his conscience, that his bones,
When he has run his course, and sleeps in blessings,
May have a tomb of orphans' tears wept on 'em.
                    HENRY VIII. ACT III., SCENE 2.

LONDON:
BURNS & OATES, PORTMAN STREET,
AND PATERNOSTER ROW.

1876.

LIVERPOOL :
PRINTED BY MATTHEWS BROTHERS, THOMAS STREET.

PREFACE.

With a feeling of extreme diffidence we devoted ourselves to the task of writing a life of that Christian hero and philosopher, the learned and estimable Sir Thomas More.

His character is one on which the mind loves to linger, so learned was he, yet so simple in his ways; full of innocent playfulness as a little child; ever unmindful of self and beneficent to others, so that he may justly be regarded as one of the best and greatest of Englishmen.

It was well for those amongst whom he lived that he was mistaken as to his vocation to a religious life, for he was doubtless destined by Providence as a bright example, to show unto others how they should educate their children, serve their country, and, at the same time, practise the christian virtues of piety, humility, and continency.

It is hoped that the Letters, and abstracts of letters written by More, which have been printed in this volume, may be perused with interest by the reader; indeed, without them, it would have seemed superfluous to publish the work, various lives of the Chancellor having already been written. The limits of this volume have forbidden the publication of more than portions of some of them, on account of their extreme length, but many are given in their entirety; and of the remainder, the pith of each has been extracted, whilst all are reproduced which have appeared in the pages of the old biographer, Cresacre More.

A far better idea of the noble and heroic character of the Chancellor may be gathered from his own epistles than from the words of others ; and it is hoped that the present humble attempt at gathering together much that has not appeared in former works may meet with a gracious reception, though some more worthy pen than ours shall perchance write hereafter of this brave English Martyr, collecting together further documents deposited perhaps in Libraries, to which we have not been so privileged as to have access.

The character of Sir Thomas More was great in all its moral aspects, for it was never sullied by ambition or avarice, and whilst bound to Henry by the greatness of the benefits that had been conferred upon him, and entirely loyal at the same time, he was proof against blandishments and threats, and though from the first moment that he thwarted the wishes of the despotic Tudor sovereign he must have been well aware that life-long imprisonment, or the block, would be the result, he yet stood firm unto the last, steady and true to the voice of his own conscience.

His famous work, the Utopia, won for him the greatest popularity at home and abroad, and one would think that some of the passages with which it abounds must needs have been unpleasant to the Tudor King.

"In the Counsels of Princes," he therein observes, "good advice proves of no avail, because the servant is never consulted by the master, except with the view of gratifying his passions." This great man was far in advance of the times in which he lived, for in his Utopia, written more than three centuries ago, he anticipates Lord Ashley's factory bill, advocating six hours for labour and the rest for recreation and study, and also condemning the heavy punishments then inflicted for small crimes of theft, &c.*

In his imaginary Republic, fathers and grandfathers, with their married sons and daughters, reside together as one family, and if such a style of living be deemed incompatible with family harmony, More's own conduct proved the contrary, for he, like a true philosopher, set the example by practising his own precepts in an exemplary manner.

His contemporaries have left the abundant proof that in More's home at Chelsea there was no strife or discord, but

* Lord Campbell.

that, on the contrary, peace, love, refinement, purity, and all the little courtesies and amenities of life were most tenderly cherished ; and that never was master more faithfully served, friend more valued, or father more beloved, than was Sir Thomas More.

In his Utopia, that fairy-land born of his imagination, every man was to be at perfect liberty to follow whatever religion he pleased, and to try to draw others to it by force of argument ; but ten years later, after the change of religion brought in by Lutheranism, and branching off into many other sectaries, had desolated Europe, a great change had taken place in the feelings of More, a prophetic fear filled his mind, and he strove by all the means in his power to stem the tide of heresy, and devoted himself with all the energy of his earnest nature to the cause of the Church.

He and the Bishop of Rochester stand foremost in the army of English Martyrs for the supremacy of the Holy See, and many of those who afterwards shed their blood in defence of the same cause declared that courage had been infused into them by their example. More's own parish priest, Dr. Larke, of Chelsea, was so struck by his glorious death, says Stapleton, that he himself shortly afterwards suffered death in the same cause.

Before concluding we must remark that in looking over extracts made from Mr. Brewer's Calendar of State Papers, from which some abstracts of letters have been taken, we were intensely surprised by observing the following remark, concerning one of More's letters to Erasmus.

"More brings forward various instances to shew that the later Church had departed from the dogmas of the Fathers."

We happened to be in Lancashire when this paragraph was observed, and reference having been made in the Calendar to "Jortin's Erasmus," vol. iii., page 365, we at once went to London to examine this book at the British Museum.

Amongst many Latin letters or rather orations of More's, for such Jortin calls them, we came at once on the letter sought for. It extends to more than thirty pages of closely printed matter, in small type.

A copy was at once made of all that portion of the letter in which the remarks appeared, and, though personally a stranger, the writer took the liberty of applying to the Rev. Father Morris, the learned and accomplished author of "Troubles of our Catholic Forefathers," begging his opinion of the justice of Mr. Brewer's summary. He most kindly responded to her request and the following remarks were made by him after perusing the passages in question :—

"No Catholic has ever thought individual fathers to be infallible, or would be surprised to find that there were points on which they differed. This is all that More says, except in the case of the Immaculate Conception. There he asks whether there was one of the ancient Saints who did not believe that Our Blessed Lady was conceived in sin, if he meant literally what he said, it was of course very wrong, for it is impossible that the Church should ever accept as generally as he says, she accepted in his time, a doctrine, the contrary of which was explicitly taught by the unanimous voice of the holy Fathers and Doctors. But the expression may be regarded as an inadvertent exaggeration in the warmth of argument. If Mr. Brewer attributes to More the statement that the modern Church had departed from the dogmas of the Fathers, such a statement would be an attack by More, not on the Fathers, but on the Catholic Church of his own time—of this there is no trace in the words you have sent me, unless it be deduced from the phrase about the Immaculate Conception ; and it would be very illogical from a particular statement, even if literally meant, to deduce so general a conclusion.

" All that can be drawn from the marked passages seems to be that More defended the statement of Erasmus that some of the holy Fathers, whom he mentions in very eulogistic terms, have fallen into occasional errors—*lapsos alicubi.*"

" If the errors were on points of doctrine, not at that time decided by the Church, I do not see what difficulty there is in his having thus defended his friend. The words cannot, without straining, be taken to mean more than this."

More's best interpreter is More himself, so we will conclude with a quotation, from a conversation on this subject held with Margaret in the Tower.*

The original may be met with in More's works, and is embodied in a very long letter, which we have copied into this volume, save about a page of which this forms part, and which would not interest the general reader.

This edition of More's works, we believe, was printed about the year 1570.

"For an example of some such matters, I have, I trow told you before now, Megg, that whether Our Blessed Lady was conceived in sin or not, was sometimes a great question amongst the learned men of Christendom, and whether it be yet decided by any general Council, I remember not, but this I remember well, that notwithstanding that the feast of her Immaculate Conception was celebrated in the

---

* It will (adds Father Morris) be regarded as thoroughly satisfactory by those who know that unity in doctrine is derived from submission to the decisions of authority. Even saints may differ, and until the Church has spoken may be expected to differ. These differences in that which is undefined bring out into the clearest relief the unanimity that follows the definitions of the Church. This is what Sir Thomas More says to his daughter, and it is what, as a Catholic, he meant to say to Erasmus, though he has expressed himself more rhetorically and with less accuracy in one case than in the other.

Churches, or at least in various provinces, yet was holy S. Bernard, which, as his manifold books written in praise of Our Lady testifieth, devoutly loved all things tending to her commendation, yet was that holy and devout man against that part of her praise, as appeareth by an epistle of his wherein he argueth against, and approveth not the institution of that feast, and he was not alone of this mind, but many other well learned men with him, and right holy men too. On the other side was the blessed and holy Bishop S. Anselm, and he not alone neither, but many well learned and virtuous were with him also. And they, Megg, be now two holy Saints in Heaven, with many more that were on either side, for neither side was then bound to change their opinion for the other, nor for any provincial Council either, but *after* the determination of a general Council, every man is bound to believe that way and to conform his conscience, to the determination of the general Council, then all they that held the contrary before, were for so holding blame-less."*

* Since the above was written a kind friend has favoured us with the following remarks—I have referred to the passage in the life and writings of S. Bernard respecting the doctrine of the Immaculate Conception. He finds fault with the Canons of the Cathedral of Lyons for introducing a new feast without authority from the Holy See. He objects in the same letter, to the Immaculate Conception, but not to the doctrine as defined by Pope Pius the 9th, and at the end of his letter, he says, "that in this as well as in every other question, he

Thus both, Sir Thomas and S. Bernard, were of one mind, namely, submission to the Roman Church.

As the plan we have adopted of giving the letters in the same type as the other portion of the work is unusual and may possibly be censured, we beg to say that we have preferred rather the convenience of the reader than the perhaps better appearance produced by the smaller type, the letters will by many persons, we feel confident, be considered very interesting. And we are equally sure that those who are advanced in life, or who are not blessed with strong sight, will be glad that they are printed in large type.

We are indebted to the courtesy and kindness of the Proprietor of the Illustrated London News, and of the Rev. R. Davis, Rector of the old parish Church of Chelsea ,for three of the Illustrations in this volume, and we take this opportunity of warmly thanking them. The former gave us his kind permission to copy by autotype process the meeting of Margaret and her father at the Tower Wharf; and the latter most kindly granted us the loan of Faulkner's Chelsea,

refers to the judgment and authority of the Roman Church, and that he is ready to retract, should he have advanced anything in opposition to the judgment which it may pass. Here is the Latin—"Romanæ presertim Ecclesiæ auctoritati atque examini *totum hoc* sicut et cætera qua ejusmodi, sunt universa reservo ; ipsius, si quid aliter sapio paratus judicio emendare."—*Epist. clxxiv.*

for engravings of Sir Thomas More's house and Monument.
The portrait of Sir Thomas was copied, by permission of
the Trustees of the British Museum, from Roper's " Life
of More."

LIST OF SUBSCRIBERS.

	COPIES.
The Right Rev. Dr. Amherst, Bishop of Northampton ...	1
His Grace the Archbishop of Cashel	1
His Grace the Archbishop of Cloyne	1
The Right Rev. Robert Cornthwaite, Bishop of Beverley	1
Rev. — Carbery, S.J.	1
Rev. P. Devlin	1
Rev. J. Duggan	1
Rev. W. Dunderdale	1
Rev. C. Dunne	1
Rev. T. Dykes, S J.	1
Rev. W. Fortuue	1
Rev. — Graley	1
Rev. E. Hannen	1
Rev. J. Hutton	1
Rev. J. Jackson, S.J.	1
Rev. D. O'Keefe	1
Very Rev. Canon Kershaw ...	1
Very Rev. Canon Last ...	1
Very Rev. Provost Doyle ...	1
Rev. Canon Browne	1
Rev. P. Lewis	1
Rev. P. Lynch	1
Rev. N. Nenci, D.D.	1
Rev. E. Purbrick, S.J. ...	2
Rev D. Ramsey	1
The Right Rev. Monsignor Woodlock	1
The Right Hon. Lord Acton ...	1
The Right Hon. Lady Arundell	·
Miss Amherst	1
Lady Bedingfeld	1
Mrs. Beckett	1

	COPIES.
Lady Blount	1
Mrs. Edward Blount	2
Mrs. Stephen Blount	1
Weld Blundell, Esq	1
J. B. Bowden, Esq.	1
L Bowring, Esq.	1
Mrs. Brady	1
N. Browne, Esq.	2
The Most Noble the Marquis of Bute	2
A. Butler, Esq.	1
Mrs. Cadman	1
The Right Hon. Lady Camoys	1
W. Campbell, Esq.	1
F. Chambers, Esq., M.D. ...	1
— Chamberlain, Esq	2
J. Chadwick, Esq.	1
Lady Chichester	1
Miss Cholmeley	1
Mrs. Coghlan	1
Convent, Cahir	1
,, Concepcion, Harbor	6
,, Clar	1
,, Clapham	6
The Right Hon. Lady Clifford	1
The Hon. Mrs. Clifford ...	2
C. Cranstoun, Esq.	2
James Cuddon, Esq.	1
Convent, Darlington	1
The Right Hon. Lady Denbigh	1
Mrs. De Lisle	4
E. H. Dering, Esq.	1
K. Digby, Esq.	1
Miss De Lys	1
C. O. Eaton, Esq.	1
C. Fairclough, Esq.	1

LIST OF SUBSCRIBERS.

	COPIES.		COPIES.
Hon. Mrs. Farrall	1	Mrs. Orme	1
The Right Hon. Lord Gainsborough	1	The Hon. Mrs. O'Ferrall	1
Right Hon. Lord Gerard	1	The Right Hon. Lady Petre	1
Mrs. Gerard	1	Miss Peel	1
Mrs. Gillow	2	The Hon. Mrs. Pereira	1
The Lady Grey	2	W. Prosser, Esq.	1
Miss Hales	1	A. Purcell, Esq.	1
Mrs. Haslem	1	Mrs. Purcell	1
C. Hargitt, Esq.	2	Convent, Plymouth	1
The Right Hon. Lady Herries	1	Mrs. Quick, English Convent, Bruges	6
The Right Hon. Lord Howard	6	The Most Noble the Marquis of Ripon	2
The Lady Holland	1	Mrs. Richardson	1
R. Hind, Esq.	1	Mrs. Rideout	1
Mrs. Hutchins	1	Miss Russell	1
Mrs. Jones	1	Mrs. Ryan	1
Mrs. Kelly	1	Convent, Roehampton	1
R. M. Kelly, Esq.	2	Mrs. Salvin	1
The Lady Henry Kerr	1	Lady Smythe	1
Convent, Killarney	1	A. Shee, Esq.	1
,, Kilkenny	1	Superioress, St. Margaret's, Edinburgh	1
Mrs. Leonard	1	Colonel Towneley	2
The Hon. Mrs. Lewis	1	— Topham, Esq.	1
The Hon. C. Lindsey	1	Mrs. Tozer	1
The Most Noble the Marchioness of Londonderry	1	Sir F. Turville	1
Miss Lightbound	2	T. H. Ware, Esq.	2
Mrs. Maher	1	Mrs. Watkins	1
T. Mapother, Esq.	1	Mrs. C. Weld	1
Mrs. Mercer	1	Miss Wilson	1
J. J. Murphy, Esq.	1	— Woolett, Esq., M.D.	1
— McVeigh, Esq.	1	Mrs. Worswick	1
Mrs. New	1	Convent, Wolverhampton	1
His Grace the Duke of Norfolk	6	,, Youghal	2
Her Grace the Duchess of Norfolk	2	Rev. S. Wells	1
— Noble, Esq., M.D.	1	Lord F. G. Osborne	1
Convent, Northampton	1	H. Whitgreave, Esq.	2
Convent, Norwood	1		

CONTENTS.

LIFE AND LETTERS

OF

SIR THOMAS MORE.

CHAPTER I.

THE BIRTH AND PARENTAGE OF SIR THOMAS MORE.

IN the year 1480, towards the close of the reign of our IVth Edward, in the, at that time, fashionable locality of Milk Street, in the Chepe, now Cheapside, a child was born, who, by the sterling virtues of his after life, diffused happiness and peace around him, and whose name will be held in reverent love and benediction as long as time itself shall endure by all who can appreciate that nobleness of mind, that generous unselfishness of spirit which shrinks from no earthly sacrifice even to the rendering up dear life itself, and considereth loss as gain, so that the path of duty be rigorously followed.

· Gifted with talents of the highest order, perceptible to those around him even in the early days of childhood, the name of the wise and just Sir Thomas More occupies a page in the history of his country, which will be read with interest and edification as long as the English language tself shall last.

" It cannot have escaped the observation of persons interested in the life of this great and good man, that his biographers are almost silent as to the family from which he sprung ; they take us no farther back than Sir Thomas's father, Sir John More, and he was no less a person than one of the superior judges, holding that dignity too for more than twelve years, and not dying till after his son had reached the highest legal position in the kingdom.

That Roper is silent cannot be attributed to ignorance, for he was not only the son-in-law of Sir Thomas, but was on terms of most affectionate intimacy with him, and it is hard to ascribe his silence to other than a delicate disinclination to expose what to weak minds he might fear would derogate from the respect with which the Chancellor was regarded. The great-grandson of Sir Thomas, now clearly proved by Mr. Hunter's investigations to be Cresacre More, endeavours to show that they were of gentle descent. He cites Sir Thomas's epitaph, commencing thus :—" Thomas More, born of no *noble* family, but of an honest stock"; but the word *nobilis* does not occur in the original, the passage stands as follows :—

" Thomae Morus, urbe Londinensi familia non *celebri* sed honesta natus," words simple enough, and which indicate that he could have his pedigree little beyond his father.

Cresacre More says Judge More bore arms from his birth, having his coat quartered, meaning, that in consequence of the marriage of one of his ancestors with the heiress of a family entitled to coat armour, he quartered the arms of that family with his own; on the monument at Chelsea, it is true, the arms of Sir Thomas are quartered, but the quartering may have belonged to Sir Thomas's mother.

The arms of Sir John, as depicted by Dugdale, from the window of the Refectory in Serjeant's Inn, Fleet Street, contain no quartering, and none of the pedigrees in Herald's College begin with an earlier name than that of Sir John, except some of a later date, which carry up the family, but without name or place, to an assumed grand-father. These, and the pedigree in the Ashmole Library, mentioned by Mr. Hunter, are evidently derived from Sir John's Will, in which he speaks of his grandmother, Joanna, daughter of John Leycester.

Looking then at the modest description given by Sir Thomas More himself, the total silence of his son-in-law, and the absence of all evidence to the contrary, it seems impossible to come to any other conclusion than that the family was an obscure one. Recent investigation has confirmed this opinion, but so far from detracting in any degree from the merit of the chancellor or the judge, it must be considered as speaking loudly to their own credit, as also that of those to whom they owed their elevation, shewing, that even in those days, virtue and learning met their due reward, and contradicting the idea that none but rich men's sons were admitted members of the Inns of Court.

Contradictory accounts are given of the Inns of Court to which John More belonged, of the bench on which he sat, and of the age at which he died.

As to the Inns of Court to which he belonged, Chauncey, in his History of Hertfordshire (p. 531) says, that he studied the law and was Reader at Lincoln's Inn ; and Dugdale, in his list of Readers at the Middle Temple names John More as one of them, naming him afterwards as one of the Judges of Common Pleas. If we examine the dates and facts we shall have a doubt whether the Judge can be identified with either.

Taking them in the order of date, John More of Lincoln's Inn, was Autumn Reader in 5th Henry VII., 1489, and Lent Reader in 1495. If this was the Judge, his elevation to the bench would be twenty-nine years after his first reading, an interval so great as to render the supposition that the Reader and the Judge were the same person highly improbable.

The name of More occurs in the Black Book, folio 1376, as early as 4th Edward IV., when a John More was raised from the office of butler to that of steward or seneschal, employed to collect the dues and keep the accounts, and in Michaelmas Term 1470, 49, (being the year of that king's temporary restoration) was admitted a member of the society, in reward for having conducted himself faithfully in the office of butler and steward, which the entry declares he had long filled, so that it may be well conceived at the date of his admission he was at least forty years of age.

He would then be progressively called to the bar, and raised to the bench, and in due time be appointed a Reader, and there can be no doubt that he was the Reader in 1489, at which time he would be about 59 years old; but were he the Judge who was appointed in 1518, he would have been no less than 88 years old.

As to the claims of the Middle Temple, Sir John More of that Society, was Autumn Reader there in 1505, and Lent Reader in 1512, dates which seems to agree with the year in which John More became a Judge, but there are two facts which exclude the idea that the Judge could have been the reader of the Middle Temple, this Judge was called · to the degree of the coif in 1503, and on that being assumed, it is well known the new serjeant leaves his original society and joins that of the judges and serjeants, and how could John More, made serjeant in 1503, be called on to read in the society he had left in 1512, after he had entered into another body?

It is difficult then to believe that either of them was the future judge.   Who then was he?

His biographers place him at Lincoln's Inn, and Roper records that, if the father and son met together at readings in Lincoln's Inn, the latter, though Chancellor, would offer in argument the pre-eminence to his father.

In the records of that Society, besides the former named John More, originally the butler, and then raised from the stewardship to be first a member and afterwards a Reader of the Society, another John More is to be found with the addition of "junior" to his name, who in 1482 (twelve years after the first John More had been admitted a member) is mentioned as *pincerna*, or butler.   It cannot be doubted that this John More was son of the first, holding as he did the same office which he had formerly filled. Fourteen years afterwards, on February 12, 1496, Thomas More, the chancellor, was admitted into the society, the entry describing him as the son of John More, without designating who John More was, leading to the inference that he was some person so well known as not to need description. That he was a member of the same society is especially apparent by the entry further stating that Thomas is pardoned four vacations at the instance of John More, his father.

His father must have been either John More, the former steward, or John More, the butler; for no other appears on the books at that time.

Presuming that the first was the father of Thomas and the father also of John More, junior, he would then have *two* sons, which would contradict the statements of all the biographers. If John More, junior, is excluded, then the birth of Sir Thomas, which is invariably fixed about 1480, must have been at a very late period of his father's life, the fact being, on the contrary, that he was the son of the first of three wives with whom his father was united. Sir Thomas therefore, being admitted in 1496, when only sixteen, could not have been the son of the elder More; the younger John must, however, have been twenty-eight or thirty in 1482, and if *he* was the Chancellor's father, it may be well conceived that, as he married early in life, he had a son two years of age, who, in 1496, would be ready to be admitted a member of the house, and to fix this parentage it only remains to account for John More, junior, being placed in such a position as afterwards to assume the coif and obtain a seat on the judicial bench.

John More, the elder, a member in 1470, must have been called to the bar long before 1482, when the younger is mentioned as butler, and as he was made Reader seven years afterwards, it is clear he was gaining an ascendancy in the Inn, and must previously have become a bencher, and with the natural feeling that he should wish his son to enjoy his own advantages, it seems almost a necessary step to his being admitted to the bench, that his son should be removed from a menial office. That no entry of his son's admission has been found may be accounted for by the carelessness with which the books were then kept, and the want of a regular list of admissions, that of Sir Thomas himself being inserted in a page devoted to other matters. Every Reader had, too, a special privilege of admitting any person he pleased into the Society,* so that no doubt can exist but that John More, junior, was admitted either before or at the time when his father became one of the Governors, or a Reader of the house ; and the interval between 1482 and 1503, when John More, the judge, was called serjeant, is amply sufficient for all the successive gradations.

A careful comparison of facts and dates leads to the only reasonable conclusion that John More, first butler, then steward, and finally the reader of Lincoln's Inn, was the Chancellor's grandfather, and that his son was the Chancellor's father, and afterwards the Judge. Not only does this descent suit precisely the "*Non celebri sed honesta natus,*" in Sir Thomas's epitaph, but it explains the silence of his biographers, and accounts for the Judge and the Chancellor attending the readings of a Society with which they had been so closely connected.

Such an investigation would be valueless if applied to an ordinary person, but it acquires a peculiar interest when a man of the highest eminence is the subject of enquiry, and who, whether he be lawyer, philosopher, or historian, will deny that title to Sir Thomas More ? Moreover, the fact is interesting, as it proves that, at a time when the barriers between the different grades of society were far more difficult to pass than in the present day, such talent united to

* Dugdale's Orig., 248.

integrity and worth, could overcome all the prejudices in favour of high descent which were the results of the feudal system.

Of the date of Sir John's elevation to the bench we have no precise information, but the uncertainty does not touch the point under discussion. He died about November, 1530, and was buried in the church of S. Lawrence in the Old Jewry. His great-grandson describes him before his death as being " near ninety years old," an idea founded on the supposition that he was the Lincoln's Inn Reader of 1489. This extreme old age all subsequent writers have adopted, without reflecting that in that case he would have been seventy-eight when raised to the bench, a time of life at which it is scarcely possible that any one would be selected for the first time to exercise judicial functions.*

On the family pictures preserved at Burford Priory and at Nostell Priory, painted in 1530, just before Sir John's death, he is described as aged seventy-six on one, and on the other seventy-seven.†

It is to be supposed that the old Judge was famous for a facetious turn of mind, which he transmitted to his son, if we credit the only saying which has come down to posterity, but let us hope he intended it rather as a compliment to the good qualities of the sex, three of whom he had chosen successively as partners, than a satire on women collectively.

He used to compare the multitude of women who are to be chosen for wives unto a bag full of snakes having amongst them a single eel : " Now, if a man should put his hand into

* Foss's Lives of the Judges.
† See Bruce's Archæologia, xxxv., p. 26.

the bag he might chance to light on the eel, but it is a hundred to one he shall be stung by a snake."

The maiden name of the mother of Sir Thomas was Handcombe, she was born in Haliwell in Bedfordshire, and died shortly after his birth, having previously become the mother of two daughters, one called Jane, who afterwards became the wife of one Richard Stafferton, and Elizabeth, wife to John Rastell, who was the mother of the future Judge Rastell.

It is said that the mother of Sir Thomas, the night of her marriage, beheld in her sleep, as it were engraven on her wedding ring, the number and faces of the children she was to have, one of which shone most brightly, by which Sir Thomas's fame and sanctity were supposed to be foreshown. Also, say the old writers, God designed to show how dear this babe was unto him, for, one day, his nurse with the child in her arms was riding over a piece of water, the horse stepping beyond its depth, put both she and her burthen in danger, and with the hope of saving the child, she flung it from her arms over a hedge into a field, and fortunately escaping herself, when she went in search of the babe she found him smiling and unhurt, so that it was said of him, "*Angels shall bear thee up, lest perchance thou hit thy foot against a stone.*"

The greatest care was taken by the Judge with respect to the education of this child of promise, and as soon as his still tender age would permit, he was placed by him in St. Antony's Free School. This school was instituted in Threadneedle Street, in the parish of S. Benet Finck, and was one of the four grammar schools founded by Henry V., a great patron of learning, in the twenty-fourth year of his reign. In the time of Sir Thomas More this school was the most celebrated in London. I myself, in my youth, says Stowe, have yearly seen on the eve of S. Bartholomew the Apostle, the scholars of divers grammar schools repair unto the churchyard of St. Bartholomew, or the Priory in Smithfield, where, upon a bank, boarded about, under a tree, some one scholar hath stepped up, and there hath opposed and answered, till he were by some better scholar overcome and put down, and then the overcomer taking the place did like as the first, and in the end the best opposers and answerers had rewards, which I observed not, but it made good schoolmasters and also good scholars diligently against such times to prepare themselves for the obtaining of that garland. I remember there repaired to these exercises, amongst others, the masters and scholars of the Free Schools of St. Paul's in London, of St. Peter's at Westminster, of Sir Thomas Acon's Hospital, and of St. Antony's Hospital, whereof the last named commonly presented the best scholars, and had the prize in those days.*

From this school various men of great reputation sprung, Sir Thomas More, Nicolas Heath, Archbishop of Canterbury and Lord Chancellor, and Archbishop Whitgift. It had fallen to decay in the time of Stowe and had come to nothing.

Not long had young More been at this school before he outstripped his companions in wit, talent, and application, making rapid advances in the Latin tongue. When he had reached his fifteenth year, his father, according to the custom of the times, placed him as page in the family of Cardinal Morton, then Archbishop of Canterbury, and Chancellor

* Stowe ii., p. 75.

under Henry VII. Here, along with some youths of the first families in England, young More waited at table, his learning and all manly exercises being well attended to meanwhile.

It was not long before the great talent and engaging parts of the youth under his care, drew upon him the notice of his master, who, though he had past the eightieth year of his age, and filled a post of the highest dignity in the realm, was not too dignified or stately to encourage the innocent amusement of his page, or to discern the extraordinary merit of the boy whose future fame he foretold, for the learned prelate often proved his wit, having at Christmas time entertainments for the recreation of his household, when the youth of a sudden would step in amongst the players, and never having studied the matter before, would invent a part for himself, so full of wit and jest that he would draw off the attention from the other players. The Cardinal at length became much attached to him, and not unfrequently said to those who dined with him, *This child here waiting at the table, whosoever shall live to see it, will prove a marvellous rare man.*

The wise prelate, however, speedily saw that, in his house, amidst the distractions of public business, young More could not profit to the extent he desired, and placed him in Canterbury College, at Oxford, now part of Christ Church, where he was instructed in Greek, a language not very commonly taught or learned at that time in England, and which Sir Thomas learned of Linacre, the famous physician. The taste for classical study was then reviving, and Oxford was the favoured spot in which the indefatigable young student contracted intimacies which were to end only with his own life.

Beneath the classic shades of his beloved university young More became acquainted with Wolsey, then bursar of Magdalen College, and the first classical scholar there, already opening his mouth in Latin disputations with Grocyn, Linacre, and Warham. He had commenced building his matchless tower, still one of the noblest monuments as a gem of architecture, amidst the groans of the Trojans, for so those were called who hated the language of Homer, and ridiculed every novelty.

His intercourse with the great scholar, or rather master, Erasmus, of Rotterdam, began about this time, as also with the young and enthusiastic student More, and the two former, truth obliges us to acknowledge, wasted their wit in ridiculing monks who were far above them in moral worth, or at pious foundations too good for their respective countries, and consequently about to be overthrown. Erasmus had proved himself no saint when he dwelt in his own monastery in Holland, whilst both he and Wolsey forgot that, amidst the tumults of the middle ages, their most admired authors would have perished had not the painstaking inmates of the cloister preserved literature from the rough grasp of the Huns and Goths, the Lombards and Vandals, or the ferocious Danes. Here it was, too, that More became acquainted with Colet, his future director. He was born of wealthy parents resident in London—his father had been twice Lord Mayor—his mother had had eleven sons and eleven daughters, of whom Colet was the eldest, and outlived them all. He was of tall and handsome person. He had studied the scholastic philosophy, Cicero, Plato, and

Plotinus, had visited France and Italy, and had diligently studied the Fathers, especially S. Augustine, and was an earnest reader of law and English poetry. On returning from Italy he lectured on S. Paul's Epistles, at Oxford, when he was of the age of thirty. Erasmus was of the same age, within a few months, when the two became acquainted. He made great advances in theology, though he took no degree, and was invited to London by Henry VII., made Dean of S. Paul's, became a great preacher, and distinguished himself by his frugality and abstinence.*

Dean Colet was, too, a man of earnest and practical piety, who made it his study to awaken a religious spirit in those around him. It was he who founded the Free School of S. Paul's, dedicating it to the Infant Jesus, and Thomas More became both his friend and penitent.

Grocyn was professor, or public teacher of Greek at Oxford, about the time Erasmus was there, afterwards becoming Master of the College of Maidstone, in Kent. Thomas Linacre lived a long while at Oxford, teaching Greek also. He founded a lecture in S. John's College, as he had founded two previously at Merton College, Oxford, and these three men became united with More in the closest bonds of friendship.

Persevering to the last degree, More fixed his attention solely on his studies, and, as his father restricted him very much with regard to pocket-money, scarcely, indeed, giving him enough to pay for the mending of his wearing apparel, he was deprived of one great incentive to the indulgence of his passions, had he been so minded, and the course his father had adopted More not unfrequently praised when he

* Er. Epis.

reached the years of manhood. It is to be observed, however, with reference to this strictness on the part of the old
Judge, that, with some natures, it would have had the contrary effect, and this spirit would have exhibited itself before
emancipation from college rules set the student free ; but it
was not with More as with many others, for whilst his disposition was full of vivacity and cheerfulness, a firm and
deep sentiment of religion prevented him from running riot
with many of those around him. He was nearly twenty
when he applied himself to the study of the law at Lincoln's
Inn, and whilst his countenance was the index of a happy
cheerful disposition, and a smile was ever on his lip, he was
practising in secret many an austerity of which the world
around him knew nothing, and had begun to lead that
" mortified life " which, with small mitigation, he continued
unto the day of his death, imitating austerities practised by
men who have forsaken the world, rather than those who,
in his age as in these our own days, seek to make its paths
most pleasant. He then began to wear a shirt of hair next
his skin, which he never wholly laid aside, even in the days
of his chancellorship.

On Fridays and fasting days he used the discipline. He
spent much time in fasting and watching, often lying on the
bare ground with a log of wood for a pillow, allowing himself
but four or five hours for sleep, treating his body hardly lest
the flesh should grow rebellious against the spirit, and using
severity to himself in this world, so that he might the better
tread the narrow path which leadeth to life eternal.

He was wont to say that his body was to be used like an
ass, with strokes and hard fare, lest provender might prick

it, and so bring his soul, like a headstrong jade, into the bottomless pit of hell.

Undecided as to whether he should not forsake the world, and devote himself wholly to God in the religious state, More, together with his faithful friend Lily, who aspired to the priesthood, fixed his abode near the Charter-house, and dwelt for four years amongst the Carthusians, frequenting all their spiritual exercises, but not binding himself by irrevocable vows.

The relaxed state of some few of the religious houses in England, may have in part deterred him from following this design, but there is no doubt that it became clear to his own mind, and that of his director, that God called him to serve Him in the busy scenes of active life, and not in the retirement of the cloister, holy as were the lives of the great majority of their inmates. And forth to the world he came, to grace and adorn it with his many virtues, and to set forth to his own and succeeding generations the pattern of a perfect Christian household—for was not the household of Sir Thomas More typical of all that is holy and beautiful in domestic life?

I have said Dean Colet was his spiritual director. The following letter will testify to the respect, nay, the love, with which he regarded him :—

"As I was walking lately in Cheapside, and busying myself about other men's causes, I met by chance your servant, at whose first encounter I was much rejoiced, both because he has always been very dear to me, and especially because, I thought he had not come to London without yourself. But when I found from him that you had not returned, nor minded to do so for a long space of time, my great joy was turned into sadness, for what could happen worse for me than to be deprived of your moral conversations, whose counsels I was wont to enjoy, with whose familiarity I have been accustomed to be recreated, by whose sermons I have been excited to devotion, by whose life and example I have been much amended in my own ; finally, in whose very countenance I have settled my trust and confidence of my progress in virtue. Wherefore, as I found myself so strengthened by these helps, so do I see myself weakened and brought low when deprived of them. For having by following your footsteps almost escaped from hell, so now, like another Eurydice, but in a contrary manner, for she was left there, because Orpheus looked back upon her, but I fall again by a fatal necessity, for 'that you cast not your eye upon me.'

"And I pray you what is there in this city that doth move any man to live well, and not rather by a thousand devices swallow *him* up in wickedness who would endeavour to ascend the steep hill of virtue. Wheresoever one cometh, what find we but feigned love, and the horrid poison of flattery in one place, cruel hatreds in another, pestiferous and hateful suits and quarrels.

"Wheresoever we cast our eyes what do we see but victualling houses, fishmongers, butchers, cooks, pudding-makers, and fowlers, who minister to our bodies, and set forward 'the service of the world and the flesh.' Yea, the houses themselves, bereave us of part of a sight of heaven, nor do they suffer us to look freely towards it, so that our horizontal circle is wholly cut short by the height of continued buildings. For which I pardon you the more easily that you do delight to remain still in the country, for you find there the society of plain souls void of the craft where-with citizens do most abound. Wheresoever you look, the earth yieldeth you a pleasant prospect, the sweetness of the air refreshes you, the very bounds of the heavens delight you, you find nothing but the bounteous gifts of nature, and saint-like tokens of innocence. And yet I would not have you so carried away with these delights, that you should be stayed from hastening hither; for, if the inconvenience of the city pesters you, yet your parish of Stepney, of which you should have great care, may afford you pleasure, like to that which you now enjoy, from whence you may quickly return to London as into your Inn, and may find great store of merit.

"In the country men are commonly more innocent and not laden with any great offence, and any physician may administer medicine unto them, but as for citizens, both because they are a multitude, and also for their inveterate manner of sinning, none can help them but he that is skilful.

"There come into the pulpit at S. Paul's divers men that promise to cure the diseases of others, but their lives do so jar with their sayings, that when they have preached a goodly process, they rather provoke to anger than assuage a sore, for they cannot persuade men they are fit to cure others when themselves, God wot, are most sick and crazy, which causes them that have uncured sores not to be touched or lanced by such ignorant physicians. But if one be courted by learned men most fit to cure in whom the sick man hath greatest hope, who doubteth then that you alone are most fit to cure their maladies, whom every one is willing to suffer to touch their wounds, and whose confidence you have sufficiently tried, and the desire every one hath that you may speedily return manifests the cause more evidently.

" Return then, dear Colet, at least for Stepney's sake, which mourneth your absence as a child does for its mother, or else for London's sake, it is your native place, of which you can have no less regard than of your own parents.

" Finally, though this be the least motive, return for my sake, who have wholly dedicated myself to your direction, and do most earnestly desire your return. In the meanwhile I pass my time with Grocyn, Linacre, and Lily, the first being, as you know, the director of my life in your absence, the second the master of my studies, the third my most dear companion. Farewell, and see you love me as you have done hitherto.

" London, 21 October."

CHAPTER II.

How Sir Thomas More Wooed his First Wife.

SHORTLY after More had elected to remain in the world, he decided on entering the state of matrimony, and the manner in which his decision was made was certainly peculiar and worthy of himself. He had become acquainted with a Mr. Colt, of New Hall, in Essex, at whose bouse he was a frequent visitor.

This gentleman had three daughters, who were all of marriageable age, they were young gentlewomen of some pretensions to personal beauty, and in whose manners there was nothing light or frivolous.

On the second of these girls, the then young lawyer fixed his affections, the choice of either of his daughters, having been previously offered to him by Mr. Colt, who doubtless anticipated the probable result of More's visits.

It was a question of the old old tale, and More, whose fancy was more particularly attracted by the second daughter, was on the point of asking her of her father in marriage, when he found his sympathies were becoming enlisted in behalf of the elder sister.

The second was undoubtedly the fairest and most highly favoured by nature's gifts, and yet—and here let us give the biographer's own words,—" he considered it would be both great grief and some shame to see her younger sister preferred before her in marriage, and he then of a certain pitie framed his mind to her, and soon after married her."* Thus

* More's Life of More.

out of pity and sympathy did Jane Colt become Mistress More.

He then sought to mould her character to his liking, for she was but young in years, and also had her education completed, for in those days the education of the daughter of a country squire was a very imperfect affair.

After his marriage he removed to Bucklersbury, still prosecuting his studies at Lincoln's Inn with indefatigable ardour, remaining there until he was called to the Bench.

In the course of a few years Mistress More presented him with four children, three daughters, the eldest of whom became the incomparable Margaret Roper, and one son, whom he named John, after his father, the Judge.

Probably his long residence amongst the Carthusians had much to do with the exactitude and regularity with which the subsequent days of More's busy and toiling life were passed. With him procrastination, "that thief of time," was known but by name, each hour of the day, so full in the world's work, as well as in preparation for that which is to come, being devoted to its own particular duty.

The day never dawned, unless sickness prevented it, which did not witness the presence of More at the holy sacrifice of the Mass, and it was doubtless owing to this careful offering of the day's first fruits to his God which shed so much peace over the life of this great and good man. So strictly, indeed, did he observe this custom, that on one occasion, when he was high in favour with the king, it is said that a messenger being sent to him while Mass was being offered up, he would not leave, though the message was twice repeated, until Mass was wholly finished, and when requested to hasten quickly for that the king awaited his coming, he calmly replied that he must first perform his duty to a King who was above all earthly princes.

At this time he was only working his way up to the future eminence he so deservedly enjoyed, and a sore trial it must have been to a man so careful of the interests of his children, and so affectionate a father, when they were deprived by death of their mother's care.

We may not then blame him as soon forgetting the young wife to whom sympathy had led him to offer his hand, and with whom he appears to have led, if but a short, still a happy wedded life, because, in little better than two years, he again entered the married state.

However devoted and affectionate a man may be to his children, and it is as a father that we love to contemplate the character of Sir Thomas More, he never can supply the void to his children occasioned by a mother's death. The busy career of a rising barrister's life led him much from home, and he wisely decided on marrying again for the sake of these motherless little ones.

Love, however, could have had no place in his heart when he espoused the widow, Alice Middleton. She was well advanced in life, plain and hard of feature, with small earthly substance. She had, too, an only daughter, and was grasping and worldly in her disposition. Something, too, was there about this second wooing almost as whimsical as about the first, for, as the story goes, More was set to woo Mistress Middleton for a friend, not for himself; but the widow promptly replied:

" Your wooing will speed better if you do it on your own account, Mr. More; go, tell your friend what I have said."

The story further goes, that More referred it to his friend, who, as he could not get the lady for himself, was well pleased More should become her husband, an event that speedily happened.

Careful and kind, however, she proved to his motherless children; and he, on his part, was a loving father to a child of hers by her first husband. Nevertheless, Mistress More was a downright shrew, and one would think that, but for the good quality we have named, More must often have regretted that he married her.

More then became under-sheriff, an office at that time judicial, and of much importance. His court, we find by a letter written by Erasmus to Hutton, which the reader will peruse when he comes to the description of More's life in his Chelsea home, sat every Thursday, and it testifies to the fact that no judge gave more righteous decisions, often remitting the fines to which he was entitled by the suitor, and the way he conducted himself in this new office endeared him extremely to his fellow-citizens.

A new life, however, shaped itself before More. After an intermission of seven years, Henry VII. called a new parliament, in order to obtain a subsidy of three-fifteenths on the occasion of the marriage of his eldest daughter, the Lady Margaret, with James, king of Scotland. More, whose abilities and talents had speedily won for him the admiration of his fellow-citizens, was returned in parliament, "for many had now taken notice of his sufficiency," and he is recorded as the first member who become famous as an orator, and who, whilst others held their peace, not daring to resist, became a successful leader of the opposition, and incurred the enmity of the court, for his arguments were so powerful *why* these exactions should not be granted, that a denial was returned to the king's request,* and Mr. Tyler, a gentleman of his privy chamber, hastening from the house, told his majesty that it was owing to a "beardless boy,"† that his expectations were disappointed. According to Tudor dealings with refractory subjects More might have been committed to the Tower for the offence, but Henry always had a keen eye to the state of his exchequer, and as More, "nothing having, nothing could lose," his grace devised a causeless quarrel with the eminent Sir John More, his unoffending old father, and placed him in the Tower till he had paid a fine of a hundred pounds.

The trouble this caused to the mind of his son may be easily conceived, and he at once sought out Dr. Fox, Bishop of Winchester, one of the Privy Council; the Bishop affecting great kindness promised him that if he would follow his advice he would get him restored to the king's favour; meaning, as it was afterwards thought, that he should confess his offences against the king, but on leaving the Bishop, More chanced to meet an intimate friend, Dr. Whitford, the Bishop's chaplain, whose advice he also asked.

Whitford instantly conjured him not to follow the Bishop's counsel, and thus serve the king's purpose, adding, "Why, my Lord, to please the king would not stick to agree to his own father's death." It is stated as a proof that More did wisely in not making any confession that he had acted

---

* Henry was entitled by the feudal customs to ask for aid to make his eldest son a knight, and to marry his eldest daughter. It was, however, so contrived that he might have the merit of moderation whilst he imposed the burden.—*Lingard.*

† Life of More, by his Great-grandson.

wrongly, that when Dudley and Empson, for their shameful exactions, were led to execution in the next reign, that the former meeting with More, said to him—-

"Oh, Mr. More, God was your good friend, that you did not ask the king's forgiveness as many would have done, for if you *had* done so, perhaps, you should have been in the like case with us now."

Henry VII. continued to watch the movements of the young patriot, so that at the first opportunity he might succeed in wreaking his vengeance against him, and justly fearing that in the end some pretext would be devised for doing so, More by degrees almost withdrew from his practice at the bar,* and passed his time in the study of the French language, in learning the viol, and perfecting himself in most of the liberal sciences, geometry, and astronomy, and he strove also to become a perfect historian.

He even meditated leaving England, but such a step was rendered unnecessary, for the death of Henry VII. preserved him for the service of his country.

---

*It appears from the Statute Book and the Parliament Roll, that this Parliament met in January, 1504, so More must then have been twenty-four years old, the age of William Pitt when Prime Minister. His early biographers say he was twenty-one.—CAMPBELL.

CHAPTER III.

IN FAVOUR AT COURT.

HANDSOME in person, generous in disposition, skilled in every martial and fashionable exercise, affable to those around him, and eminently religious, such was Henry VIII. on his accession to the throne, and it is perhaps not surprising that the usually far-seeing Thomas More regarded the young king with the same eyes as the bulk of the nation, who at that time looked forward to a long and prosperous reign.

He at once returned to the duties of his profession, discharging them with even more zest than formerly, steadily rose to eminence, and began to gain yearly, without "any grudge of his conscience," as he afterwards told Roper, £400 a-year. This sum, says Lord Campbell, considering the value of money at that time, and the relative profits of the bar, indicate as high a station as £10,000 at the present day.*

With Wolsey, the prime favourite, now rising rapidly to greatness, the reader will remember that More had become acquainted in his early days at Oxford, when *he* was the boy student, and Wolsey bursar.

Amidst his natural love of pleasure, in the early portion

---

* Roper says that he was twice chosen agent to the Still Yard Merchants, or Steel Yard. They were chiefly of Germany, and enjoyed privileges in London by charters from our kings. They were great importers of corn.—*Hunter's Edition of More's Life of More.*

 In Favour at Court.

of his reign, Henry not unfrequently occupied himself with matters of state, instead of being wholly absorbed in the amusements of the court *

Wolsey only occupied the *first* place in the royal favour, and at once fell in with the young king's wish to summon More to court. It was with difficulty, however, that he could be prevailed upon to accept the dangerous honour. His present career was yet more honourable, nay, it was more lucrative, and it was not without an inward misgiving and apprehension of future trouble, that he finally consented, and exchanged the peaceful quietude of his beloved home and the daily round of his law duties, for the life of a courtier and a statesman.

Some little time previous, More's services had been engaged in a suit of which a circumstantial account has been handed down to us. A ship belonging to the Pope had been seized at Southampton, and was forfeited to the Crown for a breach of the Law of Nations. The Pope's Nuncio at the Court of London claimed restitution, and retained More's services as counsel. The hearing was held in the Star Chamber before the Chief Justices, the Lord Treasurer, and other officers of State. To plead against the Crown must have been an onerous undertaking, but More exerted himself to the utmost, argued with precision and clearness, brought all his own learning to bear as well as availing himself of

---

* Henry saw Wolsey's talent for business, and constantly flattered him with thanks, but in everything governed for himself. Wolsey neither framed a bill for parliament, nor a despatch for a foreign court, which was not submitted to Henry, and never acted, even in domestic politics, till he had taken his pleasure.—*Sir H. Ellis's Original Letters,* p. 193, vol I.

the authorities furnished by his client, and made such an impression by his speech in behalf of his Holiness, that restitution was decreed.

The King himself was present during the hearing of this *cause celebre*, and to his credit, instead of showing mortification at the loss of his prize, he united with others in praising More for his commendable demeanour, and for no entreaty, says Roper, would he give up his services at Court.

How well did Henry's reign promise in the outset. He undoubtedly was at that time ever ready to patronise merit, his purse was open to the needy, or to reward and encourage literature, and small·wonder is it that his subjects were dazzled by the brilliant promise, and gave to him credit for more virtue than he really possessed.

In the year 1514, More left the bar, was knighted by the King, made Master of the Requests, and sworn of the Privy Council.

Amidst the public and private duties that now thronged thickly upon him, More yet found leisure for the composition of works which in his own day acquired the highest celebrity.

The shafts of envy, however, did not pass him by, his epigrams, full of pleasant and sparkling wit for which he was famous throughout, aroused the malignity of Brixius or La Brie, as his contemporary Rabelais calls him.*

In 1513, Brixius composed a poem which he called Chordigera, where, in three hundred hexameter verses, he described a battle fought that year on S. Laurence's day by a French ship *La Cordeliere*, and an English ship called *The Regent.*

* Sam Knight's Erasmus.

More, who at that time had not risen to as high a position as he filled later, composed several epigrams in derision of this poem, and Brixius, piqued at this affront, revenged himself by the *Anti Morus*, an elegy of four hundred verses, in which he severely censured all the faults he thought he had found in the poems of More.

Brixius was certainly the aggressor on this occasion as More showed in a long and spirited letter which he sent him. He also published an answer to the *Anti Morus*, but on receiving a letter from Erasmus exhorting him to treat the attack of Brixius with silent contempt, he at once suppressed the edition, and even called in such copies as were in circulation.

This quarrel produced, at a later date, a letter from Erasmus, in which he says :—

"Respecting your quarrel with More, I cannot express the great esteem I have for his learning and character. I think of More as all men do who know him, as a man of incomparable genius, possessing a happy memory, a most ready eloquence. When a boy he learned Latin, when a young man Greek, under the ablest teachers, especially Grocyn and Linacre. In divinity he has made so much progress that he is not to be despised even by eminent theologians. The liberal arts he has touched not infelicitously, in philosophy he is beyond mediocrity, to say nothing of the profession of the law, in which he yields to no one. His prudence is rare and unheard of, and for these reasons his sovereign never rested until he had brought More to be one of his council. As to the ostentatious contempt in which you profess to hold More, the world will laugh at it.

"*Antwerp*, 1520."

Extremely against his will had More been brought to court, and in a letter to his friend Fisher, Bishop of Rochester, he writes thus concerning it :—

" I have come to the court extremely against my will, as every one knoweth, and as the king himself knows, for in sport he often twits me with it, and here I hang as unseemly as a man not used to ride doth sit unhandsomely in his saddle ; but our prince, whose special and extraordinary favour towards me I know not how ever to deserve, is so affable and courteous to all who approach him, that every one, however little he may imagine it, may hope to win his love, even as citizens' wives of London do, who imagine that Our Lady's picture near the Tower smileth on them when they pray before it.   But I am not so happy as to perceive such fortunate signs of deserving his love within myself, and am of too humble a spirit to persuade myself that I deserve it, yet such is the king's virtue and learning, and so great his industry, that the more I see him increase in these high qualities, the less irksome does this courtier's life appear to me."

After he had been made Treasurer of the Exchequer, Erasmus, writing to Cochleus, says :—

" When next you write to More, you shall wish him joy of his dignity and good fortune, for being before only of the king's Privy Council, now of late by the benevolence and free gift of his most gracious prince, he, neither desiring it, nor seeking for it, is not only made knight, but Treasurer of the King's Exchequer, an office in England both honourable and also commodious for the purse."

" No man," as Erasmus truly said, " ever strove harder to gain admittance at court than More to keep out of it."

Riches and honours then lay at the feet of their unwilling, recipient, and the even tenor of his life was changed, but he was never dazzled by the glitter of worldly prosperity, or court favour, neither of which drew his great heart from God or the contemplation of eternity.

He then removed from Bucklersbury to the village of Chelsea, where he had built a pleasant country residence, for the Chelsea of the sixteenth century was truly in the country.

The mansion, with a farm attached to it, was large and commodious. It stood in the midst of pleasant grounds extending westward at the distance of about a hundred yards from the Thames. The façade of the house was alternately divided into four bay and four large casement windows, the roof having four pediments, each containing a window, a clock turret crowning the whole.

The porch over the entrance door, which gave ingress to the hall, was clustered over with jasmine and honeysuckle, and a profusion of flowering shrubs grew around in wild luxuriance, doubtless oftentimes tended lovingly by the hands of his daughter Margaret, that best-loved child of More's, whose tastes were like his own, for in one of the letters of his chosen friend, Erasmus, we are told that this great man loved flowers. The author of the "*Il Moro*" writes :—

" Along the beautiful banks of the Thames there are many delightful mansions, situated in charming places, in one of which, very near the city of London, dwelt Sir Thomas More. It was a beautiful and commodious residence, and to this place it was his custom to retire when weary of London. At this house, as well on account of its proximity to town, as for the admirable character of its owner, men distinguished for their genius, who dwelt in the city, were often accustomed to meet, and at their leisure were wont to enter into some useful argument or discourse on things pertaining to human nature. The place was charming, both from the advantages of its site, for from one part almost the whole of the noble city of London was visible ; and from another, the beautiful Thames, with green meadows and woody eminences all around, and also for its own beauty, for as it was crowned with an almost perpetual verdure, it had many flowering plants, and the branches of fruit trees which grew around, so beautifully interlaced each other, that it appeared like a living tapestry woven by nature herself."

How More must have enjoyed, when his day's toil was over, taking boat with Roper, his future son-in-law, at Westminster, and rowing back to his pleasant intellectual home on the banks of the then pellucid waters of the Thames.

At this time Sir Thomas was in the very prime of man's existence. He was daily at the court. Honours, affluence, and pleasures awaited him at every turn. His society was sought for by his prince, he was esteemed by his equals, loved by the poor, and honoured by his fellow-citizens. But let us look at the other side of the picture, and regard Sir Thomas in the bosom of his family, in his several relations of life—as husband, father, and master—and we shall find it simply impossible to imagine a more perfect type of a Christian household, than that which was governed by Sir Thomas More.

Moroseness and formalism, the condemnation of innocent and cheerful recreation, regarding it as a species of sinfulness, all this is the heritage of Puritanism, brought in with the so-called Reformation, and it found no place in More's household. Religion was, indeed, as it always should be, brought to bear on the daily events of life, but in no way interfered with the rational enjoyment of the earthly blessings bestowed on him, or cast a shadow on any innocent pleasure or cheerful relaxation, and the master mind of him who governed the household was full of cheerfulness and wit, and gifted also with a sweetness of temper which lighted up and cheered all who came within the range of its happy influence.

And having said thus much, we will devote a chapter to a description of the household of Thomas More, and insert various letters written to his daughters from the court. The letters of Erasmus to Hutton and Budaeus, and his own letter, which he sent to his friend Peter Giles, with his Utopia, will admirably bear out all that his early biographers have described of More's home life.

CHAPTER IV.

MORE'S HOME AT CHELSEA.

SOME little distance from the mansion, nestled amidst the verdant meadows which for generations past have vanished, for Chelsea has long since become merely a populous environ of the great Babylon of London, of which it is indeed a part, Sir Thomas More erected what he called "The New Buildings."

These buildings consisted of a chapel, a library, a gallery, and a home for destitute and infirm persons of the parish, for the support of whom he set aside a fixed amount, and the care and superintendence of this place devolved entirely on his eldest daughter, Margaret.

To this chapel he often retired, when he had leisure, for prayer and meditation. It was his practice to linger there, especially on the Fridays, in memory of Christ's Passion, spending much of the day in contemplation, a practice which, above all else, makes known to us the source whence he derived his unalterable patience and resignation. Much in the night, too, did he watch whilst all around him slept. On Good Friday it was his custom to call his family together in this chapel, and read to them the Passion of our Lord, pausing now and then at certain passages on which he desired to comment.

Idleness was a stranger in More's household. His numerous servants were not allowed to pass their time at games of hazard. The natural ability and talent of each one was tested carefully, and whilst the undisciplined lives of the serving-men of persons of rank were often the mainsprings which caused much trouble to the community at large, the domestics of More formed a happy exception to the general rule. Everyone was provided with the occupation best suited to him. If one had an ear for music, or another a good voice, the talent was encouraged in every possible way. Some had a particular portion of the garden to attend to. The men dwelt on one side of the house—the women on the other. It was also his wont to call them together to pray with him, ere the shades of night had fallen. He rose early himself, and all followed this most healthy and laudable example. At table one or other of his servants would read aloud, and his domestics he regarded rather in the light of children than as servants.

Very careful, too, was he of the avoidance of all singularity, and so appeared like most others in his dress and behaviour, but yet next his body he wore a shirt of hair, which, says William Roper, my sister More*, as he sat at supper, single in his doublet and hose, wearing thereupon a plain shirt, without either ruffe or collar, chancing to espie, began to laugh at it. " My wife,† not ignorant of his ways, perceiving the same, told him of it privately, and he, sorry that it had been seen, at once concealed it. Not unfrequently did he use a discipline of knotted cords, known only to my wife, his eldest daughter, and above all others he

----

* Roper's Life of More.

Anne Cresacre More, the wife of John More, aged 15.

† Margaret Roper.

specially trusted her to wash with her own hands these same shirts of hair."

His admonitions to his wife and children were delivered in his own peculiar style. "It is no great matter if you, my children, get to heaven," he was wont to say, "for every one sets you good example, and adviseth you wisely. You see virtue rewarded and vice punished, and so you are carried up thither by the chins ; but if you chance to see the day when none shall give you good example, or good advice, and you shall rather see virtue punished and vice rewarded, if *then* you stand fast, and cling close to God,—then, on my life, though you be only half good, God will count you as whole good." To foolish indulgence of those he dearly loved he never yielded, and if he heard them complain of trifling discomforts, he would say to them, "We must not look to go to heaven on feather beds. Our Lord Himself went thither but by suffering, and the servant must not look to be in better case than his master." Somewhat careless even in his own apparel, the charge of which he left entirely to his man Harris, who was at times somewhat forgetful of his duty, he was never more distressed than when he observed in his children any evidence of personal vanity, and once observing Dame Alice, his wife, take great pains to comb up her long hair to show her high forehead, and by tight-lacing to strive to make her waist small, even to her own great pain, said he, "Forsooth, madam, if God give you not hell He will do you great wrong, for it must needs be your own of very right, for you buy it very dear, and take great pains to gain it."

A sharp keen manager was this Lady More, and her husband was wont to tell her she was "penny-wise and pound foolish ; saving a candle's end and spoiling a velvet gown ;" whilst she, on her part, not unfrequently quarrelled with him for having no ambition, using a favourite and inelegant form of speech, which she often adopted: " Tillie vallie, tillie vallie ! will you sit and make goslings in the ashes. My mother has often said to me, ' it is better to rule than to be ruled.' " " Good wife," replied More, " that is well said, for I never yet found you willing to be ruled."

It was no small sorrow to More to find that, by degrees, he, for a long space of time, almost wholly lost the happiness of his own home, for he found that when he was in London, he was expected by the king to lodge within the palace, so that not only was all domestic enjoyment at an end, but he was also unable to execute the literary projects he had formed. On holidays it was the king's custom, when his devotions were over, to summon Sir Thomas to his cabinet, and converse with him on astronomy, geometry, and divinity, and, on clear nights, to ascend with him to the leads of the palace, and there discourse with him of the diversity of the courses, motions, and operations of the stars, and being of a facetious and pleasant turn of mind, the king and queen would often, after they had supped, send for him to enjoy his pleasant conversation.

Sir Thomas, however, liked his liberty far better than this unrestricted intercourse with royalty, and at length, finding that scarce once in a month he had leave to go to his wife and children, and that he could not absent himself for two days without being sent for again, he began to dissemble his mirth, and so, little by little, " to disuse himself, and from henceforth at such seasons he was no more ordinarily sent for."[*] With so tender a nature, and so sweet a disposition, he must indeed have sorely missed the home circle, and as they were chiefly written whilst he was either thus detained by the king at court, or when engaged on foreign embassies, this appears, as we said in the preceding chapter, the fittest place in which to insert the various letters written by the scholar to his children.

Sir Thomas More's daughters may be said to have led the way for the better education of the female sex. Latin was still somewhat of a living language, and an acquaintance with it was of more use than in the present day, and the " School of Sir Thomas More," as it was called by his family and their friends, gradually acquired a widely spread renown. There are many, even in our own later times, who deny to women the intelligence of the sterner sex ; granting the truth of the assertion, Sir Thomas saw in it only a reason for increased diligence on the part of women. Witness the following letter writen to their preceptor, one William Gunnell :—[†]

" I have received, my dear Gunnell, your letters such as they are wont to be, most elegant and full of affection. Your love towards my children I gather from your letters, their diligence by their own ; for every one of their epistles pleaseth me much. Yet most especially I take joy to hear that my daughter Elizabeth hath showed as great prudence in her mother's absence as if she had been present ; let her know that that liked me better than all the epistles besides, for as I esteem learning which is joined with virtue more than all the treasures of kings, to what doth the fame of being

[*] Roper.

[†] Life of Sir Thomas More, by More.

a great scholar bring us, if it be severed from virtue, other than a notorious and famous infamy, especially in a woman, whom men will be the more ready to assail for their learning because it is a rare matter, and argueth a reproach to the sluggishness of a man, who will not stick to lay the fault of their natural malice upon the quality of learning; but if a woman, on the other hand, shall join many virtues of the mind with skill in learning, as I hope all mine will do, I shall account it a more happy thing than if they had all the riches of Crœsus united to the beauty of the fair Helen, not because they were to get fame thereby, though it inseparably follows virtue as the shadow doth the body, but because they will obtain the true rewards of wisdom, which can never be taken away as wealth may, nor will it fade as beauty doth, because it dependeth upon truth and justice, and not on the words of men's mouths, than which nothing is more foolish; for as it is the duty of a good man to eschew infamy, so is it the property of a proud man to frame his actions only for praise, for that man's mind must be full of anxiety that always wavers, for fear of other men's judgments, between joy and sadness. Amongst the benefits which learning hath bestowed on men I account it the most profitable that we look not for praise to be accounted learned, but only to use it on all occasions; which the best of all learned men, I mean the philosophers, have delivered to us, though some of them have abused their science, aiming only to be accounted excellent men by the people. Thus have I spoken, my Gunnell, somewhat more of not coveting vain glory in respect of those words in your letter, wherein you say that the high spirit of my daughter Margaret's wit is not to be dejected; I am of the same opinion, but I think that he dejects his wit who admires vain objects, esteeming the shadow of good things, for want of discretion to judge true from apparent good rather than the truth itself; and I have not only requested you, dear Gunnell, who of yourself I believe would have done it, neither have I desired my wife alone, but also other friends I have entreated many times, to persuade my children to avoid the gulfs of pride, to walk through the pleasant meadows of modesty; not to be enamoured of the glitter of gold and silver, nor lament the want of it; to think none the better of themselves for all their costly trimmings, nor more meanly for the lack of them; not to lessen their beauty bestowed on them by nature by neglecting it, nor to add to it by artificial means; to esteem virtue their chief happiness, learning and good qualities the next, of which above all are piety towards God, charity to all men, modesty and Christian humility in themselves, by which they will reap from God the reward of an innocent life, so that they shall not need to fear death, and meanwhile will not be puffed up with the vain praises of men, nor cast down by slanders and disgrace. These are the solid fruits of learning, which as I confess belong not to all, but those may yet attain them who study with this intent. It matters not at harvest time whether man or woman sowed the corn, for both are reasonable beings, and therefore I do not see why learning may not equally suit either sex. Reason being thus culti- vated and (as a field) sown with wise precepts, it bringeth forth good fruit; but if the soil of woman's brain be of its own nature bad, and more apt to bear fern than corn, by which saying many terrify women from learning, I am of opinion that woman's wit is the more diligently to be culti- vated, to the end that nature's defect may be redressed by industry; of which mind were several wise and holy Fathers. S. Jerome and S. Augustine amongst others, who not only exhorted many noble matrons and honourable virgins to love of study, but, to help them, expounded to them difficult portions of Scripture; and wrote letters to tender maidens, full of so great learning that scarcely our greatest professors of divinity can well read them; which works, you will endeavour, my dear Gunnell, that my daughters may learn, so that they may know the end they ought to have in study, to place the fruits of their labours in God and a pure conscience, that at peace with themselves they be not moved with flattery nor grieved at the scoffs of the unlearned. Though I fancy you may reply that though this be true my precepts are too strong and hard for the tender age of my young wenches to listen to, for what man, be he ever so old and learned, is always so constant as not to be elated with the tickling of vain glory? For myself I consider it so hard to shake from us this plague of pride that we ought the more to endeavour to do it from our very infancy. I think there is no other cause why this mischief doth stick so fast to us, but that it is ingrafted in us even by our nurses as soon as we have crept out of our shells, fostered by our masters, nourished and perfected by our parents, whilst no one proposeth anything good to children, but they at once bid them expect praise as the reward of virtue, whence they are so used to esteem much of praise, that seeking to please the greater number, who are always the worst, they are ashamed to be good with the few. And that this plague may be banished from my children, I desire that you, my dear Gunnell, their mother, and all their friends, would still sing them this song, hammer it into their heads on every occasion, that vain glory is to be despised, nor anything more excellent than the humble modesty so much praised by Christ, which prudent charity will so guide and direct that it will teach us rather to desire virtue than to upbraid others for their vices, and make them rather love those who correct their faults than hate them for their good counsel, to obtain which nothing is more available than to read them the precepts of the Fathers, whom they know not to be angry with themselves, and with whose authority they must be moved because they are venerable for their sanctity.

"If, therefore, you will read the works of such to Margaret and Elizabeth besides their lessons in Sallust, as they, being the eldest, are of riper age, than John and Cicely, you will make both them and me every day more beholden to you ; moreover you will then make my children, dear in the order of nature, more dear for learning, and by their increase in virtue most dear unto me. Farewell.— From the Court, this Whitsun Eve."

By the above letter which I have transcribed it will be seen that Sir Thomas's chief care was to make his children virtuous, as well as learned. The following letters were addressed to themselves.

"Thomas More, to his whole School sendeth greeting.

"Behold, I have found out a compendious way to salute you all, and make spare of time and paper, which I must needs have wasted in saluting each one of you by name, which would be very superfluous, because you are all so dear to me, some in one way, some in another, that I cannot leave one of you unsaluted. Yet I know not if there be any better motive why I should love you, than that you are scholars, learning seeming to bind me more closely to you than nearness of blood. If I loved you not exceedingly I should envy your great happiness in having many great scholars for your masters. I hear that Mr. Nicolas is with you, that you have learned much astronomy of him, and have proceeded so far in this science that you know not only the pole-star, the dog, and such like common constellations, but also, which argues you as absolute and cunning astronomers, you know the chief planets themselves, and are able to discern the sun from the moon. Go forward therefore in your new and admirable skill, and whilst you daily admire the stars, I admonish you also to think of this holy fast of Lent, and let the pious song of Boethius sound in your ears, so that your minds may ascend to heaven, lest when the body is lifted up on high the soul be driven down to earth with the brute beasts. Farewell.— From the Court, this 29th of March."

And, in answer to the loving replies of his daughters, came the following.

"Thomas More, to his best beloved children, and to Margaret Giggs, whom he numbers amongst his own, sendeth greeting. The merchant from Bristol brought me yours the day after he had received them from you, with the which I was extremely delighted, for there can come nothing, though never so rude nor meanly polished, from your workshop but it yieldeth me more delight than other men's works, be they ever so eloquent, your writing doth so stir up my affection for you.

"Exclusive of this, your letters also please me well for their own worth, as full of fine wit and pure Latin phrase; therefore they all please me exceedingly. Yet, to tell you candidly what I think, my son John's letter pleaseth me most, because it was longer than the others, and also he seems to me to have taken more pains than the rest ; he not only pointeth out the matter clearly, and speaketh elegantly, but also playeth pleasantly with me, returning my jests upon me again very wittily, and this not only pleasantly but temperately withal, showing that he is mindful with whom he jesteth, to wit, his father, whom he endeavours so to delight that he is also afraid to offend.

" Hereafter I expect every day letters from each one of you, neither will I accept of such excuses as you complain of, that you had no leisure, or that the carrier went away suddenly, or that you have no matter to write. John is not wont to allege any such things, and nothing can hinder you from writing, but many things should exhort you to it. Why should you blame the carrier, seeing you may prevent his coming, and have them ready made up and sealed two days before any offer themselves to carry them? And how can you want matter of writing to me, who am delighted to hear either of your studies or your play, whom you may then please exceedingly, when, having nothing to write of, you write as largely as you can of that nothing, than which nothing is more easy for you to do, especially being women, and therefore prattlers by nature, amongst whom a great story riseth out of nothing. But this I admonish you to do, that, whether you write of serious matters or of trifles, you write with diligent consideration, premeditating it before ; neither will it be amiss if you first indite in English, for then it may be more easily translated into Latin, while the mind free from inventing is apt in finding eloquent words.

" I leave this to your choice whether you do so or no,

but I enjoin you by all means diligently to examine what you have written before you write it over fair again, examining first the whole sentence, then various parts of it, by which you will discover if any solecisms have escaped you; which being corrected, and your letter fairly written out, let it not trouble you to examine it again. By this diligence, your trifles will seem serious matters, for as nothing is so pleasing but that it may be made unsavoury by garrulity, so nothing is so unpleasant that by industry may not be made graceful and comely. Farewell, my sweetest children.—From the Court, this fifth day of September."

Amidst the distractions of a court life, and the exactions the king made upon his time, More yet found leisure to compose letters full of wisdom and fatherly love; one of his replies to Margaret ran as follows—

"Thy letters, dearest Margaret, were grateful unto me, which certified me of the state of Shaw; yet would they have been more grateful unto me, if they had told me what your and your brother's studies were, what is read amongst you every day, how you converse together, what themes you make, and how you pass the day amongst you; and although nothing is written from you but is most pleasing to me, yet those things are sweet which I can only learn through you or your brother. And in short, I pray thee, Meg, see that I understand by you what your studies are. For rather than I would suffer you, my children, to live idly, I would myself look to you with loss of my temporal estate, bidding all other cares and business farewell, amongst which there is nothing more sweet unto me than thyself, my dearest daughter. Farewell."

The following letter is addressed to all his daughters.

"Thomas More sendeth greeting to his most dear daughters, Margaret, Elizabeth, and Cicely, and to Margaret Giggs, as dear to him as if she were his own. I cannot sufficiently express, my best beloved wenches, how your eloquent letters have pleased me and not the least that I understand by them that you have not in your journeys, though changing places often, omitted any of your customs of exercising yourselves either in declamation, composing poetry, or in your logical exercises ; and so I feel convinced that you dearly love me, being thus careful to please me by your diligence, performing in my absence what you know delights me when I am present ; my return then shall be profitable to you, and assure yourselves, that amongst my troublesome and business affairs there is nothing so much delights me as when I read of your labours by which I know that to be true which your loving master writes me of you ; for unless your own epistles showed me how great was your desire to learn, I should have suspected that he had either written out of affection than according to truth, but now you make me believe and lead me to imagine those things to be true of your disputations which he boasteth of you almost beyond belief. I am very desirous to come home that I may set our scholar to dispute with you, who is slow to believe you able to answer your master's praises. But I hope—knowing how stedfast you are—that you will shortly overcome your master, if not in disputing, at least in not leaving off your strife. Farewell, dear wenches."

Nor could the loving father refrain from pouring into Margaret's ears the praises of a learned divine, and he begins as follows :—*

* Stapleton's Life of More, p. 267.

"Thomas More sendeth hearty greetings to his dearest daughter Margaret.

"I must tell you, my dearest daughter, how much your letter delighted me ; you may imagine how exceedingly it pleased your father when you understand what emotions its perusal raised in a stranger. This evening I was seated with the Lord Bishop of Exeter, a learned, and in every one's judgment a most truthful man. As we were talking together, and I taking out of my pocket a paper concerning what we were speaking of, I pulled out by chance your letter. The handwriting pleasing him he took it from me and looked at it ; when he pereeived it to be a woman's he began to devour the letter, novelty inciting him ; but having read it, and understood it to be your writing, which he never would have believed if I had not seriously affirmed it, such a letter,— but I will say no more,—yet why should I not repeat what he said ? So pure a style, such good Latin, so full of sweet affection, he was perfectly delighted with it ; and when I produced, which he read, also, many of your verses, he was so astonished that his very countenance and manner, free from all flattery and deceit, betrayed that he felt more than he could say, though he said much in your praise. Forthwith he drew from his pocket a porteguè,* which you shall receive enclosed herein. I could not possibly avoid taking it, for he desired to send it as a sign of his affection for you, though I strove to return it again ; this was the cause why I showed him none of your sister's works, fearing lest he should think I showed them on purpose that he should bestow the same courtesy on them also, for it troubled me sorely to take of so worthy a man ; but it is a happiness

* Porteguè, a gold coin of the value of £3 10s.

to please him. Write carefully to him, and as eloquently as you are able, in order to return him thanks. Farewell.— From the Court, this 11th of September, almost at midnight."

Margaret made an oration to answer Quintilian, defending the rich man he accused of having poisoned a poor man's bees with venomous plants in his garden ; and so eloquent and witty was this oration that it deserved a place beside his own. With one more letter of the Chancellor, containing strictures on his daughter's letters, I shall conclude these letters on his children's studies. It ran as follows :—

"Thomas More sendeth greeting to his dearest daughter Margaret.

"There was no reason, my dearest daughter, why you should have deferred writing for fear that your letters being barren should disgust me ; for though they had not been most curious, yet on account of thy sex any man might pardon thee, yea, even a blemish in the child's face seems often beautiful to a father. But then your letters, Meg, were so eloquently written that they had nothing in them to fear from your indulgent father. Also, I heartily thank Mr. Nicolas (a clever astronomer), and congratulate you for having in the space of one month with but small labour to learn so many wonders of that mighty and eternal work which were not discovered in many ages, but by watching in many cold nights under the open sky with much pain and labour. I am well pleased that you have resolved so diligently to study philosophy. I love you for this, dearest Meg, seeing that you will recover by diligence what negligence hath lost you. I have never found you a loiterer,

your learning showing how painfully you have proceeded ;
yet such is your modesty, that you had rather accuse yourself of negligence than vainly boast of diligence, except you
mean that in future you will be *so* diligent that your former
efforts may be called negligent.

"If this be the case nothing can happen more fortunate
to me, or more happy to you, my dearest daughter, for as I
have earnestly wished that you might spend the rest of your
life in studying physic and holy Scriptures; by which help
shall never be wanting to you to the end of your life, which
is to strive that a sound mind be in a healthy body, of
which studies you have already laid a foundation, so I think
that some of the first years of your youth still remaining
may be well bestowed in human learning and the liberal
arts, both because your age may best struggle with difficulty,
and also because it is uncertain whether at any other time
we shall have so learned and careful a master.

"I could wish, dear Meg, that I might talk with you a
long time about these matters, but those who bring in supper
interrupt me and call me away. My supper cannot be so
sweet to me as this my speech with you, were I not to
respect others more than myself. Farewell, dearest daughter ; commend me kindly to your husband, my loving son,
who makes me rejoice that he studies the same things with
you ; so that, although I am wont to advise you always to
give place to your husband, now I give you leave to strive
to master him in the knowledge of the spheres. Farewell,
again and again ; commend me to all your school-fellows,
but especially to your master.

CHAPTER V.

MORE AND HIS FRIENDS.

THE following abstracts of letters written by More, when he was in the height of his fame will no doubt be interesting, coupled as they are with the name of the scholar Erasmus, and of other celebrities, some of whose letters are inserted; they are the key to many which follow them, and abundantly testify to the fact of the poverty of this learned man, as also to the liberality of Archhishop Warham, and Fisher, Bishop of Rochester. The following bears the date of 1516, but no month is specified.

MORE TO ERASMUS.

" I have received only three letters from you direct, dearest Erasmus, since I left. Were I to lie with most solemn countenance and swear I had replied to you as often, it is ten to one you would not believe me; especially as you know me so well, how idle I am in answering letters, and not so superstitiously veracious as to reckon every white lie as black as thunder.

" Pace is on an embassy in your part of the world, yet not *wholly* so, for though not with us, he is not with you. I have a great affection for him and hope he will return safely, as between Pace and you I lose both parts of myself. I hope some great good fortune is in store for Pace, he stands so high in favour with the king, the cardinal, and all men of worth. I hope better luck too for yourself, you are partly to blame and partly in luck, as the prebend of Tournay, which Mountjoy had obtained for you, and which you now wish to have, but had formerly told me and Sampson you would rather decline, will be exchanged for a better. Shortly before you left I went to Tournay, and then heard from Mountjoy and Sampson that Wolsey, in ignorance of these arrangements, had written for that preferment to be given to some one else, to whom he had promised it. I have, however, got them to write back to him, and say it was promised to you, but Wolsey said it was not good enough for you, and promised something better. He is well-disposed towards you. I have quickened Maruffo about paying the money.

"The Archbishop has succeeded at last in getting rid of the chancellorship, which he has been labouring to do for some years. The king has nominated Wolsey in his place. My embassy has been successful but tedious. I have been away more than six months. I have written to the cardinal for my recall, and made use of Pace for that purpose ; but on my return I met Pace at Gravelines, hurrying away at such a rate we had scarce time to say, ' How do you do?' Tunstal has just returned after a stay of ten days of anxiety, and is thrust, much against his stomach, into a new legation. I compare the case of clerical ambassadors to that of a layman like myself. They have no family to burthen them, and have a chance of ecclesiastical promotion which costs the king nothing. Amongst other things which pleased me in my embassy not the least is it that I became acquainted with Buslidian, he entertained me most courteously according to his great wealth and extreme good nature ; he showed me his house most cunningly built, and enriched with costly furniture and a number of antiques, in which you know I take a great pleasure; finally, he showed me his exquisite library, yea, even his very heart he laid open to me, more stored than any library, so that I was greatly amazed.

"But in all my travels, dear Erasmus, nothing happened more to my wish than making the acquaintance of Peter Giles of Antwerp, a man so learned, so merry, so modest, and so friendly, that let me be baked if I would not purchase this man's familiarity with the loss of a good part of my estate. He is a man of good reputation amongst his countrymen, and worthy amongst the best, and being but a young man, I know not whether he be more learned or better endowed with great abilities, he is most virtuous and a great scholar. And, moreover, so courteous to all and so faithful to his friends that you would find it hard to find another to compare with him, he has also a rare diffidence, loves not flattery, candour and wisdom are united in his person, and then his conversation is so cheerful and pleasant that he greatly lessens my still over eager desire to return to my country, my wife, and my children, of the enjoyment of whose company, I am yet very anxious. I am glad to hear the New Testament gets on well.

"Linacre speaks highly of you, as I have heard from some who were present at a supper given by the king, when your praises were being sung. My wife desires to be remembered to you, also Clement, who makes great progress in Greek and Latin, and whom I hope will one day be an ornament to his country. The Bishop of Durham is grateful for the dedication of Seneca."

More to Erasmus.

"25 Feby., 1516.

"The Archbishop has ordered £20 to be sent you. I enclose his letter and the bond of Maruffo, that you may understand how liberal the Archbishop is of his money, and that I am no bad purveyor of other men's property. I have written to an Englishman to pay Aegidius £30 Flemish, which you deposited with me. Colet is earnestly studying Greek, and has made use of the services of Clement (More's page). I think you had better not write and urge Colet in his new studies. 'Solet ut eis, disputandi gratia repugnare suadentibus, etiamsi id suadeant in quod illi sua sponte maxime propendeantur.'"

From the Same to the Same.

"April 28, 1516.

"I am too much engaged, my dear Erasmus, to apply to the beauties of style. On receipt of your letter I called on Maruffo, who said that as soon as he had the money from the Archbishop he would arrange for its payment to you. I told him you *had* received notice of its payment from the Archbishop, on which, in a great fright, Maruffo gave me a bond for the money, took the letters as a security, and wrote for prompt repayment, saying he had already been some time out of pocket by advancing the money to you. I could give you a laughable account of my inter-view with the Archbishop and Maruffo's discomfiture. For every £1 you will receive 30s. 4d. Flemish. The cardinal has received with pleasure your books and letters. I am glad you like Basle. I have read the bundle of correspondence you sent me, Pace has not yet returned ; he is now the king's secretary. Clement desires his remembrances."

The following was evidently written when Erasmus visited England, and was More's guest at Chelsea, from the allusion to the wife of the latter.

Erasmus to Ammonius.

" I hope the hunting may prove as fortunate to you as it has proved unfortunate to me, for it carried away the King and the Cardinal. I angled for Urswick by sending him a New Testament, and asked for the horse he had promised me, but I found when writing to him on Monday that he had also gone hunting ; Thynne slips off in the same way, and now yourself. I beg you to break open the letter destined by me for the Pope, and to have it re-copied. I hope our projects will be successful.

" P.S. ₁I might possibly stay in England a few days, waiting for Urswick to send me the horse, were I not tired of this country, and feel that I am a stale guest to More's wife, (*sentirem me vetulum jam hospitem uxori Moricæ sup putare*)."

The Same to the Same.

" The Bishop of Rochester (Fisher) has prevailed on me to spend ten days with him, I have regretted it more than ten times. I had hoped to wheedle Urswick out of a new horse, by sending him a New Testament, as my old horse died of drink in Flanders, but whilst he was away hunting, my hunting ended in nothing. I shall not leave here before the end of the week. On leaving home I wrote to More and sent him a copy of the Epistolæ ad Leonem, but it was badly written.

" Rochester, 16 Aug., 1516.

" P.S. I shall feel greatly obliged if you will do me the service I asked of you, and thus relieve me from my anxiety."

AMMONIUS TO ERASMUS.

" I did not dare ask you to stay even two days, as you seemed in such a hurry to get away; I will venture, however, though all are not like the Bishop of Rochester. I am not at all surprised that your hunting proved unsuccessful; it is a new kind of metamorphosis to transform books into horses.

"I have received the letters you sent for More, and I will look to your business, but you must not expect haste as the passages are beset with soldiers. Give my compliments to the Bishop of Rochester.

" 26 Aug., 1516."

ERASMUS TO AMMONIUS.

" John would have gained a beating had not More stepped in in time to save him, for as soon as he heard I was in Rochester, he paid me me a visit as if he never expected to see me again. You are always catching at occasions of sending me presents; I would have sent back the last had not More dissuaded me from doing so. I am much pleased with the handsome white horse you have sent, but would rather have played the thief with the Archbishop of York, Colet, or Urswick, the last of whom promised a horse, and will certainly keep his word. I will write from Brabant to Yorke and Larke.

"Rochester, 11th Sep., 1516."

ERASMUS TO MORE.

"I send you my picture by Peter Cocles (the one-eyed), you need not give him more than ten or twelve groschen (grossi). I wish I could come myself. Whilst nursing Petrus Aegidius I have caught so bad a cold that I am almost dead with it. Dorpius is friendly, but sparing of his praises.

"Louvain, 1517."

MORE TO ERASMUS.

"Peter Cocles has brought me the picture; I am delighted with the skill of the artist. If there be one thought of ambition in my mind, it is the pleasure I feel that my name will always hereafter be intimately associated with yours. I have read your Apology, and admire it more than any of your writings. I have sent the transcriber into England with ten groats as you ordered, and I gave a noble to Peter who brought the picture. I am much affected by the death of Buslidian; I was so hampered that I could not get away to St. Omer. Tunstal has returned to England.

"Calais, 17 Oct., 1517."

MORE TO PETRUS AEGIDIUS.

"I am very anxious for your convalescence. I have written to Erasmus, and beg you will seal and send him the enclosed letters.

"P.S.—Enclosed is a copy of verses in which I compliment (Quinctinas Matsys) the painter, for his picture of Erasmus and yourself. Quinctinas has so cleverly imitated my hand that I could not do it so well myself.

"Aegidius was represented holding in his hand a letter from More."

More to Erasmus.

"I have received your letter, my dear Erasmus, written at Calais, and informing me of your prosperous voyage, the Provost of Cassell says that before he reached home you had got safely to Brussels, Maruffo grumbles that he has lost on the money paid to you. I have sent a bill for £20 more from the Archbishop, and the bearer will pay Aegidius the £20 deposited with me by you. I sent my Utopia some time since, and am delighted to hear it will come out in a magnificent form.

"Lond., 1517.

Erasmus to More.

"I sent you lately a packet of letters, with a copy of the Utopia by a friend, and I now send you by the hand of another, Reuchlin's work, Reuchlinsea Omnia, in a single volume, which you are to show to Bishop Fisher and return when read.

"I commend to your notice the Theological Propositions. I sent a letter to Marlianus, who imagined that the first book of Utopia was written by me. As soon as you have corrected the Utopia I will send the MS. to Basle or Paris.

"The Prince (Charles) will soon take his departure, and I am quite uncertain as to my own movements. Large sums are demanded of the people and immediate payment, it has been allowed by the nobles and the clergy, that is, by those who will not have to pay it. The Emperor is at hand with a magnificent army, and the fields are full of soldiers. I wish to know if Canterbury, Colet, and Rochester remain constant to me. A pest upon Maruffo and his band.

"Antwerp, March, 1817.

" Francis is in England, send back copies of the enclosed letters, and also those delivered by Lupset."

Thus did Erasmus vent his complaint concerning the money committed to him from England by the hands of a knavish Italian, who retained no small portion of it, and he then begged the Archbishop to take heed for the future what agents he employed in the affair. This good Prelate had been in pain, as his letters show, lest Erasmus should want for money, and promised to procure him another prebend. How uncommon is it for persons in high station to have any regard at all for the learned, and much more to preserve so constant an affection especially for one who is at a distance. Erasmus in his preface to S. Jerome tells his patron that as he was contented with a little; so at that time he wanted for nothing. At present, he writes, "I think myself a sort of nobleman, for I maintain two horses who are better fed, and two servants who are better clad than their master."

Living thus, it was impossible he could lay up much, for he wanted amanuensis to transcribe his works, and horses to travel himself. In appearance Erasmus was low of stature with blue eyes, and in his youth his hair was of flaxen colour. His countenance was grave ; he had a wonderful memory and without question, was the finest genius and the most learned person of his age.*

ARCHBISHOP WARHAM TO ERASMUS.

"I received your letter on the ides of February, speaking highly of your expectations ; If fortune favors you I advise you to embrace it. I would have invited you to England that I might have enjoyed in my present retirement from the bench the pleasure of your conversation, but I am unwilling to frustrate your hopes. You need not be under any anxiety about your pension, I have written to Maruffo to transmit you a sum of money free of all expenses."

"Canterbury, March 24th, 1517."

BISHOP FISHER TO ERASMUS.

"I wrote to you lately and sent you a little present. I have no control over the funds placed under my care, its expenditure being limited to certain purposes which it is out of my power to alter. So long as I have any money, however, I will not suffer you to want, who are so necessary to the University of Cambridge. Mountjoy will be sure to remember you if he has made any promise to do so. He is now at Court."

"London, 1517.

Though printed at Basle, the Greek Testament of Erasmus was strictly the work of his residence in England. In the collation and examination of MSS. required for that purpose, he had the assistance and support of Englishmen ; and English friends and patrons lent him that aid and support, without which it is very doubtful whether Erasmus would

* Da Pin.

ever have completed the work. He was not always liberal in acknowledging his obligations, yet in his New Testament, hidden away in a page where no one would have expected to find it, he bursts into a sudden fit of enthusiasm and celebrates the praises of Warham in language such as none but Erasmus could command. After descanting upon the Archbishop's modesty, labors, genius, administration of justice (for he was still Chancellor), his patronage of letters and learned men, Erasmus thus pursues the subject.

" Had it been my good fortune to have fallen in with such a Mæcenas in my earlier years, I might, perhaps, have done something for literature. Now, born as I was in an unhappy age, when barbarism reigned supreme, especially amongst my own people, by whom the least inclination for literature was then looked on as a crime, what could I do with my small modicum of talent? Death carried off Henry de Berghes, Bishop of Cambray, my first patron, my second, William, Lord Mountjoy, an English peer, was separated from me by his employments at court and the tumults of war. By this means it was my good fortune, then advanced in life and close on my fortieth year, to be introduced to Archbishop Warham. Encouraged and cheered by his bounty, I gained youth and strength in the cause of litera-ture. What nature and my country denied me his bounty supplied.*

" In one of his letters, Erasmus had complained that it was discreditable he should be obliged to beg, after spending so much time in England, but has had so much from Arch-bishop Warham, that it would be a shame to accept more if he offered it. And that Linacre, who knew he was going

* Brewer's Cal.

away with no more than six angels, and in indifferent health, urged him not to apply to the Archbishop or Mountjoy, but habituate himself to poverty. 'I could do so,' he adds, ' when health was strong, but must try now to save my life, and I will not refuse Colet's bounty.'"

"P.S. When I broached the subject of an under Master of Arts, it was said to me, ' Who would be a schoolmaster that could live any other way?' And on urging that above all others it was a christian work, my interlocutor replied, 'If a man wishes to serve Christ let him enter a Monastery;' and when I rejoined that to do good to others was charity, I was answered, 'Perfection consisted in leaving all things.' " *

MORE TO ERASMUS.

" I have spoken to Urswick, my dear Erasmus, about the horse, and he says he has none fit to send you at present. He sent you some time since Maruffo's bond, which is on more liberal terms, though neither I nor Lily, who is is a good Italian scholar, could read it. Palgrave is going to Louvain to study law, but will continue his Greek and Latin. He asked me for an introduction to you, and brings with him letters sent to you from Basle, which I have had some time."

" I am in the clouds with the dream of the government to be offered me by my Utopians, and fancy myself a grand potentate with a crown and a Franciscan cloak, (paludamentum) followed by a grand processsion of the Amauri. Should it please Heaven to exalt me to so high a dignity, I shall still keep a corner in my heart for Erasmus and

* Brewer's Cal.

Tunstal, and should they pay me a visit to Utopia, I shall make all my subjects honour them as is befitting the friends of Majesty. The morn has dawned and dispelled my dream, and stripped off my royalty, plunging me down into my old mill-round at the court."

" London, 1517."

MORE TO ERASMUS.

" I send you my Utopia, my dear Erasmus, and have delivered your letters to the Venetian Ambassador, who would have been glad of a copy of the New Testament. We paid each other long compliments on meeting, but I like him very much. I have heard nothing yet from the Archbishop. Colet has not spoken to me about you, but he has spoken with Wolsey, who was profuse in your praise. My agent (John) will deliver to you at Michaelmas the money deposited with me. If you print my Epigrams a second time, would it not be better to omit those relating to Briarius."

" London, 3 Sept., 1517."

COLET TO ERASMUS.

" I have received your letter by the one-eyed (Peter) I did not know till then where he was. Your edition of the New Testament is much sought after, some approving some condemning it, using the arguments of Martin Dorp. I have read it with mixed feelings, glad of the new light, sorry for my ignorance of Greek. I look anxiously for S. Jerome. I approve of your work De Institutione Christi Principis, and I wish you quietly settled. The Archbishop, whom I visited a few days since, talked much about you. He is rid of all business and lives in happy retirement. *(otio felicissimo)*

I have read your comment on Ps. 1, and admire your *Copia.*
I wonder you should praise my fortune, which is far from
ample, and scarce sufficient for my necessary expenses. I
hear you are learning Hebrew."

" From my mother's house at Stepney. She is a cheerful
old lady and often talks of you."

" London, 1517."

ARCHBISHOP WARHAM TO ERASMUS.

"I have received two letters from you, one in Westminster Hall, the other by so bald a man that he had
scarcely a single hair on his head, who stated that you were
suffering from a cough. I send you twenty gold angels to
cure you, '*inter quos Raphaelem salutis modicum reperies.*'
I am glad to hear that you intend visiting London next
January.

" Lambeth, 11 Nov., 1517."

MORE TO ERASMUS.

" 15 Nov., 1517.

" I have received your letters for Colet and Fisher, with
a book for the latter. I wonder you have not written to
the Archbishop yourself, for you have more influence with
Warham than any one else has, but I will do it, if you think
I can do more in person than you can by letter ; but you
will have to wait, as it is usual for an ambassador, on his
return, to visit the King first, and not even casually call
upon any one else. Business also at Calais proceeds so
slowly that I fear I shall have to stay a long time. I will
manage that your pension shall be paid by Maruffo. I do
not think it advisable to redeem it, as it may offend the

Archbishop. I am glad your Paraphrase is in the press. Pace has not yet returned, nor do I know when he will. I cannot think what business he has on hand. As far as I can hear he has none with the Swiss or the Emperor, and he has now been more than a year at Constance. I am glad you liked the verses on the picture. 'A friar had criticized them on account of More comparing the two friends to Castor and Pollux.'"

MORE TO ERASMUS.

" I make no doubt that Palgrave has given you my letters. I am glad to find that Dorpius, who would not be quieted by mild usage, has yielded to sterner treatment. Such is the way with some. Lupset has given me certain sheets which he had belonging to you, e.g. Julii Genius, De Pueris Erudiendis, he affirms he has nothing else. Linacre will send his translations of Galen to Paris to be printed under the care of Lupset, and is very much pleased at the notice of his books by you. Lately, in a large concourse of people, the Bishop of Winchester (Fox) affirmed that your version of the New Testament was worth more to him than ten commentaries. I expect my Utopia.

" London, 15 Dec., 1517.

" I have sent your letter to Latimer. My wife desires a million of compliments, especially for your careful wish that she should live many years. She says she is the more anxious for this as she will live the longer to plague me."

ERASMUS TO PETER AEGIDIUS.

" I am sorry to hear, my dear Aegidius, of your father's death. The Archbishop Warham writes me that I am to receive £20, and if I send a receipt the money shall be paid immediately. I beg you to send to John Crull to pay the money, and take my receipt. It is to be paid to my agent in England. More is still at Calais involved in tedious business, this it is to be loved by kings and blessèd by cardinals. Pace has been in banishment with the Swiss for two years. The Paraphrase is nearly finished. You are not to send the books to N. at present, until I see More; he is now at Cambridge intending to lecture on Greek.

"Louvain, 17 Dec., 1517."

Erasmus to Archbishop Warham.

"I am going to Venice through Germany; the road is dangerous from robbers and sickness. I intend to increase my store of books. Should it be my fate to return, I shall visit England and settle there. I beg your Grace's liberality. I am sorry to hear of the death of Grocyn. I think the war against the Turks is a mere blind; Lorenzo, the Pope's nephew, is attempting to occupy Campania, and has married the daughter of the King of Navarre. I wish I had such a horse as you once sent by me to the Abbot of St. Bertin's. People seem to wonder that at my age I am going to undertake such a toilsome journey, whilst I am much more astonished that the Bishop of Paris, who is now nearly seventy, should engage himself in a task much more burthensome, for purposes not half so important in my judgment."

"Louvain, 5th March, 1518."

More to the University of Oxford.

"When I was in London I heard that certain scholars of the University in contempt of Greek literature had banded together under the name of Trojans, taking the titles of Priam, Hector, Paris, and the like. After I had followed the king to Abingdon, it was repeated to me that this folly was beginning to become serious, and that in the public sermons made in the sacred season of Lent, much nonsense has been uttered against learning generally, one cannot but denounce in severe terms the folly of a preacher who has distinguished himself by an attack on the studies of the University and especially on Erasmus. There is every necessity for a liberal education for the proper study of theology."

" Abingdon, 4 Kal. April, 1518."

ERASMUS TO HUTTON.

" More is greatly delighted with your writings and at your request, difficult as is the task, I send you the following description of him :—He is somewhat below the middle height but perfectly symmetrical in all his limbs ; of a fair complexion, face inclined rather to fairness than palor, with very little red except a slight bloom ; hair inclining to black or dark brown ; thin beard ; grey eyes covered with specks, which, as a mark of genius, is much admired in England, and indicates a generous nature. His inside corresponds to his out. He has a pleasant smiling look, and to tell you the truth is more inclined to pleasantry than gaiety, though he is entirely free from buffoonery. His right shoulder is a little higher that the left, especially when he walks—not a natural defect but an acquired ill habit. As compared with the rest of his person, his hands are a little clumsy. He has always been careless of his dress. I became acquainted with him when he was twenty-three, he is now near forty, and you may guess from this description how handsome he was in his youth. He has good health, but is not robust, and is likely to live long, as his father is a very hale old man. He is indifferent in the choice of his food, generally drinks water, and sometimes, to please others, beer, little better than water, out of a tin cup. As it is the fashion to drink healths in England, More has learned to pledge his guests *summo ore*. His favourite diet is beef, salt meats, and coarse brown bread well fermented ; he prefers milk and vegetable diet, and is fond of eggs. His voice is penetrating and clear, but not musical, although he is fond of music, his speech plain and distinct. He wears no silk, purple, or gold chains, except when he cannot avoid it, and dislikes all ceremony. At first, he was disinclined to Court life, through hatred of tyranny and love of equality, and would not be induced to take service at Court except after great solicitation from Henry VIII. He likes liberty and ease, but no one is more active or more patient than he when occasion requires it. He is friendly, accessible, and fond of conversation, hating tennis, dice, and similar games. He is very much given to jesting ; wrote and acted little comedies when a lad, and loves a jest even when made at his own expense. It was he who induced me to write my Praise of Folly. He is equally at home with the wise and the foolish, and in female society he is full of his jokes. No one is less led by the judgment of the vulgar, and yet no man has more common sense. His chief pleasure is in watching animals; he has a variety of them, for instance, an ape, a fox, a ferret, &c. Any rarity or exotic he purchases readily, and his house is well furnished with curiosities. He has always been fond of female society and female friendships.

" As a young man he devoted himself to Greek, for which he was nearly disinherited by his father, who wished to bring him up to the law, a profession, which above all others in England, leads to honour and emolument, but requires many years of hard study. He lectured on St. Augustine *De civitate Dei*, and was fitting himself by a course of study and seclusion for the priesthood ; but as he had a wish to enter the married life he abandoned this design.

"He married a young girl of good family, quite uneducated, as she had been brought up entirely in the country, had her instructed, and made her an accomplished musician, when he unfortunately lost her, after she had given birth to three daughters, Margaret, Elizabeth, and Cicely, and a son named John. Unable to live alone, he married a widow some months after, neither young nor handsome (*nec bella, nec puella*, as he himself is fond of saying) but a good housekeeper to look after his family, with whom, however, he lives on very amicable terms. Nothing can show his influence over her more completely than that, though she is advanced in life, and very attentive to housekeeping, More has prevailed upon her to learn various musical instruments.

"He manages his whole household in the same admirable way, there is no noise nor contention, no vice nor bad repute, and perhaps no family can be found where father, step-mother, and son live together on such excellent terms. Moreover, his father has just married a third wife, and More swears he has not seen a better one.

" When he lived entirely by his profession, he gave every man true and faithful advice, urging them to make up their differences though it was contrary to his own interest

When that was not possible, as some persons take pleasure in litigation, he showed them how to proceed at the smallest cost. He was for some time a judge for civil suits in London, an easy and an honourable post, as he sits only on Thursday till dinner time, and well did he behave in this post till he was sent on various embassies by the King, who takes great pleasure in his company and conversation.

"With all this favour, More is neither proud nor boastful, nor forgetful of his friends, but always obliging and charitable. He wrote his Utopia, to show the perils to which governments are exposed, but he especially aimed at his own country; the second book was written first. He is a good *ex tempore* speaker, has a ready wit, and a well-stored memory, so that he speaks without hesitation. Colet is accustomed to say of him that he is the only genius in England. In his devotions he prayed *ex tempore*, and he talks with his friends on a future life with perfect sincerity and assured hope.

"Such men as More, Mountjoy, Linacre, Pace, Colet, Stokesley, Latimer, Tunstal, and Clerk are a credit to the Court of Henry VIII.

"Clumsy as is this description, it will not be tedious to you, considering the subject. You can send by no one better than Pace, whether I be in Brabant or Brittany. I hear you are in great favour with Cardinal Cajetan.

"Antwerp, 10 Kal., Aug., 1519."

In another letter to Erasmus, More writes as follows :—

"When I returned from my embassy to Flanders, the king would have given me a yearly pension, which, inasmuch as one respects honour and profit was not to be lightly esteemed, yet have I refused it, and shall continue to do so, for I should be sorry to forsake my present means derived from the city, which I prefer to better, or else I must keep it with the chance .that my fellow citizens may distrust my sincerity, should any future controversy arise between them and the king on the subject of their privileges."

About the year 1516, More wrote in Latin, his Utopia, a book so much admired that it was speedily translated into French, Italian, Dutch, and English.

This Utopia described a complete commonwealth in an imaginary island, supposed to be lately discovered in America; but More's pen, however, depicted it in such glowing colours, that many persons mistook what was merely romance for reality. Raphael, who is the traveller, and the relater of the laws, customs, and manners of the Utopians, or non-existing republic, is More himself, who, depicting a kingdom in a New World, which no one had seen or would see, obliquely censures the faults and defects in the old one.

The first book is full of striking and beautiful passages, serving to excite the attention and give the reader an eager desire to know what Raphael had seen in his voyages.*

The following letter was addressed by More to his friend Petrus Aegidius (Peter Giles), whom he puts forward as having been with himself the auditor of Raphael in his Utopia.

" I am almost ashamed, my dearest Peter Giles, to send you this book of " The Utopia or Commonwealth," after about a year's delay, when you no doubt looked for it in about six weeks; for as you are sensible that I had no occasion to make use of my invention, or to arrange my subject methodically, but to repeat exactly what I heard Raphael

* Jortin's Erasmus.

relate in your presence, so a studied elegance of expression would have been unnecessary, as he delivered the matter to us in a careless style ; he, being, you know, a better master of Greek than of Latin, the plainer my words are, the more they will resemble his simplicity, and consequently be nearer to the truth. This is all that I think depends on me, and the only thing in which I think myself concerned.

"I confess I had very little left for me to do ; for the invention of such a scheme would have cost a man—whose learning and capacity was of the ordinary standing—some pains and much time.

"But had it been necessary that this relation should have been consistent with truth as well as elegantly expressed, it could never have been performed, even after all the time and pains that I could have bestowed upon it ; for my part in it was so small, all that belonged to me being only to give a full and true account of the things that I had heard, and, though this required little of my time, yet even that little was denied me by my other duties which press much upon me. For, while in pleading, hearing, judging, or deciding causes, or arranging disputes as an arbitrator, in waiting on some men on business, and on others out of respect, the greatest part of the day is spent in other men's affairs, the remainder must be given to my family at home, so that I can reserve no part of it to myself, that is, to study. I must gossip with my wife and chat with my children, and find something to say to my servants, for all these things I reckon a part of my business, unless I were content to become as a stranger in mine own house ; for with whomsoever either nature, or chance, or choice, hath engaged a man in any relation of life, he must endeavour to make himself as acceptable to them as he possibly can ; and yet so demeaning himself towards them as not to spoil them by excessive gentleness, so that his servants may not become his masters.   In such like occupations days, weeks, months and years slip away, what is then left for writing ? And yet I have said nothing of the time that must be for sleep and meals, indeed, all the time that I can gain for myself is that which I steal from each, and because that is not much, I have made but a small progress ; yet is it somewhat.   I have at last got to the end of my Utopia, which I now send to you, and expect that after you have read it, you will let me know if you can put me in mind of anything that has escaped me, for though. I should think myself happy if I had but as great powers of invention and learning as I know I have of memory, yet I do not rely so entirely upon it as to think I can forget nothing.

"My servant, John Clement, has started some things that shake me ; you know he was present with us, as I think he ought to be, at every conversation that may be of use to him ; for I promise myself great things from the progress he has made so speedily in Greek and Latin.   As far as my memory serves me, the bridge over Amidor at Amaurot, was, according to Raphael's account, 500 paces broad, but John assures me he spoke only of 300 paces, therefore pray recollect what you can of this, if you remember nothing of it I will not alter what I have written, because it is to the best of my remembrance, for as I will take care that there may be nothing falsely written down, so if there is anything doubtful, though I may, perhaps, tell a lie, I am sure I will not *make* one, for I would rather pass for a good man that a wise one.

" I have another difficulty that presses upon me more, and

makes it necessary you should write to him. I know not whom to blame for it, whether Raphael, you, or myself, for as we did not think of asking it, so neither did he of telling us, in what part of the New World Utopia is situated. This was such an omission that I would gladly redeem it ; at any rate I am ashamed, that after I have told so many things concerning this island, I cannot let my readers know in what sea it lies. There are some amongst us that have a mighty desire to go thither, and in particular one pious divine is very earnest upon it, not so much from a vain curiosity of seeing unknown countries, as that he may advance our religion, which is happily begun to be planted there, and to do this regularly, he intends to procure a mission from the Pope and be sent there as their bishop.

" In such a case he makes no scruple of aspiring to that character, but thinks such ambition meritorious when actuated solely by a pious ; zeal he desires it only as the means of advancing the christian religion, and not for any honour to himself; therefore if you meet with Raphael, or know where he is, be pleased to write to him, and inform yourself of these things that there be no falsehood in my book, or any important truth wanting. Perhaps it will not be unwise to let him see the book itself, for as no man can correct any errors that may be in it so well as he, so by reading it, he will be able to give a more perfect judgment, and you will be able to discover whether this undertaking of mine is acceptable to him or not, for if he intends to write an account of his travels, perhaps he will not be pleased that I should prevent him in that part which belongs to the Utopian Commonwealth, since if I should do so, his book will not surprise the world with the pleasure which this new discovery will give the age. I am so little fond of appearing in print, that if he desires it I will lay it aside, and, even though he positively approves it, I am not positively determined as to the publishing it. Men's tastes differ much, some are of so morose a temper, so sour a disposition, and form such absurd judgments, that others of cheerful and lively temper, who do not indulge their genius, seem much happier, than those who waste their time and strength in order to publish a book, which, though of itself useful or pleasant, will be sure to be either laughed at or censured. Many know nothing of learning, others despise it. A man that is accustomed to a coarse and harsh style, thinks everything stupid that is not barbarous. Our trifling pretenders to learning think little of that that is not dressed up in obsolete words, some love only old things, and many like nothing but what is their own. Some are so sour that they cannot endure jests, others so dull that they can bear nothing that is not sharp ; while others are as fearful of any-thing gay or lively, as a man bit by a mad dog is of water ; others are so light and unsettled, that their thoughts change with every movement of the body. Some, when they meet in taverns pass censures over their cups upon all writers, and with a supercilious liberty condemn everything they do not like, in which they have an advantage, like a bald man who can catch hold of another by the hair, while the other cannot do the same by him. They are safe as it were from gun-shot, since there is nothing in them solid enough to be taken hold of. Others are so thankless that even when they are well pleased with a book, they think they owe nothing to the author, and are like those rude guests, who having been well entertained at a good dinner, when they have satisfied their appetites, go away without thanking him that treated them. But who would charge himself with making a feast for men of such nice palates who are so forgetful of the civility paid them. But do you clear up these points with Raphael, and then it will be time to consider whether it be fit to publish it or not, for since I have been at the pains to write it, if he consents to its being published, I will follow my friend's advice and chiefly yours.

"Farewell, my dear Peter, commend me kindly to your good wife, and love me still as you used to do, for I assure you I love you daily more and more."

CHAPTER VI.

Ambassador and Statesman.

It was during the five years in which More was engaged in embassies on the Continent that many of the interesting letters given in the last chapter were written by himself or his friends. He had spent, with how great unwillingness, several passages in these letters have shown the reader, much time both in France and in the Netherlands, the Low Countries forming part of the possessions of the great Emperor Charles V.

Henry loved nothing better than to be attended by More during the Royal progresses, and at Oxford and Cambridge, where he was received with eloquent Latin orations, he was the man appointed by his Majesty to reply to them *ex tempore*. When he accompanied Henry to France to meet the French King, and the monarchs embraced each other in a hollow friendship at the tedious splendours of the Field of Cloth of Gold, More was employed to make the speech of congratulation; and when the Emperor Charles V. landed in England to visit his aunt, Queen Catharine, his welcome was so eloquent and graceful as to excite the admiration of the Emperor as well as of his foreign attendants. Amongst his other virtues we must notice the generosity and meekness of this great man, it not unfrequently happened that those who entered into learned disputations with him had the worst part of the argument, and it was then his custom, when he perceived this, to wittily turn the subject and discourse on some other matter, indeed so great was his love of learning that he rather preferred that others should deem him worsted than discourage scholars in their studies. The next step in the way of worldly promotion was the Chair of the House of Commons. The real object for calling the Parliament which met in April, 1523, was to obtain money. Henry, following the example of his father, had governed during eight years without the aid of the great council of the nation, but his necessities now compelled him to summon a parliament.

Very much depended on the Speaker, for he not only had great influence with the assembly, as he was their president, but was also wont to take part in their discussions. With the Commons themselves the choice of the Speaker rested, but in reality it was dictated by the Court, and at this time Sir Thomas was chosen from the fact of his being so popular, and from his having had a part in the administration of Wolsey, who as yet had not been liable to much exception. The Commons testified the greatest delight by the recommendation, and presented their favourite More as Speaker to the King whilst sitting on his throne in the Upper House.

But More's modesty and love of retirement made him attempt to disqualify himself, and he cited the story of Phormio the philosopher, who desired Hannibal to come and hear his lectures, and so, when the latter consented Phormio began to read the *Re di Militari* of chivalry, whereupon Hannibal called the philosopher an arrogant fool to presume to teach him, who was already master of chivalry, and of all the arts of war, and so, quoth Sir Thomas :

" If I should presume to speak before his majesty of learning, and the well ordering of the Government, or such like matters; the King, who is so deeply learned, might say to one, as Hannibal to Phormio, and so I do beseech your Majesty to order the Commons to choose another Speaker."

The Chancellor by the King's command replied—

" His Majesty, by long experience of your service, is well acquainted with your wit, learning, and discretion, and believeth the Commons have chosen the fittest person amongst them to be their Speaker."

More, then seeing it was useless to attempt to decline the honourable office, made the following speech. It is copied from the original MS., and is curious as an authentic specimen of the state in which the English language then was, and the kind of oratory that prevailed.*

" Sith I perceive, most redoubted Sovereign that it standeth not with your pleasure to reform this election and cause it to be changed, but have by the mouth of the Most Reverend Father in God, the Legate, your Highness's Chancellor, thereunto given your most royal assent, and have of your benignity determined—far above that I may bear for this office to repute me meet, rather than that you should impute it to your Commons that they had incorrectly chosen, I am ready obediently to conform myself to the accomplishment of your Highness's pleasure and commandment.

"I dare to beg a favourable construction on all my own words and actions, and favour for the plain and homely speech as well as privilege for the Commons.

" Much care has been taken to elect men of discretion according to the exigency of the writs.

" Whereby it is not to be doubted but there is a very sub-

* Campbell.

tantial assembly of right wise, meet, and politique persons;
yet, most precocious Prince, sith among so many wise men,
neither is every man wise alike, nor among so many alike
well witted, every man well spoken ; and it often happeth
that as much folly is uttered with pointed polished speech,
so many boistrous and rude in language give right substantial counsel ; and sith also in matters of great importance
the mind is often so occupied in the matter that a man rather
studieth what to say, than how : by reason whereof the
wisest man and best speaker in the whole country fortuneth,
when his mind is fervent in the matter, somewhat to speak
in such wise as he would afterwards wish to have been
uttered otherwise, and yet no worse will had when he spake
it, than he had when he would so gladly change it.   Therefore, most generous Sovereign, considering that in your High
Court of Parliament is nothing treated but matter of weight
and importance concerning your realm and your own royal
estate, it could not fail to put to silence from the giving of their
advice and counsel many of your discreet Commons, to the
great hindrance of your common affairs, unless every one of
your Commons were utterly discharged of all doubt and
fear how any thing that it should happen them to·speak
should happen of your Highness to be taken.   And on this
point, though your well known and proved benignity putteth
every man in good hope, yet such is the weight of the
matter, such is the reverend dread that the timorous hearts
of your natural subjects conceive towards your Highness,
our most redoubted King and undoubted Sovereign, that
they cannot in this point find themselves satisfied, except
your gracious bounty therein declared put away the scruple
of their timorous minds, and put them out of doubt.   It

may therefore like your most abundant Grace to give to all your Commons here assembled, your most gracious licence and pardon freely, without doubt of your dreadful displeasure every man to discharge his conscience, and boldly in every thing incidental among us to declare his advice ; and whatsoever happeneth any man to say, that it may like your noble Majesty, of your inestimable goodness, to take all in good part, interpreting every man's words, how uncunningly however they may be avouched, to proceed yet of good zeal towards the profit of your realm and honour of your royal person; and the prosperous state and preservation whereof, most exultant Sovereign, is the thing which we, all your Majesty's humble loving subjects, according to the most bounden duty of our national allegiance, most highly desire and pray for."

More has been blamed for servility for this speech, but the phrases addressed to the king are only in accordance with the habit of the times in which he lived; and Sir Thomas evinced no cowardly feeling when he craved liberty of speech, while he levelled a few hits at the country squires over whom he was placed.

At this Parliament Wolsey felt himself much aggrieved at the independent spirit shewn by the Commons, and complained that nothing could be said or done in either House, but that it was at once made the subject of discourse in every road-side ale-house.

A subsidy of the enormous sum of £800,000 had been demanded for the purposes of war, to the amazement of the Commons, who declared it to be more than the current coin of the whole realm ; and, enraged at their tardy compliance, and trusting to overcome them by his presence, Wolsey resolved to go to the House himself with his accustomed lordly retinue. He had complained of breach of privilege in publishing parliamentary debates, and the wit of More made him resolve that the future blame should lay only with his followers.

"My masters," said he, "the Cardinal hath lately laid to our charge, the lightness of our tongues for things uttered out of this House, and in my mind it will not be amiss to receive him with all his pomp, his maces, his poleaxes, his pillars, his cross, his hat, and the Great Seal, to the intent that if he find the like fault with us again, we may lay the blame on those whom his Grace bringeth with him."

To this advice the House agreed, and the Cardinal was received accordingly, and exerted all his powers of eloquence to prove how necessary it was that the demand should be granted, and proceeded to shew that a smaller sum would not serve the prince's purposes.

All the members, however, remained in their seats, and observing an obstinate silence answered not a word, and seeing no intention on their part to grant his request, he added—

"Masters, you have amongst you many wise and learned men, and sith I am from the King's own person, sent hither for the preservation of yourselves and all the realm, I think it but meet you should give me a reasonable answer. "Still, however, every man held his peace when he addressed himself to one Marney, afterwards Lord Marney."

"How say you, Master Marney," he exclaimed, "but Marney also was silent, and the Cardinal, in no little vexation of spirit, then addressed himself one by one to those who were the most influential, and considered the wisest of the assembly, but none of them answered a word, they having of one accord agreed before to reply only by the mouth of their Speaker."

"Masters," then said the Cardinal, "unless it be the manner of your House, as very likely it be, by the mouth of your Speaker, whom you have chosen for trusty and wise (as indeed he is) in such cases to utter your minds, here is without doubt a marvellous obstinate silence." Then requiring answer of the Speaker, More reverently kneeling, according to the custom of the times, excused the silence of the House, abashed at the presence of so noble a personage, who was able to manage the most learned and wisest in the realm; then More went on to prove that for them to make reply was neither expedient nor agreeable with the ancient liberty of the House, showing in the end that, though they had all with their voices trusted him, that except they could put in his one head all their individual wits, he alone in so weighty a matter was quite unable to reply to His Grace's demands until he had received their instructions."

"Thereupon," says the old biographer, "the Cardinal departed in a rage, much displeased with Sir Thomas, who had thus frustrated his wishes. To the indignation of the King and himself the matter was adjourned from day to day, and Wolsey again repaired to the House ; they listened to what he had to say, and finally made a grant not at all equivalent to the exorbitant demand which had been made them, but which they were compelled to pay at once, contrary to former customs.

Wolsey did not conceal his anger, for when he met More in the gallery at Whitehall, he exclaimed,

"Would to God you had been at Rome, Master More,

when I made you Speaker." "Your Grace not offended," replied More, with his usual calmness, " so would I too, my lord, for then I should have seen the place I long have desired to visit;" adding, to give a turn to the subject, " This gallery of yours, my lord, pleaseth me much better than your other at Hampton Court."

Roper, however, charges the Cardinal with endeavouring to remove More out of his way, by advising the King to send him as his ambassador to Spain, recommending him for his learning, wisdom and discretion. More, however, had no desire to be promoted in this fashion, and begged him to excuse him on the plea that the climate of Spain disagreed with him, though, he added, he was still ready to do his Majesty's pleasure, to which the King replied, " It is not our pleasure, Master More, to do you hurt, but to do you good we would be glad ; we will therefore employ you otherwise." We must add, however, to the credit of Wolsey, that the Cardinal soon overcame his anger, for when the session was concluded he wrote the following letter to Henry, for the usual reward of £200 to the Speaker.*

Wolsey to Henry VIII.

"I have shown the bearer, Sir Thomas More, divers matters to declare to your Grace.

"It has been usual, even when the Parliament is right soon finished, to give the Speaker a reward of £100 for his household, besides the £100 ordinary.

" Your Grace is aware of the faithful diligence of More, in the late Parliament, about the subsidy, so that no man could

---

* State Papers.

deserve it better. I will, therefore, cause the sum to be advanced on learning your Grace's pleasure.

"I am the rather moved to put your Highness in mind thereof, because he is not the most ready to speak and solicit his own cause."

"Hampton Court, 24th August."

It is certain, however, that there was a great jealousy on the part of the Cardinal, after he had been thwarted by the keenness of the Chancellor of the Duchy; yet there was never anything approaching to an open rupture between them, for nothing could bear down the calmness of More. The Cardinal once showed him the draft of a treaty with two of the continental powers, asking his opinion, and pressing him to say "whether there were anything to be misliked." Sir Thomas, misled by his apparent sincerity, was taken off his guard, and imagining that he really *did* desire his advice, pointed out some great blunders which occurred in it. His astonishment may be imagined, when starting up in a fit of anger, Wolsey exclaimed,

"By the mass, thou art the veriest fool of all the council."

"God be thanked," replied More, with his usual equanimity, "that the King, our master, hath but one fool in his council."

The fascinating charm of More's conversation, his engaging and lively manners, and ready flow of wit and humour, endeared him to Henry, who with his queen, not only coveted his company at the palace during the evening hours, but he was even wont on certain occasions to throw aside the etiquette of royalty, and steal on Sir Thomas in his domestic privacy at Chelsea.

Without any previous warning or notice of his intention,

he would come and dine with him; and after dinner, in the pleasant summer evening, would enjoy a ramble in the garden, where with his arm thrown around the neck of More, with the affection of a son or a brother, the monarch would abandon himself to the pleasure of unrestricted friendly intercourse.

On one of these occasions after the departure of Henry, his son-in-law, Roper, spoke with delight of the King having manifested his partiality for him in a more pointed manner than he had seen him do with any other man, unless it might be the Cardinal, with whom he had been once seen to walk arm in arm."

"I thank our lord, son Roper," replied he, "I find his Grace, my very good lord indeed, and I believe he doth as singularly favour me as any other within the realm. Howbeit, son Roper, I may tell thee I have no cause to be proud, for if my head would win him a castle in France, it should not fail to go."

This anecdote is told by Roper himself, and clearly shows the penetration of More, aided by the opportunities which unrestricted freedom of intercourse gave him of being present with the King. when he was off his guard, and not endeavouring to throw a mask over his real character, enabled him to read his disposition, such as it really was. Doubtless the wisdom of More discovered that beneath this show of outward affability and good temper there lurked an innate selfishness and cruelty, which, were he thwarted would break through all restraints, so that he would not scruple to crush the offender, however dear he might previously have been to him. For a time however, More was in a manner necessary to the happiness of the capricious and despotic Henry.

It must have been during one of these familiar visits of the king at More's house that Holbein, the painter, was introduced to him by Sir Thomas ; the latter had been anxiously longing to see Erasmus in England, he having been often prevented from coming in consequence of the prevalence of the sweating sickness.   He then wrote to him with much earnestness for his picture, and Erasmus, who desired to forward the interests of Holbein, the painter, who, though a great master of his art, had at Basle but small encouragement, yielded to More's request, sat for the portrait, and sent Holbein over with it, giving him letters of recommendation to his friend.

Holbein, however, lingered so long at Antwerp, that he reached England in a state of destitution, having literally almost begged his way thither.

Sir Thomas received him with the warmest welcome, and kept him in his house nearly three years, during which time he drew the portraits of his kind patron and his family.

Sir Thomas having enriched his house with Holbein's productions, adopted the following method of introducing him to the King.   He invited Henry to an entertainment and hung up all Holbein's pieces in the great hall of his mansion.   The King upon his first entrance was so charmed with the sight, that he asked Sir Thomas if the artist who had given such expression and life to his paintings were now living, and if so, was he to be had for money ; on which Sir Thomas at once introduced him to the King, who immediately engaged him for his own service.

In the few letters that we are now about to give, it may be easily gathered how weary his spirit must have grown of the political intrigues in which he was compelled to bear a part, in the discharge of his irksome duty of ambassador and politician ; and his frank and upright spirit must often have shrunk within itself at the hypocritical deceit and artifice in which he was made to join.

Many, perhaps, of those who may glance over these pages will turn aside from the dry details of state matters with which the following letters are filled, whilst others will gladly peruse them, and smile at the chicanery and artifice which they reveal, the three several courts of England, France, and Germany endeavouring to outvie and outwit each other.

The following letters, it will be observed, must have been written when More was with the court in England, sad in spirit at his absence from his Chelsea home.

Sir T. More to Cardinal Wolsey.

" My Singular Good Lord—I was commanded last night by the king to deliver to your servant, Forest, a complaint sent to him by the men of Waterford against the town of New Ross, in Ireland, for disturbing them in the use of a grant of prize wines, made to them by the king's progenitors. The king remembers the men of Waterford in the rebellion against his father, and that there is a great grudge against them in Ireland, so that they cannot resort to those parts where the laws are administered for fear of the wild Irish. He wishes you to examine it in the Star Chamber, or commit it to some justices. When I, on my return, spoke to the King, his grace was very glad that you retained your health notwithstanding your continued labour, of which I know more than those who only see you at Westminster. He saith, " that you may thank his counsel thereof, by which ye leave the often taking of medicines that ye were wont to use, and while ye do so, he saith, ye shall not fail of health.'"

" 5 July, 1519."

SIR THOMAS TO CARDINAL WOLSEY.

" My Singular Good Lord—This Wednesday, the ambassador of the King of Castile declared certain news on his master's behalf, and the King desires you to devise letters of thanks. The ambassador has asked his advice of the King of Castile, 'concerning the matter of the last Diet, in which the great Master of France deceased,' and for letters of credence to declare the same, but the King thinks it better his advice should be communicated by letter ; he wishes you to know that he told the ambassador he would persevere in his amity to Charles, but if the latter should do anything contrary to the amity between him and the French king, he will 'think himself bounden to regard the friendship of none earthly man so highly as his oath given to God.' The ambassador rode from court after dinner, and will be with you shortly.

" Okyng,* 6 July."

SIR T. MORE TO CARDINAL WOLSEY.

" My Singular Good Lord—Yesterday the King received a letter from his Vice Admiral, dated 14th Aug., and is very well satisfied with the proceedings. He agrees with your grace as to the war ships to be sent under Sir Anthony Pointz, and is satisfied with your answer to the imperial ambassador and thinks that the Emperor should not allow any safe-conduct for traffic between his subjects and France. One Thomas Murner, a Franciscan friar, who wrote in defence

* Okingham, or Wokingham, Berkshire.

of the King against Luther, is come over to England, having been told by a simple fellow that the King wished to see him. The King desires out of pity that he should return, for he is one of the chief stays against the faction of Luther, and requests your grace to pay him £100.   The same simple person has now brought with him to England a baron's letters from Duke Ferdinand, desiring a pension for the Duke of Mecklenburgh.   He boasted that he was the King's servant, and now says he is in the service of the Emperor's Majesty, but the King does not know him, and he wishes the advice of your Grace on these points.

The King has ordered that besides my fee of £100 as Speaker, I shall receive £100 out of the Exchequer."

"Easthampstead, 26 Aug.

"To my Lord Legate's good Grace."

Sir T. More to Cardinal Wolsey.

" My Singular Good Lord—I have received your grace's letter, dated 31 Aug., with letters from the Lord Admiral, and the copies of those between his lordship and the Queen of Scots, with your grace's reply to them.   I read them all to the King, who well liked them, especially that written in his name to the Queen of Scots. I hever saw him like thing better, and, so help me God, in my poor fantasy, not causeless, for it is, for the quantity, one of the best made letters, for words, matter, sentence, and couching that ever I read in my life.

"The King is glad that your grace 'touched' the Admiral and Dacre, ' for letting of the great roode,' contrary to your advice, for it would have been productive of some good, as appears by the Queen's letter ; and he notes 'not only remiss dealing, but also some suspicion,' in that Dacre so little esteemed the Queen's opinion. He is of your grace's mind that the Admiral should set forth his enterprise at once, as he is not satisfied with his excuses. I also read to the King your grace's letter to Dr. Knight, touching the money for the 10,000 lances. He approves your foresight in doubting lest this delay is only a device of the Emperor to spare his own charge, and entertain the Almains at the King's cost. I also read your letter to Sampson and Jerningham, advertising them of the setting forth of the King's army, also the letters in the King's name to Don Fernando, the Duke of Mecklenburgh, and the Duke of Ferrara, in case the last accept the Order of the Garter. The King said he perceived what great labours your grace had taken, when the only reading of these papers held him more than two hours."

" Okyng, 1 Sept."

"To my Lord Legate."

Sir T. More to Cardinal Wolsey.

" My Singular Good Lord—I have received your letter of the 2 Sep., and the congratulatory letter to the Duke of Venice, drawn up by your grace for the King, who has signed it and sends it back, announcing 'his substantial draught and ornate device therein.' I also read your letter to his grace which his highness gladly heard, and said your grace deserved more thanks than he could give you. He was glad you were pleased with the venison he sent you, and wished it had been much better."

" Okyng, 3 Sep."

Sir T. More to Cardinal Wolsey.

"I have received your grace's letter of the 4th, and those from Suffolk to the King, with a letter of Lady Margaret to the same; I read them all to the King, who was well pleased with your grace's politic counsel, and were it not for the plague raging at Calais, he would not be in haste to remove his army out of his own pale into the enemy's frontier, but as the plague is so fervent, his highness resolves to follow your counsel. He requests your grace to write to Suffolk, thank him for his endeavors and advertise him of the King's and your opinion that he should march diligently out of the English pale, but without letting the enemy know his intentions, until he be joined by the Burgundians, whose coming your grace is to accelerate by letters to the Lady Margaret, in your prudent manner. Suffolk is then to turn suddenly on Boulogne. I am grateful that my services are so well liked by your grace."

"Okyng, 5 Sep."

Sir T. More to Cardinal Wolsey.

"Last night, after supper, I presented to the King Suffolk's letter to your grace, Iselstein's letters to Suffolk and the King, and your letter to myself, dated 11 Sept. Notwithstanding the reasons of Lord Iselstein and Lady Margaret and the Emperor's opinion, the King is resolved to have the siege of Boulogne experimented, for reasons stated by your grace. He is not content to have all the preparations for that purpose set aside and his army sent into a distant land to be dependent for provisions to those 'of whose slackness and hard handling' he has had proof already."

His Grace saith that your Grace hit the nail on the head when ye write that the Burgundians would be upon their own frontiers to the end our money should be spent among them, and their frontiers defended and themselves resort to their houses.' Touching defence of the Low Countries, the King says that, if all things be well ordered they will have no cause to fear for the reasons mentioned by your grace. He requests you to advertise Suffolk and Iselstein of his resolution, and I will send the letter to the Venetian ambassador as soon as the King has leisure to sign it."

"Okyng, 12 Sep., 1523."

" To my Lord Legate."

Sir T. More to Cardinal Wolsey.

" My Singular Good Lord—I have received your letters of yesterday and six others devised by you, addressed to noblemen of the Emperor's army, which I return signed. Yesterday, the king received a letter from my Lord of Shrewsbury, enclosed, dated the 8th, but containing nothing new, excepting that as the King's ordnance could not pass over Staynes More, towards Carlisle, the council then determined that my lord and his company should invade Scotland by the East Marches, till they met the Duke on his return from the west borders to Edinburgh, unless they were compelled to relieve Dacre at Carlisle. This was not likely, as he had 20,000 men with him, whose coming the Lord Steward considered timely. I wrote by the King's command to the Lord Steward that the King had great doubts, and thought the division of his army impolitic, as either of the two portions might have to face the whole enemy; but left it to his discretion. The King hoped that his lack of money was relieved by the arrival of the £10,000, and of the £6,500 afterwards sent by yourself which, with the proceeds of the loan should be sufficient; and that the army would not hesitate to advance a day's journey or two when assured that the money was on the way, as they were free from the taxes imposed elsewhere, and assured him that he should have money whenever he wanted it. I have given the substance of my letter from memory, as the King caused it to be delivered immediately 'to my said lord's servant tarrying, and incessantly calling for it.'

"Newhall, 14 Sep."

"Add : My Lord Legate's good Grace."

Sir T. More to Cardinal Wolsey.

"I have received your letters dated the 19th, with a minute of a letter to be written by the King to the Emperor, instructions for the King's ambassadors there, letters from Pace and two letters by you, devised 'for the gentleman of Spruce,' (Prussia). I read to the King the same morning the letters 'which it liked your grace to write to me, in which it mych liked his grace that your grace so well liked and approved his opinion concerning the overtures made by the French king unto the Emperor.' After your grace's said letter read when he saw of your grace's own hand, that I should diligently solicit the expedition of those other things, for as mych as your grace intended and would gladly despatch the post this present Sunday, his Grace laughed, and said, 'Nay, by my soul that will not be, for this is my removing day; at Newhall I will read the remnant at night.'

"After the King had returned and dined, I attended him at six o'clock at night, when he signed the letters to the

Emperor, and for the gentleman at (Spruce), and put off the rest till this morning. On leaving I received a letter from your grace, addressed to the King, with which I forthwith returned into his chamber, where his Grace read openly my Lord Admiral's letter to the Queen's grace, which marvellously rejoiced in the good news, and especially in that, that the French king should be now towards a tutor, and his realm to have a governor. In the communication whereof, which lasted about an hour, the King's grace said, ' that he trusted in God to be their governor himself, and that they should by this means make a way for him, as King Richard did for his father.' I pray God, if it be good for his grace, and for this realm, that then it may prove so, and else in the stead thereof, I pray God send his Grace an honourable and profitable peace. I read the King this morning your grace's prudent and eloquent instructions, for which I return hearty thanks. In the instructions he would have introduced a clause, touching the Emperor's leaving Milan, to the French king, only that your grace, could, as he said, ' better furnish it and set it forth.' He thinks the Venetians are only waiting to see which way the world goes."

" The King wishes your grace to look to one Dodo, a Venetian, who, under the pretence of being a denizen, is sending out of the realm the goods of others, his countrymen." "Sunday, 20 Sept.

" To my Lord Legate's good Grace."

Sir T. More to Cardinal Wolsey.

" I have received a packet containing your grace's letter to myself, dated 12 Sep. ; two letters of Sir John Russell, and a copy of the letter of Chastean to the Imperial Ambassador here, all which I read to the King. He is of opinion that Bourbon could not do other than dissemble his purpose, and is not likely to be reconciled to the French King. He is glad that he was deceived in his fears, lest the French King might have perceived this practice with Bourbon, which it is clear he does not, 'for if he had, he would either not have come into his house, or not so departed thence.' As it is now in so many men's mouths, he is afraid it will not long be kept secret, and if the French King suspected it, the Duke might be suddenly distressed, and the whole matter fail. 'He thinks, Sir John Russell might be used to advertise the Duke that many people in Flanders know of it, and the King deems it right to warn and put him on his guard ; advising him either to declare himself or provide for his safety. 'He thinks the intelligence about Guienne is a mere excuse.'

'He is of your grace's opinion that for any solicitation of Lady Margaret and the Emperor, no money be dispensed till the declaration is made.'"

Sir T. More to Cardinal Wolsey.

"The King has received the letter of your grace by the hands of Sir John Russell 'of whose well achieved errand his Grace taketh great pleasure,' containing your advice for abandoning at present the siege of Boulogne, and to march to some places devised by the Duke of Bourbon, which your grace has been informed may easily be taken. The King is by no means displeased that you have changed your opinion, 'as his highness esteemeth nothing in counsel more perilous than for one to persevere in the maintenance of his advice, because he hath once given it.' He therefore commendeth and most affectiously thanketh your faithful diligence and high wisdom 'in advertising him of the reasons which have moved you to change your mind.'"

Then follow many considerations which Henry submits to Wolsey, after which continues Sir Thomas :

" The King thinks you should send a good round letter to Lady Margaret, taxing her with slackness in the common affairs. He says that such dealing so often used, may well give him cause hereafter to be cautious, ere he undertake any charge for their defence."

" Abingdon, 21 Sep."

" To my Lord Legate's good Grace."

Sir T. More to Cardinal Wolsey.

"After the King had supped I read him your grace's letter to myself, two letters of the Queen of Scots, directed to the King, two directed to Surrey, and two written by your grace in the King's name to the Queen herself. As in reading Lord Surrey's letter to your grace, ' the King noted that my said lord had already written unto the Queen of Scots answer unto both her letters, his Grace requireth yours, that it may like you to send him the copies which his letters specifieth to have sent unto your grace. He thinks that the Homes and Douglas should be received as suitable hostages, and attempts made to win the Chancellor and other lords from the Duke. He also wishes to see your instructions to Surrey, and that he should be advertised of the declaration of the Duke of Bourbon, and the same be inserted, with exaggeration of the French King's tyranny, in the letter which the Queen of Scots is to shew to the lords. The King requires your grace to consider well that clause in the Queen's letter in which she desires to be received in England."

"Woodstock, 22 Sep."

"To my Lord Legate."

Sir T. More to Cardinal Wolsey.

" I have received and presented to the King your grace's letter to himself, and copies of Surrey's letters to the Queen of Scots, for all which the King sends your grace most hearty thanks, and has signed the letters devised by you to the Queen, his sister."

"Woodstock, 24 Sep."

Sir T. More to Cardinal Wolsey.

" After the King had supped I presented him your grace's letter to myself, dated yesterday, with letters of the Queen of Scots to Surrey. The King is glad that Surrey now perceives that 'the lords of Scotland intend but only to drive over the time of their annoyance,' the King would have been glad if Surrey had perceived this before. He does not like that Surrey, in his letter written to the Queen, to be shewn to the lords of Scotland, 'appointeth them the time and place where they shall send to him to Jedworth,' as the Scots will thus be prepared. The King is sorry for the plagues and agues which have befallen the army, and thinks it must be supplied with horsemen of those parts. I should be very unkind and blind if I did not perceive the gracious favours that your grace has done me with the king.

"Woodstock, 26 Sep."

"To my Lord Legate."

"My Singular Good Lord—Yesterday I came to the King who was very glad to hear of your good health. His Grace was surprised at my telling him you had sent no word by John Joachim.

"'No word,' quoth he, 'I marvel at it, for John Joachim had a servant come to him two days ago.' I replied that you had despatched me yesterday afternoon with letters from Knight and Pace, and wished to have them back to shew to Joachim, 'for the contents be such as will do him little pleasure.' I read all the letters and commented on them to the Queen, who said she was glad that the Spaniards had done something in Italy in return for their departure from Provence. I said you thought Francis would lose in his estimation, finding his enemies strong, being twice repulsed at Pavia, and disappointed of the money he expected at Milan, and that Louise will have to send for him back again. The King laughed, and said he thought it would be hard for him to get thence.

"To Knight's letter he said not much, but that if Bewreyn came he would be plain with him, if not, he desires *you* to be very plain with him on imperial matters. He is glad to find the affairs of Scotland are in a good train, and will be sorry to have them ruffled by Angus; he approves of your advice to make Angus an instrument for the due management of Scotland. I spoke about Mr. Burke, who I perceive has promised the King not to marry without his advice, as he is intended for one of the Queen's maidens.

"Hertford, Nov. 29."

The following letter affords an amusing instance of the *sang froid* with which a lady's hand might be disposed of in marriage by a Tudor sovereign:

Sir Thomas to Cardinal Wolsey.

" It may like your grace to be advertised that the King's Highness, going this night to his supper, called me to him secretly, and commanded me to write to your grace; that as it hath pleased our Lord to call to His mercy Mr. Myrfyn, late alderman of London, his grace greatly desireth, on account of the special favour which he beareth towards Sir William Tyler, that he should have the widow of the late alderman in marriage."

" For the furtherance whereof, his Highness, considering your grace's well approved dexterity in bringing to pass what he desireth, commanded me to advertise your grace that his Highness requireth that it may like you to devise and pursue the most effectual means by which his Grace's desire may in this matter be brought about, and take effect; wherein he saith you shall do him a right special favour; and bind the said Sir William during his life to pray for your good grace.   This much hath his Highness commanded me to write to you, whom both our Lord long preserve in honour and health together."

"At Easthampstede, the xvii. day of September, Your humble orator and much bounden bedesman,

" Thomas More."

CHAPTER VII.

THE many estimable qualities which adorned both the public and private character of Sir Thomas More, gained him the love and affection of all who came within the range of his influence, and as letters given, as far as possible, *in extenso* (and the greater portion, by far, of those printed in this volume appear in their entirety), present the best key to the character of him who wrote them, it is hoped they will interest the reader. To Cuthbert Tunstal, Bishop of Durham, he was tenderly attached. The following letters will shew how strict was the bond of friendship that united the two :

" Although every letter which I receive from you, most dear friend, is very grateful unto me, yet that which you last wrote was most welcome, for besides the other commendations which the rest of your letters deserve in respect of their eloquence, and the friendship they profess towards me, this last of yours possesses peculiar grace, for it continues your peculiar testimony (I would it were as true as it is favourable) of my ' Common Wealth.' I requested my friend Erasmus to explain the matter to you in familiar talk ; yet I charged him to press you not to read it hastily, not because I would not have you to read it at all (for that is my chief desire) but remembering your prudent purpose not to take in hand the reading of any modern work until you had fully satisfied yourselves with the works of ancient authors, but if you remember the profit you have made of what you have read, surely you have accomplished your task, but if by affection, then you will never bring your purpose to a perfect end.

"Thus I was afraid, that, seeing the excellent works of others could not allure you to read them, you would never be brought to condescend willingly to the perusal of my trifling work, and surely you would never have read it but that your love of me drove you to it more than the worth of the thing itself.

"Therefore I give you exceeding thanks for reading so diligently my Utopia, because you have for my sake bestowed so much labour, and no less thanks truly do I give you that my work hath pleased you, for not less do I attribute this to your love, because I see you have rather testified to me what your love suggested, than the authority of a censor. However the matter may be, I cannot express how much I rejoice that you have cast your whole account in liking my doings, for I almost persuade myself that all you say is true, knowing you to be far from all dissembling, and myself more mean than that you should need to flatter me, and more dear to you than that I should expect disguise ; so, whether you have seen the truth unfeignedly, I rejoice heartily in your judgment, or if your affection for me hath blinded your judgment, I am none the less delighted in your love, and truly great and extraordinary must that love be that could deprive Tunstal of his judgment."

Again to the same, he writes :—

"You deal very courteously with me in giving me, in your letter, such hearty thanks, because I have been careful to

defend the causes of your friends, exaggerating the small
good turn I have done you therein, by your great bounty,
but you think too lightly of the love which is between us
if you imagine you are indebted to me for anything I have
done, and do not rather challenge it to be of right due to
yourself. The amber which you sent me being a precious
sepulchre of flies, was for many respects most welcome, for
the matter may be compared in colour and brightness to a
precious stone, and the form is excellent, because it represen-
teth the figure of a heart, as it were the hieroglyphic of our
love, which I interpret as your meaning, that between us it
will never fly away, and yet be always without corruption,
because I see the fly (which hath wings like Cupid, the son of
Venus, and is as fickle as he) so shut up in this amber that
it cannot fly away, and so embalmed that it cannot perish.
I am not at all troubled that I cannot send *you* the like gift,
for I know you do not expect any change of tokens, and I
am willing to be still in your debt, but it troubleth me a little
that my state and condition is so mean that I am never able
to shew myself worthy of your singular friendship, so that I
cannot give testimony myself before others. You must be
satisfied, therefore, with my own expressions of affection,
and your gentle acceptance of the same."

His dedication of one of his works to the same Bishop
runs as follows :—

" When I considered, dear Tunstal, to which of my friends
I should dedicate these, my collections out of many authors,
I thought it most due to you, on account of the familiar
conversations which for a long time have passed between us,
as also for your sincerity, because you would always be ready
to take thankfully whatever seems good to you in this work,

and whatever should be worthless you would place a courteous construction on, and what was displeasing you would be willing to pardon."

To the intense grief of Sir Thomas, this Bishop went the same way as the rest in the reign of Henry VIII. ; he lived to see Queen Elizabeth on the throne, to whom he had stood godfather, and witnessing her persecution of the members of the Catholic church, he came up from Durham in his old age, and strongly admonished her not to throw off her religion, warning her she would lose God's blessing if she did so.

The iron-hearted Queen was of course ill pleased with his admonitions, and ordered him to be cast into prison, with others of the Bishops, in which prison he died as a confessor of the faith, atoning thus for his schism in the time of her father.

The love of More for the great Fisher, Bishop of Rochester, continued with the bitter, or rather, to them, may we not write, glorious end. Two of their letters run as follows. The good Bishop writes :—

"I pray you, dear More, allow our Cambridge men to have some hope that through you they may be favoured by the King's Majesty, that our scholars may be stirred up to learning by the countenance of so worthy a prince. We have few friends in the Court who can, or will commend our cause to his royal highness, and amongst them we account you the chief, for you have always favoured us greatly, even when you were in a meaner place ; now then, shew what you can do, raised as you are to the honour of knighthood, and in such great favour with the prince, at which we greatly rejoice, and congratulate you on your happiness.

"Give favour to this youth, who is both a good scholar in divinity, and also a sufficient preacher to the people; he hopes in your favour that you will procure him great advancement, and that your recommendation will help him to notice."

Sir Thomas's reply was as follows :—

" Respecting this Priest, Reverend Father, whom you write to be suitable for a Bishopric, if he might have some worthy suitor to speak for him to the King, I imagine that I have so prevailed in his behalf that his majesty will be no hindrance thereto. If I have any favour with the King, and truly it is but little, but whatsoever I have, I will employ all I can in the service of your Fatherhood, and your scholars, to whom I send constant thanks for their never ending affection to myself, so often testified by their loving letters. My house shall be open to them as if it were their own.

" Farewell, worthy and most courteous prelate, and see you continue to love me as you have hitherto done."

To his friends Reginald Pole and Dr. Clement, a celebrated physician, whom he brought up in his own house, he writes :—

" I thank you much, my dear Clement, for your care of my health and that of my children, also that you prescribe in my absence what meats are to be avoided by us. And to you, my friend, I render double thanks, both because you have sent us in writing the advice of so good a physician and also have procured the same for us from your mother, a most excellent and noble matron, worthy of so great a son, so as you do not seem more liberal of your counsel than in bestowing on us the thing itself, concerning which you advise us. I love and praise you both for your bounty and fidelity."

To Dr. Lee, afterwards Archbishop of York, he was a firm friend, although he had written against his most dear friend Erasmus's Annotations on the New Testament. He writes him as follows :—

"Good Lee, you request me not to suffer my regard for you to be diminished, trust me it shall not, though of myself I incline rather to him who is impugned, and as I could wish this city well free from your siege, so will I always love you, and be glad you so much esteem my friendship."

Of Lupset, a great scholar of his time, he writes to Erasmus :—

"Our friend Lupset reads with great applause in both languages at Oxford, having a great auditory, for he succeedeth my John Clement in that charge."

To Croke, who was Henry VIII.'s master in the study of Greek, he writes :—

"Whosoever it was, my Crocus, who hath signified to you that my love is lessened, because you have omitted a long time to write to me, either deceives himself or strives to deceive you, and although I have great comfort in reading your letter, yet I am not so proud that I should challenge such interest in you, as if it was your duty to salute me every day in this way, nor so wayward nor full of complaint as to be offended with you for neglecting a little this your custom of writing, for I were indeed unjust if I exacted letters from others when I know myself to be a sluggard in writing them, so take this for granted, never hath my esteem for you waxed so cold, that it needs to be kindled and heated by the continual blowing of epistles to and fro, yet shall you do me a great pleasure by writing to me as often as you have leisure, though I shall never urge you to devote that time in writing to friends you have allotted to study or to your scholars. As for the place you wish I should procure you, both Pace and I, who esteem you much, have put the King in mind of it."

To John Cochleus he writes as follows :—

"It cannot be expressed, most worthy sir, how much I am indebted to you for acquainting me of those occurrences which happen in your country. Germany now daily bringeth forth more monsters, yea, more prodigious things than Africa was wont to do; for what can be more monstrous than the Anabaptists; yet how have they risen forth and spread for many years together. I, for my part, seeing these sects daily increase, expect shortly to hear that there will arise some who will not scruple to preach that Christ himself is to be denied, neither can there arise so absurd a knave but he shall have disciples, the madness of the people is so great.*

"I would have you know, dear Cochleus, that I have not received any letter from our friend these many years more grateful than your last was to me, and this for many reasons; the first, that I see your sincere regard for me; I was sure of it before, but now I see it more perfectly, and I regard it as a grest happiness, and esteem highly the favour of having

---

* In this letter he seems to see, as with the spirit of prophecy, David George, the Hollander, who called himself Christ, and the Englishman, Hackett, whose disciples were Arden and Coppinger. For this man's madness and impiety, see " Camden's Hist." vol. 4, p. 450, and Collier's " Ecclesiastical Hist.," vol. 2, p. 627.

such a friend ; and secondly, because you give me news of the doings of many of the continental princes."

To the famous Budæus, one of the privy council to the French King, he writes :—

" I know not, my good Budæus, whether it were good for us to possess anything very dear, except we might always keep it. I have imagined I should be a happy man, if I could but once see Budæus, whose beautiful picture, the reading of his works represented to me. Just when God had granted me my wish, it seemed to me I was more happy than happiness itself; yet, afterwards our business was so urgent, I could not gratify my desire often to enjoy your sweet conversation, and our friendship was scarce began but it was shortly ended, the affairs of our Prince's calling us from each other, so that it is now hard to say whether we shall again meet, each of us being forced to wait on our own Prince, by how much the more joyful was our meeting, so much the more deep was my sorrow in our parting, which you may somewhat lessen, if you will please to make me often present by your letters, yet dare I not urge you to send them, though my desire to have them is very great." *

ERASMUS TO BUDÆUS.

I found many of my friends at the meeting of the Emperor at Bruges, among the rest " *Non minus humanum quam magnum, hoc est, non minus amandum quam reverandum*

*This letter is extracted, originially, from Stapleton's *Vit. Th. Mori,* and is copied from More's *Life of More,* it bears no date, but Budæus and More had not met each other when the following letter, dated 1521, was written by Erasmus to Budæus ; it contains an interesting account of More and his family.

Cardinalum Eboracensem," * who was received by the Emperor with regal magnificence. Tunstal, More, Mountjoy, and many others were also there. More was in great hopes he should have found you at Calais in the French embassy.

" The arrival of the Cardinal was the more pleasant to me, because I hoped that the heart-burnings amongst Princes would be composed by his wisdom and authority, but I know not what to think as matters now stand. The Emperor and the French King are not on good terms. More is now made treasurer with a liberal salary. The King gave him the appointment in preference to another who would have taken it without a salary, he has also made More a knight.

" Unmarried men are more easily advanced, but More is so wedded to wedlock that nothing can emancipate him. When he lost his first wife he married another, *viduus viduam.* He has three daughters, the eldest who is named Margaret, is just married to a young man (Roper) of good fortune and unspotted morals, and with an inclination to learning. More had all his daughters educated from their infancy; first paying great attention to their morals and then to their learning. He brings up another girl as a companion to his daughters. He has also a step-daughter, of great beauty and genius, now married some years to a young man '*non indocto sed cujus moribus nihil sit magis aureum.*† He has a son by his former wife, aged thirteen, the youngest of his children. He ordered them a year ago to write to me on their own responsibility : the subject was not supplied, nor were any corrections allowed. When they showed their father their exercises, all he did was to have them fairly copied without

* The not less learned than great, not less amiable than venerable Cardinal of York.

† Not unlearned, and of most excellent morals.

changing a syllable, and seal them and send them to me, and I greatly admired them. They read Livy and similar authors; his wife, who is an excellent housewife, manages the household; you complain that he has brought a scandal upon learning, because it has entailed on him two evils—ill health, and ill husbandry. More, on the other hand, produces the opposite impression on me.

" He says that his health is the better for study, and that he has more influence with the King, more popularity at home and abroad, is more pleasant and useful to his friends and relations, abler for the business of politics and life generally, and more thankful (*gratior*) to heaven. It has been said that learning is unfavourable to common sense; there is no greater reader than More, yet you will not find a man who is more complete master of his faculties, on all occasions, and with all persons, more accessible, more ready to oblige, more quick-witted in conversation, or who combines so much true prudence with such agreeable manners. His influence has been such that there is scarce a nobleman in the land who considers his children fit for their rank unless they have been well educated, and learning has become fashionable at court.

" I once thought with others, that learning was useless to the female sex. More has quite changed my opinion. I now think that nothing so completely preserves the modesty or so sensibly employs the thoughts of young girls as learning. By such employments they are kept from pernicious idleness they imbibe noble precepts, and their minds are trained to virtue. Many from simplicity and inexperience have lost their chastity before they knew that such an inestimable treasure was in danger, nor do I see why husbands should fear lest a learned wife should be less obedient, except they would exact from their wives what should not be exacted from honest and virtuous dames.

"I think that nothing is more intractable than ignorance, to say nothing of the fact that similarity of tastes and literary inclinations are a much stronger bond of union between husband and wife than mere sensual affection. I have heard of women returning from church who wonderfully admired the preacher, but could not repeat a word he had said, or explain the course of his argument, while More's daughters, and such as they, can form an opinion on what they have heard, and discriminate between the good and the bad. When I once told More that he would grieve more deeply if he lost his daughters, after he had bestowed on them so much care, he replied, 'he would rather they died learned than unlearned;' this put me in mind of Phocian's answer to his wife, who lamented that her husband was to suffer innocently. 'Wife,' said he, 'Would it be better that I should die guilty?'" · "Antwerp, 1521."

The following letter to Archbishop Warham was written to the latter by More, on his resignation of the Great Seal:

"I have always esteemed your most Reverend Fatherhood happier in your courses, not only when you executed with great praise the office of Chancellor, hut also more happy now, when being rid of that care, you have betaken yourself to a desirable quietude, the better to live to yourself and to serve God more easily. Such repose is not only more pleasing than worldly business, but in my opinion more honourable than the honours you formerly enjoyed, the greater the authority and power of one who has filled the high office of Chancellor, the more numerous the slanders he is exposed to, to resign such an office voluntarily, none but a modest-minded man would, nor any but a guiltless one dare do.   Many, with myself, admire your resolution, and I know not whether your humility is greater that you would willingly forsake so magnificent a place, or your spirit more heroic in that you continue it, or innocent that you feared not to resign it, but most prudent were you in doing so.

"I rejoice and congratulate you that you have obtained so rare a happiness by sequestering yourself far from worldly business, and tumult of Causes of others, so as to spend the rest of your days with a peaceable conscience as to your life past, and in quiet calmness and Christian philosophy, which contented state of yours, my own misery maketh me daily more and more to long for; (he was then of the Privy Council, Treasurer of the Exchequer, and employed in many embassies).   I am so troubled daily with business that I have not leisure to visit you, or to excuse myself by letter, indeed scarcely was I able to write this to you.   I commend my little book of Utopia to your Reverend Fatherhood, which an Antwerpian friend of mine, love swaying his judgment, hath printed without my knowledge, which I am emboldened to send you, though it is unworthy of your learning, relying on your courteous nature, also trusting in your tried love to me, by which I hope though the work in itself should not be cared for, that yet for the author's sake you will like it.   Farewell, most honourable prelate."

Of Beatus Renanus, another scholar, he writes :—

"I esteem Renanus much, and am greatly in his debt for his Preface.   I would have thanked him a long time ago, but that I have been troubled with such a gout of the hand, that is to say, idleness, that by no means could I over-come it."

The learned Cranvilde, one of the Emperor Charles V.'s Privy Council, was introduced to More by Erasmus; he thanks Erasmus, as follows, for this favour—

"I cannot but thank you greatly with these my (rude) letters (you the most learned in all sciences) for your singular benefit lately bestowed on me, which I shall always bear in remembrance, and which I esteem so much I would not lose it for the wealth of Crœsus."

" You will ask, dear Erasmus, what benefit that was, truly this, that you have brought me to the acquaintance and sweet conversation of your friend More, but now I will call him mine. After your departure, I often met him, because he frequently sent for me, and bountiful the entertainment at his table, I esteem not so much as his learning, his courtesy, and his liberality. I reckon myself, therefore, deeply indebted to you, and pray God I may be able to make you a grateful return for this good work done me. He sent my wife a gold ring the English motto of which is ' All things are measured by good-will.'

He gave me also several old pieces of gold and silver coin, in one of which was engraven the picture of Tiberias, in another that of Augustus. I tell you this because I have you to thank for all."

Erasmus replied as follows :—

"There is a vulgar adage, ' I have by means of one daughter got two sons,' you thank me because through me you have got such a friend as More ; and, he on the other hand, thanks me also becanse I have procured him the knowledge of Cranvilde. I knew well enough that because your wit and manner were alike, there would easily arise a dear friendship between you, if you did but know each other, but as the having of such friends is precious, so is the keeping of them as rare."

The letter of Sir Thomas to Cranvilde was as follows :—-

" I see and acknowledge how much I am in your debt, my dear Cranvilde, for you always do 'what is most pleasing to me, namely, keeping me informed of your affairs.'   For what can be more acceptable to Thomas More in his adversity or more pleasing to him in his prosperity than to receive letters from Cranvilde, except I could speak with him, learned as he is, far above other men.   But as often as I read your writings, I am as enchanted with them, as if I were conversing with you present with me ; so that nothing troubles me more than that your letters are not longer, but that I have found a remedy for, because I read them over and over again, and I do it at my leisure, so that my pleasure may last the longer.   But enough of this.   What you tell me respecting our friend Vines, and your opinion of his discouse on 'wicked women,' I quite agree with.   I think one cannot live without innocence even with good women, for if a man be married he shall not be without care in my opinion. Metellus Numidicus spoke not untruly of wives; and I would more willingly say it if many of them were not made the worse through our own faults.

" Vines, however, has so good a wife, that he may not only avoid, as far as is possible to man, all the troubles of marriage, but also he may receive great happiness, for men's minds are so busy with public matters whilst the fury of war rages everywhere, that no man has much leisure to think of his private affairs, so that if family troubles have hitherto oppressed them, they are now forgotten in the common mischief. But enough of this. I return to yourself, for your courtesy and friendship to me, as often as I dwell upon it, driveth from me all sorrow. I thank you for the book you sent me, and I wish you much joy with your new child, not for your own sake only but for that of the Commonwealth, to whose benefit it is that such a parent should increase it with plenty of children, for from such as you only good ones can proceed. Farewell, and commend me heartily and sincerely to your good wife, to whom I pray God to send happiness, health, and strength. My wife and children also wish you health. From what I have told them you are as well known and as dear to them as to myself. Again farewell. "London, August 10, 1524."

Again to the same, he writes :—

"I am ashamed, God help me, my dear Cranvilde, of your great courtesy that you write to me so often, so lovingly and carefully, and I so rarely answer you, especially seeing you may allege quite as many cares and as much business as myself, but so great is your courtesy, that you are ready to excuse all things in your friends, whilst you yourself faithfully perform every duty ; but be persuaded, good Cranvilde, that if anything happen at any time wherein I may testify the esteem I have for you, then, God willing, I will not be wanting. Commend me to my mistress, your wife, for I dare not now invert the order began, and to your whole family, whom mine do with all their hearts salute.

"From my house in the country, this 10th day of June, 1528."

Erasmus thus commends to Sir Thomas More, one Goclenius, a Westphalian :—

"I praise your disposition, my dearest More, exceedingly,

for your joy is to be rich in sincere and faithful friends, and you esteem it the greatest felicity of this life. Some take great care that they may not be cheated with counterfeit jewels; but you, contemning all such trifles, seem yourself to be rich enough if you can but get an unfeigned friend; for there is no man taketh delight, either in cards, dice, chess, hunting or music, so much as you do in conversing with a learned companion, full of pleasant conceits, and although you are stored with riches of this kind, yet because I know that a covetous man hath never enough, and that his manner of dealing hath luckily happened both to you and me on many occasions, I deliver to your custody one friend more, whom I would have you accept with your whole heart. His name is Conradus Goclenius, a Westphalian, who with great applause and no less fruit, hath taught rhetoric at the college newly erected at Louvain, called Trillingue. I hope that, as soon as you have a real knowledge of him, I shall have thanks from you both; for so I had of Cranvilde, who so entirely possesseth your esteem that I almost envy him for it."

But amongst all others, Erasmus himself more especially won his love and affection, the letters which are copied, some of them in full, in this volume, testify to the strength of the attachment which subsisted between these two great men, an attachment, however, which was somewhat cooled on More's part towards the end of his life, by the free opinions of his friend, who though he lived and died a Catholic Priest, rendered himself so remarkable for his satires on the clergy, that he has been said to have hatched the eggs which Luther laid.

Whilst he was in England, and the guest of More, many

were the good offices done him by Sir Thomas, both by word and by purse, "but," says his early biographer, "in course of time the affection of Sir Thomas cooled, by reason that he saw him still fraught with inconstancy with respect of religion, so that Tindal objected to Sir Thomas, that his darling Erasmus had translated the word *Church* into *Congregation*, and *Priest* into *Elder*, as himself had done." Sir Thomas replied, "And if my darling Erasmus hath translated these words with the like wicked intent that Tindal hath done, he shall be no more my darling but the devil's darling." And finally, having found in his works many things which ought to be amended, he counselled him to imitate the example of the great St. Augustine, and publish a book of Retractations, to correct what he had unavisedly written in the heat of youth, but not possessing the humility of that great doctor of the Church, he never followed More's advice.

Erasmus, however, never relapsed into heresy or led a thoroughly worldly life. Some of his writings are masterpieces of eloquence and piety, and the following extract from a letter to Lord Mountjoy, bearing date 1521, will shew that he resented being counted as a supporter of the men who were preaching heretical tenets :

"I understand that I am accused of favouring Luther, and am requested to clear myself from the charge by writing against the reformer. I distinctly deny the charge. I think Luther was justified in exposing the evils of the times, which were patent to all, but I dislike his manner of doing it. I am not the author of any of the writings attributed to me, for I have never published anything anonymously, and least of all would I oppose the decrees of the Pope."

In Cresacre's More's life of his great ancestor, we are told that they once met at the Lord Mayor's table, and during dinner they began to argue together, Erasmus defending the worst side, but he was so sharply opposed by Sir Thomas that he broke out with *Aut tu es Morus aut nullus?* to which Sir Thomas replied *Aut tu es Erasmus, aut diabolus?*

He had sought to defend false propositions, and scoffed at religious matters, for which cause he was termed Erransmus.* This story, however, cannot be authentic, unless one or both of them were much altered, as it will be remembered they were intimately acquainted in More's student days at Oxford.

With another extract from a letter of Erasmus I close this chapter; he is writing to his friend Hutton.

"More, my dear Hutton, seems to be made and formed for friendship. He is a most sincere follower and fast-keeper of it, neither doth he fear to be taxed with having many friends, which thing Hesiod praiseth not. Every man may have his friendship, he is not slow in choosing, is apt in nourishing, constant in keeping them; and if by chance he becomes the friend of one whose vices he cannot correct, he loosens the bonds of friendship little by little rather than by a sudden rupture. Those whom he findeth sincere and of accord with his own good disposition, he is so delighted with that all his earthly pleasure seems to consist in conversing with them, and though he is very negligent in his own temporal affairs, yet none is more diligent than he in advancing his friend's cause. Why need I speak many words? If any are desirous to have a perfect pattern of friendship, none can find it better than in More. In his society there is such

* Hoddesdon's Hist. of More.

rare affability, and such sweet behaviour that no man's nature is so harsh, but that his discourse is able to make him merry ; no conversation so unpleasant, but he with his wit can take from it all tediousness.

.   .   .   .

.   .   .   .

" His house appears to enjoy the happiness that all who live therein become better in their moral character, as well as improved in condition, and no stain has ever fallen on their reputation. You might imagine yourself in the academy of Plato, but I do the house injury by comparing it with the school of Plato, where only abstract questions and sometimes moral virtues were the topics under discussion, I should rather call it a school of christian religion, a theatre for the exercise of all christian virtues. Its inmates apply themselves to liberal sciences, and no quarrelling or angry words are ever heard, every one does his duty cheerfully, and the discipline of his home is enforced by More by kindness and courtesy, neither is sober cheerfulness ever wanting. Such a household deserves to be called a school of the Christian religion."

CHAPTER VIII.

The Men of the New Learning.

The diligent assiduity of Sir Thomas More in the discharge of the manifold duties of his high station did not prevent him from using his pen and bringing his talents to bear against the heresies which, like a torrent, spread far and wide. They commenced in Germany and Flanders, and from thence deluged England. The age was rife with heresy, and the authority of the Church was treated by many with derision and contempt. The fiery heresiarch Luther had burned the bull of the Pope, in which his propositions were condemned as false, scandalous, and heretical, and he, on his part had stigmatized the sovereign Pontiff as a blasphemer, an apostate and as antichrist.

Then the heroic Fisher, Bishop of Rochester, he, the story of whose life presents a record of unbroken piety, charity, and benevolence, came forth to preach, and stem as far as possible the plague-spot of disunion, division, and discord, which has grown on and on since this great rupture with the old, old faith, till the sectaries who sprung from the intemperate and fiery monk, Martin Luther, number more offshoots from Protestantism than can well be told.

Fisher's sermons arrested many wavering souls ; and the King himself took pen in hand, and published against the doctrines of the apostate monk, his celebrated work the

Defence of the Seven Sacraments, which he submitted to the reigning Pontiff, receiving from him the Papal Bull, conferring on him the title of Defender of the Faith.

Then Luther wrote a coarse and scurrilous reply, in which he styled the King, a fool, an ass, a blasphemer, and a liar, and More then appeared in the lists, and in the following year published a work at Rome, under the feigned name of Rosseus. Cresacre More, the old biographer, says, "to see how he handleth Luther under the name of one Rosseus would do any man good;" but few at the present day at least, will endorse the same opinion, for certainly the polished pen of the great philosopher and statesman, strove to vie with that of his adversary in scurrility of language, so that it has been said by Bishop Atterbury that "they had the best knack of any men in Europe at calling each other bad names in good Latin."

And it must have been hard work to come up to Luther, after all. The King he designated as a "Thomistical ass,"from his study of scholastic divinity, " that he was not worthy to wipe his shoes," with other scurrilous speeches. Indeed, his flowers of rhetoric are sometimes of a filthy nature, which in these days would not be tolerated in any writer. The school men he abhorred, calling them sophistical locusts, caterpillars, frogs, and lice.* And it is to be regretted that the learned More, whose knowledge of theology fitted him for controversy of a very different description, should have striven to do battle with Luther in inelegant and coarse language.

His knowledge of scholastic divinity was extensive. He had diligently studied the Fathers of the Church, and his

* Jortin's Erasmus.

secretary, John Harris, a man himself noted for his judgment and sound piety, relates how, when he was one day going in his barge from Chelsea to London, an heretical book, just published was being examined by him, and pointing with his finger to a passage in the work, he exclaimed—"Look here, how the knave draws his arguments out of St. Thomas, in such and such a place, the solutions are added soon after, and those, too, the fellow must have seen and has not copied." Amongst other works of the same kind there came out a pamphlet entitled "The Supplication of Beggars." It was at once followed by Sir Thomas, by his *Supplication of Souls.*

The notorious Fishe was the author of the former work, the intent of which was to shew to his own satisfaction that the poor would be the better off when the Church was deprived of her revenues, and abbeys and religious houses be overthrown, and that the mendicant orders were in annual receipt of £43,333 6s. 8d. More answered with his own withering sarcasm, and averred that an ocean of mischief was about to deluge the whole realm. " Then," saith he, " shall Luther's gospel be preached, and Tindal's Testament be read ; false heresies shall be preached ; the sacraments be set at nought ; fasting and praise be neglected ; the holy saints reviled, and Almighty God be angered ; virtue shall be held in derision, and vice reign supreme ; youth shall forsake labour, folks wax idle, and thieves and beggars, increase ; servants shall set their masters at nought, and the unruly rebel against them ; mischief and insurrection shall arise ; whereof what the end will be the Lord knoweth."

As to Fishe and his mendicant friars, he says his calculation is about the same as to suppose "that every ass has four heads."* The book also contains a defence of the Catholic doctrine of purgatory. Satirical as he undoubtedly was, yet More always treated his adversaries fairly, and his old biographers notice the fact that he never wrested the words of his opponents to the worst, or made their arguments appear at the weakest, but gave them the benefit of as much sense as they really possessed.

He also published a defence of the Real Presence against the writings of Frith, and an Apology against Friar Barnes, under the name of Salem and Byzance. His Dialogue, a work against the errors of Tindal, brought upon him a reply of a very personal nature, and it drew upon him the trouble of a long controversy, in which he refuted the errors of his adversary with an unsparing hand.

Long before the change took place which so desolated the Church in England, Sir Thomas, with that seeming spirit of prophecy which so distinguished him, foretold what was about to pass. We would wish these words, however, to be taken in a somewhat modified sense, for without thus investing the words of this Christian philosopher, it is certain that he looked farther into the future than did those around him, and could see the result of the change which was steadily making way. The question of the divorce, which was in itself the cause of the separation of this kingdom from Catholic unity, was but recently mooted; and Roper, whilst one day walking in the pleasant garden at Chelsea with his father-in-law, burst out in praises of the happy state of England in possessing so Catholic a prince, and such a learned and virtuous clergy, so grave and sound a nobility,

* Fishe became a convert, and died penitent.

and such loving and obedient subjects, all bound up in one faith, although they had but one heart and one soul.*

"It is true, son Roper, as you say," was the reply, " and yet I pray God that some of us, as high as we seem now to sit upon the mountains, treading heretics under our feet like ants, may not live to see the day when we would gladly wish to make this league with them, to suffer them to have their churches quietly to themselves, so they would be content to let us have ours peaceably too."

" After this I begged him," says Roper, " to consider that he had no cause to say so."

" Well, said he, "I pray God, son Roper, some of us live not to see that day," showing me no reason why he should doubt it ; to which I replied —

" By my troth, sir, it is very desperately spoken, that vile term, I cry God's mercy, did I give him."

Seeing me in such a fume, he then said merrily to me—

" Well, son Roper, it shall not be so, it shall not be so."†

Little did William Roper then think that he himself would for some time be a cause of sorrow to his father-in-law, and his own matchless wife.

A sore trial it must have been to Sir Thomas and his best loved daughter, Margaret, when the errors of the time led away William Roper himself, that most favoured son-in-law, on whom he had bestowed the hand of his priceless pearl, Margaret.

Roper embraced for awhile the novelties of the times, for, says Cresacre More, "he had used austerities to himself beyond what discretion allowed, and then he grew weary of Catholic

* Roper's Life of More.
† Roper's More.

fasts and religious discipline, and hearing of a new and easy way to heaven, he diligently read some of the heretical works spread in every part of England, " took the bridle into his teeth, and ran forth, like a headstrong horse, thirsting very sore to publish his new doctrine, and thought himself very able so to do, if even it were at St. Paul's Cross. Yea, for the burning zeal he bore to the furtherance and advancement of Luther's new broached religion, and for the pretty liking of himself, he longed so sore to be pulpitted, that to have satisfied his mind's affection and desire, he could have been contented to have foregone a good portion of his lands."

"This fall into heresy, Mr. Roper thought afterwards, first grew of a scruple of his own conscience, for lack of grave and better knowledge, as some do upon other occasions. He then did use immoderate fasting and many prayers, which, with good discretion, well used, had not been to be misliked, but using them *without* order and good consideration, thinking God thereby now to be pleased, did wear himself even *usque ad servitia*.

"Then did he understand of Luther's work, brought into this realm, and as Eve, of a curious mind, desirous to know both good and evil, so did he, for the strangeness and delight of that doctrine, fall into great desire to read his work ; amongst others, he had read a book of Luther's, *De Libertate Christiana*, and another, *De Captivitate Babylonica*, and was so with them bewitched, that he did then believe only matter set forth by Luther to be true.

"And he was with these books, ignorance, pride, allegations, sophistical reasons and arguments, and with his own corrupt affections, deceived and fully persuaded, that faith only did justify, that the works of man did nothing profit, and if **man** could once believe that our Saviour Christ shed his precious blood and died on the cross for our sins, the same only belief should be sufficient for our salvation. Then thought he, that all ceremonies and sacraments in Christ's Church were very vain, and was at length so far waded into heresy, and puffed up with pride, that he wished that he might be suffered publicly to preach, thinking, as we have said, that he should be better able to edify, and profit the people than the best preacher that came at Paul's Cross, and that in Luther's doctrine he was able to convince the best doctors in the realm, and so much the rather, for that he had reviled some that were doctors of divinity, and thought there could be no truth but that which came forth from Germany, who, for his open talk, and keeping company with people of his own sort of the Still Yard, and other merchants, was with them had up before Cardinal Wolsey and convicted of heresy, which merchants openly abjured their opinions at St. Paul's Cross.

"Yet he, for the love borne by the Cardinal to Sir Thomas More, his father-in-law, was in a friendly warning, discharged. And albeit he had married the oldest daughter of Sir Thomas More, whom then of all the world he did, during that time, most abhor, though he was a man of much mildness and notable patience. Now these easy, short, and very pleasant lessons cast him into so sweet a sleep that he was loath to wake from it.

" And he so well liked it that he soon after gave over his fastings and prayer, and got to him a Lutheran Bible, wherein upon holidays instead of his prayers he spent his whole time, thinking it sufficient for him only to get knowledge to be able amongst ignorant persons to babble and talk (as he thought)

like a great doctor.   And so continned he in his heresies
awhile until upon a time that Sir Thomas More privately in
his garden talked with his daughter Margaret, and amongst
other sayings said he, ' Meg, I have borne a long time with
thy husband.   I have reasoned and argued with him on divers
points of religion, and still given to him my poor fatherly
counsel, but I perceive none of all this able to call him back,
and therefore, Meg, I will no longer argue or dispute with
him, but will clean give him over, and get me another while
to God and pray for him." *

Meanwhile, Roper came to prefer a request to Sir
Thomas that, as he was high in the King's favour, he would
get him a license to preach, for he was sure God had sent
him to instruct the world, not knowing "God wote," says the
old biographer, Cresacre More, " anie reason for this his
mission, but only his private spirit."   " Is it not sufficient, son
Roper, was the reply, that we who are your friends should
know that you are a fool, but that you would have your folly
proclaimed to the world."   He still did his best, however, to
bring him to reason, but at last, said he, " I see, son, no
arguing with thee will do thee good, henceforth, therefore, I
will dispute with thee no more, I will only pray for thee, that
God will touch thy heart," and so committing him to God's
mercy they parted.

" And soon after, as he verily believed, through the great
mercy of God and the devout prayers of Sir Thomas More,
he perceived his own ignorance and folly, and turned him
again to the Catholic faith, wherein (God be thanked) he
hath hitherto continued." †

A valiant champion of the faith, too, was William Roper

* Harleian MS.S.   † Harleian M.SS.

ever after, and as compassionate and charitable to the poor as was the good Sir Thomas himself.

This is one out of two instances noticed by the early biographers of the marked answer granted to the prayers of one, who, living in the heart of the world, and to all outward seeming, absorbed in the world's cares, was yet not of it.

Margaret was once seized with illness, she had fallen ill of what was termed the sweating sickness, of which thousands of persons were then dying, her life was despaired of, and[*] "her father, he that most loved her, being in no small heaviness of heart at last sought for remedy of this most desperate case from God; wherefore going, as was his custom, into his new building, there in his chapel upon his knees with many tears he besought Almighty God, to whom nothing is impossible, of his goodness, if it were his blessed will, graciously to grant his petition." In the patient's most dangerous state she could not be kept from sleep, whilst he prayed, it flashed across his mind that there was a certain remedy that would save her life. It was administered whilst she slept, and when she awoke, though bearing upon her marks which were an evident and undoubted token of death, she was almost miraculously restored to perfect health.

More had declared in the depth of his grief, that if it should please God to take from him his " jewel " Margaret, he would never more meddle with worldly matters, whilst she always referred her recovery to her father's earnest prayers.[†]

* Cresacre More.   † Harleian MS.

CHAPTER IX.

Queen Katherine.—" Heaven witness
I have been to you a true and humble wife,
At all times to your will conformable ;
The King, your father, was reputed for
A prince most prudent, of an excellent
And unmatched wit and judgment.   Ferdinand,
My father, King of Spain, was reckoned one
The wisest prince, that there had reigned by many
A year before. . It is not to be questioned
That they had gathered a wise council to them
Of every realm, that did debate this business,
Who deemed our marriage lawful.

Shakspeare—Henry VIII.

The King's Divorce.

Erasmus to Queen Katherine.

" The nobility of your Highness's birth, your exalted rank and marriage with a most prosperous sovereign, are as nothing in contributing to your happiness, compared with your Majesty's own gifts.   It is most rare to find a lady born and brought up at Court, placing all her hopes and solace in devotion and the reading of scripture.   Would that others, widows at all events, would take an example by your grace, and not widows only, but unmarried ladies—by devoting themselves to the service of Christ.   He is a solid rock, the spouse of all pious souls, and dearer to each than the nearest earthly tie.   The soul that is devoted to this husband is not less grateful in adversity than in prosperity.   He knows what is expedient for all, and is often more propitious when he changes the sweet for bitter.   Everyone must take up their cross; there is no entering into heavenly glory without it. These are blessings which none can take away.   I hope the book which I have dedicated to your Majesty will receive your favorable attention.

"Basle, 1 March, 1528."

"Even when the Queen had lost his heart she never forfeited his esteem.   The reputation which she had acquired on the throne did not suffer from her disgrace.   Her affability and meekness, her piety and charity, had been the theme of universal praise; the fortitude with which she bore her wrongs raised her still higher in the estimation of the public." *

And various have been the eulogiums such as these which have been passed on the truly unfortunate Katherine of Arragon; such was she who was put aside for her maid of honour, Anne Boleyn, such was the right royal lady to divorce himself from whom the Eighth Henry wrung the fair appanage of England from the Church, and caused the heads of two of the most noble and heroic of men to fall beneath the headsman's axe — Fisher, Bishop of Rochester, and Sir Thomas More.

When Henry the Eighth married Katherine of Arragon, daughter of the late King of Spain, and aunt to the reigning Emperor Charles V., she was then in her twenty-sixth year.   She bore him three sons and two daughters, all of whom died in their infancy, except the Princess Mary, who survived both parents, and afterwards ascended the throne.

* Lingard.

Katherine had been previously contracted to his elder, brother, who died a few months after the solemnisation of their marriage, and all impediments to Henry's union with her had been removed by a Papal dispensation. The question had been set at rest by the decision of his counsel, but his passion for the beautiful maid of honour, Anne Boleyn, led him to reconsider the subject.

"Whether the idea of a divorce arose spontaneously to his mind, or was suggested by others, is uncertain ; but Wolsey offered his aid, and ventured to promise success. *His* views, however, were very different to those of his sovereign : *he* looked forward to the political consequences of the divorce ; and that he might perpetuate the alliance between England and France, had selected Renèe, the daughter of Louis XII., for the future queen of England. When he learned from Henry that he wanted no French princess, and that Anne Boleyn was to be queen if the divorce could be obtained, he received the intelligence with grief and dismay, and on his knees he besought the King to recede from a project which must cover him with disgrace ; but, aware of the royal temper, soon desisted, and became a convert to the measures which he could not avert.*

The King's treatise, or case, was then laid before the first literary man in the kingdom, Sir Thomas More, but when consulted by the King he waived the dangerous subject, saying that it was a question fit only for theologians, referring to writings of St. Augustine and other distinguished doctors of the Church. Henry, whose whole heart was bent on making the fair Boleyn his wife, and whose conscience though made the plea, was not at all in the question, did

* Lingard.

not, however, intend More thus quietly to escape, but showed him all the passages of Scripture that seemed to bear him out in what he termed his conscientious scruples. To pacify the King he promised to consider the subject, but abstained from expressing any decisive opinion.

He has been charged by some persons with a concealment of his own ideas, but how could he have acted otherwise than he did? His path was surrounded with difficulties, out of which he could by no means see his way, and intimate as he *must* have been with Henry, from his constant intercourse with him, he must have clearly seen and feared how the matter would end.

After a short time the King made known his doubts respecting his marriage to several canonists and divines, who easily discovered the real wish of their Sovereign through the thin disguise with which he affected to cover it— "the scruples of a timorous conscience and the dangers of a disputed succession." * Many, from passages in scriptures, contended both for and against the matter in question. It is not our purpose, however, to give other than the merest outline of the circumstances connected with "the King's secret matter," as it was called, which occasioned, as we have before said, for it led directly to it, the disruption of England from the See of Rome.

The unfortunate Katherine had been kept in the dark hitherto respecting his intentions to repudiate her, but she at last with her own eyes witnessed his partiality for her maid, and in a fit of passion reproached him with the baseness of his conduct. After a "shorte tragedie" Henry appeased her for a time.

<hr>

* Lingard.

The King's "secret matter" was then disclosed by Wolsey to the prelates of Canterbury and Rochester, and the latter, unlike More, spoke out his mind plainly to the King. It is well known that this prelate was a zealous defender of the Catholic Church against the attacks of the Lutherans. He wrote against the new opinions with spirit and acuteness, and backed his arguments with the weighty evidence of an untainted and irreproachable life. In an age by no means distinguished either for morality or learning, he was at once eminent for virtue, and respectable as a scholar. That he was an encourager of learning in others is well-known by his patronage of Erasmus, and his assiduity in the foundation of Christ's and S. John's Colleges, Cambridge, the Lady Margaret's Professorships, and other scholastic endowments, and his personal affection for literature, may be inferred from the fact of his collecting one of the best libraries in England, and also from his undertaking the study of Greek, when the knowledge of that language was revived in England, although he was then above sixty years of age.[*]

"He had the notablest library of books in all England, two long galleries full. The books were sorted in stalls and a register of the name of every book was at the end of each stall."[†]

Fisher's reputation was equivalent to his merit. Henry VIII. held him in peculiar esteem, and had inquired of Cardinal Pole whether in all his travels he had ever found a prelate of equal ability and worth with the Bishop of Rochester. It appears from the state papers lately published that upon the first whisper of the meditated divorce between Henry and Katherine, Fisher, although unwilling to interfere,

[*] Bruce's Archæologia.　　　[†] Harleian MS.

was applied to by the Queen for advice.   He was afterwards one of her counsellors upon the hearing before the Legate at Blackfriars, and in that character drew upon himself the displeasure of the King.   The opposition which there can be no doubt he offered conscientiously against Henry's subsequent proceedings, not merely eradicated the King's former feeling of affection for him, but even increased his displeasure to dislike and hatred.   In the convocation and afterwards in the Parliament, though almost alone, Fisher was a strenuous opponent to every measure which tended "to break the bonds of Rome," and, notwithstanding his advanced age and infirm health, appears to have maintained the contest eloquently and with vigour *

The earnest-minded Fisher, in the conversation alluded to above, addressed the prelates as follows :—

" May it not seem displeasing to your eminence, and the rest of these grave and reverend fathers of the Church, that I speak a few words, which I hope may not be out of season.   I had thought that when so many learned men came together, some good matters would have been thought of for the weal of the Church, that the scandals that lie so heavy on her members, and the disease that takes such hold on their advantage, might have been at once removed. But who hath made any, the least proposition against the ambition of those men whose pride is so offensive, while their profession is humility or against the licentious lives of those who are vowed to chastity.   How are the goods of the Church invested?   The lands, the tithes, the other oblations of our people's devout ancestors wasted, to the scandal of their posterity, in riotous expenses.   How can we exhort

* Bruce's Archœlogia.

our flocks to fly the pomps and vanities of the world, when we, that are Bishops, set our minds on nothing more than that which we forbid.

If we should teach according to our doings, how absurdly would our doctrines sound? And yet, we teach one thing and do another. Who shall believe our report? We preach humility, sobriety and contempt of the world, and the people perceive in the same men that thus speak, pride and haughtiness of mind, excess of apparel, and an abandonment to the pomps and vanities of the world, so that they know not whether to follow what they see or what they hear. Excuse me, reverend fathers, I blame herein no man more than I do myself, for many times when I have settled myself to the care of my people, to visit my flock, to govern my Church, to answer the enemies of Christ, there hath suddenly come a message to me from the Court, that I must attend such a triumph, or receive such an ambassador. What have *we* to do with the courts of princes? If we are in love with majesty, is there a greater excellence than Him whom we serve? If we delight in stately buildings, where are there higher roofs than those of our cathedrals? If in goodly apparel, is there a greater ornament than that of the priesthood, or is all this better company than the communion of saints? Reverend fathers, what these things may work in you I know not, but this I know, that to *me* they are impediments to devotion, and I think the time is come for us, who are the heads, to give example to the inferior clergy in these particulars, whereby we may be better conformable to the image of God; for, in this trade of life we now lead, there can neither be any likelihood of perpetuity in the state wherein we stand, or safety to the clergy."

Wolsey, with all his love of pomp and pride, could ill have relished this speech of the intrepid prelate; some there were, alas, unworthy of the garb they wore, but there were many, like the monks of the Charter House, ready to die the martyr's death. The Church was fettered by the state, kings, and parliaments had warred against the authority of the Holy See, and in proportion as her prelates became subservient to the crown, they became worldly, luxurious, and time serving.

Sir Thomas More and Bishop Fisher were men of too great worth, influence and learning, to be set aside, and Henry continued to embrace every opportunity of trying to gain them over to his cause. He began by flattering Fisher respecting his learning and virtue, and ended by speaking of the tortures of his own conscience.

The prelate exerted all his powers to soothe and reassure him, told him the matter was too clear to admit of any doubt, and ended by saying, " there be worthy and learned men in your kingdom, who, if they dared speak out, hold it a perilous and unseemly thing that a divorce should be so much as spoken of."

The King abruptly quitted him ; he had spoken out, and there is no doubt but that his constant opposition made him exceedingly troublesome to a Court little accustomed to have its measures thwarted.

All, whether for or against, were, however, of one mind that the marriage, having been originally celebrated under a Papal dispensation, it could only be dissolved by the Holy See. The Pope had been led to believe that the suit of Henry proceeded from sincere scruples, and a commission was ultimately prepared in the most ample forms which the

Papal Council would admit, authorising Wolsey, with the aid of any one of the other English prelates, to enquire without judicial forms into the validity of the dispensation granted for the marriage, and to pronounce in defiance of exception or appeal, the dispensation sufficient or surreptitious, to divorce the parties, if it were invalid, but to legitimate their offspring if desired.

"When Dr. Fox, the King's almoner, and an earnest advocate for the divorce, returned to England with these instruments, the King declared himself satisfied, and Anne Boleyn expressed her gratitude for the agent's services, but Wolsey received the commissions with alarm and vexation. Every clause was examined, corrections suggested, and a request made that Cardinal Campeggio, as a prelate experienced in the forms of the Roman Courts, should be joined in commission with himself. He now began to hesitate. He had persuaded himself a divorce might be justly pronounced now; he declared to the King that, though he was under obligations to him, he owed more to God, and if he found the dispensation sufficient, so to pronounce it, whatever might be the consequence. Henry at the moment suppressed his feelings, but in a short time gave vent to his anger in language the most opprobrious and alarming. Without a divorce Wolsey's power, perhaps his life was at stake. With it, the prospect was equally bad. Anne was not his friend. Her relatives were *his* enemies and rivals, and to be prepared for the worst he hastened to procure the legal endowment of his colleges, saying, as soon as the King's matter was settled, he should retire from Court, and devote the rest of his days to priestly duties. During the various negotiations which preceded the arrival of

Cardinal Campeggio, as joint legate with Wolsey, the King and Queen outwardly lived on the same terms as heretofore. Katherine carefully concealed her feelings, and Henry was induced by a sense of decency to send his mistress a second time from Court. We here insert curious fragments of a letter copied from Sir Henry Ellis's Collection, showing the anxiety of the Queen for the Legate's arrival.

Katherine of Arragon and Henry the Eighth to Cardinal Wolsey—A Joint Letter, 1527.

The mutilated joint letter now presented to the reader is one of the most curious fragments which these volumes will preserve. The first part forms a note from the Queen, anxious for the coming of Campeggio, steadfast in the hope that her cause would be affirmed, and kind and caressing to Wolsey. It is entirely in Katherine's hand-writing, but breaks off abruptly, Henry the Eighth having consented to her importunity, and taken up the pen to finish it.*

"Here we have another added to the many proofs already known, that whatever were Henry's scruples really, however blinded by lust or determined in his heart to get rid of Katherine, his heart respected her.†

"My Lord in my most humblest ways that my heart can think . . . . Me that I am so bold to troubyl you with my sympyl . . . . . ytt to proceed from her that is muche desirus to kno . . . . . . I perseave by this berar that you do the wiche I . . . . as I am moste bounde to pray, for I do know the g . . . . . you

* MS. Cotton.

† Original Letters from Sir Henry Ellis, vol. 1, first series, p. 274.

have taken for me bothe day and nyght . . . . . . my part, but all only in loveing you next on to the . . . . . creatures leveng and I do not dought but the . . . . . · shall manifestly declare and affirm my Wrgte . . . . . · trust you do thynke the same. My Lord I do assure y . . . . from you som neues of the Legat for I do hope and . . . . . . shall be very good, and I am seur that you desayre . . . . . . and more and ytt waer possibel as 1 know it is not . . . . In a stedfast hope I make an end of my letter . . . . . of her that is most bounde to be."

Here Queen Katherine's part ends, the rest is in the hand-writing of Henry VIII.

"The wrytter of this letter wolde not cease tyll she had . . . . . to sett to my hands, desyryng you thought it be short to t . . . . I assure you ther is nother ol us but that grettly desiry . . . . . . muche more rejoyse to hear that you have scapyd thys plage . . . . the fury thereoff to be passyd, specially with them that k . . . . . as I trust you doo. The nott heryng off the the Leg's arywall . . . . . . us somewhat to muse nott withstandyng we trust by your dilyg . . . . (with the assysstence of All myghty God) shortly to be easyd owght . . . no more to you att thys tyme, but that I pray God send you . . . . . and prosperyte as the wryters wolde. By your lovyng So . . . . Frende

'H. E. N. R.

The following, copied from the State Papers, were probably written to Anne Boleyn about the same time as the joint letters given above. The King was, of course, longing as impatiently for the arrival of Campeggio as the unfortunate Katherine :—

1528—Henry VIII. to Anne Boleyn.

"The bearer and his fellow are dispatched with as many things to compass our matter, and bring it to pass as wit could imagine, which being accomplished by their diligence, I trust you and I will shortly have our desired end. This would be more to my heart's ease and quietness of my mind than anything in the world. I assure you no time shall be lost, for *ultra posse non est esse.* Keep him not too long with you, but desire him, for your sake, to make the more speed, for the sooner we shall have word from him the sooner shall our matter come to pass. And this, upon trust of your short repair to London, I make an end of my letter, mine own sweetheart. Written with the hand of him that desireth as much to be yours as you do to have him."

1528.—From the Same to the Same.

"Darling,—The approach of the time which has been delayed so long, delights me so exceedingly that it seems almost already come. Nevertheless, the entire accomplishment cannot be till two persons meet, which meeting is more desired on my part than anything in the world, for what joy can be so great as to have the company of her who is my most dear friend, knowing likewise that she does the same. Judge then what that personage will do whose absence has given me the greatest pain in my heart, which neither tongue nor writing can express, and nothing but that can remedy. Tell your father on my part that I expect him to abridge by two days the time appointed, that he may be in Court before the old term, or at least upon the day prefixed, otherwise I shall think he will not do the lovers turn as he said he would, nor answer my expectation. No more for want of time. I hope soon to tell you by my mouth the rest of the pains I have suffered in your absence. Written by the hand of the Secretary, who hopes to be privately with you, &c."

FROM THE SAME TO THE SAME.

Darling,—The reasonable request of your last letters, with the pleasure also that I take that I know them true, causes me to send you news. The Legate, which we most desire, arrived at Paris on Sunday or Monday* last past, so that I hope by next Monday to hear of his arrival at Calais, and then I trust within a while after to enjoy that which I have so longed for to God's pleasure."

Campeggio was so severely afflicted with gout on his arrival, that he was carried in a litter to his lodgings, and was confined to his bed for a fortnight, of course to the great uneasiness of the King. Throughout the whole of this time Sir Thomas More had not interfered, declaring himself that " the matter was in hand by the ordinary process of spiritual law, whereof," he adds, " I have little skill."

An embassy to the Netherlands took him from the scene of strife, and he was made colleague of his friend, Tunstal, to arrange the treaty of peace between England, France, and the States of Charles the Fifth.

It was upon this occasion that, whilst staying at Bruges, he is said to have puzzled a pragmatical professor of the university, who gave a universal challenge to dispute with any person in any science, *in omni scibili et de quotibi ente.*

* Campeggio reached Paris on Monday, 14 Sep.

Upon which More sent him this question—*Utrum averia carucæ, capto in vetito namio, sunt irreplegibilia?* Whether beasts of the plough, taken in *withernam*, are incapable of being replevied? *

The braggadocio, however, of course did not understand the terms of our common law, and made himself a laughing stock to the whole city for his bragging.

Meanwhile the divorce matter, which was to bring such ruin to many, made its first victim of Wolsey, whom Anne had never forgiven for his opposition to the match; but before the arrival of Campeggio to animate his exertions in her behalf, she had written him as follows :—" All the days of my life I am most bound, of all creatures, next the King's grace, to love and serve your grace, of the which I beseech you never to doubt that I shall vary from this thought as long as there is breath in my body. And as touching your grace's trouble with the sweat, I thank our Lord that those that I desired and prayed for have scaped, and that is the King and you. . . . And as for the coming of the Legate, I desire that much ; and if it be God's pleasure I pray him to send this matter shortly to a good end, and then I trust, my lord, to recompense part of your great pain."

Again she writes :—

" I do know the great pains and trouble that you have taken for me, both day and night, is never like to be recompensed on my part, but alonely in loving you, next to the King's grace, above all creatures living."

In a third she writes :—

" I assure you, that after this matter is brought to pass, you shall find me, as I am bound in the mean time to owe you my services, and then look what thing in the world I

* Blackstone, vol. iii., p. 149.

can imagine to do your pleasure in, you shall find me the gladdest woman in the world to do it."

When the Legate, Campeggio, arrived in England, Katharine, in an interview with him, became aware that the Pontiff had been falsely told that she wished to enter a convent; the line of conduct she adopted proved that she had never entertained such an idea, and it provoked a burst of fury from the King. Thus seven months had passed since the Legate's arrival, Katharine had been dismissed from Court, and Anne was required to return, and had a princely establishment allotted to her, with richly furnished apartments, contiguous to those of the King, and he exacted of his courtiers that they should attend her levees in the same manner that they had attended those of the Queen. On the 29th of May 1529, the Court summoned the royal parties, the Legates, Wolsey and Campeggio, each had a chair of state covered with cloth of gold, the King answered by two proctors; the Queen appealed from them as prejudiced and incompetent judges to the Court of Rome, and then departed. The Court sat every week, and heard arguments on both sides, but seemed as far off as ever in coming to a decision. On the 18th of June the King and Queen were again cited to appear, and the Queen again answered by protesting against the legality of the Court, and, before she withdrew, she made a pathetic and passionate appeal to the King.

Katharine was again summoned before the Court on the 25th of June, and, refusing to appear, was declared contumacious An appeal to the Pope, signed in every page in her own hand, was, however, given in. She also wrote to the Emperor, declaring that she would sooner suffer death than compromise her child's legitimacy, the perplexed Legates

then stopped their proceedings, they declared the Courts
never sat in Rome from July to October, and that they must
follow the example of their head. At this delay Anne so
worked on the feelings of her lover, that he was in an agony
of impatience, and, sending for Wolsey, he remained an hour
with him, while he stormed in all the fury of unbridled
passion. At last Wolsey returned to his barge, and the
Bishop of Carlisle, who was waiting in it at Blackfriars
observing that it was warm weather :

"Yea, my lord," was the reply, "and if you had been chafed,
as I have been, you would say it was *hot.*"   That night when
he had been two hours in bed, Lord Wiltshire, Anne Boleyn's
father, called him up, in the name of the King, to repair instantly to Bridewell palace in order to wait on the Queen
with Campeggio in the morning, with proposals for a private
accommodation.   Wolsey was imprudent enough to rate
him soundly for his eagerness."*

"In the morning the Legates spent much time with the
poor Queen, but accommodation was as far off as ever, when
the long interview was over, she, however, gained over both
Legates to her cause, and this was the real cause of the
King's enmity to his former favourite Wolsey, who had found
ere now that all the pains he had taken to injure Katherine,
were but to exalt Anne Boleyn, his active enemy. The King's
counsel, when the Court resumed its sittings, pressed the
Legates to give judgment, but Campeggio refused, declaring
the matter should be referred to the Pontiff. The Court
was then dissolved, and Suffolk, the King's brother-in-law,
striking the table so violently with his fist, as to make every-

* Agnes Strickland.

one start, swore no good had ever befallen England since Cardinals came there, to which Wolsey retorted :

"That if it had not been for one Cardinal at least, the Duke of Suffolk, would have lost his head, and not had the opportunity of reviling Cardinals at that time."

Meanwhile More had returned to England, and whilst at Woodstock, where the Court then was, tidings of the news was brought to him that his barns and store-houses—which were well filled with corn—had been destroyed by fire. His letter, which shewed his christian resignation and philosophy in every line, ran as follows :—

"Mistress Alice,—In my most hearty wise I recommend me to you. And whereas I am informed by my son Heron, of the loss of our barns, and of our neighbours also, with all the corn therein ; albeit (saving God's pleasure) it is a great pity of so much good corn lost, yet, since it has liked Him to send us such a chance, we must not only be content, but also glad of His visitation. He sent us all we have lost, and since He hath by such a chance, taken it away again, His pleasure be fulfilled. Let us never grudge thereat but take it in good part, and heartily thank Him both in prosperity and adversity. And, peradventure, we have more cause to thank Him for our losing than our winning, for His wisdom seeth better what is good for us than we do ourselves. Therefore I pray you be of good cheer, and take all the household with you to church, and there thank God both for what He hath given us and for what He hath taken away ; and for all He hath left us, which He can easily increase when He sees fit, and if He pleases to take more from us—His blessed will be done. I pray you diligently enquire what our poor neighbours have lost, and desire them not to be sad, for I will not see any of them damaged by any mischance of my house, even if it should leave me without a spoon. I pray you be cheerful with all my children, and family, and take counsel of our friends, as to how corn is to be procured for our household; and for seed this year coming, if we think well to keep the ground still in our hands, but whether we do so, or not, I do not think it expedient suddenly to give it up, and put out our workmen from our farm till we have taken counsel thereon."

"If we have more workmen now than we have need of, such may be dismissed, if they can be conveniently placed with other masters, but I will not suffer any to be sent away at random without a place to live in. On my return to the King I found things so happening, that it is likely I shall stay with him a long while, but, on account of this mischance, perhaps, I shall get leave to come and see you some time this next week, when we will confer at leisure, about these our household affairs.   Farewell.

" From the Court at Woodstock, 13 Sept., 1529."

CHAPTER X.

The Chancellor.

On the return of Sir Thomas More from his successful negociation at Cambray, the King resumed his former importunities, saying, that though the dispensation he had received to marry his brother's widow, was good with regard to the laws of the Church, yet now it was found to be against the law of nature, as Doctor Stokeley (who, by the way, for raising this objection was preferred to the Bishopric of London) would inform him.

Ultimately More, who, do what he would, could not escape, agreed to confer on the matter with Tunstal and Clarke, the Bishops of Bath and Durham, and with others of the Privy Council, but he remained inflexible, and when he came to Court, when talking with the King, said More :

"To be plain with your Grace, neither my lords of Durham nor of Bath, though I know them to be wise, virtuous and learned prelates, or myself, with the rest of the council, being your Grace's own servants, bound to you for many benefits, are in my mind, meet councillors. If your Grace mean to know the truth, such councillors should you have, as neither for their own worldly advancement, nor for fear of your authority, will be inclined to deceive you."

Such a mode of reasoning was correct enough, but it was not what the King wished for ; and though he affected to take

More's advice in good part, the storm raged within his breast, and he ceased not to adopt every means in his power to bend his virtuous statesman to obedience to his will.

As to Wolsey, his good fortune had now abandoned him, and Henry was still smarting under his disappointment, when an instrument arrived from Rome forbidding him to pursue his cause before the Legates, and citing him to appear by attorney in the Papal Court, under a penalty of 10,000 ducats. The whole process was one of mere form, but the King deemed it a personal insult, and insisted Wolsey should prevent it from being served upon him, and from being made known to his subjects. The Cardinal in vain strove to recover the royal favour.

Anne Boleyn openly avowed her hostility, and seconded the attempts of the Dukes of Norfolk and Suffolk, and her father, Viscount Rochford, to precipitate the downfall of the minister, nor did she let the King have any peace till she had extracted from him a solemn promise that he would never more speak to the Cardinal.

His enemies did not rest till they had stripped him of every office and dignity; he then resigned the Great Seal into the hands of the Dukes of Norfolk and Suffolk, and was told that the King meant to reside at his house at York Place, and that he might retire to Esher, a seat belonging to his Bishopric of Winchester. To appoint a successor to Wolsey in the Chancery was of great importance, and the office was given to Sir Thomas More, the Treasurer of the Household, and Chancellor of the Duchy of Lancaster.

There is no doubt but that Cardinal Pole was correct in

saying that this honourable post was conferred on More, in order the better to bring him within "the bent of the King's bow," with respect to the contemplated marriage with Anne Boleyn. With a delicate conscience, and a high sense of duty, Sir Thomas was surely not a fit associate for his less timorous colleagues, the difficulties which in two years compelled him to retire from office, must even now have stared him in the face. As a scholar he was celebrated throughout Europe; as a lawyer he had long practised with applause and success; his merit was acknowledged by all, even Wolsey declared he knew no one more worthy to be his successor, but there were few instances in which the seals had been entrusted to any but dignified churchmen.

As More possessed no hereditary rank or judicial reputation beyond that acquired as under Sheriff of London, an apprehension was felt lest his office should be thought lowered by the prejudices of the vulgar, after having been held by a Cardinal Archbishop, the Pope's Legate, and Prime Minister of the Crown.* And a splendid pageant was got up for the installation of the new Lord Chancellor, whose exaltation to so high a post was acknowledged by all. The Duke of Norfolk, the first peer in the realm, headed the procession, together with the King's brother-in-law, the Duke of Suffolk, the nobility resident in and near London followed, together with the judges, and professors of the law.

On arriving at Palace Yard, the Chancellor, wearing his robes of office, was conducted between the two Dukes up Westminster Hall to the Stone Chamber, where were the marble table and marble chair, and then taking his place in the high judgment seat, the Duke of Norfolk, by command

* Lord Cardinal Pole.

of the King, spoke as follows to the people, who had gathered together " with great applause and joy."

" The King's majesty, which I pray God may prove happy to the whole realm of England, hath raised to the dignity of Chancellorship, Sir Thomas More, a man for his extraordinary worth and sufficiency, well known to himself and the whole realm, for no other but that he hath plainly perceived all the gifts of nature and grace to be heaped upon him, which, either the people could desire or himself could wish for the discharge of so great an office.

" For the wisdom, integrity, and sincerity joined with pleasant facility of wit that this man is endowed with, have been known to all Englishmen, from his youth, and for these many years to the King's majesty himself. This, the King hath found in many weighty affairs which he hath happily despatched at home and abroad, in many offices he hath borne, in embassies he hath undertaken, and in his daily counsel and advice on other occasions ; so that he hath found no one in his realm more wise in deliberating, more sincere in revealing his thoughts, or eloquent in speech. Wherefore, because he saw in him such excellent endowments, and out of a special care he hath that his people should be governed with equity and justice, integrity and wisdom, he hath graciously created this singular man Lord Chancellor, that, by his worthy performance of this office, his people may enjoy peace and justice, and that honour may redound to the whole kingdom. It may perhaps seem strange that this dignity should now be bestowed on a layman, not of the nobility, because formerly learned prelates and great noblemen have possessed it, but what is wanting in this respect, the admirable virtues and matchless gifts,

and wisdom of the man doth amply atone for. For his majesty hath not regarded how great, but the kind of man he
was, not the nobility of his blood, but the worth of his person,
he hath respected his qualities, not his profession, and finally
he would shew by this his choice that he hath some rare
subjects amongst his gentry, who are worthy of managing
the highest offices in the realm, which bishops and noblemen
think they only can deserve."

"The rarer it was then, he hath held it to be the more
excellent, and to his people he thought it would be the more
grateful. Wherefore, receive this your Chancellor with joyful
acclamations, at whose hands you may expect all happiness
and content."

The worthy Sir Thomas was not a little abashed at
having to listen to his own praises declared so pompously,
and recollecting himself for a moment, replied as follows :—

"Most Noble Duke, Right Honourable Lords, and worthy
Gentlemen, I know all these things are very far from me,
which the King's highness hath been pleased should be
spoken, and which your grace hath exaggerated, and I wish
with all my heart I did possess them for the better performance of so great a charge. And though this your speech
hath aroused greater fear in me than I can well express in
words, yet this favour of my dread sovereign, by which he
shews how well he thinketh of my weakness—having commanded that my mean birth should be so greatly commended,
cannot but be acceptable to me, and I cannot choose but
give your grace exceeding thanks that what his Majesty
willed you briefly to utter, you, out of the abundance of
your love have enlarged on in a long and eloquent oration.
As for myself I cannot take it otherwise than that it proceeds

from his Majesty's great favour towards me, and the good-will of his royal mind, by which he hath for many years constantly favoured me, hath alone, without any merit of mine, caused this my new honour, and your grace's undeserved praise.

"For who am I, or what is the house of my father, that the King's highness should heap upon me, through such a stream of affection, these high honours?

"I am far less than the meanest of the benefits he hath showered on me, how then can I think myself fit or worthy of this peerless dignity. I have been drawn forcibly, as the King's majesty hath often said, to his Highness' service, to become a courtier, but to take this dignity upon me is most of all against my will, yet such is his benignity and bounty, that he esteems the small service of the meanest of his subjects, and seeketh to reward his servants, not only such as deserve well, but even such as have a desire to deserve well at his hands, amongst which number I have always wished myself to be reckoned, because I cannot consider myself one of the former, so that you may all see how great a burden is laid on my back, so that I must strive by diligence and duty to correspond with his royal benevolence, and to respond to the expectations which he and you have of me, wherefore these high praises are so much the more gracious to me, because I know the greatness of the charge I have to make myself worthy of, and the small means I possess to make them good. This weight is hardly suitable for my weak shoulders, this honour does not correspond with my poor deserts, it is a burthen, not a glory, a care, not a dignity; the one I must bear as bravely as I can, the other I must discharge as well as I am able.

" The earnest desire which I have always had to satisfy by all possible means for the ample favours of his Highness, will greatly excite me to diligent performance, which I trust I shall be better able to do, if I find your good will and wishes both favourable to me and conformable to the King's royal munificence, for my serious endeavours to do well, united with your good will, will ensure that whatever is performed by me, though in itself but small, will seem praiseworthy; for those things are always well achieved which are willingly accepted, and those fortunately succeed which are received courteously, and as you hope for great and good things at my hands, so, though I dare not pro-mise any such, yet I promise truly and affectionately to do the best that I am able."

Then turning his face to the judgment-seat of the Chancery, he thus continued,--" But when I look upon this seat, and think of the greatness of the personages who have filled this place before me, when I call to mind who *he* was that last occupied it; his wisdom, and experience, what prosperous fortune he had for a great space, and then so grievous a fall, I have sufficient cause to think this honour but slippery, and this dignity not so grateful to me as it may seem to others, for it is a hard matter to follow a man of such admirable wit, prudence, and authority, to whom I may seem but as the lighting of a candle when the sun hath set, and also the sudden and unexpected fall of so great a man doth terribly put me in mind that this honour ought not to please me too much, nor the lustre of his glittering seat dazzle mine eyes, so that I occupy it as a place full of labour and danger void of true honour, and by which the higher it is the more I have to fear a fall, as well in respect of the thing itself as of the late example before me, and truly at this first step I might stumble, but that his Majesty's favour and your good wills manifested by the joyful countenances of this honourable assembly, doth revive my spirits, otherwise this seat would be no more pleasing to me than was that sword to Damocles, suspended over his head by a single hair, when he had store of delicate viands before him, seated in the throne of Denis, the tyrant of Sicily, this, therefore, fresh in my mind will I have before mine eyes, that this seat will be honourable and full of glory, if with care, and diligence, fidelity, and wisdom, I try to do my duty; and I shall remember that the enjoyment of it may be short and uncertain, the one whereof my own labour ought to perform, the other my predecessor's example may easily teach me, and this being the case you may easily perceive what great pleasure I take in this high dignity, or in this most noble Duke's praises."

His words again seem invested as with the spirit of the prophets of old. The character of the King, must, by this time, have been read by More in its true light, nay, long years since, for his own speech to Roper, when the latter congratulated him on the favor of Henry, makes this manifest; and in the future, amidst all the glittering pomp, and parade, and splendours of this day, so far removed from the humbleness and simplicity which his great soul prized, he may have beheld in spirit the bitter end, the Tower, the dungeon, and the block, to which the fatal liking of himself of the despotic sovereign whom he served, was so surely leading him.

More's elevation was as popular abroad as at home, congratulations were showered on him from all sides, a single sentence addressed by Erasmus to John Fabius, Bishop of Vienna, sufficiently proves this, it runs as follows :—

" Concerning the new increase of honour experienced by Thomas More, I should easily make you believe it, were I to shew you the letters of many famous men, rejoicing with much alacrity, congratulating the King, the realm, himself, and also me, on his promotion to be Lord Chancellor of England."

" Then did all present behold the spectacle of this wise and learned man kneeling, each morning for his father's blessing, before he occupied his own seat as Lord High Chancellor, for in the adjoining room to his own was seated his venerable father, over whose head the snows of many winters had passed. The senior of the Judges of England was this Judge More, and his son, Sir Thomas, delighted to render him this act of filial piety. *

Soon after his installation he was called upon to open the Parliament summoned for the impeachment of his predecessor ; and thus ran his speech :—

" Like as a good shepherd, who not only tendeth but keepeth well his sheep, but also provideth and foreseeth against everything which may be hurtful to his flock, or may preserve and defend the same against all chances to come, and considering how divers laws by long mutation of things and continuance of time, were now grown insufficient and imperfect, and, also, that by the frail condition of man,

---

* I am old enough to remember that when the Lord Chancellor left his Court, if the Court of King's Bench was sitting, a curtain was drawn and bows were exchanged between him and the Judges, so that I can easily picture to myself " the blessing scene " between the father and son.—*Lord Campbell's Lives of the Chancellors.*

divers new enormities were sprung up amongst the people for which no law was made to reform the same, was the very cause, he added, why, at this time the King had summoned his High Court of Parliament. He likened the King for this cause to a shepherd or herdsman; if a King be esteemed only for his riches, he is a rich man, but compare him to the multitude of his people, and the number of his flock, then he is a ruler, a governor of might and power, so that his people maketh him a prince, as of the multitude of sheep cometh the name of a shepherd. And as you see that amongst a great flock of sheep, some may be rotten and faulty, which the good shepherd sendeth from the sound sheep, so the great WETHER, which is lately fallen as you all know, juggled with the King so craftily and untruly, that all men must think that he imagined himself that the King had no sense to perceive his crafty doings, or presumed that he would not see or understand his fraudulent jugglings and attempts. But he was deceived, for his Grace's sight was so quick that he not only saw him, but through him, both within and without; so that he was entirely open to him. According to his desert, he hath had a gentle correction, which small punishment the King would should be an example to other offenders, but openly declareth that, whoever, hereafter should make the like attempt, or commit the same offences shall not escape with the like punishment.* Articles of charge were then brought against Wolsey, Audley being Speaker, and Sir Thomas, Chairman."

Lord Campbell, in his Lives of the Chancellors, says, that the articles, numbering forty-four, were many of them frivolous, and that the Cardinal's violation of the law by

* Parl. Hist. 491.

raising taxes without authority of Parliament, and other excesses of the prerogative were passed over without any proof; these articles were unanimously agreed to by the House of Lords, where the ex-chancellor was particularly odious, on account of his haughty bearing to the ancient nobility, and even to his brother prelates.

By the Lower House they were rejected at the instance of Cromwell, formerly the Cardinal's servant.

Campbell alludes to the ungenerous language in which More expressed himself concerning his fallen predecessor, but adds that with regard to his speech when Parliament was assembled, he might have felt himself compelled to consult the feelings of those whom he addressed, to whom the late Chancellor had rendered himself most odious.

As chief law-officer of the Crown, More's name was affixed to the bill; there can be no doubt that one so simple in his own tastes and habits, and who held in horror all that appertained to luxury and worldliness, can have felt but small respect for Wolsey in his ecclesiastical character, still the remarks made in his speech are barely justifiable even when viewed in the light in which Lord Campbell considers them.

More at once proceeded to business, and several statutes were speedily passed to put down extortion on the probate of wills, and in the demands for mortuaries, and to prevent the clergy from engaging in trade, and, to his great relief, the session was closed on the 17th December. Not being a member of the House, he did not openly take any part in the debates, but he was named on committees, and the proceedings of the Lords were entirely governed by him.

Left to attend to the business of Chancery, he began by

an order that no *subpœna* should issue till a bill had been filed, signed by the attorney, and he himself having perused it, had granted a fiat for the commencement of the suit; abuses had multiplied during the late chancellorship, writs of subpœna had been granted on payment of the fees, without examining whether there was a chance of the innocent being involved in the misery of Chancery suits, several causes had stood over even for twenty years, and people were wont to say that "no one could hope for a favourable judgment unless his fingers were tipt with gold,"* caused probably by the fees and gratuities demanded by the Cardinal's servants. Once, a very foolish bill was brought to More, who at once combined humour and justice, for it was signed " A. Tubbe," and he wrote immediately above the signature, " A Tale of."

The attorney being told that the Lord Chancellor was satisfied with his bill, took it at once to his clients, who immediately detected the jest.*

He was cautious in granting injunctions whilst he was Lord Chancellor, and, says Lord Campbell, it was his opinion that law and equity might be beneficially administered by the same tribunal, and he strove to induce the common law judges to relax the rigour of their rules, so as to meet the justice of particular cases, and, not succeeding, he resolutely examined their proceedings, stayed trials and executions, wherever it seemed to him that wrong would be done, from their refusal to remedy the effects of accident, to enforce the performance of trusts, or to prevent secret frauds from being profitable to the parties concerned in them.

These new rules, however, occasioned some murmuring

More's Roper.

from various of the Judges, which came to the ears of Roper, and were by him made known to his father-in-law. "They shall have little cause to find fault with me for that," said Sir Thomas, and he at once ordered one Mr. Crooke, chief of the six clerks, to make a dockett * containing the whole number and causes of all such injunctions as in his time had already passed, or at present depended in any of the King's. Courts at Westminster before him. This being done, he invited all the Judges to dine with him in the Council Chamber at Westminster Hall, and after they had dined, told them the reason why he had made so many injunctions, when they one and all declared that in his place they would have done no less. He then promised them that if they, who could so easily modify the rigour of the law, would use their own discretion, and mitigate its severity where needful, he would grant no more injunctions, to which, on their refusing, then said More :—

"You, yourselves, my lords, drive me to this necessity, so do not blame me if I seek to relieve the poor whom I may find in need." To Roper he afterwards said :—

"I can see, son, why they do not like this, they think that by the verdict of a jury they may cast off all blame from themselves on the poor men who hold it, whom they rely on as their defence. So I am obliged to abide the chance of their blame."†

Very seldom had he any leisure time, for so honest and indeed perfect was he in the discharge of his duties as judge, that not only was his court thronged by suitors, but

---

* A small piece of paper or parchment containing the effect of a larger writing.—*Cowel's Law Interpreter.*

† Roper.

when the hours devoted to his public duties were over, he acted in his own house as arbitrator. One may fancy this great and good man, in the quietude of his own beloved home at Chelsea, stealing away from his family to some chamber kept for the use of unfortunate persons who had no money to pay the expenses of a lawsuit, and there, seated before the contending parties, or pacing up and down the room, listening to the tale of each, acting as umpire, reconciling them, adjusting their differences, and sending them contented to their homes.

This novel mode of procedure, however, did not always please those around him, and on one occasion Dauncey, one of his sons-in-law, represented to him that when Cardinal Wolsey was chancellor, not only those of his privy chamber, but also his door-keeper, made great gains under him, and seeing he was the husband of one of his daughters, and still attended upon him, he thought he ought in all reason to do the same. " But he was so ready to hear every man's cause, both rich and poor, and would keep no doors shut from them, that he could find no gains at all, which discouraged him exceedingly. Some for friendship, some for relationship, and others for profit, would gladly have had him help to bring them to his presence." But," added he, " were I to take anything of them, I should do them a great wrong, for they can do as much for themselves as I can do for them, which state of things, though commendable in you, sir, is to me unprofitable." "I do not mislike, son, that your conscience is so scrupulous," replied Sir Thomas, " but there may be many other ways in which I may do good to you, and be of use to your friend. Sometimes by a word I may help him, or else by a letter, if he hath a cause depending before myself. At your entreaty I may hear his cause before that of another. And if it be not one of the best, I may urge the parties to accommodate their differences by means of arbitration; but, of this be certain, that if those before me require justice and equity, then, although my father (whom I dearly love) were on one side, and the devil (whom I hate) were on the other, his cause being first, the devil should have his right."

Indeed his love of justice was so great that he never digressed one iota from it for any tie of kindred or friendship, thus, when another son-in-law, Heron, had a cause in Chancery pending before Sir Thomas, he trusted on being favoured because he was "the most affectionate of fathers," and could not be persuaded to agree to any reasonable decision, but at length Sir Thomas made a flat decree against him.

All who chose to come before him with their petitions were allowed to do so, and he gave them redress when in his power, according to law and his conscience, and "The poorer and the meaner the applicant was, the more affably he would speak unto him, the more heartily he would hearken to his cause, and with speedy trial dispatch him.* Not only did he himself refuse all corrupt offers that were made to him, but he took stringent means to prevent those connected with him from doing so also, and this it was which called forth the remonstrance of his son-in-law quoted above."

Owing to his quickness and diligence, in the course of a few terms all the old arrears were subdued, and every cause

* More.

decided as soon as ready for hearing. He examined all cases that came before him like an arbitrator. On once being told by the officer that there was not another cause or petition to be set before him, he ordered the fact to be entered on record, as it had never happened before, and a prophesy was then entered which has been fully verified :

> When MORE some time had Chancellor been,
>   No *more* suits did remain ;
> The same shall *never* more be seen
>   Till MORE be there again.

"Nor did this great man despise a practical joke. While he held his city office he used regularly to attend the Old Bailey Sessions, where there was a tiresome old justice, ' who was wont to chide the poor men that had their purses cut for not keeping them more warily, saying that their negligence was the cause that there were so many cut-purses brought thither.' To stop this prosing, More at last went to a celebrated cut-purse then in prison, who was to be tried next day, and promised to stand his friend if he would cut this justice's purse while he sat on the bench trying him. The thief being arraigned at the sitting of the court next morning, said he could excuse himself sufficiently if he were but permitted to speak in private to one on the bench. He was bid to choose whom he would, and he chose that grave old justice, who had then his pouch at his girdle. The thief stepped up to him, and while he rounded him in the ear, cunningly cut his purse, and, taking his leave, solemnly went back to his place. From the agreed signal, More, knowing that the deed was done, proposed a small subscription for the poor needy fellow, who had been acquitted, himself setting a liberal example. The old justice, after some hesitation, expressed his willingness to give a trifle ; but, finding his purse cut away, expressed the greatest astonishment, as he said he was sure he had it when he took his seat in court that morning. More replied, in a pleasant manner, ' What ! will you charge your brethren of the bench with felony ?' The justice, becoming angry and ashamed, Sir Thomas called the thief and desired him to deliver up the purse, counselling the worthy justice hereafter not to be so bitter a censurer of innocent men's negligence, since he himself could not keep his purse safe when presiding as a judge at the trial of cut-purses."

Of course the household at Chelsea possessed the ancient appendage of a Fool, and Pattison, for such was his name, appears in Holbein's painting of the More family, an anecdote of whom appears in the Il Moro, before quoted, and has been copied into the various biographies of More, affording an instance that the folly of these simple beings must sometimes have made them a source of real annoyance and mortification. Sir Thomas relates in the Dialogue in the work I have named that " Pattison was yesterday standing by the table while we were at dinner, and seeing a gentleman among the company, with an unusually large nose, after he had gazed for some time upon the gentleman's face, he said aloud, to my great annoyance, ' What a terrific nose that gentleman has got.' As we all affected not to hear him, that the good man might not be abashed, Pattison perceived that he had made a mistake and endeavoured to set himself right by saying, ' How I lyed in my throat, when I said that gentleman's nose was so monstrously large ; on the faith of a gentleman—it really is rather a small one.' At this, all being greatly inclined to laugh, I made a sign that the fool

should be turned out of the room.   But Pattison, not wishing
for his own credit's sake that this should be the termination
of the affair (because he was always accustomed to boast,
as above every other merit he possessed, that whatever he
commenced he brought to a happy conclusion), to bring this
affair to a good end, he placed himself in my seat at the
head of the table, and said aloud, ' There is one thing I
would have you know, that gentleman there has not the
least atom of a nose.'

The unpretending nature of the private life of Sir Thomas
More was in keeping with the simplicity of his career in
public.   The surroundings of his Chelsea home underwent
no change, and the guests who partook of the bounteous
liberality of the Lord Chancellor, observed that he himself,
partook but of one dish, and that was generally salted beef,
indeed coarse brown bread and cheese, with perhaps a little
fruit and milk, was the food he best liked.

Wine he rarely touched, and so far from his health
suffering from so singularly abstemious a diet, it is possible
the great powers of his mind, and the rapidity with which
he discharged his multiplied and arduous duties may be
ascribed to this mode of life.

Early rising and temperate habits injure no one, and
assuredly prolong life ; had More been a lover of the table
and risen late, he never could have got through so vast an
amount of work, or have maintained the powers of his mind
in full vigour.

Unlike his predecessor, whose love of pomp and display
was so great, that crosses, pillars, and poleaxes were borne
before him when he went to administer justice, More avoided
all outward parade and shew of ostentation, and even on

Sundays, whilst in his high office as Lord Chancellor, instead of striving to outvie the nobles at the Court, then held at Greenwich, he would walk on foot to church. It was a favourite practice of More's to serve the Mass of his friend Dr. Larke, when in his parish church at Chelsea, and himself to bear the cross in procession around it, or assist in bearing the canopy in processions of the Blessed Sacrament.

In Rogation Week, when they were necessarily very long, and he had followed those who carried the rood round the parish, being advised to use a horse on account of his high dignity, he replied—"It beseemeth not the servant to follow his master, prancing on cock-horse, whilst his lord is going on foot." During the celebration of High Mass at Chelsea, when he was with his family at the parish church, he would put on a surplice, and, entering the chancel, he always sung along with the choristers.

On one occasion, when the Duke of Norfolk was coming to dine with him, coming into the church on his way, he was surprised to find him thus employed, and as they walked home together, after Mass was over, the Duke, unable to appreciate the motives that actuated More, who knew that even small actions become great when done in God's service, with a pure intention, and whose worldly mind led him to view More's conduct in the light of one who was practising a voluntary self-abasement, exclaimed—"God save us, my Lord Chancellor! God save us, my Lord Chancellor, a parish clerk! A parish clerk? You dishonour the King and his office." "Nay," replied Sir Thomas with a smile; "your grace must not think that the King, your master and mine, will be offended with me for serving *his* master, or thereby account his office dishonoured."

The inflexible love of justice by which More was distinguished, and which was never known to waver for friend or foe, and to which we have alluded before, is strikingly manifested in an amusing anecdote told by Lady More.

It happened that she had become possessed of a little dog, of which she had become very fond, and she had kept it carefully enough for some two or three weeks. It was, in fact, the property of a beggar-woman, who, finding out in whose keeping the animal was, presente dherself before the Chancellor, as he was sitting hearing causes in his hall, telling him that his lady withheld her dog from her. Dame Alice was presently sent for, together with the dog, which Sir Thomas, holding in his hands, bade his wife stand at the upper end of the hall, and the beggar at the lower end, and ordered both of them to call the animal.

The dog ran immediately to the beggar-woman, thus making it clear to all present to whom he really belonged.

On seeing this, said More—" Be contented, Dame, for the dog is none of yours."

The lady, however, expressed dissatisfaction at the Chancellor's judgment, and made the beggar an offer of a piece of gold, sufficient to have paid for three dogs, so she remained mistress of the animal, this time by good right. "Solomon himself could not have delivered a more equitable judgment." *

It is said that a friend of his had taken great pains about a dull and heavy book ; he would not take any denial, but was resolved Sir Thomas should read it before it was printed, with a safe conscience the Chancellor could not

* Campbell.

praise the work, and seeing nothing in it worth printing, he said :

"If it were in verse, it would be better, methinks." On which the author took it away and turned it into verse, and bringing it to him again, Sir Thomas, looking it over, said, "Yea, marry now it is somewhat, for it is rhyme, and before it was neither rhyme nor reason."

Meanwhile the Lord Chancellor had his hours of anxious musing respecting the King's contemplated divorce, a matter which also preyed heavily on the mind of Pope Clement, who had hoped that the Cardinal, in virtue of his ordinary powers, would have pronounced judgment without asking his consent or interfering with his authority. At length, yielding to the solicitations of the Emperor, he forbade Henry to marry before the sentence of divorce was published, and in the interim to treat Katherine as his wife. Ambassadors from Henry then visited the Pope, amongst whom was the Earl of Wiltshire, Anne's father. He received them graciously, but when they were presented to the Emperor, who was with the Pope, that prince did not attempt to conceal his feelings at the sight of the father of his aunt's rival.

"Stop, sir," said the Emperor, "allow your colleagues to speak ; you are a party to the cause." The Earl replied firmly that he did not come there as a father defending the interests of his child, but as a subject representing the person of his sovereign. As the price of Charles' consent to the divorce, the ambassador offered him 300,000 crowns, the restoration of the marriage portion paid with Katherine, and security for a maintenance suitable to her birth during her life. He replied indignantly, "He was not a merchant to sell the honour of his aunt."

The new ministers then condescended to profit by the advice of Wolsey, whom they had supplanted, and to obtain in favour of the divorce, the opinions of the universities and the most celebrated divines in Europe. In Italy the King's agents were numerous, their success and failure were nearly balanced; from the Pontiff they had procured a breve exhorting every man to speak his mind without fear or favour.* In the states of Germany they were less successful, even the reformed divines, with a few exceptions, condemned the divorce, and Luther wrote to Barnes, the royal agent, that he would rather allow the King to have two wives at once than separate from Katharine to marry another woman. In France, after a bribe of two millions of crowns, the assent of the University of Paris was won only by the basest manœuvres.

It had been originally intended to lay before the Pontiff this mass of opinions as the voice of the christian world, but Clement knew (and Henry was aware that he knew) the arts by which they had been extorted, so a letter was sent to the Pope instead, subscribed by the lords spiritual and temporal and the most influential of the commoners, complaining of the delays of Clement, representing the evils of a disputed succession, and threatening to remedy the evil without his interference.

Clement's reply was mild, but firm, he answered that if lawless remedies were used, those who employed them must answer for the result; that he would shew the King every indulgence and favour, but would not, through gratitude to man, violate the commandments of God.

The King was then informed that the Imperialists were

* In every city from Venice to Rome royal agents were to be seen distributing money in reward for a signature.—*Lingard.*

most urgent in their solicitations, and that Clement was about to issue a breve forbidding any ecclesiastical court from giving judgment in the case. It was observed that the King became pensive, he began to waver and appeared inclined to give up the struggle, his half formed resolve reached the ears of Anne Boleyn, her ruin and that of her advocates was imminent, but they were saved by Cromwell, who, as the King's evil genius, determined, to use his own words, "to make or mar," and he asked for an audience of Henry.

"Affection and duty would not suffer him to be silent," said he, "when he witnessed his sovereign's anxiety, why not throw off the yoke of Rome, and declare himself the head of the Church within his own realms."

Henry listened with a glad surprise to this evil genius; his passion for Anne Boleyn was flattered, his thirst of wealth, his greed of power. He thanked Cromwell and ordered him to be sworn of his Privy Council. It was evident, however, even to Cromwell, that this change would meet with much opposition, but his cunning soon contrived a plan to secure submission.* When the statutes of premunire were passed, a power was given to the Sovereign to modify or suspend their operation at his discretion, and it had been usual for the King to grant letters of license to individuals who meant to act, or who had acted, against these statutes. Hence Wolsey had taken out a patent under the great seal authorising him to exercise the legantine authority, nor did any one for fifteen years accuse him of violating the law, When, however, he was indicted for the offence, he refused on motives of prudence, to plead the royal permission, and suffered judgment to pass against him. Now, on the ground

* Lingard.

of his conviction, it was argued that all the clergy were guilty, as, admitting his jurisdiction, they had become his fautors and abettors, and an information was filed, ordered by Henry, against the whole body in the Court of King's Bench, though he had himself requested the dignity of Legate for his once favoured minister. A present of 10,000 pounds was offered in return for a full pardon, but to the grief and astonishment of the clergy Henry refused the proposal, unless in the preamble to the grant, a clause were introduced acknowledging him to be the protector and only supreme head of the Church in England. Three days were spent in useless consultation, and the King then sent a positive message that he would allow of no alteration than the addition of the words "under God." Fisher and Warham, by their strong language, caused an amendment to be introduced, with the King's permission, which was carried by consent of both houses. Tunstal, Bishop of Durham, had the courage to protest against the assumption of this title by the King. The grant was then made in the usual manner, and the following clause was adopted, " so far as the law of God will permit," *quantum per legem Dei licet.*

The introduction of these words served to invalidate the whole recognition, but a beginning was made, and the above clause, the King felt, might be expunged later.

More's own words make known to us, that in the earlier part of his life he had not such clear views of the supremacy of the Pope, his later studies, however, on that point, carried perfect conviction to his mind. In the midst of his numerous avocations, he now set himself to expose the false doctrines of the sectarians around him, and exposed himself to the enmity of all who were joining the new religionists, thus the Water Bailiff of the city, who had formerly been in his employment, could not restrain his anger at the malicious and envious speeches which he heard from certain merchants, regarding his old master, and unable to contain himself he vented what he felt in the following manner, on accompanying Sir Thomas to his barge.

"Were I in your place, and high in favour and authority with the King, I would not allow myself to be so villainously slandered. You should summon them before you and punish them."

But nothing could shake the imperturbable calmness of More, who replied, with a smile, " Why, Mr. Water Bailiff, should you want me to punish these men. I receive greater benefits from them than from all of you who are my friends, let them, in God's name, speak as foully of me as they list ; and, as long as their arrows do not hurt me, what need I care ; but if they once hurt it would indeed be a trouble ; but, by God's help, I hope that will never be. I have more cause, my good friend, to pity than to be angry with them."

But the aspect of the outer world raised grave fears in the otherwise calm and well tempered mind of this christian philosopher and statesman. Of himself, as he truly said, the world might talk as it listed, but the peace of the State, above all the peace and prosperity of the Church, to which he was so firmly attached, harrassed him not a little ; and so Roper tells us that, one day when they were walking together by the banks of the Thames, at Chelsea, said he,

"Upon condition that these things were well established in christendom, I would to our Lord, son Roper, that I were put in a sack and cast in the Thames."

"What great things be these, sir," quoth I, "that you so wish."

"Wouldst thou really know, son Roper?"

"Ah, marry with a good will, sir, an it please you to tell me."

"In faith, son, they be these : the *first*, that whereas the great majority of Christian kings are at war, that they were all in universal peace ; the *second*, that even as the Church of Christ is sore afflicted with many errors and heresies, it were well settled in perfect uniformity of religion ; and the *third*, that, as the matter of the King's marriage is now come in question, it were to the glory of God and peace of all parties brought to a happy conclusion." "Whereby," continues Roper, "as far as I could understand, he judged that otherwise it would disturb great part of the Christian world."

More has been charged with being a persecutor. The charge, however, rests on the notoriously false Fox, the Martyrologist, Burnet, and others of the same stamp.

"It is," says Erasmus, "a sufficient proof of the clemency of More, that whilst he was Chancellor no man was executed for these pestilent dogmas, whilst at the same time many were put to death in France, Germany, and the Netherlands."

The notorious libel-monger, Fox, speaks in his Martyrology of a certain tree in the Chancellor's garden, which he called the "Tree of Truth," to which he says More was in the habit of having obstinate heretics tied and whipped, and that three men were confined as prisoners in his own house. Burnet and Fox were noted for their utter disregard of truth, and consequently we must not be surprised that the character of this great man has been thus blackened by them, but unfortunately the charge has been handed down even by impartial writers to the present time.

More, in his *Apology*, extracts from which we shall insert later, writes—"There are divers who say that such as were in my house while I was Chancellor, I used to examine with torments, causing them to be bound to a tree, and there piteously beaten. This tale some of these blessed brethren so caused to be blown about that a good friend* of mine heard it commonly spoken of."

He was, indeed, charged with having converted his house at Chelsea into a sort of inquisition. Of Burnham, one of the reformers, Fox relates that he was "carried out of the Middle Temple to the Chancellor's house at Chelsea, where he continued in free prison awhile, till the time that Sir Thomas More saw that he could not prevail in perverting him to his sect. Then he cast him into prison in his own house, and whipped him at the tree in his garden, called the 'Tree of Truth,' and after sent him to the tower to be racked."*   A story always gains by repetition, and thus it is that the scourgings said to have been inflicted by the tolerant Chancellor at the "Tree of Truth" have been received as undoubted facts.

* Mart. vol. ii., p. 287.

In More's defence of himself in respect of his treatment of the reformers, he admits the imprisonment, but denies the ill-treatment of them, except in two cases, not ill-defended. The defence ought to be read by all who speak of More. See it in Cayley's Memoirs of him, p. 137. He distinctly denies the story of the "Tree of Truth." "The lies are neither few nor small," says More, "which many of the blessed brethren have made, and daily yet make of me.—*Campbell.*

The crimes against religion for which he gave over offenders to the officers of the Marshalsea Prison were robbery, sacrilege, and murder, stealing a pyx, and profaning the Blessed Sacrament. But concerning heretics, save only their safe keeping, he writes—" I never caused any such thing to be done to them in all my life, save one of them, a child, and servant of my own. This child had previously served an Apostate priest, who had taught him to blaspheme the Holy Sacrament, which heresy he began to teach another child in my house, who declared the thing." The punishment which More gave the child was a good whipping.

The other case was of one who, from heresy, had become raving mad. He had been for some time in Bedlam, where, by the harsh treatment used in those days, he for a time recovered. After a while, however, his crazy fancies returned. He wandered into the churches, and during the most solemn part of the Mass disturbed the people. More, shrewd as he always was, guessed that this violent fanatic was not so mad as he appeared, in short, that it was put on to annoy others, so on the next outbreak he caused him to be taken by the constables, bound to a post, and beaten. " Then," adds More, " it appeared that his memory was good enough, except that it went about grazing till it was beaten home. Of all that ever came into my hands for heresy, not one of them, so help me God, had any stripe or stroke given them, no, not so much as a filip on the forehead, all I had to do was the sure keeping of them, and yet not so sure either, but that George Constantine found means to steal away from me, and some say that when he was gotten away, I was fallen for anger in a wonderful rage. But surelye, though I would not have suffered him to go, if it had pleased him to have tarried still in the stocks, yet neither was I then so heavye for the losse, but that I had youth enough left me to wear it out, nor so angry with any man of mine that I spoke them any evil word for the matter, more than to my porter. That he should see the stocks mended and locked fast, that the prisoner stole not in again. I will never be so unreasonable as to be angry with a man who, ill at ease, changes his position for a better." *

About this time Sir Thomas lost his father, who had reached a good old age, the death of the judge however, brought no accession of worldly wealth to his son, the small property left by Sir John More, being settled on his wife as long as she lived; she survived the Chancellor by several years.

Sir Thomas was, for his rank, a poor man; his charity and liberality was unbounded, whilst himself living abstemiously he kept a bountiful table; for his elevated rank obliged him to entertain the rich and powerful. Of his professional income, once so large, nothing was laid by, and Cresacre More, tells us that his benefactions to the poor, and his liberality to the Church, made great demands on his purse.

Can we not fancy the distress of Lady More when the barns were burnt, with the store of corn housed up for use, and that she, the careful, keen, shrewd housekeeper, was counting up at what cost to herself and her husband, who set so little store by that which she so valued, for, † Roper says,

---

* More's English Works, page 902, vol. 1.

† Roper.

that in ready money he had not the worth of one hundred pounds, and had made no purchases of land beyond the value of twenty marks a year, previous to his acceptance of the Great Seal.

The poverty of More was indeed so well known as to make the Bishops resolve to make him an offering from their own purses, on remembering the pains and labour he had taken to serve the Catholic faith, by his writings in its defence; they therefore called together many of the clergy, and agreed to make him up from among themselves as much as four thousand pounds, to the payment of which (and such a sum in those days was no trifling matter) every bishop and abbot, with each of the clergy, contributed to the best of their power.

Then, those of his most intimate friends amongst the bishops called upon him at Chelsea, telling him they considered themselves bound to reward him for the pains he had taken in helping them, with his pen, to battle against the prevalent errors of the times, adding, that it was not, indeed, in their power to requite him as he deserved, but that they presented him with this small sum on behalf of the members of the Convocation, begging him to take it of them in good part.

And the Chancellor answered them as follows :—

" It is no small comfort to me, my lords, that men so wise and learned have so well accepted of my simple doings, for which I never thought of any reward save from God alone. So give I most humble thanks unto your lordships, for all your bountiful and friendly consideration, but I purpose not to receive anything from you."

" But I pray you refuse not our offering," said the Bishop

of Bath, "truly it is but a poor acknowledgement of the matchless services you have rendered to the Church, and those who have contributed to raise this sum as a feeble testimony of their personal regard for you, will feel grieved by your refusal." But More was still inexorable.

"Then, my Lord Chancellor," said Tunstal, Bishop of Durham, "I beseech you take it to bestow upon your wife and children, and we will be well content."

In this remark the Bishop of Bath concurred.

"Not so, my lords," replied the still obstinate Chancellor, "I had rather see it all cast in the Thames than that I or mine should touch one penny of it, for though your offer, my lords, is indeed most honourable, yet have I so much regard for my pleasure and so little for my profit, that I would not for much more money, have lost the rest of so many nights as was spent upon the same, and yet, on condition all heresies were suppressed, I am quite willing that all my works be speedily burned."

Finding it impossible to make More revoke his determination, the Bishops were fain to depart, and restore to each of the contributors the sum he had advanced. A rumour soon got about, however, to the effect that the clergy had paid him a large sum of money, and the men of the new opinions at once declared that More had been bribed to write against them. In his Apology, before alluded to, in answer to these calumnies, he writes:—"As for all the landes and fees that I have in all England, besides such as I have of the King's most noble grace, they are not at this day worth, yearly, nor shall be while my mother-in-law liveth, the sum of full fifty pounds, and thereof have I some by my wife, and some by my father, whose soul our Lord assoil, and some also have I purchased myself, some few have I of temporal men, and thus may every man well guess that I have no very great part of my living by the clergy to make me partial on their side."

"And over than this, shall I truly say, that of all the yearly living that I have of the King's gracious gift, I have not one groat by the means of any spiritual man, but farre above my deserving have had it, onlye by his own singular bounty, and goodness and special favour towards me."

And verily, of any such yearly fees as I have to my living at this time or any other, I have not had one groat granted me since I first wrote, or went about to write, my dialogue, and that ye wot well, was the first work I wrote on these matters."

"But, then," say the brethren, as their holy father writeth and telleth also divers whom he talketh with, " I have taken great rewards in readye money, of divers of the clergye, for making of my booke. In good faith I will not say nay, but that some good and honourable men of them, would, in reward of my good will and my labour against these heretics, have given me much more than ever I could or did deserve. But I dare take God and themselves also to record, that they all could never fee me with one penny thereof (but as I plainly told them) I would rather have cast their money in the Thames than take it, for, albeit, as indeed they were both good men and honourable, yet look I for my thanks of God, that is their better."

Meanwhile there were many persons who were, doubtless, aware that in the end, as far as this world went, his inflexibility would cost him dear, and they did not scruple to reproach him with ingratitude to the King, thus, Lord

Manners, who had without scruple supported all the new measures, and was loud in favour of the divorce, sarcastically taunted him, saying, "But so says the old proverb, *Honores mutant Mores.*"*

"Yes," replied More, who was always ready with a quick. witted answer, " it is a trite proverb, if rightly translated, for *Mores* is Latin for Manners."

He was never at a loss for witty answers. Little care had he indeed for money, nevertheless, having lent a large sum to a person of means, who shewed no disposition to repay the sum advanced, More asked him for the amount, to which his debtor replied by bidding him " remember that he should die, God knoweth," he added " how soon," adding the sentence in Latin, *Memento Morieris.*

" How say you, Sir ?" replied his witty creditor, " Methinks you put yourself in mind of your duty, by saying *Memento Morieris*, remember More's money."†

He always uttered his jests with a grave countenance, yet none could converse with him but were filled with mirth at his witticisms.

Meanwhile More's position as Chancellor became every day more painful, the inhibitory breve had been signed by the Pope, and published with the usual solemnity in Flanders ; the most furious discussions raged amongst all classes, the Duke of Norfolk espoused the side of the King, the Duchess that of the Queen, indeed the women of all classes,

---

* Honours change Manners.

† The learned reader will understand that the point of the pun lies in the word *Morieris* (thou shalt die), for which the Chancellor substituted the words *Mori Aeris.* Anglice, More's brass, More's money.

from high to low, ranked themselves amongst the partisans of Katharine.

The horror More entertained of heresy, and his belief that wholesale disorder would follow in the wake of religious dissension made him shrink with terror from whatever would tend to disruption with the supreme Pontiff. The increasing distraction on the Continent, where the change to heresy was making progress, strengthened these feelings. He had agreed, however, to the plan of consulting the universities, and to the late address to the Pope and was prevailed upon by the King and Cromwell to go down with twelve spiritual and temporal Peers to the House, and then deliver the following address, meant to prepare the world for what might follow :—

" You of this worshipful house, I am sure you be not so ignorant, but you know well that the King, our Sovereign Lord, hath married his brother's wife ; for she was wedded to his brother, Prince Arthur, and therefore you may surely say that he hath married his brother's wife, if this marriage be good—as so many do doubt. Wherefore the King, like a virtuous Prince, willing to be satisfied in his conscience, and also for the surety of his realm, hath, with great deliberation, consulted with great clerks, and hath sent my Lord of London, here present, to the chief universities of all Christendom, to know their opinion and judgments in that matter; and, although the universities of Oxford and Cambridge had been sufficient to discuss the cause, yet this being in his realm, and to avoid all suspicion of partiality, he hath sent into the realms of France, Italy, the Pope's dominions, and the Venetians, to know their judgment in that behalf, which have concluded, written, and sealed their determinations, according as you shall hear read."   A box was then opened, and .

many opinions were then read—all on one side, holding the marriage void. Whereupon the Chancellor said, "Now you of this Commons House may report in your homes what you have seen and heard, and then all men shall perceive that the King hath not attempted this matter of will or pleasure, as some strangers report, but only for the discharge of his conscience, and the security of the succession of his realm. This is the cause of our repair hither to you, and now we will all depart."

Whoever reads this address must perceive the Chancellor's embarrassment must have been great, and his anxiety distressing at having to speak on this subject without saying anything by which he might be compromised, either with the King or the Church. In his office as Lord Chancellor he must have felt that he was unable to refuse to address the House. Several lords were then deputed to wait on the Queen, and to request that, for the quiet of the King's conscience, she would refer the matter to the decision of four spiritual and four temporal peers. "God grant him a quiet conscience," said she, "but this shall be your answer : I am married to him by order of Holy Church, and so I will abide until the Court of Rome, which was privy to the beginning, shall have made thereof an end."

A second deputation was sent with an order for her to leave the palace at Windsor.

"Go where I may," she answered, "I shall still be his lawful wife."

In obedience to the King she repaired to Ampthill, where, if she was no longer treated as Queen, she no longer witnessed the ascendancy of her rival.

"The first that *openly* resisted or reprehended the King

touching his marriage with Anne, was one Friar Peyto, a simple man, yet very devout of the order of the Observants; this man, preaching at Greenwich, on the 22nd chap. of the third book of Kings thus addressed Henry, saying—

"Even as the dogs licked the blood of Achab, even so shall the dogs lick thy blood, O King," and therewithal he spake of the lying prophets which abused the King.' I am, quoth he, ' that Micheas whom thou wilt hate, because I must tell thee truly that this marriage is unlawful, and I know I shall eat the bread of affliction, and drink the water of sorrow, yet because our Lord hath put it into my mouth.' Then when he had strongly inveighed against the King's second marriage to dissuade him from it, he also said, ' there are many other preachers, yea, too many, who preach and persuade thee otherwise, feeding thy folly and vain affections upon hope of their own worldly promotion, and by that means they betray thy soul, thy honor, and posterity, to obtain fat benefices, to become rich Abbots, and get episcopal jurisdiction, and other ecclesiastical dignities, these I say are the four hundred prophets, who in the spirit of lying seek to deceive thee, but take good heed lest thou, being seduced, shalt find Achab's punishment, which was to have his blood licked up by the dogs,' and adding, 'it was one of the greatest miseries of princes to be daily abused by flatterers.' The King being thus reproved bore it patiently, and did no violence to Peyto, but the next Sunday, being the 8th of May, Doctor Curwin preached in the same place, who most sharply reprehended Peyto and his preaching—called him dog, slanderer, base beggarly Friar, rebel, and traitor,' saying, ' that no subject should speak so maliciously to princes, and having said much more to that effect, and in commendation of the King's marriage, thereby to establish his progeny in his seat for ever.' He then supposing he had utterly silenced Peyto and his partisans raised his voice and said, 'I speak to thee, Peyto, who makest thyself Micheas, that thou mayest speak evil of kings, but now thou art not to be found, having fled for fear and shame, as being unable to answer my arguments.'" But whilst he thus spoke—one Elstow, a brother Friar to Peyto, who was standing in the roodloft, with a loud voice replied to Doctor Curwin,—

"Good Sir, you know that Father Peyto, as he was commanded, hath gone to a provincial council, holden at Canterbury, and *not* fled for fear of you, for to-morrow he will return again ; in the meantime I am here as another Micheas, and will lay down my life to prove all these things true, which he hath taught out of the Holy Scriptures, and to this combat I challenge thee before God and all equal judges, even unto thee, Curwin, I say, which art one of the four hundred prophets into whom the spirit of lying hath entered, and seeketh by adultery to establish succession, more for thy own vainglory, and hope of promotion, than for discharge of thy clogged conscience, and the King's salvation."

"Elstow waxed hot, and spoke earnestly, so they could not make him cease speaking until the King bade him hold his peace, and gave orders that he and Peyto should be convened before the council, which was done the next day, and when the lords had rebuked them, then the Earl of Essex told them that they deserved to be put in a sack and cast into the Thames, at which Elstow smiled and said, "Threaten these things to rich and dainty folk which are clothed in purple and fine linen, who fare deliciously and have their hope in this world, but we esteem them not, and rejoice, that in the discharge of our duties, we are driven hence, and thank God we know the way to heaven to be as near by water as by land, and so we care not which way we go."

" These Friars, and all the rest of their order, were shortly after banished, and after these none openly opposed themselves against the King. Dr. Curwin was made Dean of Hereford, after that, Archbishop of Dublin, and after that, Bishop of Oxford, in Queen Mary's time." *

Each recurring day made it evident to More that a rupture with Rome must surely happen, his situation became more and more embarrassing, he had been again pressed by Henry regarding the divorce, and falling on his knees, he had reminded him of his own words when delivering to him the Great Seal, bidding him—-

" Look first to God, and after God to him," adding :

" And God knoweth how much it paineth me that in this matter I cannot serve your Grace."

Henry on this occasion had agreed that when the subject was introduced in the Council Chamber, More should be allowed to withdraw ; but he soon observed a coldness in the King's manner to himself, and felt the necessity of taking a step to which we will devote another chapter.

* Stow's Chronicles.

CHAPTER XI.

Giving up the Great Seal.

The aversion More felt to his late task, made him alive to the fact that others still more painful and repugnant to his feelings, would have to be gone through should he continue in office ; to remain a faithful Catholic, and at the same time act as Chancellor and Minister to the King, was simply impossible.

He therefore urgently entreated his intimate friend, the Duke of Norfolk, to plead with the King for leave to retire from office, and he felt the task the easier, inasmuch as he had lately suffered from a complaint of the chest, brought on, it was supposed, by constant stooping over the writing table.

After repeated solicitations, the Duke obtained the desired leave, and Sir Thomas waited upon the King at Greenwich to deliver up the Great Seal, which he courteously received ; and Henry, as he received it from the hand of the Chancellor, thanked him for his good services, adding, "In any future suit which you may hereafter have, which may affect either your honour or your profit, you shall not fail to find me a good and gracious lord."

"How true these professions were," says Cresacre More in the life of his great ancestor, "let others judge, as the King not only never bestowed on him the value of a single penny, but robbed him and his posterity of all they possessed." He might have added, of his head also, for surely his life was of more consequence than his fortune.

Dignities and honours had been thrust on an unwilling recipient, the tenor of More's whole life shewed this, but it would have been a difficult matter for him to have shirked the honours showered upon him by a Tudor Sovereign; and we must needs think he acted for the best, when he took upon him the onerous charge of the Chancellorship.

However, one may imagine the joy that must have filled his heart, when he was once more free, free for his beloved studies, free for his sweet domestic joys, free for his dear Margaret, whose name even has been so long banished from these pages, whilst we have been looking over the great event which dismembered England from the centre of Catholic unity, and which, as it led afterwards to the very death of her great and good father, we have noticed as far as the length of our humble volume permitted.

Free! what joy is comprised in that word, how More's heart must have bounded with joy as he passed out from Eastgreenwiche, and wended his way back to Chelsea, what joy as he folded Margaret in his arms, she whom he loved so well, for never were father and daughter more closely united than were these two, she *must* have known this secret, as she did all others, and how, for his dear sake, she must have rejoiced when he whispered in her ear :—" Sweet Meg, I am free."

The next day was a holiday, probably the Feast of the Ascension, for More resigned the Great Seal on the 10th of May, and he doubtless dreaded to confront Dame Alice, with what she was sure to consider the saddest of all sad news, so he resolved to break it to her in Chelsea church; a novel expedient, but the manner in which it was done, was quite in keeping with the humourous character of the ex-chancellor.

When Mass was over, More being generally in the chancel with the choristers, it was the custom for one of the attendants to go to the seat used by Lady More and her family, and inform her if "my lord," had already gone, " but on this day, the first day that he was "free," he went himself and cap in hand, with a low bow, said he to Lady More " May it please your ladyship to come forth, for my lord has gone."

Mistress Alice naturally thought my lord was jesting with her, according to his old fashion, but on their way home, he told her the truth in sober earnest, explaining to her that in very truth, he was "my lord" no longer.

One can well imagine the feelings of *such* a woman as Lady More is described at *such* an announcement; her husband's large emoluments were gone, her own dignity, also; one may really pity her for what she must have felt, when she ascertained that what she had considered as a jest, was the sober unvarnished truth.

Was not her inelegant phrase but too true; did she speak amiss when she had said, "you are always making goslings in the ashes?"

More must surely have found it a hard matter to stop her shrewish tongue on this occasion, in which the patience of far more amiable and gentle women would have been tried, so he turned the conversation and began to criticise the fashion of her dress, saying, he espied a great fault in it that morning.

For a few moments it changed the topic on which Lady

More's thoughts were bent, and she called her daughters to her, bidding them say " what was amiss in her costume," and she being angry that none of them could see anything wrong, Sir Thomas then said, " Do you see, children, that your mother's nose is somewhat awry." At these words poor Lady More broke from him in a great rage.

All which he did to make her think the less of her decay of honour, which else would have troubled her sore.*

Now to face his family and dependents, and tell them they must all disperse, must here have been *the* trouble, and the only trouble More felt in his altered position ; as usual, he tried to get over his task in his humorous way ; so he called his household together, his children, servants, and retainers, many of whom, according to the custom of the times, were men of family and position, and telling them that he was no longer Lord Chancellor, and that in future he could not keep up such an establishment as hitherto, he demanded of them individually what kind of service they wished to procure, and whether they would like to enter that of any nobleman, as if so he would try to settle each one to his liking.

Moved even to tears, they declared they would sooner serve him for nothing than others for a salary, but to this he would not agree, and he arranged so as to place them all in good situations.

But the greatest trial was to part from his children, those children who had dwelt beneath his roof even after they had entered the married state ; but mastering his emotion, he called them all about him, and bade them consult with him as to what they had best do, as now he had resigned

* **More.**

his office, he could not keep them with him as he had hitherto done.

But neither sons nor daughters spoke a word. "Then will I shew unto you all my mind," said he, "I have been brought up at Oxford, at an inn of Chancery, and Lincoln's Inn, and also in the King's Court, and so have gone from the lowest degree to the highest; and yet have I in yearly revenue at this present little left me above a hundred a year, so that now, if we live together, we must look to be contributors together. But my advice is that we fall not to the lowest fare first. We will not descend to Oxford fare nor to the fare of New Inn, but we will begin with Lincoln's Inn diet, where many right worshipful men of great account and right good years live full well. If we cannot maintain that we will go a step lower, and come down to Oxford fare, wherewith many an ancient father and learned doctor has been contented, and if our united purses will not do that much, then will we with bags and wallets go a begging together, hoping that for pity some good folks will give us charity, and at every man's door we will sing a *Salve Regina*, whereby we shall still keep company and be merry together." *

Silent and tearful those whom he loved stood around him, whilst throwing a veil over the grief he must needs have felt, the good Christian still with an innocent jest on his lips sought to infuse into their souls somewhat of his own spirit of cheerful contentment. Looking on More's past life with the eyes of the world, his practical and shrewd

---

* He here alludes to the practice of begging adopted by the poor scholars of Oxford, who used to go begging through the streets, singing the *Salve Regina*.

wife was in the right, he *had* been hospitable and charitable *far* beyond what even his very ample means had allowed, when first he entered the service of the King he threw up a handsome income of £400 a year, which, in those far off days, represented some thousands of our money at its present worth. He then engaged in weighty causes concerning the King and the realm, toiling away many of the best years of his life in other countries, in like matters, and thus consumed the gains of his whole life ; so that at this time he had positively not sufficient for necessaries for himself and those belonging to him, for, previous to his acceptance of the Great Seal, he had not purchased land above the value of twenty marks a year, and after paying his debts, his gold chain of office excepted, he had only about the value of £100.*

It may well be imagined that the contemplated change was a heavy blow to his family, and that the breaking up of his extensive household was not effected without great sorrow. One was located here, another there, all apart, except Margaret and her husband, who hired for their use a house immediately adjoining his own, so that the ex-chancellor and his eldest daughter enjoyed each other's society almost as much as hitherto.

Thus, having settled his family and disposed of his servants, in the houses of others, not forgetting his fool, Pattison, who was now no longer necessary in his humble establishment, More sold much of his furniture and other property, and devoted the rest of this year of 1532, the year which preceded his great trials, to acts of mortification, prayer, and study.

* Roper.

A letter to Erasmus from More, written about this time, runs as follows :—

" I have a good while expected, if any man could accuse me of anything, since I gave up the office of Chancellor, but as yet no man hath come forward to complain of any act of injustice. Either I must have been so innocent or so crafty that my enemies must suffer me to glory in the one, if they abide, I should glory in the other. The King's Majesty also, as well in private conversation as twice in public, hath witnessed for that, which I am ashamed to say for myself; he commended the Duke of Norfolk, when my successor (an excellent man) was settled in my place, to testify this to all the assembly, that he, with difficulty, at my earnest entreaty, suffered me to go ; and, not content with that favour, he caused it to be referred to again in his own presence, when at a meeting of the Nobility and Commons, my successor made his first speech in Parliament."

In another letter to Erasmus he writes :—

" From childhood unto this day, I have constantly desired, my dear Desiderius, to be freed from public affairs, so that I might for some time live only to God and myself; I have now, by the special grace of God and the kindness of my Prince, obtained this favour. Having often thought I must resign my office or fail in the performance of my duty, for that I could no longer dispatch its business, but by endangering my life, I resolved to forego one rather than both. So that as it was necessary to be as careful of the public affairs as of my health, I earnestly begged the King, that because I began to grow weary of my burthen, I might be rid of it, honourable office as it was, whereto his favour had raised me, as far above my deserving as it was wholly out of my seeking. I beseech, therefore, all the saints in heaven, that by their intercession, God would reward the affection of the King for me, and that He will give me grace to spend the rest of my life profitably, and not idly or vainly, granting me bodily health, so that I may take greater pains therein."

To his friend Cochleus he wrote as follows :—

" I have been of late sorely sick for months together, not so much to the sight of others as to my own feelings, an infirmity of which I need scarcely allude to, now that I have resigned my office, for I could not hold it and discharge my duties without danger to my health.

" The hope of final recovery, and the fear I had that my health would interfere with the justice due to the public, moved me to resign my office, aware that I should greatly hinder the former, if, being sick, I endeavoured to look to business matters as when in stronger health, and the leisure which the benignity of my most gracious Prince hath granted me, I propose to dedicate wholly to study and the honour of God."

As if aware of the peril that still lay before him, for the King shewed a certain coolness of manner towards More such as he had never before exhibited, he seemed desirous to withdraw himself daily more and more within the bosom of his family, and with them even, he became more grave and serious than of old, often talking with them of the joys of the bright hereafter, of the lives of the holy martyrs, of their wondrous patience and happy death, and that it was an honour for the love of our Lord to suffer loss of goods, imprisonment, lands and life, adding, that it would be a comfort to him if his wife and children would encourage him to die in so good a cause. Then he would speak of the kind of death which might happen to him, intending by so doing to take off the sharpness of the sorrow whensoever it should happen, for said he, "*shafts foreseen hurt us not so much.*"

Cromwell had taken his place in the favour of the King, and, coming to him once with a message from the latter, when he was taking his leave, Sir Thomas said:—

"Mr. Cromwell, you are entered into the service of a wise, noble, and liberal Prince; if you will follow my poor advice, you will, when giving counsel to his Majesty, always tell him what he *ought* to do, but, never what he is *able* to do; in this way you may prove yourself a true and faithful servant, and a good counsellor, for if a lion knew his own strength, hard would it be to rule him."

The straightforward More, however, poured his advice into unwilling ears, for Cromwell always gave the King the advice that would please him best, and not that which was lawful.

CHAPTER XII.

Queen Anne Boleyn.

After her expulsion from Court, Queen Katherine wrote a letter to the Pope to apprise him of the treatment she had received, when the Pontiff, in the most forcible but affectionate terms, addressed a letter to the King, painting in its true colours the infamy he was stamping on his character, by introducing his mistress to the court in place of his wife, and requesting him to recall his Queen and dismiss her rival. This was a duty he owed to himself, but Clement declared he would receive it as a signal favour to himself. The King, however, no longer sought to conciliate, and, assembling his parliament, an act was passed for the abolition of the annates, or first fruits, an ecclesiastical impost paid to the Roman see.

Then Cromwell proceeded to other matters hostile to the clergy, and the interests of the Pontiff, by annexing to the Crown supreme jurisdiction in ecclesiastical matters, and it was enacted that if any prelate should pay first fruits to Rome, he should forfeit his personalities to the King, and the profits of his see as long as he held it. A promise from convocation was also exacted never to enact or enforce any constitutions without the royal authority and assent.

In the September of 1532, the King had created mistress Anne, Marchioness of Pembroke. On the 25th of the next

January, Dr. Lee, one of the royal chaplains, received orders to celebrate Mass in a room in the west terrace of Whitehall, there he found the King attended by Anne. Lee, we are told, made some opposition when he discovered *that he was to marry the King privately*, but Henry calmed his scruples by declaring he had the papal instrument in his closet.*

Warham, who was zealously attached to the ancient doctrines, was now dead, and Henry found a ready tool in Cranmer, a chaplain of the Boleyns, whose book in favour of the divorce, and the boldness with which he had advocated it, and his zeal in soliciting signatures in its behalf when in Italy, made both Henry and Anne believe that in him they should possess an Archbishop subservient to their will. He was now raised to the Archbishopric, the papal confirmation was obtained, the bulls were expedited from the Pope, to whom he took the customary oath of fidelity, and he at once entered on his new career by a solemn act of perjury ; for he called four witnesses into the chapter-house of St. Stephen's, and declared that by the oath of obedience to the Pope, which for the sake of form he should take, he did not mean to bind himself to anything contrary to the law of God, against the rights of the King, or of such reforms as he might judge useful to the Church of England. He then went to the high altar and took the pontifical oath, after which he was then consecrated, and again reminding the witnesses of his protest, he took the oath a second time, and received the pallium from the hands of the papal delegates.†

* Lee was made Bishop of Chester and was afterwards translated to Lichfield and Coventry—Lingard, Stowe.

† Some of our historians, endeavouring to palliate this matter, make an

Cranmer was fully aware as to what was expected of him, and Henry at once proceeded with the divorce. To prevent Katherine from opposing any obstacle to Cranmer, an act was passed forbidding appeals from English spiritual judges to the Court of the Pontiff; a hypocritical farce was then enacted between Cranmer and Henry, and the former as if ignorant of the purpose for which he had been made archbishop, wrote a letter of fatherly reproof to the King " for scandalising the world by his unlawful union with Katherine, it was a duty which he owed to her and himself, to put an end to all doubt, and he begged the King to hear the cause of the divorce in his own archiepiscopal Court," the King of course graciously assented, but at the same time reminded the primate that, " the sovereign had no superior on earth, and was not subject to the laws of any earthly creature." *

To this Court Katherine was repeatedly cited to appear, but she carefully avoided any admission of the Archbishop's jurisdiction ; finally, she was declared contumacious, and the sentence was passed that her marriage was null and void, and had never been good, and five days later, he confirmed the private marriage already celebrated with Anne. Henry

apology for him, after an odd sort of a manner. Dodd, Part 1, Art 2, p.213. If this seemed too artificial for a man of his sincerity (?) yet still he acted fairly and without deceit.—Echard, 1,675. If he did not *wholly* save his integrity, yet it was plain he intended no cheat, but to act fairly and above board.—Burnet, 1,124. But how a man can act fairly, and yet not save his integrity is farther than I can discover ; and, therefore, with due regard to Cranmer's memory, it must be said, there was something of human infirmity in this management.—Collier, 11,74.

* State Papers, 1390-3.

had not the heart to proceed against Katherine. His repudiated wife was the only person who could brave him with impunity. *

No sentence of divorce had been pronounced, nor act of parliament passed to dissolve the first marriage.

An attempt has been made to show a marriage on the 14th Nov. 1532, nine months before the birth of Elizabeth, 7 Sep., 1533, but this is disproved by the testimony of Cranmer himself. †

On the news of the marriage of the King reaching the ears of More, said he to his son-in-law :—

" God give grace, son, that these matters be not confirmed on oath." A remark at which Roper felt grieved, for so often did matters turn out as Sir Thomas feared they would.

More, shrewd and keen as he was, watched, in the quietude of his Chelsea home, the sad signs of the times, and felt sure that matters would soon be pressed to extremity on hearing of the preparations for the approaching corona-tion. He then received a letter from the three Bishops of Durham, Winchester, and Bath, requesting him to be present with them at the coronation of the new queen, and asking him to accept the sum of twenty pounds, which they sent him to buy him a dress suitable for the occasion ; the money he thankfully accepted, but he stirred not from his house, and on their next meeting, said More to these Bishops :—

" In your late letter, my Lords, you requested of me two things, the one I was well pleased to grant you, that the other I might the better deny, for I took you to be no beggars, and I knew myself to be no rich man ; for the . other, take heed, my Lords, that being present at the corona-

<hr>

* Lingard.　　　　　† Hallam's Court Hist. p. 841.

tion you do not presently preach about it, as for myself, they may indeed destroy me, but by God's grace I will take care that they hurt no other than the body."

Possibly these words may have reached the ears of Anne, at any rate he was a marked man, as Wolsey had been before him; by not being present at her coronation he increased her deadly hatred, and the King listened more readily than of old to her remarks against him.

Whitsunday, the first of June, 1533, was the coronation day. That great day on which the hopes of Anne Boleyn had for so long a space of time rested, had at last arrived.

It was a bright, glorious summer morning, when all nature was in unison with the sweet future of happiness and joy which seemed to stretch itself before this beautiful and ambitious woman.

Very early indeed must she and her ladies have been astir, for at the early hour of eight, she entered Westminster Hall and stood beneath her canopy of state, in her mantle of purple velvet lined with ermine, and a circlet of rubies on her head. Then came the Monks of Westminster in copes, and Bishops and Abbots in copes and mitres. The ray cloth was spread all the way from the daïs in Westminster Hall, through the sanctuary and palace up to the high altar in the Abbey.* A glorious day for her doubtless, but what a day of anguish for the poor repudiated wife.

But for the time being all was bright as the summer sun-shine, and Mistress Anne was crowned by Cranmer, the King's ready tool, who proclaimed her divorce two short years later, as easily as he had pronounced her rival's marriage

* Agnes Strickland.

null and void, but a short time since; but this day was *her* day of triumph. With unusual magnificence did Henry celebrate the coronation of his beloved Queen, it was attended by all the nobility of England, and there was no lack of processions, and triumphal arches and tournaments; his pride was gratified, and he hoped to have his darling wish of a male heir to the throne at last fulfilled.

How would Anne Boleyn have shrunk from his touch could she have seen into the dreary future, could she have beheld the death-warrant, *her* death-warrant signed by the hand of him who now caressed her; how would she have shuddered, when she a few days previous to her coronation, landed at the Tower in much state, attired in cloth of gold, when Henry with a countenance full of love received her at the postern by the water side, could she have but seen as in second-sight her own self when she entered that gloomy fortress as a prisoner after so brief a space, could she but have beheld herself as she was a short time later still, when led out upon the Tower Green, that spot at which one shudders still to look; poor soul, how would she have shrunk within herself, torn the crown from off her head and lamented as she did later, that she had ever striven to gain so giddy a height of human greatness.

When the tidings of the coronation reached Rome, the Pope annulled Cranmer's pretended divorce, pronounced the marriage with Katherine to be valid, and called on the King to take her back as his legitimate wife. But the die was cast, the final question had not been settled till ten months after Cranmer's sentence, and a resolution had been taken to erect an independent Church within the realm. Act after act derogatory from the papal claims had been debated and passed in parliament, and the kingdom was severed by legislative authority from the communion of Rome long before the judgment given by Clement could have reached the ear of Henry.

CHAPTER XIII.

MORE AND FISHER.

THERE can be no doubt but that the King strove by every means, even by conferring the office of Chancellor upon More, to win over both himself and Fisher to his cause, and had failed with each. The reader will remember that in a letter to Erasmus after he had withdrawn wholly from public life, More congratulates himself that no accusations were brought against him; time, however, and the smouldering anger of the King which had long been ready to burst forth in a flame, effected a change, and the first sign he had of the trouble which hung over him was a rumour that he had received bribes and gifts when Lord Chancellor, and he was summoned to answer the first charge before the Earl of Wiltshire, the Queen's father, and his own declared enemy.

He, the very soul of integrity, and who carried his notions of honour to an extent that was even fastidious, was accused of having accepted a silver gilt cup from the hands of one Mistress Vaughan.

Sir Thomas confessed that he *had* taken the cup some time after judgment had been given. " It was intended," said he, as a New Year's Gift, and out of very shame I could not refuse it.

The countenance of his ancient foe beamed with delight, and unable to restrain his pleasure at the thought that he should be able to convict him, he exclaimed, "There, my Lords, did I not tell you the matter would be found true?"

"I beg you, my Lords, as you have heard one-half of my story, to tarry patiently for the other,' said More, 'I did indeed take the cup, but I immediately ordered my butler to fill it up with wine, which, being done, I drank to the lady's health, and afterwards she drank to me, and I then returned the cup into her hands, to carry back as a New Year's present to her husband.'"

Then Mistress Vaughan was called upon to give evidence, and she attested to the truth of what More had said.

There was too one Mistress Croaker, a rich woman, to assist whom—and at no small cost to himself, More had obtained a decree in Chancery against Lord Arundell. This lady, in the excess of her gratitude, had brought him a pair of gloves filled with fourscore golden angels.

He accepted the gloves, but refused the money, saying—

"It would be, Madam, against all rules of gentlemanly courtesy to refuse the gloves, as they are a lady's New Year's gift, but as to the lining I must beg to return it."

There were other cases of the same kind maliciously brought against the incorruptible ex-chancellor, but the result was the same in every case, an honourable acquittal from the slightest imputation of bribery. Such charges as these, though they might be unpleasant and annoying at the time, could have no evil effect in the end; but there was another, which attacked both himself and the venerable Bishop Fisher; this was of a far more serious nature, and had also something in it of a semblance of justice.

Alone, amongst all the other bishops Fisher stood firm. He was nearly eighty years of age, the last survivor of the councillors of Henry VII., and the wise prelate to whose care the Countess of Richmond had on her death-bed recommended the youth and inexperience of her royal grandson. For many years the King had revered him as a parent, and boasted that no prince in Europe possessed a bishop equal in virtue to the Bishop of Rochester; but his opposition to the divorce gradually effaced the recollection of his merit and services; and the case of Elizabeth Barton, the Nun, or Holy Maid of Kent, as she was called, was laid hold of by the King's advisers as an opportunity of at any rate silencing, if not crushing him.

This young woman, a native of Aldington, in Kent, had been subject to fits, and the contortions of body which she suffered on these occasions were attributed by her ignorant neighbours to some supernatural agency. In a short time they considered in the nature of prophecies the expressions she used, she herself partook of the illusions, and denounced impending judgments against the King, should he proceed with the divorce, and the fame of her sanctity won for her the above appellation. She had applied to many persons of influence, and bade them carry her remonstrances to the King, and had then repaired to Fisher at Rochester, who obtained for her an interview with Sir Thomas, and the latter became thus mixed up in the matter.

As soon as the ex-chancellor heard of such a charge (for it was now made high treason to slander the King's marriage) he sent the following letter to Cromwell.

"Right Worshipful—After my most hearty recommenda tion, with thanks for your goodness, I perceive that of your

further favour towards me it pleased you to break to my son
Roper that I had communication not only with many that
were acquainted with the maid of Canterbury, but also with
herself; and, beyond that, by my letters declared favour
towards her, and gave her advice and counsel.   And of my
demeanour towards her as you are content to take the trouble
to hear, by my own pen, the truth, I right heartily thank you,
and consider myself beholden to you very deeply.

"It is I suppose about eight or nine years ago, since I
heard of that housewife first, at which time the then Bishop
of Canterbury, God absolve his soul, sent unto the King's
grace a roll of paper, in which were written certain words of
hers, that she had, as report said, spoken in her trances,
whereupon, it pleased the King to deliver me the roll, com-
manding me to look thereon and afterwards let him know
what I thought; and at another time his highness asked me.
I told him I found nothing in those words that I could regard
or esteem ; a right simple woman might in my mind speak
it of her own wit well enough ; nevertheless, I said, it was
constantly reported for a truth that God wrought in her, and
that a miracle was showed upon her, and I durst not be
bold in judging the matter.

"From that time till about last Christmas twelvemonths,
there was much said of her and of her holiness, yet I never
heard of revelation of hers or of miracle, saving that in my
lord cardinal's days, that she had been both with his lordship
and with the King, but what she had said either to the one
or the other I never heard a word.   But, as I was about to
tell you, about Christmas was twelvemonth, Father Risby,
friar Observant, then of Canterbury, lodged one night at my
house, where after supper, a little before he went to his cham-

ber, he fell to talking with me about the maid, commending her holiness, and saying that it was wonderful to see and understand the works that God wrought in her; which I answered I was very glad to hear of. Then he told me she had been with the lord legate in his lifetime, and with the King's grace too, and had told the legate a revelation of hers, of three swords that God had put in his hand, which if he ordered not well would be laid to his charge. The first she said was ordering the spirituality under the pope as legate, the second the rule that he bore in order of the temporality under the King, and the third was the meddling he was en-trusted with by the King concerning the matter of his marriage.

"I told him that any revelation of the King's matters I would not hear of, doubting not but that God would direct him that the thing should take such an end as He should be pleased with, to the king's honour and the good of the realm.

"Then he told me that God had specially commanded her to pray for the king, and spoke again of her revelations concerning the cardinal, that his soul was saved by her mediation, and so went forth to his chamber; and he and I spoke not again of the matter. And since his departing on the morrow I never saw him after, to my remembrance, till I saw him at Paul's Cross.

"After this, about Shrovetide, there came to me, a little before supper, Father Rich, friar Observant, of Richmond; and as we fell into conversation I asked him of Father Risby, how he did, on which he asked me if he had told me anything about the holy maid of Kent. I answered yes, and that I was glad to hear of her virtue. 'I would not,' said he 'repeat what you have heard already, but God hath wrought great graces in her, and by her to others'; and then he asked me if Father Risby had told me of her having been with the cardinal. I answered yes. 'And he told you of the three swords?' 'Yes,' quoth I. 'And of her revelations concerning the king's grace?' 'Nay, forsooth,' said I, 'and if he would I would not have given him the hearing; and since she hath been with the King himself and told him, it is needless to tell me or any other man.' And when Father Rich saw that I would not hear of her revelations, he talked on a little of her virtue and let them alone; and supper was set on the board, but he would not tarry, but departed to London. After that I talked with him twice, once in my own house, and once in his own garden at the Friars, but not of any revelations touching the King but only of mean folk, some of which things were very strange and others childish. However, he said he had seen her in her trances in great pain, and had been spiritually comforted by her communications; but he did never tell me she had told him these tales herself; if he had I would have both liked him and her the worse. I little doubted but that some of the tales I heard of her were untrue, but that nevertheless many of them might be true.

"After this, being one day at Sion, and talking with several of the fathers at the grate, they told me she had been with them, and showed me various things some of them disliked in her; and whilst talking they said they wished I had spoken with her, they would fain know how I liked her. Whereupon, when I heard she was again there, I came to speak to her and see her myself. At which communication, in a little chapel, there were none present but we two. In the beginning I told her my coming to her was not of any curiosity, or to know of such things as it pleased God to reveal and show her, but for the great virtue that I had heard so many years every day more and more reported of her; therefore, I had a mind to see her and be acquainted with her, that she might have the more cause to remember me to God in her devotions. Whereto she answered that, as God of His goodness did far more by her than she, poor wretch, was worthy of, so she feared that many spoke of their own favourable minds far above the truth, and that she had heard so many things of me that already she prayed for me, and always would, for which I thanked her.

"Then said I : ' Madam, there is one Helen, a maiden dwelling at Totnam, of whose trances and revelations there hath been much talk. She hath been with me, and showed me that she was with you, and that after rehearsing such visions as she had seen, you showed her they were no revelations, but plain illusions of the devil, and advised her to cast them out of her mind. She gave credence unto you, and leaneth no longer to visions of her own, saying she findeth your words true, for she hath been less visited with such things than she was wont.' To this she answered me, 'Forsooth, sir, there is in this no praise due to me; the goodness of God hath wrought much meekness in her soul, which hath taken my rude meaning so well, and not grudged to hear her spirit and her visions reproved.'

"I liked her better for this answer than for many of the things I had heard reported of her. Then she said : ' Persons have great need that are visited with such visions to take heed and prove what spirit they come of.' We spake no word of the King's grace, or of any other but of her and of myself, and after no long conversation, my time came to go home, and I gave her a double ducat, prayed her to pray for me and mine, and never spoke word with her after. But I had a good opinion of her, and held her in high estimation.

"And because I often heard that many right worshipful folks had much communication with her, and many are curious, and fall sometimes into talking, and better were to forbear, therefore I wrote her a letter, which, since peradventure she tore or lost it, I shall insert the very copy in this letter :

"Good madam and dearly beloved sister in our Lord,—I beseech you take my mind in good worth, and pardon me that I am so homely as, unrequired and without necessity, to counsel you, of whom for the revelations it hath pleased God to give you, as many wise and learned and virtuous testify, I myself have need to ask advice. I showed you that I was neither curious of any knowledge of other men's matters, least of all of any matter of princes or of the realm. It sufficeth to put you in remembrance of these things, and the Spirit of God shall keep you from talking with high persons of things pertaining to princes' affairs or the state of the realm, but only to talk of such with persons high or low, as may be profitable for you to show or them to hear. At Chelsea, this Tuesday, by the hand of

"Your loving Brother and Beadsman, •

"THOMAS MORE, Knight."

"Soon after there came to my house the Prior of the Charter House at Sheen, and one Brother Williams, who talked of nothing but her virtue and revelations ; but at another time Brother Williams came to me and told me a long tale of her being at the house of a knight in Kent, that was troubled with temptations to destroy himself. On another day when I came to Sion one of the fathers asked me how I had liked her: I answered that I liked her very well in her talking, but she is never the nearer tried by that; she were likely to be very bad, an she seemed good, ere I should think her the reverse.' That is my manner; unless I were set to search and examine the truth or likelihood of some cloaked evil, when, though I nothing suspected the person myself, I would search to find out the truth, as yourself hath prudently done in this matter, doing a meritorious deed in bringing to light such detestable hypocrisy, whereby every other wretch may take warning and be afraid to set forth their devilish falsehood under colour of the wonderful work of God; for this woman so handled herself, with help of that evil spirit that inspired her, that after her confession delivered at St. Paul's Cross, when I sent word to the prior of the Charter House that she was undoubtedly proved a false hypocrite, the good man had had such an opinion of her that he could not at first believe it.

"I remember me further that I counselled Father Rich that in such things as concerned such folk as had come unto her, to whom she said she had told the cause of their coming ere they themselves spoke, and such good fruit as they said men had received by her prayers, he and such others as reported it, should first cause the things to be well examined by the ordinaries, so that it might be surely known whether the things were true or not. 'That she *is* a good virtuous woman I hear many folk report; I verily think it is true, and think it likely God may work good and great things by her; but you wot well, these strange tales are *no* part of our creed; and before you see them proved, see you wed not yourself so far to the belief of them as to report for true, lest, it should hap they be afterwards proved false, it might minish the estimation of your preaching.'

"Thus have I, good Mr. Cromwell, declared to you as far as I can remember, all that ever I have said or done in the matter. If any one report of me any word touching breach of my truth and duty to my sovereign, I will make good my answer. Whilst I live neither man nor woman shall make me digress from my truth to God and to my natural prince.

"I beseech our Lord long to preserve you.

"MAISTER THOMAS."*

Another parliament was called; and to the dismay of More's family and friends, he discovered that a bill of attainder was brought into the House, attainting the maid and her abettors, and charging himself and Bishop Fisher with misprision of treason; when he at once wrote the following letters to Cromwell and the king :—

"Right Worshipful,—

"I am informed that there is a black plot put in against me in the Higher House before the Lords, concerning my communications with the maid of Canterbury and my writing to her, whereof I not a little marvel, the truth of the matter being as God and I know it is, and as I have plainly declared unto you by my former letter.

"I desire you to favour me that I may have a copy of the bill, which seen, if I find untrue surmise therein I may

---

* See his letters in his printed works, p. 1423.

make humble suit unto the king's grace and declare the same. I am so sure of my truth to his grace that I cannot mistrust his goodness to me, being myself so innocent, whatsoever should happen me. At Chelsea, this present Saturday, by the hand of heartily all your own,

"THOMAS MORE, Knight.

And thus ran his letter to the King's grace :—

"It may like your highness to call to your gracious remembrance that at such time as of the office of your chancellor you were so good as to disburden me, it pleased your highness to say that, in any suit I should after have to your grace that should concern mine honour (the word it liked your highness to use) or should pertain unto my profit, I should find your highness a good and gracious lord unto me. Now is my most humble suit to your highness, that of your accustomed goodness no sinister information move your noble grace to have any more distrust of my truth and devotion to you than I shall during my life give cause. For in this matter of the maid of Canterbury I have to your trusty counsellor, Maister Cromwell, by my writing as plainly declared the truth as I possibly can. In my most humble manner, prostrate at your gracious feet, I beseech your grace, with your own prudence and accustomed goodness, consider and weigh the matter. And if in your so doing your own virtuous mind should tell you, that, notwithstanding the goodness your gracious highness hath by so many ways used unto me, I were a wretch of such monstrous ingratitude as to digress from my bounden duty of allegiance to your grace, then I desire no further favour at your hands than the loss of goods, lands, liberty, and life.   But if in the considering of my cause your gracious goodness perceive that I have not demeaned myself towards your royal majesty, I beseech your most noble grace that the knowledge of your persuasion may relieve the torment of my present heaviness, conceived out of the dread and fear (by that I hear such a grievous bill is put by your learned council into the High Court of Parliament against me), lest your grace might, by some sinister information which your highness do not, as I trust in God and your great goodness you will not.   Then in my most humble manner I beseech your highness further (albeit that in respect of my former request this other thing is very slight), yet since your highness hath of your abundant goodness heaped and accumulated on me (though I was far unworthy) from time to time both worship and great honour too, sithI have now left all such things, and nothing seek or desire but the life to come, and pray for your grace the while, it may like your highness of your benignity somewhat to tender my poor honesty and never suffer (by means of such a bill put forth against me) any man to take occasion hereafter against the truth to slander me, which should do themselves more hurt than me, which shall, I trust, settle my heart with your gracious favour, to depend upon the comfort of the truth and hope of Heaven, and not upon the fallible opinion or hastily spoken words of light and changeable people.   And thus, most dread and dear sovereign lord, I beseech the blessed Trinity preserve your most noble grace, both body and soul, and all that are your well-wishers, and amend all the contrary, among whom if ever I be or ever have been one, then pray I God that he may with my open shame and destruction declare it."

Fisher's name was removed from the bill on payment of three hundred pounds to the Crown. It would seem that More's name had been introduced as a threat to terrify him into submission to the King, but he boldly demanded to be allowed to plead at the bar of the House. He was not allowed, however, to defend himself publicly, and the hearing of the case was given to Cranmer, Audley, Cromwell, and the Duke of Norfolk.

Roper and Margaret, fearing lest he should throw away his life by the dauntless avowal of his principles, besought him, as far as he could do so conscientiously, to get his name put out of the bill. He promised them that he would do so, but yet never urged the matter.

The Lords Commissioners requested him to be seated, a courteous permission which Sir Thomas declined. Their object was to win him over to the King's party, and they began by reminding him of the many proofs he had received of his favour, of the King's wish still to retain him in his service, and to heap yet greater benefits upon him, than those he had already received, and that he could ask no worldly honour and profit at the hands of his sovereign, which he would not grant, provided he added his sanction and consent in favour of the marriage, which had already been given by the Bishops, the Universities, and the Parliament.

"My lords," replied Sir Thomas, "there never lived a man who would feel more pleasure at doing that which would be acceptable to his highness than myself, for he hath been most bountiful and liberal to me; but I had hoped I should never more have heard of this matter, as from the very outset I truly declared my mind to his Majesty, who accepted my opinion graciously, not minding, as he said to me, to trouble me any more concerning it, since which time I never found cause to change my opinion; if I had, none would be more joyful than myself."

Long they tried to make Sir Thomas yield; but when they saw they could not do so, Cromwell exclaimed:

"The king's majesty hath bid us tell you, if you continued obstinate, that never before was there a servant so villainous to his sovereign, or a subject so traitorous to his prince, as you. By your subtle and sinister conduct you most unnaturally procured and provoked the King to set forth his book on the seven sacraments and the maintenance of the Pope's authority, thus causing his Majesty to put a sword in the Pope's hands, wherewith to fight against himself to his own dishonour."

Sir Thomas had so lively a sense of the ridiculous that it is a matter of wonder how he kept his countenance. That the King, now grieving over the success of his own literary labours, should turn upon him with the charge of villainy for having helped him when he aspired to the fame of authorship, and urge it against him that he had maliciously provoked him to write a book, was about one of the strangest things that was ever entered in a bill of attainder.

"My lords," said More calmly, "these threats might terrify children, but not me. But, to make answer to your last charge against me, I cannot think the King's grace will ever lay that book to my door; in that point none can say more for my discharge than himself, who knoweth right well I never promoted or counselled it; only, after it was finished by his grace's appointment I sorted out and placed in order the principal matter thereof. And when I had found the Pope's authority highly advanced and defended with the strongest arguments, I said to his grace,* 'I must put your highness in remembrance of one thing, and that is that the Pope is, as your Majesty knows, a prince, as you are, in league with all other Christian princes. At some future time it may happen that your grace and he may differ on some points of the league, when there may be breach of friendship between you; therefore I think it best that portion be altered, and his authority more lightly touched on. 'Nay,' replied his grace, 'we are too much bound to the See of Rome, and cannot too much honour it.' I then reminded him how part of the Pope's pastoral authority had been pared away,† to which he replied, 'Whatever impediment there may be, we will set forth our authority to the utmost, for we have received from that see our crown imperial, which (till his grace with his own lips told me) I had never heard before, and these things being considered, I trust his highness will never speak of it again, but will himself clear me from this charge."

To his great surprise not a word passed from any of the Council respecting the real charge for which he had been brought before them, namely, his having countenanced and been an abettor of Elizabeth Barton.

In great good spirits he left the Council Chamber, and took boat with Roper for Chelsea, though yet unconscious

---

* More altered his opinions later, after studying the matter by the king's own wish; in fact he laid down his life in defence of the Pope's supremacy. He here speaks of opinions uttered by him fourteen years previously, before he had studied the question.

† He alludes to the statute of "præmunire," passed in the reign of Edward III., by which it was forbidden to receive bulls from Rome, or to act on their provisions, by appointment to ecclesiastical benefices or bishoprics, without consent of the King.—Lingard.

as to what the result of his defence might be, Roper was amazed at seeing him so cheerful, and persuaded himself that his name was struck out of the bill, so when they had landed from the boat and had entered the garden, he leaning on his son-in-law's arm, the latter said :—

"I trust, sir, all is well, since you are so merry."

"It *is* well, son Roper, and I thank God for it."

"Are you then put out of the parliament bill, sir?"

"By my troth, son, I never remembered it," rejoined Sir Thomas.

"Never remembered that, sir, which affects you so nearly, and *us* for your sake ; I am sorry to hear it, I trusted when I saw you so merry that all was well."

"Wouldst thou know, son, why I am so joyful? By my troth I never remembered the bill, but I have given the devil a foul fall, because when I was before these lords, I went so far that without great shame I can never go back."

This then was the cause of his joy, it was his confidence in God that He would give him strength to suffer. At these words of his, says Roper, " I waxed sad, for though *he* liked them well, yet they liked me but a little."*

As soon as the Lords of the Council made their report to the King of the conduct of Sir Thomas before them, in one of his fits of passion he demanded that his name should be kept in the parliament bill, and for a time would not listen to their advice, for they declared that the conviction on the minds of all in the Upper House, was so in favour of the late Chancellor, that if his name were not cast out of the bill, it would be of no force against the rest who were included in it.

* Roper's Life of More.

Much would Henry have given could he but have bent to his will the inflexible More, and he yet insisted on retaining his name in the bill of attainder, adding with a passionate exclamation, which we cannot repeat in these pages, that he would himself be present at the passing of it.

Then the Lords cast themselves on their knees imploring his Majesty not to carry out his threat, urging that if he, in his own presence, should see the bill thrown out, it would not only encourage his subjects to contempt of his authority, but would dishonour him throughout all Europe, adding, that they doubted not that the time would come when they might find "some fitting matter" against him, for in this case of Elizabeth Barton, every one thinks him perfectly innocent, and that his conduct is rather worthy of praise than the reverse."

The King then condescended to grant their petition, but his anger against Sir Thomas was rather increased than lessened by the necessity which he felt really existed for him to yield to the counsel of the Lords.

On the morrow, Secretary Cromwell met William Roper, and made the good man's heart glad, by telling him that the name of his father-in-law was put out of the bill. The message was at once sent to Chelsea, and Margaret hastened to her father with the joyful news. He answered calmly :

" In faith, Meg, *quod differtur non aufertur.** The ex statesman was deeper versed in the wiles of Henry's court than was his daughter. He knew well enough that he was not put out of the bill for love or favour, but that right soon some little matter would crop up, upon which to work more safely.

* That which is deferred is not dismissed.

A few days later the Duke of Norfolk called to see him, perhaps, as he called himself More's friend, with the hope of inducing him to comply with Henry's wishes, and leading the conversation to the trouble from which he had just escaped, he said :—

" But, by the mass, Sir Thomas, it is perilous striving with princes, therefore I could wish you, as a friend, to conform to the King's pleasure, for, by the rood, *Indignatio principis mors est.*"*

" Is that all, my lord ?" replied More with perfect calmness. " Then in good faith there is no more difference between you and me, than that I shall die to-day and you to-morrow. If the anger of a prince causeth but temporal death, we have greater cause to fear that which is eternal, which the King of heaven can condemn us to if we scruple not to displease Him by fearing an earthly prince."†

This remark of the unflinching More established in the duke's mind the opinion he had already formed that it would be, as it were, a trial of strength between the King and his ex-minister, and that the latter must inevitably be the loser; and he bade him farewell with the conviction that the crisis would soon arrive, and that that crisis would cost More his head.

* " The anger of a prince bringeth death."
† Roper, More.

CHAPTER XIV.

THE FITTING MATTER.

AND the "fitting matter" was the oath of the King's supremacy, the denial of which brought to the block Sir Thomas More, and John Fisher, Bishop of Rochester.

"This fitting matter," alluded to by Chancellor Audley, when advising the King to allow the name of More to be erased from the bill, was to force him to declare the lawfulness of the King's marriage with Anne Boleyn, thus rendering illegitimate his daughter Mary; and he was to be made to do this by taking the oath of succession.

A few days previously the maid of Kent, with Brocking, Masters, Deering, Rich, Gold and Risley, who were considered her abettors, were executed at Tyburn. To sustain the charge of treason it was held that the communication of such prophecies had in view the bringing the King in peril of his life; and the being acquainted with them, and yet concealing, amounted to the offence of misprision of treason. The accused were, however, never brought to trial; no defence was allowed; and the bill received the royal assent. Barton died confessing her delusion.

Once, when More took it into his head to try and prepare his family for what he felt in his inward heart would sooner or later inevitably happen, he had hired a person to come as a pursuivant, whilst they were all at dinner, and knocking hastily at his door, to warn him to appear before the Commissioners ; *now* the pursuivant did come in earnest.

If formerly he had laid awake by his wife's side, while she and all around him slept, still more of late had he watched and prayed through the live-long night, reckoning up the cost of an unwavering fidelity to principle, praying that he might not be wanting in strength to overcome his natural frailty, which, as he himself said, "could not endure to suffer."

And so it fell out that on the 13th of April, 1534, the long-expected summons came. The hour was one of supremest trial ; its waiting, however, had been almost as terrible in its varied alternations of hope and fear, as was the certainty at which they had now arrived.

He spoke cheerfully to his wife and daughter, after having calmly received the summons, and then he turned his steps to Chelsea Church, made his confession, communicated, and heard Mass ; returned home, made a frugal meal, and prepared to take boat for Lambeth. More was a good Christian, and a wise philosopher, but had no stoicism in his composition ; on this morning, for the life of him, he could not say the customary "Good-bye."

He had evermore been used at his departure from his wife and children, whom he tenderly loved, to have them conduct him to his boat, and there to kiss them, and bid them all farewell,* but that day he suffered none of them to follow him, but pulling the wicket after him, never looking back, shut them all from him. Margaret had indeed lingered, but her father gave her no chance of bidding him farewell, or increased his own pain by gazing .

---

* Roper.

on her tearful, pallid face, but with a sad countenance, and a heavy heart, he followed Roper to the boat.

Silent and sorrowful was he for a time, for full well he knew he had for ever left his once happy home. He was now alone with Christ in the garden !

Then, Roper, who was buried in his own painful thoughts, observing the sadness of his father-in-law, was suddenly roused from his reverie by feeling his ear smartly pulled, and looking round, he saw that dear, kind face wearing its usual glad expression.

" Son Roper, I thank our Lord *the field is won.*"

" I am very glad, Sir," said Roper answering at random, scarce able at the moment to guess his meaning, but later he saw cause rightly to believe that More had alluded to the conflict which was going on within him, and the struggles of natural affection, which for awhile made itself heard.

There is something very sweet and tender in the character of More, his affectionate heart was full of grief, and as soon as he had become wholly master of himself, his childlike simplicity and love of innocent mirth again manifests itself by that little action by which he attracted the attention of Roper.

And now appears in view the grey walls of Lambeth Church and Palace, and very full was he of anxious thoughts as he entered the great gate, and made his way at once to the Commissioners.

It was a great grief to More to behold, when brought before them, a throng of timorous clergy, amongst whom were several bishops, who without stay or hindrance unhesitatingly took the oath. The Commissioners were Boston the abbot of Westminster, the Archbishop Cranmer, and

Audley the chancellor. *Two only* of all that appeared before the Commissioners stood firm to their principles; one of them was a Dr. Wilson, the king's own confessor, who was at once on his refusal "genteely sent straight into the Tower," the other was Bishop Fisher.

The bishop had two days before received a letter from the primate, summoning him to his presence; and aware what the termination *must* be, he composedly put his house in order, and made his will as one who is about to die. Then he set out for Lambeth, and passing on his way through Rochester, he was met by a multitude of persons to whom he gave his blessing, riding amongst them bareheaded. After he had journeyed some twenty miles, he stopped for rest and refreshment on the brow of Shooters Hill, then mounted his horse again, and arrived in London in the evening. And when he went to Lambeth Palace on the morrow, the first person he encountered was Sir Thomas More.

"Well met, my lord," was the exclamation by which he was greeted, "I hope we shall soon meet in heaven."

"This should be the way, Sir Thomas," replied the bishop, "for it is a very strait gate we are in."

On the oath being tendered to him, he asked for time to consider it, and after some hesitation on the part of the Commissioners, he was allowed five days. Then he withdrew to his own house in Carlisle Place, Lambeth Marsh, then a pleasant spot in the midst of rural scenes, now one of the lowest and most densely populated districts in the extensive parish of Lambeth.

More was again called upon, and a long list exhibited of persons who had assented to the propositions of the oath. "We are sorry," said the Lord Chancellor, "that you should refuse to take this oath, which all other persons have sworn to."

More then consented to give his reasons, provided the King should assure him that then his motives should not be taken as an additional offence.

"The King," replied Cromwell, "cannot save you from the penalties provided by the statutes against those who refuse the oath."

"But," said More, "if I cannot explain my motives without danger, it is not obstinacy which silences me ; moreover, I blame no one for taking it." He then offered to swear to the succession alone, but not to every particular contained in the Act. He was then remanded whilst the oath was tendered to the clergy, he being the only layman who had been summoned, and was told he could walk in the garden for awhile, perhaps with the hope that a little quiet commune with self would bring him to a different frame of mind. But More wished to be quite alone, one would suppose, for he wandered away to a small desolate apartment which had been partly consumed by fire ; it overlooked the gardens, the river, the fine old abbey on the opposite bank of the Thames, Westminster Hall, the spots on which our own eyes have rested, aye, well nigh a thousand times, some of them so like still to what they were these three centuries and a half ago, altered not, save in their surroundings, for the majestic abbey, the ancient hall, the everflowing river, the grey walls of the old church in which Mass and Vespers oftimes used to be sung, are still as then they were.

More's mind, one would think, must have wandered to far other scenes, for yonder is the hall in which he sat as Chancellor, when his name was on the lips of thousands, and when the poor were made happy, because he heard their appeals. His courtier life too, must needs have rushed back upon him with all its dissipation, its turmoil, its frivolity, in which his inmost heart had so little share. How he must have wished, one would think, that King Henry had let him rest, he was unwilling to go to court, and it had brought him nought but sadness and woe, and to his family misery unspeakable.

There are voices in the gardens of his grace, the Archbishop, and he sighs deeply as he beholds various members of the clergy with whom he was acquainted, discoursing with each other ; their consciences, like that of Boston, the Abbot, who was one of the Commissioners, had not stood at all in their way.

It must have been a trial to the fidelity of the layman, Thomas More, to see that throng of ecclesiastics fall away.

The noble and venerable Fisher is not amongst them !

Again he stands before the Commissioners, and Cranmer triumphantly exhibits a list of those who have just sworn the oath, warning him of the King's anger should he remain obstinate.

More, however, is true to his colours, nor archbishop, nor priest, nor abbot, nor chancellor, can lead him other than the voice of his conscience shall direct ; and for four days he is committed to the safe custody of Boston, the Abbot of Westminster.

It has been said that the King at this time would fain have discharged him, but that Queen Anne urged him to show him neither mercy nor favour.

CHAPTER XV.

THE TOWER.

FOUR days later the oath was again tendered, and refused, and More's term of remand having expired, he leaves the custody of Boston for a prison lodging in London's time-worn fortress, the Tower. He must have known full well the morning he left his home at Chelsea, never venturing to look back, that he was leaving it for ever, but strange yearning emotions must have filled his soul; as he left the abbot's custody and entered the boat; *now* steered in the direction of the city, instead of, as of old, to Chelsea, he now realized, for the first time, that he was a prisoner, and that home (such a home as his was too), for it comprised all that can constitute its charm, was gone from him for *ever*. Yes, all was gone now, for he was accompanied by Sir Richard Wingfield to the Tower of London; but he called his christian philosophy and resignation to his aid, and in this, the most trying moment in his life, More was composed and even cheerful.

And now the boat shoots swiftly under one of the arches of old London Bridge, and the ancient fortress, the walls of which could tell, if they could speak, such terrible tales of sin and wrong, frown down upon good Sir Thomas More.

In the direction of the Traitors' Gate the boat was steered. A wicket formed of heavy beams of massive oak was opened, only a step from thence to the block, he must have surely thought.   The dull splash of the water beating against the sides of the arch, the frowning fortress, the prospect of, perhaps, a life-long incarceration, or of a shorter imprisonment, to be ended by an ignominious death, must have struck terror into the hearts of all who have been doomed to pass beneath that gate ; and in this wise More's thoughts must have run.

Before the usual form of delivering the warrant, and receiving an acknowledgment for the body of the prisoner, was gone through, Sir Richard, observing his gold chain around his neck, kindly advised him to send it home to his family.

" Nay," was his reply, " that will I not, for if my enemies take me on the field I should like them to have somewhat for their pains."   Indeed More was perfectly well aware that whether in his house at Chelsea, or in the Tower, all his personal effects would go ; his home had already, according to the infamous custom of the times, been searched and ransacked by the King's officers, and it mattered nothing to him whether he was plundered there or where he now was.

As he landed at the Tower steps, the process of fleecing him, under the name of " garnish," was at once commenced by the porter demanding of him his outer garments as a perquisite.

" Marry, porter," said More, taking off his cap, " here it is, and I am sorry it is not a better one."

"No, no, sir, by your leave, it is your coat that I must have."

Without a word More submitted to be robbed, and following his conductors, ascended a narrow spiral staircase, lighted at intervals by small loopholes in the outer wall, and which led to the prison lodging in which he was to be confined.

On entering his cell it was with a sigh of relief that he beheld on a small wooden table, beneath the grated loophole which served as a window, a writing desk, with pen, ink, and paper.   It was removed later by the gaoler, but not until Sir Thomas had bequeathed to posterity some interesting letters and writings, all of which show us how entirely resigned he was to suffer persecution for justice sake.   He was allowed the unusual privilege of an attendant, one John à Wood, an old servant of his own, who could neither read nor write, and who was sworn by the lieutenant that should he see or hear anything against the King he should declare it to him at once.

The use to which Sir Thomas applied his pen and ink was, without delay, to write the following letter to Margaret :—

"April 17, 1534.

"My dearest Daughter,—When I was before the lords at Lambeth, I was the first called in ; though Master Doctor, the vicar of Croydon, and several others, had come before me.   After they had declared to me why I was sent for (at which I wondered), seeing there was no other secular man there but myself, I asked to *see* the oath, which they showed me under the great seal, as also the act of the succession, which was delivered me in a printed roll.   I then read them to myself, and considered the act with the oath, and showed them that my purpose was not to put any fault in the act or he that made it, or in the oath or any man that swore it, nor to condemn any man's conscience ; but, as for myself, my conscience so moved *me*, that though I

would not deny to swear to the succession, yet to the oath
I could not swear without jeopardy to my soul.   And that
if they doubted if I refused the oath for the grudge of my
conscience or for any fancy, I was ready to satisfy them on
my oath, which if they trusted not, what should they be the
better for giving me an oath; and if they trusted I would
swear true, then I hoped they would not move me to swear
the oath they offered me to swear, it being against my
conscience.   To this my Lord Chancellor* said, they were
all very sorry to see me refuse the oath, saying, I was the
very first who *had* refused it, which would cause the King's
highness to conceive great suspicion and great indignation
towards me ; and then they showed me the roll, with the
names of the lords and commons who had sworn and subscribed their names already.   And seeing—I still refused
to swear the same myself, not blaming any that *had* sworn,
I was bid go down into the garden ; but I tarried in the old
chamber that looked into it, and would not go down on
account of the heat.   And then I saw Master Doctor Latimer come into the garden, walking about with various other
doctors and chaplains of my lord of Canterbury ; and very
merry I saw he was, for he took one or two about the neck
right handsomely.   After that came Master Doctor Wilson
forth from the lords ; and he was with two gentlemen sent
straight unto the Tower.   What time my Lord of Rochester
was called in before them I cannot tell ; but at night I
heard he had been before them ; but where he remained
until sent hither, I never heard.   I heard also that
Master Vicar of Croydon and the remainder of the
priests of London that were sent for were sworn,

* Sir Thomas Audley.

and that they had such favour at the hands of the council that they were not detained and made to dance attendance to their own cost, as suitors are sometimes wont to be; but were speedily dismissed. And that Master Vicar of Croydon, either for joy, or for thirst, or else that it might be seen *quod ille notus erat pontifici,** went to my lord's buttery bar, called for drink, and drank *valde familiariter.*†

" As soon as they had played their pageant, and gone out of the place, I was called in again, and was told what a number had sworn since I had left, without any scruple, for which I blamed no man, answering only for myself as before. Then again they spoke of my obstinacy, that since I refused to swear, I would not declare any special part of the oath that pricked my conscience. And I told them that I feared the King's highness would, as they said, take displeasure enough only for refusing the oath; and if I should say why, I should but further exasperate him, and would rather abide all the harm that might come unto me than occasion his highness further displeasure than the offering of the oath to me constrained me of pure necessity. Then many times they imputed obstinacy to me, that I would neither swear nor say why I declined; and rather than I would be thus accounted, I said I would declare the cause in writing upon the King's gracious licence, or such commandment of his as might be my sufficient warrant that my declaration should not offend him, nor put me in danger of any of his statutes; and above that, I would give an oath in the beginning that if I might find those causes by any man answered as might satisfy my conscience, I would after swear the principal oath

---

* " That he was known to the chief priest."

† Right jollily.

also. To this they said that, though the King would give me licence under his letters patent, yet would it not serve against the statute. To which I said, that if I had them I would stand to his honour; but if I may not declare the cause without peril, then to leave them undeclared is no obstinacy.

" My Lord of Canterbury then took hold of my saying that I did not condemn those who swore, saying it showed that I did not take it for a certain thing that I might not swear, but as very doubtful; but you do know for a certainty, without doubt, that you are bound to obey your sovereign lord and king, and so are bound to leave off the doubt of your uncertain conscience in refusing the oath : take the sure way, obey your prince, and swear it. Now in my own mind not convinced, yet this argument, coming suddenly out of so noble a prelate's mouth, I could only answer I thought I might not do so, because in my own conscience this was not a case in which I *should* obey my prince, whatsoever others, whose conscience or learning I would not take on me to judge, thought in the matter; the truth seemed to me on the other side, for I had not informed myself suddenly, but by long leisure and diligent search; and if that reason may conclude, then have we a sure way to avoid all perplexities; for in whatever matter the doctors stand in doubt, the King's command, given on whichever side he liketh, solves the doubts.

"Then said my Lord of Westminster, howsoever the matter seems unto your mind, your mind is erroneous, when you see the great council of the realm determine the contrary; and you ought to change your conscience.

" To this, said I, were there not one on my side, and the

whole parliament on the other, I would be sore afraid to lean to my own mind; but I have on my side as great a council, and the greater; so I am not bound to change my conscience, and conform to the council of one realm against the whole of Christendom.

"Then Master Secretary swore a great oath, that he had rather that his only son had lost his head, than that I should have refused the oath; for that the King would hold me in suspicion, and think the matter of the nun of Canterbury contrived by me.

"The contrary is well known, said I; and whatever shall happen me, it is not of my power to help it without peril to my soul.

"My Lord Chancellor then repeated before me my refusal to Master Secretary, as he was going unto the King's grace; and in the repeating said I denied not, but was content to swear to the succession.

"As for that point, I will be content, said I, so that I may see my oath so framed as may stand with my conscience. When said my lord:

"'Marry, Master secretary, mark that, so he'll not swear that either, but under some certain fashion.'

"Verily, no, indeed, quoth I, I will see it made in such a manner first, that I shall know I am neither forsworn nor swear against my conscience. As to swearing to the succession, I see no danger; but it is reasonable that to my oath I look well myself, and take counsel also and never swear for a piece and set my hand to the whole; but, so help me God, as regards the whole oath, I never led any man *from* taking it, nor advised any to *refuse* it, nor put any scruple in any man's head; but leave every man to his own conscience.

And methinks it were right every man should leave me to mine."

It was on the 17th of April, 1534, that More was committed for trial. The following prayer bears the date of the same year, but the month is not named, probably it was the outpouring of More's heart to his God, when first he became an inmate of his prison lodging in the Bell Tower, which tradition names as the place of his confinement. Therefore we will insert it here ; and the letters, according to the dates, shall follow in rotation. It is headed as follows :—

"A godly meditation, written by Sir Thomas More, Knight, whilst prisoner in the Tower of London, in the year of our Lord 1534."

"Give me thy grace, good Lorde, to set the worlde at nought.

" To set my mynde fast upon Thee.

" And not to change upon the blaste of men's mouthes.

" To be content to be solitary.

" Not to long for worldlye companye.

"Lytle by lytle utterly to cast off the worlde, and rydde my mynde of all the busyness thereof.

" Not to longe to hear of any worldlye thynges, but that the hearing of worldlye thynges may be to me displeasant.

"Gladly to be thynking of God.

" Piteously to call for His help.

'·To leane unto the comfort of God, and busily to labour to love Hym.

" To knowe myne own wretchedness.

"To humble myself under the myghte hand of God.

"To bewail my sins passed.

" For the purging of them, patiently to suffer adversitye.

" Gladly to bear my purgatory here.

"To be joyful of tribulations.

" To walk the narrow way that leadeth to lyfe.

" To bear the crosse with Christ.

" To have the laste thyngs in remembrance.

" To have ever before my eyes my death, that is ever at hande.

" To make death no stranger to me.

" To foresee and consider the everlasting pains of hell.

" To pray for pardon before the judge cometh.

" To have continually in mynde the passion that Christ suffered for me.

" For His benefittes incessantly to give Hym thanks.

" To lyve the time again that I before have lost.

"To abstaine from vaine conversations.

" To eschew light foolish mirth and gladness.

"Recreations not necessary, to cast off, worldly substance, frendes, liberty, lyfe, and all, to settle the losse at right nought for the winning of Christ.

" To think my worst enemies my best frendes."

" For the brethren of Joseph could never have done hym so muche good with their love and favour, as they did hym with their malice and hatred.

" These mindes are more to be desired of every man, than all the treasures of all the princes and kynges, christian and heathen, were it gathered and layde together all in one heape."

The following bears no date :—

" My dearest Daughter—Our Lorde keepe me continually true, faithfule and playne, to the contrary whereof I beseech hym heartily never to suffer me to live. For as for long lyfe,

as I have often told thee, Megge, I nayther looke for nor long
for it, but am well content to go, if God call me hence
to-morrow; and I thanke our Lord I knowe no person living
that I would have endure one filip for my sake, of whiche
minde I am more glad than of all the worlde besyde.

"Recommend me to your shrewde Will and mine other
sonnes, and to John Harris, my frende, and yourself knoweth
to whom else, and to my shrewd wife above alle, and God
make and keepe you all His servantes."

A few days after his imprisonment in the fortress, Margaret
wrote him a letter, in which she appeared to endeavour to
persuade him to take the oath, by so doing she won a certain
degree of credence with Cromwell, so that in the end she
obtained liberty to have free access to her father, a permission which she profited by during the greater part of his
imprisonment.　Cromwell, doubtless, believed he could
practise on More through the affections of his daughter.
The reply of Sir Thomas to Margaret's letter, alluded to
above, was as follows :—

OUR LORD BLESSE YOU.

"If I had not been, my dearly beloved daughter, at a
firm and fast point, I trust in God's great mercy, this good
great while before, your lamentable letter had not a little
abashed me, surely far above all other things, of which I
have often not a few terrible ones.　Surely none of them
ever touched me so near nor were so grievous to me as to
see you, my well beloved child, in so vehemently piteous a
manner labouring to persuade me to the thing concerning
which I have for pure necessity, for respect to my own soul,
so often spoken precisely to you.

" Concerning the chief points of your letter I can make

no reply; for I doubt not you well remember that the matters which move my conscience (without declaration whereof I cannot touch upon the points) I have often told you I will disclose to no one. Therefore, daughter Margaret, I can in this do nothing, but as. you labour and entreat me to follow your mind, again to desire and pray you to desist from such labour, and with my former answers to keep yourself content. A deadly grief to me, much more deadly than to hear the decree of my own death (for the fear of that, I thank our Lord, the fear of hell, the hope of heaven and the passion of Christ daily more and more assuage) is, that I perceive my good son your husband, and you, my good daughter, and my good wife, and my other good children and innocent friends, are held in great displeasure, and are in great danger of harm thereby. To hinder which resteth not with me, I can but commit all to God (*Nam in manu Dei*, saith the Scriptures, *cor regis est, et sicut divisiones aquarum quocunque voluerit impellit illud*),* whose great goodness I most humbly beseech to incline the noble heart of the King's highness tenderly to favour all of you, and to favour me no better than God and myself know that my faithful heart towards him and my daily prayers for him deserve ; for if his highness might see my mind such as God knows it to be, it would, I trust, soon soothe his great displeasure. But while I am in this world I can never thus show it, so that his grace might think differently of me ; I can but leave all in the hands of Him, for fear of whose displeasure, for the safety of my soul, without reproaching any one, I now endure this trouble ;

* For in the hand of God, saith the Scriptures, is the heart of the King, and as the division of the waters he inclines it.

out of which I beseech God to bring me when it pleaseth
Him, into His endless bliss in heaven; and meanwhile to
give me grace, and you also, in all our agony and trouble
devoutly to dwell on the remembrance of that bitter agony
which our Saviour suffered before His passion on the
Mount; and if we do so diligently, I verily trust we shall
find therein great comfort and consolation.   And so, my
dear daughter, may the blessed Spirit of Christ, of His
tender mercy, govern and guide you all, to His pleasure and
your weal and comfort, both body and soul.

> " Your tender, loving father,
>
> " THOMAS MORE, Knight."

And this was Margaret's reply :—

" Mine own good Father—It is to me no little comfort,
since I cannot talk to you as I would, at least to console
myself in this bitter time of your absence by such means as
I may, by as often writing to you as shall be expedient, and
by reading again and again your most fruitful and delectable
letter, the faithful messenger of your very virtuous and
spiritual mind, rid from all corrupt love of worldly things,
and fast knit only in the love of God and desire of heaven,
as becometh a true worshipper and a very faithful servant of
God, who I doubt not, good father, holdeth His holy hand
over you, and shall (as He hath) preserve you both body
and soul (*ut sit mens sana in corpore sano*),* now when you
have cast away all earthly consolations, and resigned yourself willingly, gladly, and fully for His love to His holy pro-
tection.   Father, what think you hath been our comfort
since you departed from us?   Surely nothing but the
experience we have had of your life past, your godly con-

---

* That you may have a sound mind in a sound body.

versation, wholesome counsel, and virtuous example, and a certainty not only of a continuance of the same, but also a great increase by the goodness of our Lord to the great rest and gladness of your heart, devoid of all earthly dross, and garnished with the noble vestures of heavenly virtues, a pleasant place for the Holy Spirit of God to rest in. May He defend you (as I doubt not, good father, of His goodness He will) from all trouble of mind and body, and give me, your most loving, obedient daughter and handmaid, and all us your children and friends, to imitate all that we praise in you, and to our only comfort remember you, that we may meet with you, mine own dear father, in the bliss of heaven, to which our most merciful Lord hath brought us with His most precious blood.

" Your own most loving and obedient daughter and petitioner, Margaret Roper, who desireth above all worldly things to be in John à Wood's place to do you some service. But we live in hope that we shall shortly receive you again. I pray God heartily we may, if it be His holy will."

The joy of the father and daughter on again meeting each other may be better imagined than described. Always devotedly attached to her father by more than even the usual love which binds the child to its parent, Margaret beheld him endued with a new character, which won her especial veneration, that of a confessor, whom she doubted nothing in her own mind, would soon wear the crown of a martyr.

He was changed both in person and in character, suffering and imprisonment had left their trace upon his features ; his face was more pallid than of old, but his keen grey eyes bright as ever ; there was no longer, however, his old joyous spirits, these had sobered down into a quiet, calm cheerfulness; ever and again too those features which she had been used to behold all aglow with gladness, and radiant with happiness were shadowed over with a gravity she had never seen them assume in other days.

Taking her by the hand when she entered, he made her kneel down, and then ere he touched upon the subject nearest their hearts; they prayed together.

"The seven Psalms and the Letany sayde," he rose, gazed lovingly on this daughter of his fondest affection, embraced her, and sitting down beside her, said he to Margaret :—

"I believe, Megg, that they who have put me here think they have done me a great displeasure, but I assure thee on my faith, mine own good daughter, that if it had not been for my wife and children, whom I account the chief part of my charge, I would not have failed long ere this to have closed myself in as straight a cell as this, and straighter too, and since I have come here without my own will, I trust that God of His goodness will discharge me of my care, and graciously supply the want of my presence amongst you. Methinks, Megg, God dealeth with me as with a wanton child, and doth dandle me as He dandleth his best friends, even as He hath done S.S. Peter and Paul, and all His holy martyrs, whose example may He make me worthy to imitate."

Little by little somewhat of his own calm composure communicated itself to the unhappy Margaret, and she strove to rally her spirits, drive back the tears which ever and again welled up into her eyes, and even to force a smile as some playful sally ever and again fell from the lips of this saintly christian and philosopher, who even in the hour of direst anguish knew how to extract sweets from his sorrows, and so well practised that first and most essential virtue, entire resignation to the will of God. And then, having craved his fatherly blessing and affectionately embraced him, she took her leave, and wended her way out from the cruel Tower back to the busy scenes of life, pausing yet, as she stood upon the Tower green, to gaze in the direction of the prison lodging, which confined him whom she held so dear.

He was no longer with her to cheer her with his smile, and she turned away at length, sad and sorrowful, and mingled with the throng of wayfarers in Tower Hill.

After this first interview Margaret was for some months allowed free access to her father. The following letter, said to have been written with a coal, was probably given very soon after the permission to visit him had been accorded.

. It is addressed :—

" To all my lovinge frendes—Forasmuch as being in prison I cannot tell what need I may have, or what necessity I may hap to stand in, I hartily beseech you all, if my well beloved daughter, Margaret Roper, which onely of all my frendes hath by the Kyng's gracious permission, license to resorte unto me, do anything desire of any of you, of such things as I shall hap to nede, that it may like you no less to regard and tender it than if I moved it unto you, and required it of you personally present, myself, and I beseech you all to praye for me, and I shal praye for you."

"Your faithful lover and poor bedesman,

"THOMAS MORE, Knight, prisoner."

It is necessary here to advert to Bishop Fisher, who was also committed to the Tower about the same time as Sir

Thomas, these friends and fellow-captives were lodged in the Bell Tower, and the confinement of the bishop was more rigorous from the first than was that of the ex-chancellor.

Both these illustrious captives Anne Boleyn is said to have regarded with the deepest resentment. She knew that from the first Fisher had expressed his aversion for the divorce in most unqualified terms of disapprobation, whilst More, who though he so far temporised as to consent to investigate the matter with the bishops appointed by the King, never yielded, and as well he had no doubt wounded her female vanity, by refusing to be present on the day of her coronation.

CHAPTER XVI.

LADY ALLINGTON'S LETTER.

THE following letters, extracted from the works of Sir Thomas, will, we are sure, be read with much interest :—

"In August, in the year of our Lord 1534, the Lady Alice Allington, wife to Sir John Allington, Knight, and daughter to Sir Thomas More's second wife, wrote the following letter to Mistress Roper—

"Sister Roper,—With all my heart I recommend me unto you, thanking you for all kindness : the cause of my writing is to show you that two hours after my coming home, my Lord Chancellor did come to take a course at a buck in our park, the which was a great pleasure to my husband. Then, when he had taken his pleasure and killed his deer, he went to Sir Thomas Barnstow's to bed, at whose house I met him the next day at his desire, to which I could not say nay, for he begged me heartily and most especially, because I would speak to him of my father. And when I saw my time, I besought him as humbly as I could, that he would be still good lord unto him. First, he answered, that he would be glad to do for him even as for his own father, and he said he appeared very well when the matter of the nun was laid to his charge, and as to the other matter he marvelled that my father was so obstinate in his own conceit, for that every one went forth, save only the blind bishop and he ; 'and in good faith,' said he, 'I am very glad that *I* have no learning,' but I know a few of Esop's fables, of which I will tell you one. There was a country in which there were none but fools, saving a few men which were wise, and they by their wisdom knew that theyre should fall a great raine, that should make all them fools that should be wet therewith : they seeing that, made them caves under ground till all the rayne was past. Then they came forth thinking to make the fools do what they list, and to rule them as they woulde. But the fools would none of that, but would have the rule themselves for all their craft. And when the wise men saw that they could not obtain their purpose, they wished that they had been in the rayne and had wetted their garments with the fools. When this tale was told, my lord laughed merrily, and I replied, 'for all this meny fable, I have no doubt but that he would be good lord to my father, when he saw his time (opportunity).'

"I would not have your father so scrupulous of his conscience, said he, and then he told me another fable of a lion, an ass, and a wolfe, and how they went to confession ; first the lion confessed that he had devoured all the beasts he could meet with, his confessor absolved him because he was a king, and it was his nature so to do ; then came the poor ass, and said that he took but one straw out of his master's shoe for hunger, by which means he thought his master did take cold, this great trespass the confessor could not absolve, but sent him to the bishop ; then came the wolfe and made his confession, and he was strictly forbidden to exceed the cost of sixpence at a meal, but when the wolfe had used this much of diet, at a time, he waxed very hungry, insomuch that on a day when he saw a cow with her calf come by him, he sayd to himselfe, 'I am very hungry, and fain would I eate, but that I am bound by my ghostly father; notwithstanding that, my conscience shall judge me, and then if that be so, then my conscience shall be this, that the cow doth seem to me now but worth a groat, then is the calf but worth twopence.' So did the wolfe eate both the cow and the calfe. Now, my good sister, hath not my lord told me two odd fables. In good faith, they pleased me not at all, nor I wist not what to say, for I was ashamed of this answer, and I see no better suit than to Almighty God, for He is the comforter of all sorrows, and will not fail to send comfort to his servants when they have most need. Thus fare ye well, myne owne good sister.

"Written on Monday after S. Laurence in haste.

"Your Sister, ALICE ALLINGTON.."

The following reply to the above letter makes known to us the communication that passed between the prisoner and his daughter :—

"Sister Allington,—When I next visited my father, I thought it proper and requisite to show him your letter, proper, that he may see for himself how lovingly you take his case to heart, requisite as he may thereby perceive that if he still stand in such scruple of conscience (as it is tenderly called by many that are his frendes and wyfe), all his frendes that seem most able to benefit him, either will finally forsake him, or perchance not indeed be able to do him any good at all. For these reasons, at my next being with him after receiving your letter, when I had talked with him awhile of his old disease in his chest, and of his pre-

R

sent internal complaint, and also of the crampe that many nights grips him in the legs, and that I found his bodily pains had not increased but continued as formerly, sometimes very painful, sometimes less, and at this time finding him pretty well, after oure seven psalms and the letany sayde, beginning to talk and be merry first with matters about the comfort of my mother, and the good order of my brother and sisters, that he hoped disposed themselves daily more and more to set little by the world and draw more closely to God, and that his family, his neighbours, and other good frendes, diligently remembered him in their prayers, I said—

"I pray God, dear father, that their prayers and ours may purchase grace of God, His grace that you may in this great matter, for which you are in this trouble, and for which also we all who love you, may take such means, as agreeing with the will of God, may content and please the King, whom you have always found so singularly gracious to you, but if you stiffly refuse to do the thing that would please him, which God not offended, you might do (as many great, wise, and learned say that you may), it would be a great blot in you in every wise man's opinion, and as I have heard some say, whom you have always, held for good and learned, a peril to your soul also.   But as for that point, dear father, I will not be so bold as to dispute upon it, for I trust in God, and your own good heart, that you will look surely to it, and your learning is such that I well know you can.

"But there is one thing, father, which I and your friends perceive, which, if it be not shown you, you may peradventure to your soul's peril mistake, and hope for less harm (for as

for good I wot well that in this world you expect none)
than I fear may fall upon you. For I assure you, father,
I received lately a letter from my sister Allington, from
which I clearly see that if you do not change your mind
you are likely soon to lose all those friends that are able to
do you any good ; and if you do not lose their good will,
you will lose its effects for any benefit they might be able
to do you.

"'What, Mistress Eve,' said my dear father with a smile,
'hath my daughter Allington played the serpent with you,
and with her letter set you to work to come and tempt
your father again, and for the love that you bear him set
him to swear against his conscience, and so send him to
the devil.'

"Then he looked very sad, and said to me earnestly—

"'Daughter Margaret, we two have talked over this
matter twice or thrice, and the same tale that you tell me
now, with the same fear have you told me before ; I have
twice told you that if in this matter it were possible for me
to do the thing that would content the King's grace, God
not offended, then hath no man taken this oath more gladly
than I would do, as one that reckoneth himself deeply
beholden to the King's highness for his goodness many
ways shown me, more than all others. But in conscience
I can in no way do it, and for my own instruction in the
matter I have not slightly looked over, but have studied
and consulted many of the fathers, but can find nothing,
nor shall I ever, to induce me to think other than I do. I
have no remedy. God hath put me in this strait, that
either I must deadly displease Him, or abide any worldly
harm that He shall for mine other sins under this matter

suffer to fall upon me. As I have told you, Margaret, before I came here, I did not leave unthought of, or unconsidered, the very worst that could by any possibility fall upon me ; and although I know my own frailty well, and the natural weakness of my heart, yet if I had not trusted God would give me strength to suffer rather than sore offend Him by swearing against my conscience, you may be very sure I had not come here. I look only to Him, it matters not to me that men shall say if it pleases them, that it is not conscience but a foolish scruple.'   Then said I—

"In good faith, father, it cannot become me either to mistrust your mind or your learning, but as you speak of some terming it a scruple, you shall see by my sister's letter that one of the highest state in the realm, a learned man too, as I dare say you will think when you know who he is, you have already proved him to be your friend, accounteth your conscience in this matter as a right simple scruple, you may be sure he saith it with no small cause. 'You say,' he says, 'your conscience holds you to this, while all the nobles of the realm, and all other men also, go boldly forth and stick not thereat, save only you and one other, who though he be right good, and very learned, gives you advice against all others to lean to his mind alone.' With these words I showed him your letter that he might see I spoke not of myself, but used the words of one whom he highly esteems.

"He read your letter twice, sister, making no haste over it, but reading it leisurely, pondering over every word, then said he—

"'Forsooth, daughter Margaret, 'I find my daughter Allington such as I have found her, as I trust I. ever shall, thinking of me as tenderly as you, who are mine owne. Howbeit, I verily deem her as mine, as I married her mother, and brought her up from a child, as I brought up you, in other things, as well as learning, and I thank God she findeth now the good of it, and bringeth up her children well and virtuously. I thank God he hath sent her good store. May he preserve them all, and my good son, her husband too. I am her daily bedesman (so write her for all), in this matter she hath behaved like herself wisely, like a very daughter to me, and at the end of it she giveth as good counsel as any man would wish, God reward her for it.

"Now daughter, Margaret, as for my lord, I not only think but have always found, that he is undoubtedly my friend. In mine other business concerning the nun, as my case was clear, so was he, my good lord, and Master Secretary my good master too, for which I shall ever be a faithful bedesman for them both, and pray for them as for myself. And should it ever happen, which I trust in God it never may, that I be other than true to my prince; let them never favour me again; it would not become them to do so. But to tell the truth, Megg, between thee and me, my lord's Æsop's fables do not move me a bit, but as he in his wisdom, for his pastime, told them merely to mine own daughter, so shall I for mine, answer them to thee, Megg, for thou art mine other daughter.

"The first fable of the rayne that washed away all their wits, I have heard before; it was a tale often told to the King's council by my Lord Cardinal, when his Grace was Chancellor, and I cannot soon forget it, for in past times when there was variance between the Emperor and the

French king, so that they were likely and indeed did go to war together, and that there were various opinions held in the council, in which some were minded that it would be wise to sit still and let them alone, but more against that plan, my lord told this fable of the wise men, that because they would not be washed with the rain that should make all the people fools, went and hid themselves underground; but when the rain was gone and they came out and would utter their wise sayings, the fools conspired together against them, and would rule over the wise men; 'and so,' said his Grace, 'if we would be so wise as to sit still whilst the fools fought, they would not fail by and by to make peace and fall upon us. I will not dispute as to his Grace's counsel. I trust we never made war but when we were obliged by good cause, but this fable put in *his* fashion, did in his day help the King and the people to the spending of many a fair penny; but those years have passed and his Grace is gone, our Lord absolve his soul, and now I come to that Æsop's fable, as my lord merrily laid it out for me. To speak the truth, Meg, before the rayne came, if the wise men thought all the rest would turn into fools, and were so silly that they would, or so mad as to think they should rule over fools, and lacked wit enough to remember that there are none so unruly as they that are short witted, then were those wise men stark fools themselves before ever the rayne came. However, daughter Roper, whom my lord taketh to be wise men, or whom soever he taketh to be fools, I cannot very well guess, I cannot read such riddles. For as Danus saith in Terence *Nonsum Œdipus,** I may say you *wot* well, *Nonsum*

* I am not Œdipus.

Œdipus * *sed Moròs*, which name of mine what it signifieth in Greek I need not tell you. But I trust my lord reckoneth me amongst the fools, and so reckon I myself, as my name is in Greek, and I find, I thank God, reasons not a few, wherefore I should be so in very deed, but surely amongst those that long to be rulers, God and mine own conscience clearly knoweth that no man may truly reckon or number me. And I ween every man's conscience may tell him the same, since it is well known that of the King's great goodness I *was* one of the greatest rulers in the realm, and only at mine own great trouble of his goodness discharged ; and I pray God make us all so wise that we may each so wisely rule ourselves in this sad time, and in this vale of misery, this wretched world in which as Bœthius saith, ' one man to be proud that he rules over another man, is as if a mouse in a barn were to be proud to rule over other mice,' God, I say, give us grace so wisely to rule ourselves here, that when we shall haste to meet the bridegroom, we be not taken asleep and for lack of light in our lamps, be shut out of heaven amongst the foolish virgins.

" The second fable, Margaret, seemeth not to be Æsop's, for by it the matter hangeth all upon confession, it seemeth to be since christendom began, for in Greece before Christ's days they used not confession, no more the men then than beasts now. And Æsop was a Greek, and died long ere Christ was born ; but whoever made it matters little, I envy not that Æsop hath the name, but it is too subtle for me, for whom his lordship understandeth by the lion and the wolf, who both confessed themselves of devouring all that

* I am not Œdipus but a fool.

came into their hands, and the one enlarged his conscience
at his pleasure, in the matter of his penance, nor who by
the good discreet confessor who enjoined the one a little
penance, and the other none at all, and yet sent the poor
ass to the bishop, of all these things can I nothing tell.   But
by the foolish, scrupulous ass that had so sore a conscience
for the taking of a straw for hunger out of his master's
shoe, my lord's other words of my scruples declares that he
meant it for me, signifying as it seems, by that similitude,
that out of folly my scrupulous conscience taketh for a
perilous thing for my soul, if I should swear this oath which
his lordship thinketh but a trifle.   I suppose, Margaret, as
you told me just now, and so many think beside, as well
spiritual as temporal, that of these who for their learning
and virtue I myself esteem, and yet though I believe I am
right, yet believe I not every man doth not so think.   But
though they did, daughter, it matters not to me, even
should I see my Lord of Rochester say the same, and swear
the oath before me, too, for you told me but now, that such
as love me would not advise me, that against all others I
should lean to his mind alone, and truly, daughter, I do
not; for though I hold him in respectful veneration and
esteem, no man in wisdom, learning, or virtue, fit to be
matched or compared with him, yet in this matter I was in
no way led by him, as is plain, because I refused the oath
before it was offered him, and also when you told me that
his lordship was content to have sworn the oath, verily,
daughter, I never intend, by God's help, to pin my soul to
another man's back, not even the best man living, for I
know not whither he may chance to carry it, there is no
living man of whom while he lives one can make sure.

Some may yield for favour, and some for fear, and so might carry my soul a long way, and some might chance to frame themselves a conscience, and think that while he hid it in fear, God would forgive it, and some may think that if they say one thing and think the contrary, God will regard the heart more than the tongue, and that their oath will depend on what they think, and not on what they say. As a woman reasoned once, I trow, daughter, you were standing by. But in good fayth, Margaret, I can use no such wayes in so great a matter, but like as if mine own conscience served me, I would not let to do it, though other men refused, so though others refuse it not, *I* dare not do it, my conscience standeth against me. If I had, as I tolde you, looked but lightly into the matter, I shold have cause to feare, but now have I so looked and so long, that I purpose at the least to have no less regard for my soule, than had once a poor honest countryman, whom they called Company. Saying this, Alice, he told me a tale, and I ween I must tell it to you agayne, because it hangeth upon some foims and ceremonies of the law. As farre as I can call to mind, my father's tale was this. There is a court belonging of course to every fayre. This court hath a pretty fond name, but I cannot happen upon it, but it beginneth with a P, and the rest goeth much like the name of a knight that I have known, I wis, and I trowe you too, for he hath often been at my father's at such time as you were there, a metely, tall, dark man, hys name was Syr William Pounder. But let the name of the court go for this once, or call it if ye will a court of Syr William Pounder. But thys was the matter, that upon a time at such a court holden at Bartylmewe fayre, there was a London escheator that had arrested a man that was outlawed, and had sealed hys goods that he brought to the fayre. Thyss man that was arrested was from the North, and through hys friends he caused the escheator himself to be arrested, he had done something, I wot not what, and so was he brought before the judge of the court of Syr William Pounder, and at last the matter came to a certain ceremony to be tryed by a quest of XII men, a jury, as I remember they call it, or a perjury. Now, the clothman from the North had by favour of the officers found the means to have the quest almost made of the Northern men, such as had their boothes standing in the fayre. It had come to the after-noon of the last day, and the XII men had heard both par-ties, and theyre council tell their tales at the bar, and from thence they were had in a certain place to talk in common and agree as to their understanding, nay, let me use better terms, for I trow the judge giveth sentence, and the quests' tale is called a verdict.

"They had come in together, but the Northern men were agreed, and, indeed, the others too, to cast out the London escheator. They thought they needed no more to prove that he had done wrong than the bare name of his office, but there was amongst them an honest man of another quarter, that was called Company, and because the fellow seemed but a fool and sate still, and sayd nothing, they made no reckoning of hym, but sayd, 'come, we be agreed now, come let us give our verdict.' Then the poore fellow said that they made such haste, and his mind nothing gave him, that way that theirs did, if their minds were as they said, he prayed them to tarry and talk upon the matter, and give him reasons that he might think as they did, and when he should so do, he would be glad to say with them, or else they must excuse him, for sith he had a soule of his own to keepe as they had, he must say as he thought for hys, as they must for theirs. When they heard him talk thus they were angry with him.

" ' What ! good fellow,' quoth one of the North country-men, ' be we not eleven here, and thou but one alone, and all we agree, wherefore shouldst thou stick ; what is thy name, fellow ?'

" ' Masters,' quoth he, ' my name is called Company.'

" ' Company,' quoth they, ' now by thy teeth good fellow, play thou the good companion, come forth with us, and pass for good company.'

" ' Would God, good masters,' quoth the man, ' that there lay no more weight thereon, but when we shall go hence and come before God, and He shall send you to heaven for acting according to your conscience, and me to hell for acting against mine, in passing here at your request for good company, now, if I shall then, Master Dickenson, say to you all, "Masters, I went once with all of you for company's sake, so do some of you go with me now, would you go, Master Dickenson ? Nay, by our Lady, nay, never one of ye all, and so must you pardon me from passing as you pass, for if I think not in this matter as you do, I dare not, for the passage of my soul surpasseth all good company.'"

" When my father had told me of this tale, he further said—

" I pray thee now, good Margaret, wouldst thou wish thy poor father, being at least somewhat learned, less to regard the peril of his soul than did this simple and un-learned man ; I meddle not, you wot well with the conscience of any man that hath sworn, if I, on the contrary, with *my* conscience should pass on and swear with them, when our souls hereafter shall pass out of this world, and stand in judgment at the bar before the most high judge, if He judge them to heaven and me to hell, because I did as they did, not thinking as they thought, shold I then say as the good man Company said. "Mine own good lords and frendes," calling on them by name, yea, and bishops peradventure, of such as I love best, I swore because you swore, and went that way because you went; do now for me likewise, let me not go alone, if there be any friendship in you; come, some of you, come with me, by my troth, Margaret, I may say to you in secret between us two, but let it go no further, I find the friendship of this wretched world so fickle, that for all I might entreat and pray for friendship, amongst them all, I ween I should not find one, and if so, Margaret, I think best it is, were they twice as many as they are, that I should have respect for my own soul.'

" 'But surely, father,' I replied, ' you may be bold enough to swear without scruple for, father, they that think you should not refuse to swear the thing that you see so many good and learned men swear before you, do not mean that you should swear to keep them company, but that the esteem you may reasonably give to them, and their good qualities, should lead you to think the oath such as any man may take without danger, if *their* conscience be not the hindrance, and you have good cause to conform yours to theirs, being such as you know them to be, and sith father, it is commanded by a law made by the parliament, *they* think that you be on peril of your soul bound to reform your conscience, and conform it to that of others.'

" ' Margaret, Margaret,' he replied, ' for the part you play, you play it not amiss, but, my daughter, as to the laws of the land, though every man born and dwelling therein is bound to keep them under temporal punishment, and in many cases under God's displeasure too, yet is no man bound to swear that every law is well made, nor bound on pain of His displeasure to perform such points as were unlawful, of which kind there mayhap to be many in any part of christendom.'

" But, Margaret, for what cause I refuse the oath, that thing, as I have often told you, I will never show you, neither you nor any one else, except the King's highness should command me, but daughter, I have and do refuse it for no cause save one, this I am sure is already well known, that of them that *have* sworn some of the most learned before the oath was given them, plainly affirmed the contrary of such things as they have now sworn, and that upon their truth, and their learning, not in haste nor suddenly, but often after greate diligence done to find out the truth.

" ' That might be, father,' I replied, ' and yet since then, they might see,' —— He interrupted me, saying—

" I will not dispute, daughter, nor misjudge any man's conscience ; it lieth in their own heart far out of my sight, but this will I say, that *I* never heard the cause of their change, they had, I suppose, well weighed matters before they swore. I am glad for their sakes, but anything *I* ever believed before seemeth at this day as formerly ; therefore, though they may do otherwise yet, daughter, I may not, some say I may less regard their change, because the keeping in favour with the King, avoiding his anger, fear of losing their worldly wealth, and the unhappiness of their kinsfolk and friends may make some swear other than they think, or frame their conscience anew. Such opinion I will not hold of them, I have better idea of their virtue, for if such things should have turned them, the same had been likely to make me turn, for truly I know none so faint-hearted as I am ; and so, Margaret, I will think no worse of others than I do of myself, and as I know well my own conscience causeth me to refuse the oath, so will I trust in God that according to *their* consciences *they* have been able to receive and swear to it.

" But, Margaret, you urge that there are so many more on the other side ; but yet, thinking as I do, surely for your own comfort you should not suppose that your father casteth himself away like a fool, that he would jeopardise the loss of his property, and perhaps his life, without cause of peril to his soul, but rather endangering it thereby; but indeed, Megg, I nothing doubt that though not in this realm, yet throughout Christendom of the virtuous and learned men living the greater portion are of my mind. Besides, ye wot, it were possible that some in this realm too think not the contrary so clear as they have sworn to by the oath they have taken. So far for the living, go we now to them that are dead, and that are I hope in heaven ; I am sure they are not the fewest who all the time they lived believed as I do ; and I am sure of this, Megg, that of those holy saints and doctors which are in heaven long ago no Christian man doubteth, whose books at this day show they thought as I do. I pray God that my soul may follow theirs. I do not say all, Margaret, that I could, but for the rest, my daughter, as I have often told you, I take not upon myself to define or dispute. I rebuke or impugn no man's actions ; I never wrote or spoke in any company one word of reproach concerning anything that had passed through Parliament. I meddle not with any who say or think contrary to me ; but for myself, for thy comfort I say to thee, Margaret, my own conscience in this matter is such that it may stand with my salvation, of that, Megg, I am as sure as there is a God in heaven ; and . as for all the rest, goods, lands, and life (if it should so hap), since conscience speaks for me, I verily trust in God, He shall strengthen me to bear the loss rather than to swear against it, sith all the causes that I perceive move other men to the contrary make in me no change."

At hearing all this I felt very sad, for I promise you, sister Allington, my heart was full heavy at the peril of his life, for i' faith I feare not for his soule ; then he smiled, and said :

"How now, daughter Margaret, how now, mother Eve, upon what is your mind fixed ; sit not musing there with some serpent in your breast, intent upon some new persuasion to offer father Adam, the apple yet once again."

"In good faith, father," quoth I, "I am, as Cressida saith in Chaucer, coming to Dulcarno, even at my wit's ends ; for sith the example of so many wise men cannot move you, I see not what more to say unless I shall persuade you by the reason Master Harry Pattison made. He met one day one of our men, and asking where you were, and hearing you were in the Tower still, he waxed angry, and said : 'Why what aileth him that he will not swear, I have sworn the oath myself?' And in good faith I can go no further myself neither, but say with Master Harry, why should you refuse, father, for I have taken the oath myself."*

* Margaret took the oath, coupled with the clause, as "farre as it would stande with the lawe of God."

On my saying this he laughed, and said "that was like Eve too, for she had offered Adam no worse fruit than she had eaten herself."

"But father," said I, "I feel *very* sad, this matter will bring you into wondrous heavy trouble, you well know as I told you, Master Secretary sent you word as your friend to remember that the Parliament still lasteth."

To this, sister, he said:

"I thank him heartily, Margaret; but, as I have often told you, I have not left this matter unconsidered, albeit, I know that if they made a law to do me harm, that law could never be lawful, but God shall, I trust, keep me in grace, that, as concerns my duty to my King, no man shall do me harm; and then, as I told you, this is like a riddle, a case in which a man may lose his head and have no harm; but I have good hope that God will not surely suffer so good a Prince in such wise to requite the service of a true and faithful servant, yet sith there is nothing impossible, I forget not in this matter the counsel of Christ in the Gospel, that as I began to build this house for the safety of my soul, I should reckon up what the cost would be. I counted up, Margaret, in many a restless night, while my wife slept, what danger were possible to befal me, so far that I am sure it cannot be exceeded; and in thinking on it, daughter, my heart was very heavy; but still, for all that, I thank God I never thought to change, though the very worst might happen that I could possibly fear."

"To this, sister, I said sorrowfully:

"No, father, it is not the same to think on what *may* be, as it is to think on what *shal* be, as you shal later, Our Lord help you, if the case do so happen; then, perchance, you may think other than you do now, and peradventure it will be too late."

"My words, sister, touched him sensibly. 'Too late, daughter Margaret," he cried out. 'I beseech, O Lord, that if ever I *do* change, it may, indeed, be too late ; for well do I know the change would not be for the good of my soul, a change which groweth out of fear, and so I pray God that in this world I never benefit by such a change, for, inasmuch as I suffer here, I shall suffer less hereafter ; and if it were so that I should slip, and fall, and out of fear swear, then do I wish to be in danger by first refusing, as I shall have better hope of grace to rise again ; and though I well know that for my past sins I am well worthy God should let me fall, yet do I trust in His great goodness, that as He hath strengthened me hitherto, and made me content to lose all rather than to forswear my conscience, and hath put the King in that gracious mind to take from me only my liberty, by which his grace hath done me good by the spiritual profit it gives me (so that i' faith I reckon my imprisonment the greatest benefit). I cannot, therefore, doubt but that God will still keep the King in that same mind to do me no harm ; and if it be his will that I should suffer innocently, then his grace will strengthen me to bear it patiently, aye, and even gladly, too, and that, in union with the sufferings of His bitter passion, He will make it to serve as a release from the pains of purgatory, and moreover increase my reward in heaven. Mistrust Him, Meg, I will not, even though I should feel me faint—yea, even if I feel my fear so great as on the point of overthrowing me, I will yet call to mind how S. Peter began to sink for want of faith, and called on Christ to help him ; and thus will I, too, call on

Him, and He will grasp me with His holy hands, and amidst the stormy seas will bear me up from drowning; and, Margaret, were He to suffer me to fall and swear, and forswear, too, (which God forbid, for His tender Passion's sake,) and let me so fall that I may never win, yet will I trust that after all He will cast on me a loving glance as He did on S. Peter, and make me stand again and abide the shame and confusion of my fault; and once for all, Megg, this know I for certain, that without I so will, He will not let me forswear myself, and with good hope I commend myself to Him. But even were He to suffer me to perish, I shall yet serve to praise His justice; but truly, Margaret, I trust His tender pity will keep me safe, so to His mercy I commend me. Therefore, mine own good daughter, never trouble thyself for anything that may happen me in this life, for nothing *can* happen but that which God willeth, and I am very sure that whatever that may be, let it *seem* ever so bad, it shall, indeed, be the very best; and so, my dear child, I beg you, with all my heart, you and your sisters, and my sons also, comfort and help your good mother, my wyfe, of the minds of your good husbands in this matter, I have no doubt. Remember me to all of them, to my good daughter Allington and all my other friends, nieces, nephews, and relations, and to all our servants and children, and our acquaintances abroad. And I pray that both you and they may serve God, and be glad, and rejoice in Him; and if anything happen me that you would be loth to see, pray to God for me, but trouble not yourself, and I will pray earnestly to God for all of us, that we may meet in heaven, where we shall rejoice for ever, and never, never more, have any trouble or sorrow."

The above letter sent by Mistress Roper to her half sister,

Lady Allington, is an evidence that learned and virtuous as she was, Margaret had but a woman's heart and head, and so thoroughly and devotedly did she love her father, that there is small reason to doubt that her ardent desire to save his life, made her willing to shirk any close reasoning on the matter, for which he was ready to lay, if needs be, his head on the block. It is quite clear that she used every argument she could think of to persuade him to take the oath, and it is also plain, that with the majority of the best of those who had taken it, she had not entered deeply into the importance of the question it involved.

How any one can be found to express a doubt that More died a martyr, and for conscience sake, we can with difficulty understand, his own words, showing plainly that he did so; letters speak for themselves, and show far better the character of the person who wrote them than the opinions of others ; and all More's letters testify to one truth, namely, that at this time his mind was *so* settled, his convictions *so* firm, from the seven years' study of the question to which the King himself had led him, that no power on earth could now shake the one or disturb the other.

CHAPTER XVII.

SIR THOMAS MORE AND DR. WILSON.

THE following letters were addressed by More to Dr. Wilson, and we are sure will be read with interest. The latter had been the King's confessor, and was in the Tower on account of his refusal to take the oath :—

"Our Lord be your comforte.

"I perceive by sundry means that you have promised to swear the oath, I beseech Our Lord give you good fortune; I never gave any man contrary counsels, nor any way put scruples in the consciences of other folk concerning this matter.

"And as I perceive that you would gladly know what I intend to do, you wot well what I told you when we were both free, that I wished neither to know your mind nor any other man's, for I would not take part with any one, nor will I ever, but leaving all to their own consciences, I will myself with God's grace follow mine. Against mine own to swear, would be at the risk of damnation, and of what mine shall to-morrow be, I myself cannot be sure. And whether I shall have the grace to act according to it or not, dependeth on God's goodness and not on my own. I beseech you commend me to Him in your devout prayers, as I shall, and do now daily remember you in mine, such as they be. As long as my poor short life shall last, anything that I have you shall share therein."

ANOTHER LETTER FROM MORE TO THE SAME.

"Good Maister Wilson, in right hearty wyse, I commend me to you, and very sorry am I to see that beside the trouble you suffer by this imprisonment, with loss of liberty, goods, revenues of your living, and comfort of the company to your friends, you have fallen also into such anguish and trouble of mind through doubts, that trouble your conscience of your great heaviness of heart, as I (to no small grief of my own mind for your sake) do well perceive. And, good Maister Doctor, I am so much the more sorry for you because it lieth not in me to give you any kind of comfort, as it seems to me you desire and look for at my hands.

"You in your own doubts would know somewhat of my mind, but I am a man very little meet at present.

"You know well, good Maister Doctor, that at the time the matter came in question, and that my opinion was asked amongst that of others, you and I many times talked together thereof, and when I did by the King's gracious command seek out, and read, and commune, with such as I know were privy to the matter, to discover what I might, and by impartially weighing every thing as far as my poor wit and learning would serve me, to see to which side my conscience would incline and my mind guide me, so as to report to his highness what I should think therein, for in truth other commandment in this matter his grace never gave me saving this, to which he added, 'that I should look first to God, and after God to him,' which speech also was the first his Grace gave me when I first came into his noble service, and a more impartial commandment on a more gracious lesson, never to my mynde could King give his

servant ; but as I told you a long time since, I cannot now
tell how many years, or with whom I have conferred with of
this matter, also consulting the Scriptures and the holy
doctors, with the councils, and laws that also spoke thereof.
One whom I most conferred with was, as you wot well yourself, for with none did I associate so much, and so often, as
with you, both on account of your substantial learning and
your mature judgment, and because I perceived that no
man could have a more faithful respect to the King's honour
and safety, both of soul and body, than I saw that you had.
And beyond many things that I admired in you, one
especially was your careful secret manner in the thing the
King's grace entrusted you with, for I had heard (I wot not
from whom) that you had written a book on that matter,
and had sent it his grace from Paris, yet in all the long
years of our acquaintance, and often talking and reasoning
on the thing, I never heard you once make mention of that
book.   But else, except there were many other things in it
that you perchance did not think of afterwards, I suppose
all that ever came to your mind I might take in the matter
we considered together, as comprised in the Holy Scriptures
or taken from the ancient doctors.   I remember now well,
that of those points you now call afresh to your remembrance, there was not one at that time forgotten, also by
our constant conferences in the matter, that all the time in
which you and I studied the question, we were in every
point agreed.   I also remember well that the laws and
counsels and the words of S. Austin, *De Civitate Dei*, and
the epistle of S. Ambrose, *ad paternum*, the epistle of
S. Ambrose from the Greek, and the writings of S. Gregory,
we diligently studied together, and beyond these the

Scriptures, both Leviticus and Deuteronomy, the Gospels, and S. Paul's Espistles. Moreover various portions of S. Austin, which you will remember, in which he toucheth on the matter expressly, with the words of S. Jerome and S. Chrysostome, and I cannot recollect how many more.

"I think as regards you, and I am very sure of myself, albeit it had perchance been too long to read with you every man's book (that I read by myself or which others trusted me with, not giving me leave to show them further), as you perhaps also did by me, yet you and I having both one command to consider everything by Scripture and the Doctors, I faithfully communed with you as I suppose you did by me.

"So that from me, good Maister Doctor, though I had every point as fresh in my mind now as I had then, yet could you no new thing hear more than you have often heard before. Now, it standeth with me in far other case, for when I had signified to the King my own poor opinion in the matter which his highness took very graciously in good part, and that I did not see that I could do his grace further service in the matter to his pleasure, and meddle against his pleasure I would not, I resolved to rid my mind of any useless studying or thinking further about it, and thereupon I returned all the books that I had, save some that I burned by consent of the owner, so that, good Maister Doctor, I am not now able to discuss these points again, though were I so minded, sith many things are now out of my mind which I do not intend to look for again, and if I would, should not be likely to find. Besides, all that ever I looked for was, you well wot, concerning two or three questions to be pondered and weighed by the study of the

Scriptures, and the interpretations of the same, save some that had been affected by the canon laws of the Church. But then, there were other things at that time, faults found in the bull of dispensation, by which the King's counsel learned in the spiritual law, reckoned the bull defective partly by reason of false suggestion, partly of insufficient learning, concerning which points I never meddled, for I neither understand the doctors of the law, nor can well turn their books. Many things have since grown out of this matter, of which I am neither learned nor informed enough of the facts, and I am not one to murmur, grudge, make assertions, or entertain suspicions about the matter, but, like the King's poor humble subject, daily pray for the preservation of the King and Queen's grace, their noble offspring, and for the whole realm.

" Finally, as touching the oath, no man wotteth the causes for which I refused it ; they be secret in my own conscience, others perchance than those which men may ween, and such as I never disclosed, nor ever intend to do. Moreover, as I said to you before the oath was offered, when we met in London by chance, I would be no sharer with you in the matter, but for my own self follow mine own conscience, for which I must answer to God, and leave every man to his own. Every learned man knows well, that there are matters in which every one is at liberty, without peril of damnation, to think which way he listeth, till a certain point be determined by a general council, and I am not the man to define or determine of what nature everything is that this oath containeth, nor am I so presumptuous as to blame the consciences of others, their truth, nor their learning, no, I meddle only with mine own conscience, and of none else. I cry God mercy, I find in my own life matters enough to think upon. I have lived methinks a long life, and I neither look nor long to live much longer. Since I came into the Tower, I thought once or twice I should have given up the ghost ere this, and truly, mine heart waxed lighter with hope thereof, but forget I not that I have a long and great reckoning to give account of. But I trust in God, and in the merits of His bitter passion, and I beseech Him to give and keep me in the mind to long to be out of this world, and to be with Him, for I can never believe that he who longs to be with Him will not be welcome to Him; and furthermore, I am minded that any that shall come to Him, must full heartily wish to be with Him ere ever he shall come at Him. I beseech Him to fill your heart with such rest and quiet as may be to His pleasure, and the welfare of your soul, and that also, if it be His holy will, He will incline the King's noble heart to be gracious and favourable both to you and me, sith we two be of true and faithful mind to him, whether in *this* matter we be both of one or differ. And if the will of God be of either of us otherwise to dispose, I need give you no counsel nor advice. For myself, I humbly beseech Him, to give me grace patiently to conform my mind to His good pleasure, that after the troublesome storm of this tempestuous time, His great mercy may lead me to the sure haven of the blissful joys of heaven, and (if I have any) all my enemies also. For there shall we love together easily enough, and for myself I thank our Lord, so do I here to. Be not angry now, though I pray not the same for you, you may be sure I wish my friends should fare no worse than my enemies, nor they no worse than myself.

"For our Lord's sake, good Maister Wilson, pray for me, for I pray for you daily; sometimes, when I would be sorry for you, if I thought you not asleep. Console yourself, good Maister Doctor, by remembering God's great mercy, and the King's usual goodness. Verily, I think that all his grace's council favor you in their hearts. I cannot in my own mind judge so badly of any of them as to mean you otherwise than well. And, in conclusion, in God is all my hope, *Spes non confundis*. I pray you pardon my scribbling, for I cannot always write so well as I may at times. And I beg you, when you see time convenient, to answer me this rough billet."

The following letter was written by Sir Thomas to one Master Leder, a virtuous priest, the 16th of January, 1535 :—

"The tale that is reported, albeit I cannot but thank you, though you wold it were true, is, I thank God, a very vanity.

"I trust in the mercy of God that He will never suffer it to be true. If I had been obstinate I would not (let) scruple for any shame, plainly to confess the truth, for I do not depend on the praise of the world, I thank God that I do it for the weal of my soul, because I cannot think other than I do, concerning the oath, if ever I should swear it (I trust our Lord will never suffer me), ye may safely reckon it were extracted by rough handling. As for the goods of this world, I thank God I set no more store by them than I do by dust. I trust they will use no violent and forcible ways to me, and that if they do, God of His grace (the rather a great deal through the prayers of good folks) will give me strength to stand, for this, I am quite sure, if ever I should swear it, I should swear deadly against my conscience, for I am very sure my mind will never change. It hath been shown me that I am reckoned wilful and obstinate, because since coming hither, I have not written to the King's grace to make suit myself to his highn ess.I n good faith I do not forbear out of obstinacy, but rather from a reverent and lowly mind, because I see that I could write nothing but that which I fear his grace were likely to feel displeased with than otherwise, whilst he rather believeth me obstinate than that my conscience stands in my way; but God, to whom I commend the whole matter, knoweth better. *In cujus manu corda regi sunt.** I pray God that all may prove as true and faithful subjects to the King that *have* sworn, as I am very sure they be who have refused to swear. In haste, this Saturday, the 16th day of January, by the hand of your bedesman,

"THOMAS MORE, Knight, prisoner."

More did not neglect to point out to Margaret the utter illegality of his imprisonment. *No particular form* of the oath of succession had as yet been prescribed by the statute, either from accident or design, and Henry, taking advantage of the omission, afterwards modelled and re-modelled it at his pleasure, and a clause was added by which the clergy were required to declare that the Bishop of Rome had no more authority in the realm, than any other foreign bishop, and to acknowledge the king as supreme head of the Church.†
In autumn the parliament again assembled, and it was made treason for anyone to wish, or will *maliciously* against the

---

* In whose hand are the hearts of kings.
† Without the saving clause, " as far as the law of God will allow."

supremacy, and henceforward the oath of succession and the supremacy were included under one.*

" I may tell thee, Megg," he had once said to Margaret, "they who have committed me hither for refusing an oath not agreeable with their own statute, are not able by their own law to justify my imprisonment; it is a great pity that a Christian prince should be drawn to follow his affections by bad counsel, or by a frail clergy who lack grace, for want of which they fall away from learning, and abuse themselves with flattery."

The defect in the statute was remedied, as we have said above.

From time to time the unhappy Margaret visited her father, conveying to him such sums as she could bring from her own means or from the kindness of friends.

After several unavailing efforts Lady More at last obtained leave to see her husband.   Her first greeting could not have been pleasant to the prisoner, but most certainly it was characteristic of herself.

" What the good gear, Mr. More?" said she. " I marvel that you who have always been taken for a wise man now chose to play the fool. Abiding here indeed in this close and filthy prison, among the rats and mice, when you might have your liberty with the favour and good-will of the king and the council, if you would but do as others have done as learned as you, and seeing you have at Chelsea a

---

* It was not till after some struggle that the king yielded to the insertion of this qualification " maliciously." Arch. xxv. 795. At More's trial, however, the judges contrived to render it useless, by declaring that a refusal to acknowledge the supremacy was a proof of internal " malice."—LINGARD.

right fair house, your library, your garden, and all other necessaries about you ; and might be merry with your wife, your children, and your household !   I wonder why in God's name you tarry longer here."

Very calmly More heard this long speech ; then he said to her cheerfully :

"I pray thee, Alice, tell me one thing.   Is not this house as near heaven as my own ?"

Of course poor Lady More could not agree with her husband's lofty aspirations, so she uttered her usual ejaculations when angry, scornfully exclaiming :

" Twittle twattle, will this gear *never* be left ?"

" But say, Mistress Alice, is it not the truth ?"

" *Bone Deus*, man, will it never cease ? "

" Well then, Alice, if it be as I have said as near to heaven as my own house, why should I not be as happy here as there ? For were I but under the ground some seven years, and then to arise and go to that fair house of mine, I should not fail to find some therein that would bid me get out of it, and tell me it was none of mine.   What cause then have I to like a house that would so soon forget its master?   Again, tell me how long you think we may live to enjoy it."

"Some twenty years, may be."

"Truly; now an you had said a thousand, that would have been somewhat; and yet methinks he would be a bad merchant that would put himself in danger of losing eternity for a thousand years : how much the more if we are not sure to enjoy it for one day !"

Poor Lady More, however, she did her best for her husband in her own way, as we may see from the following

letter to Cromwell, written on account of her extreme
want.

"Right honourable and my especial gud Maister Secretarye,
—In my most humble wyse I recommend me unto your gud
maistershypp, knowlegying myself to be most deeply
boundyn to your gud maistershypp for your manyfold
gudnesse and lovying favor, both before this tyme and now
dayly and always shewyd towards my poure husband and
me. I pray Almyghtye God to continue your gudnes so
still, for thereupon hangith the greatest part of my poure
husband's comfert and myne. The cause of my wrytynge
at this tyme is to certyfy your espescial gud maystershypp
of my great and extreme necessyte, which on and besydes
the charge of my own house doe pay weekly 15 shillings
for bord-wages of my poure husband and his servant for the
mayntaining whereof I have been compellyd of verey
necessyte to sell part of myn apparell for lack of other
substance to make money of. Wherefore my most humble
petition and sewte to your maistershypp at this tyme is to
desyre your maistershypp's favorable advyce and counsell,
whether I may be so bold to attend upon the King's most
gracyouse highness. I trust theyr is no dowte in the cause
of my impediment, for the younge man being a ploughman
had been dyseased with the aggue by the space of three
years before that he departed. And besides this, it is now
fyve weeks sith he departed, and no other person dyseased
in the house sith he left. I humblye beseeche you especyal
gud maistershypp (as my only trust is, and as know not what
to doe, but utterly in this world to be undone) for the love
of God to consider the premisses; and thereupon of your
most abundant gudness, to shewe your most favourable helpe

to the comfortyng of my poure husband and me in this our
great hevynes, extreme age, and necesstye.   And thus we,
and all ours, shall dayly duryng our lyves pray to God for
the prosperous successe of your ryght honourable dygnyte.

By your poure contynuall Oratryx,

To the Ryght Honorable,   DAME ALIS MORE.

and her especyall gud Maister,

MAISTER SECRETARYE.*

" I wist a woman once," said Sir Thomas, writing of his
wife, "that came into a prison to visit of her charity a poor
prisoner there, who she found in a chamber, to say the truth,
meetely fair, and at leastwise it was strong enough, but
with matts of straw the prisoner had made it so warm, both
under the foot and round about the walls, that in these
things for the keeping of his health she was on his behalf
glad and well comforted.

" But among many other displeasures that for his sake she
was sorry. for, she was angry that he should have the
chambèr door upon him by night made fast by the gaoler,
'for by my troth,' (quoth she), 'if the door should be
shut upon me, I would ween it would stop up my breath.'

" At these words of hers, the prisoner laughed in his mind,
but he durst not laugh aloud, nor said he anything to her,
for somewhat, indeed, he stood in awe of her, for he had his
living there in much part of her charity for alms, but he
could not but laugh inwardly, while he wist well enough
she shut her own chamber door and windows too, and used
not to open them all the night, what difference then as to
the stopping of the breath whether they were shut within or
without ?   Thus it was, Eve supplanted and overthrew by

* Leonard Howard's Coll. of Letters.

her pleasant persuasions her husband, our first father Adam, yet could not this woman anything infringe or break the constant settled meekness and humility of this worthy man, no one in his extremity and adversity (no more than blessed Job's wife) could shake and overturn any part of his good patience. And yet surely no stronger or mightier temptation in all the world is there than that which proceedeth from the wife."*

We cannot but sympathise with the necessity and trouble of good Lady More, but how unfit was she to be the wife of such a man as Sir Thomas. An anecdote, translated from the Il Moro, and which we will quote as well as we can from memory, will show how little she could have appreciated those brilliant qualities and that glorious intellect which charmed all who came in his way, and which won for him the fatal esteem of the King, and his entrance within the Court circle. And yet a wife *ought* to be the intelligent companion of her husband's leisure hours.

" You were reading to your daughters," said one of More's friends, " on the nature of a line, and trying to make them understand that it consisted only of length, without breadth or thickness, when he had done, your lady called them into the hall, and said to them :—How very clever you are, children, where was the necessity for your father to worry his brains for an hour to show you what a line is ; look here, stupid children that you are, here is a line, pointing, as she spoke, to a beam of wood that crossed the hall."

* Harleian M.SS.

CHAPTER XVIII.

BEFORE THE COUNCIL.

IN spite of the vigilance of his gaolers, More not unfrequently exchanged letters with another of his fellow prisoners, the Venerable Bishop Fisher. That holy prelate was deprived of the common necessaries of life, and one of the tricks devised by Cromwell and the council was to lead each prisoner to think that the other had taken the oath. On one occasion, Margaret was on her way to the council-chamber with a petition she was about to present on her father's behalf, when she was met by Audley, who, aware of the cause of her being there, said to her—

"Your father is much to be blamed. Fisher resembled him, but he has become wiser, and has taken the oath."

"Are you quite sure of it, my lord?" said Margaret, giving a spring for joy, says Fisher's biographer.

"Yes, I am quite certain; Fisher is now with the King. You will soon see him in liberty and in great favour."

Margaret at once hastened to her father, and exclaimed in triumphant tones :

"Father, my Lord of Rochester has taken the oath."

"Silence, daughter," said More in accents of surprise, "it is not possible."

"The Lord Chancellor has just told me so."

"Away, away, thou foolish one," said More; "thou art not used to their tricks; but understand, if the bishop had done so, it would be no precedent for me."

Fisher was more simple, and believed those who told him that More had taken the oath; but though it added to his grief it did not shake his constancy.

"I am sorry that his courage hath failed him," said he; "yet should I not blame him, not being beset by the temptations of wife and children; but anyway, it affecteth me not, for unless I would make shipwreck of my conscience I cannot take your oath."

The communication between the holy prelate and his friend was, however, finally discovered, and the bishop's servant, who had carried the letters to and fro, was closely imprisoned, and even threatened with death. He is said to have been a simple countryman, and asked his gaoler, with an air of such perfect innocence and simplicity, if a new statute had been made to hang a servant for serving his master, that he obtained his liberty on condition that he should be the bearer of no more letters.

More had refused to believe the story concerning Fisher when told it by Margaret, but later he was called before the commissioners, who repeated it to him with unblushing deliberation. More then asked to speak with him, and was told he should do so as soon as he himself had taken the oath. "Let me see his signature, my Lords," was the next request, to which Audley replied that it had been taken to the King.

"Then, my Lords, I will candidly tell you," said More, "that I do not believe that my Lord of Rochester has either subscribed his hand or taken the oath; *and if he has done both I can do neither."* He was then taken back to his cell.

The following letter, addressed to Margaret, bears date May 3, 1535 :—

"OUR LORD BLESSE YOU, MY DEARLY BELOVED DAUGHTER.

"Doubtless you have heard that there came hither lately the king's councillors to examine three fathers of the Charter House, who be now judged to death for treason, whose causes I know not. Mayhap this may put you in trouble and fear concerning me being here prisoner, especially as it is not unlikely you may have heard that I also was myself before the council. So I thought it necessary to advertise you of the truth, so that you should neither conceive more hope than the matter giveth, lest upon another turn it might aggrieve your heaviness; nor more grief and fear than the matter giveth on the other side.

"Shortly ye shall understand that on Friday, in the last day of April, Master lieutenant came in here unto me, and showed me that Master secretary would speak with me, whereupon I shyfted my gown, and went out with him into the gallery, where I met many, some known and some unknown, in the way. And in conclusion coming into the chamber where his mastershypp sat with Master attorney, Master solicitor, Master Bedyll, and Master Doctor Tregonnell, I was offered to sit down with them, which in no wise I would. Master secretary then showed unto me that he doubted not but that I had by such friends as had resorted unto me seen the new statutes made at the sitting of the last parliament. I answered : 'Yes, verily; howbeit, forasmuch as being here I have no conversation with any people." I thought it little with need for me to bestow much time upon them, and therefore I gave back the book, and the effect of the statutes I neither marked nor studied to remember. Then he asked me if I had not read the *first* statute, of the King being head of the Church, whereunto I answered 'Yes.'

"Then his mastership declared unto me, that since it was now by act of parliament ordained that his highness and his heirs be and ever of right *have* been, and perpetually *should* be supreme head on earth of the Church of England under Christ, the King's pleasure was that those of his council there assembled should demand my opinion and what my mind was therein. Whereunto I answered that in good faith I had well trusted that the King's highness would never have commanded any question to be asked of me, considering that I from time to time declared my mind to his highness, and also your mastership, Master secretary, by mouth and by writing. And now I have in good faith discharged my mind of all such matters, and neither *will* dispute king's titles nor pope's ; but the King's true faithful subject I am, and will be, and daily I pray for him, and all his, and for you all that are of his honourable council, and for all the realm, and otherwise than this I never intend to meddle. Master secretary answered, that he thought this manner of reply would not content nor satisfy the King's highness, but that his grace would exact a more full answer, and his mastership added, that the King's highness was a prince, not of rigour but of mercy and pity ; and though he had found obstinacy at some time in any of his subjects, yet when he should find them at another time submit and conform themselves, his grace would show mercy ; and that concerning myself his highness would be glad to see me take such conformable ways, as I might be abroad in the world again amongst other men, as I had been before. Whereto I answered, I would never meddle in the world again, to have all the world given me; and as to the rest of the matter I have fully determined never to meddle or study any worldly concern, but that my whole study should be on the passion of Christ and my own passage out of the world.

"They then sent me away for a while, and after called me in again, when Master secretary said: 'Though you are a prisoner condemned to perpetual imprisonment, you are not discharged of your obedience to the King's highness;' and he asked of me whether I thought that the King's grace might not exact of me upon like pains as other men. Whereto said I, 'I will not maintain the contrary.' And said he: 'Even as the King's highness will be gracious to them that be found conformable, so will his grace follow the course of law to such as be obstinate,' adding, 'your demeanour in this matter is such as very likely makes others as stiff as they be.' Whereto I answered, 'I give no man cause to hold any point one way or the other, nor never gave any man advice or counsel.' And, in conclusion, I could no further go, whatsoever pain should come thereof. 'I am,' quoth I, 'the King's true faithful subject and daily bedesman, and pray for his highness and all his and all the realm; I do nobody no harm; I say none harm, I think none harm, but wish everybody good. And if this be not enough to keep a man alive, in good faith I long not to live. And I am dying already, and have since I came here been many times in the case that I thought to die within one hour. And I thank our Lord I was never sorry for it, but rather sorry when I saw the peril past, and therefore my poor body is at the king's pleasure. Would God my death may do him good.'

"After this Master secretary said : ' Well, ye find no fault in that statute, find you any in any of the *other* statutes after?' I answered : ' Sir, whatsoever thing should seem to me other than good in that, or in any of the other statutes, I will not declare what fault I find, nor speak of it.' To which he said gently, that of anything I had spoken there should be no advantage taken ; and whether he farther said that there was none to be taken I am not well remembered ; but he added that report should be made unto the King's highness, and his gracious pleasure known Whereupon I was delivered again to Master lieutenant, which was then called in, and so was I brought again into my chamber. And here am I yet in such case as I was, neither better nor worse. That that shall follow lieth in the hands of God, whom I beseech to put in the King's grace's mind that thing that may be to His high pleasure, and in mine to mind only the weal of my soul with little regard of my body, and you with all yours, and my wife, and all my children, and all our other friends, both bodily and spiritually heartily well to fare. And I pray you and them all to pray for me, and take no thought whatsoever shall happen me, for I verily trust in the goodness of God, seem it never so evil to this world, it shall indeed in another world be for the best.

"Your loving Father,

"Thomas More, Knight."

Another letter, written by Sir Thomas to his daughter, Mistress Roper :—

"OUR LORD BLESSE YOU AND ALL YOURS.

" Forasmuch (dearly beloved daughter) as it is likely that you have heard that the council were here this day, and that I was before them, I have thought it necessary to send you word how the matter standeth. And verily, to be short, I perceive little difference between this time and the last, for, as far as I can see, the whole purpose is to drive me to say precisely one way or the other.

"Here sat my lord of Canterbury, my Lord Chancellor, my lord of Suffolk, my lord of Wiltshire, and Master secretary. And after my coming Master secretary told me he had reported unto the King's highness what had been said by his grace's council unto me, and my answers to them, which I heartily thanked him for. Whereupon he added that the King's highness was neither content nor satisfied with me, but thought I had been the cause of much grudge in the realm, and that I had an obstinate and an evil mind towards him, that my duty being his subject was (and he had sent them in his name to command me on my allegiance) to make plain answer, did I think the statute lawful or not, that he should be supreme head of the Church of England, or else utter plainly my malignity.

"' I have no malignity, and so can none utter,' said I. ' And as to the answer, I can make none other than I have made before. And very grieved I am his highness should have such opinion of me, howbeit, I shall comfort myself with considering that the time will come when God shall declare my truth before his grace and all the world ; and though haply it may seem small cause of comfort, because

I must take harm here first, in the meanwhile, I thanked God I was very sure I had no corrupt affection, looking first upon God, then upon the King, according to the lesson his highness taught me at my first coming to his noble service, the most virtuous ever prince taught a servant. The opinion he has of me now is to my great grief ; I have no means to help it, in this matter further I could not go, nor other answer make.'

" ' But,' said both the Lord Chancellor and Master secretary, ' the king may *compel* you to make a plain answer one way or the other.'   Whereto said I : ' I will not dispute the King's authority, but verily, under correction, it seemeth to me, if my conscience give me against the statute (wherein it giveth me I do not say), that, I nothing doing or saying against it, it is hard to make me say for or against, to the peril of my soul or the destruction of my body.'

"To this said Master secretary : ' When you were in office you examined heretics and malefactors, whether they believed the Pope to be the head of the Church, and compelled them to make a precise answer ; and why should not the King, sith it is a law made that his Grace is head of the Church here, compel men to answer now as they were then compelled to answer about the Pope ?'

" ' I protest,' quoth I, ' that I wish not to stand in contention ; but there is this difference, that here, as through the whole of Christendom, the power of the Pope was considered an undoubted thing, not like a thing agreed on in this realm.'   To which said Master secretary, they were as well burned for denying that as beheaded for denying this, and as good reason to make them answer one as the other. ' A man is not so bound in conscience by a law of one realm,' said I, 'when there is a law of all Christendom to the contrary, touching a point of belief, though there hap to be made in some place a law to the contrary.'

"Then they offered me an oath, by which 1 should make true answer to such things as should be asked me on the King's behalf.

"'Verily, I never mean to swear any book oath more, as long as I live,' said I.

"'Then,' said they, 'I was very obstinate, for of all those brought to the star-chamber there are none who have not taken a similar oath.'

"'Very true,' said I; 'but I can understand what your questions will be, and as good to refuse them at first as at last.'

"My Lord Chancellor said he thought I guessed the truth, and I should see them. There were but two; the first was, had I seen the statute? the second, did I believe it lawfully made? At once I refused the oath, saying that the first I had confessed to, to the *second* I would make no answer.

"This was the end of my examination, and I was sent away. In the former communication it was wondered at that I should take thus much on my conscience; whereto I said I was very sure my conscience, informed by much diligence, might stand with my salvation; I meddle not with the consciences of those who think otherwise, I am no man's judge.

"And they also said: 'If you had as lief be out of the world as in it, why not speak out plain? It appears you are not content to die, though you say so.' 'The truth is,' I replied, 'I have not led so holy a life as to bold enough to offer myself for death, lest God for my temptation suffer me to fall; therefore I put not myself forward, but draw back. Howbeit, if God draw me to it Himself, then trust I in His great mercy, that He will not fail to give me grace and strength.'

"'I like you much worse to-day than I did the last time,' said Master secretary; 'then I pitied you, now I think you mean not well.'

"But God and I know both that I do mean well, and so I pray God do by me. I pray you and mine other friends be of good cheer, whatsoever befal me. Take no thought of me, but pray for me, as I do for you and all of them.

"Your tender loving father,

"Thomas More, Knight."

After the examination recorded above, the councillors looked significantly at each other, and withdrew, pausing as they left the Tower to bid Kingston exercise strict vigilance over Sir Thomas; the lieutenant at once understood that there was small hope for the ex-chancellor.

This Kingston was one of those good souls who never forget a service rendered to them. In the days of the ex-chancellor's prosperity he had never been repulsed by him, More always feeling pleasure at granting various requests made to him. And now that so sad a reverse had befallen Sir Thomas, he strove, when unseen, by every means in his power to soften the severity of his imprisonment. One day he himself carried to More's cell a delicate little dish, and complained in a whisper of bringing him no better cheer; but, he added, "I am watched, and walls have eyes as well as ears. I cannot alter matters without incurring the King's displeasure, so must beg you to accept my good will."

"I believe you, good Kingston," answered More; ' and I thank you most heartily for it. Assure yourself I do not mislike my ordinary fare ; when I do, then spare not to thrust me out of your doors."

"And notwithstanding their new law was worse than the former, yet was there no matter (I will not say) by right and justice, but not so much as by their own unlawful and unjust law, to be found in him, that their adversaries might with any outward honest appearance have, what they sought for, that was, his life's blood, for he neither spoke or did any thing to bring himself within the least compass and danger of the said law."

The usual quiet of More's prison lodging was one morning disturbed by the sound of many footsteps, and looking through the narrow barred window of his cell, he beheld in the court yard beneath, these same monks of the Charter House, and Father Reynolds, of Sion, being led out of the Tower. They were then bound, and taken to Tyburn, about three miles from London, to be executed.

" For the withstanding of which about two months before Sir Thos. More suffered, the Prior of the Charter House of London, the Priors of the Charter House of Benold and Spain, and Father Reynolds, a singular learned divine, well seen in the Latin, Greek, and Hebrew tongues, a virtuous religious father of Syon, and one Mr. John Hall, vicar of Thistleworth, were the 29th of April condemned of treason, and executed the 4th day of May."

"Afterwards the 9th of June were there other of the said

Charter House of London, hanged and quartered, and eight or nine of the said house died by reason of the closeness and filthiness of the prison in Newgate."*

"Look, Meg," said More, to his daughter, who was with him, "Dost thou not see those good Fathers† going to death as if they were bridegrooms about to be married. See then, good Margaret, what a difference there is between such as have spent their life religiously, and such as have, like thy poor father, spent their time in ease and pleasures. For God, considering their long life in continued penance, will not suffer them longer to inhabit this miserable world, but taketh them speedily hence; whilst thy poor father, not worthy of so great happiness, is condemned still to continue in this vale of wretchedness and sin !"

This spectacle, which met the eyes of More in the presence of his daughter, only preceded his own execution by about six weeks, most probably it was almost Margaret's last visit, for his confinement appears to have become more rigorous henceforth.

A few moments later Cromwell, the King's minister of evil, entered More's cell, anxious to see the effect that the execution of the Carthusian victims might have on the prisoner, but his countenance was radiant with joy. In the name of the King, Cromwell remonstrated with More on the course he was pursuing, for on this day he did not venture on threats, and for his comfort told him that the King was still his good and gracious Lord, and did not urge him on any

* Harleian MSS.

† These three orders of the Carthusians, Briggitins, and Observants (Reformed Franciscans) had a reputution for the greatest regularity.— Campbell.

matter in which he could have cause of scruple.   As soon as Master Secretary had departed, to express the kind of comfort his words had given him, he took a piece of coal, and wrote the following lines :—

> Aye, flattering fortune, look thou ne'er so fair,
>   Or ne'er so p'easantly begin to smile ;
> As though thou would my ruin all repair,
>   Throughout my life thou shalt not me beguile.
> Trust I to God to enter in a while
>   His haven of heav'n, sure and uniform ;
>   Ever after calme, look I for a storm.

CHAPTER XIX.

'TWIXT EARTH AND HEAVEN.

WINTER brought with it many hardships to the aged prelate. Fisher had been for many months confined in the Bell Tower, and he was now reduced to a state of destitution, in which he had not sufficient clothes to cover him, and he was repeatedly and treacherously examined by commissioners with regard to his private opinions relative to the supremacy, and left almost without food to eat, sometimes supplied by More with a portion of his own ; he was never allowed a drop of wine, his clothes were tattered and falling to pieces, and after many supplications he at last obtained a pen and a sheet of paper, on which he traced a few trembling lines to Cromwell.

"Have mercy on me," writes the aged man, "I have neither shirt, linen, nor garments, I am ashamed of my nakedness, but I could bear with my poverty, if I could get warmth for my body. I have not enough to eat, and God knoweth, at my age one hath many wants, if I am thus left in want of common necessaries, I must speedily sink. I beseech you in the name of common charity beg of the King to restore me his gracious bounty. I should feel very grateful if he would take me from this cold prison. Two favours I ask of yourself: one is to let me see a priest to whom I may make confession for the approaching feast of Christmas, also that a volume of prayers be lent me; and may our Lord grant you a happy New Year and many of them."

"Though both Sir Thomas More and the Bishop of Rochester refused the oath of supremacy, both offered to swear another oath for the succession of the Crown to the issue of the King's present marriage, because *that* was in the power of Parliament to determine, Cranmer foreseeing well the ill effects that would follow on contending so much with persons so highly esteemed by the world, and of such a temper that severity would bend them to nothing, did by an earnest letter to Cromwell, dated the 27th of April, move that what they offered might be accepted; for if they once swore to the succession, it would quiet the kingdom, for *they* acknowledging, all other persons would acquiesce and submit to their judgments."*

If some of the historians are to be believed, Henry waited awhile, hoping that a natural death would deliver him from Fisher, but death did not seize upon him, he was to receive the crown of martyrdom at his hands.† Clement VII. was no more, and Paul III. had succeeded him. One of the first thoughts of the new Pope, was to reward by a Cardinal's hat the heroism and virtue of Fisher. Hearing that a messenger was on the road in order to bring the emblem of this dignity to the Bishop of Rochester, the King forbade him to land at Dover, and then in order to ascertain what impression the news of this favour from the Pontiff would have on the aged Bishop, he sent Cromwell to visit the prisoner.

* Weever Monuments, p. 504.
† Audin.

"What would you say, my lord," said the latter, "if I told you that the Pope is sending you the hat of a Cardinal. Would you accept it?"

"I should consider myself unworthy of it," replied Fisher, "but if the Pope did such a thing, *I would receive it on my knees,* with respect and gratitude."

This answer was carried back to Henry, who, enraged at the Bishop's dauntless conduct, exclaimed—

"Mother of God, he shall wear it on his shoulders then, for I will see he hath never a head to set it on."*

We have already quoted from the Harleian MSS. respecting the library of valuable books possessed by Fisher, all his property had been seized by the royal tyrant, and as the pursuivants wandered through the house, searching for valuable property, they hit upon a chest in his chamber, bound with iron. Fancying it contained valuable property, they broke it open, but found that it contained only a hair-shirt and some disciplines. It was a source of great vexation to Fisher, who said that had he but remembered it in the hurry of his leaving home, the contents of the chest would never have been found.

It was hoped that the great sufferings of the bishop would have made him lose his courage, but he remained inflexible, and eventually Rich, the solicitor-general, was sent to him as bearer of a message from the King. He entered the captive's dungeon with a smile upon his face, saying that his Majesty desired to know the mind of so enlightened a prelate as to the supremacy which parliament had recognised as an attribute of royalty. "The prince has

---

* Tytler.

many scruples," added Rich, begging the prisoner to speak out fearlessly.

The old prelate grew courageous. " More than once," said he, "have I spoken on this subject with his Majesty ; it is not now, when my days are numbered, that I can change my former opinions. I think now, as I did formerly, that if the King is solicitous about his salvation he will put away this notion of spiritual supremacy."

To this remark Rich made no reply, but at once withdrew.

Audley, under the great seal, issued a special commission for the trial of Fisher and More, placing himself at the head of it. As less skill was apprehended from the aged prelate in defending himself, and there was a colouring against him from the infamous arts of Rich, the wary Audley began with him first, although the conviction of the ex-chancellor was an object of far greater importance. Scarcely able to stand at the bar of Westminster Hall from age and weakness, he was charged with having traitorously attempted to deprive the King of his title by maliciously speaking these words : "The Kyng oure Soveraign Lord is not supreme Hedd yn Erthe of the Cherche of Englande."

The only witness for the Crown was Rich, the solicitor-general, who, though supposed not to have exceeded the truth in stating what had passed between him and the prisoner, covered himself with infamy, for he had the baseness voluntarily to swear that in a private conversation he had held with the bishop when paying him a friendly visit in the Tower, he heard the prelate declare that he believed in his conscience, and by his learning he assuredly knew, that the King neither was nor by right could be supreme head of the Church of England. He now saw the snare that had been laid for him by Rich, and then this aged prelate, bending beneath the infirmities of age, pleaded his own cause without the aid of counsel, which could not be permitted against the crown.

"Mr. Rich," said he, "I cannot but marvel to hear you come and bear witness against me of these words. This man, my lords, came to me from the King, on a secret message as he said, with kindly words and commendations from his grace, declaring what good opinion his Majesty had of me, and how sorry he was for my trouble, and then broke the matter of the supremacy, telling me the King had sent him in the most secret way to know my opinion; and when I warned him the new act of parliament might endanger me if I said aught against its provisions, he replied 'that the King willed him to assure me, *upon his honour and on the word of a King*, that whatsoever I should say unto him I should not abide peril for it, though my words were ever so against the statute;' and the messenger gave me his most solemn promise that he would repeat my words to no living soul save the King alone. And therefore my lords, seeing it pleased his Majesty to send to me thus secretly to know my poor advice and opinion, methinks it is very hard to allow the same as sufficient testimony against me to prove me guilty of high treason."

Then observed Rich:

"I said to him no more, my lords, than his Majesty commanded, and I argue, as counsel for the crown, that assuming the statement to be true, it is no discharge in law against his Majesty for a direct violation of the statute."

The malicious Audley then decided, and his opinion was shared in by the other judges, that this promise from the King neither did nor could by rigour of law discharge him. He had declared his mind and conscience against the supremacy; yea, though it were at the King's own request. he committed treason, and nothing could save him but the King's pardon.

"But," still urged the venerable prelate, "it is only treason *maliciously* to deny the King's supremacy; I cannot surely be guilty for expressing an opinion to the King himself by his own order."

" Malice does not mean spite or ill-will in the vulgar sense, but is an inference of law," replied Audley; "if the King's supremacy be spoken against, that speech is to be held and understood as malicious."

" But in my case," urged the prelate, " there is but one witness, which in treason you know is insufficient."

His objection puzzled the court; but, determined to have the old man's blood, Audley replied, with a shameless violation of the rule :

" This is a case in which the King *personally* is concerned ; the necessity for two witnesses does not hold good ; the jury will consider the evidence, and as they believe or disbelieve so will you be acquitted or condemned."

The bright glorious sunshine flashed across the wan and haggard face of the venerable prelate, as he raised his sunken eyes to the infamous Audley and the parasites who sat beside him.

Audley had indeed so scandalously aggravated the case, straining it to high treason, that the jury at once perceived the verdict they must return, unless prepared to heap danger on their own heads, which none of them cared to brave.

Yet in the crowded court that day were many present whose faces were bathed in tears when they looked on that venerable father of the Church, about to be sentenced to a cruel death on evidence given contrary to all faith, and the promise of the King himself.

The jury in a short time returned; they brought in a verdict of *guilty*.

The aged prelate lifted his emaciated hands to heaven, and prayed God to forgive those who persecuted him unto death. And Audley arose, and putting on a grave and solemn countenance, he passed sentence of death in the revolting terms usual on such occasions, ordering that his head and four quarters should be set up where the King should appoint, and ending by the mockery of a prayer that God would have mercy on his soul.

The Bishop was no longer placed in the Bell Tower, but conveyed to a dreary dungeon beneath the fortress, wherein he was confined till the day fixed for his execution. Early one morning the lieutenant came to bid him prepare for his approaching end. "One day, more or less my lord," said he in a broken voice, "the will of his Grace is that this morning."

"Thanks, I understand; at what hour?"

"At nine, my lord."

"What is the hour now?"

"Just five."

"I will then sleep two hours longer."

"The will of the King is that you should not address the people"

" His Grace may rest content."

And the Bishop again fell asleep.

At seven he arose and dressed himself carefully, clothes having been given to him, and on the rugged walls of that fearful dungeon, within which we have reverently stood, for it has been hallowed by the presence of the holy bishop, he scratched these words :

" Here I put on my garments, and am led forth to be executed."

And then he leaned him against the dungeon wall with breviary in hand. As he left the Tower he opened a copy of the New Testament, at the 17th chapter of S. John's Gospel :

" *Now this is life eternal, that they might know Thee the only true God, and Jesus Christ, whom Thou has sent. I have glorified Thee on the earth : I have finished the work which Thou gavest me to do.*"

At length the cart, in which he was conveyed, reached Tyburn, and having ascended the scaffold, he turned him to the people saying,

" I die for our holy faith, pray for me ; may God receive my soul, and save the King and his people."

And the bright beams of the morning sun shone on the face of the holy prelate, and clasping his hands, and raising his eyes to heaven, he exclaimed,

" *Approach unto Him and be enlightened, and your faces shall not be confounded.*"

Then he sung the *Te Deum Laudamus* in so loud a voice that the spectators wondered when they gazed on his emaciated frame, and the glorious hymn of praise concluded, as also the Psalm *In te Domine Speravi*, the executioner

bound a handkerchief about his eyes, and the holy
prelate raised his heart to heaven, for his lips were seen to
move in prayer, then laying his venerable head on the block,
he received the blow which severed it from his body at a
single stroke.

His remains were at once stripped, left exposed on the
scaffold throughout the day, and then buried with every
kind of indignity in a grave in All Hallows Church, Barking,.
the soldiers having dug it with their halberds. The head
was said to be preserved from corruption, the lips remaining
red, and the king after a time ordered it to be thrown into.
the Thames.

CHAPTER XX.

Looking for the End.

MEANWHILE the time was fast approaching which should decide the fate of the other illustrious captive, whom the King was so vindictively pursuing; if until now, Margaret and her father had counted on the latter being contented with the incarceration of his victim, the fate of the venerable prelate, eminent as he was in learning and virtue, must have assured them that there was scant ground for hope that imprisonment alone would content the ruthless Henry.

Never was he left long at rest. Soon came to his cell Mr. Rich, Sir Richard Southwell, and one Palmer, deputed by the King to take away all his books.

Whilst Southwell made up in a parcel the books and manuscripts, Rich took Sir Thomas aside and led him towards the window of his prison, signing to his companions to pay attention to whatever the prisoner might say.

But Southwell and Palmer, touched with pity, did not care to listen, they looked with compassion on the bent form of the venerable prisoner, and turned away as if intent on their work.

A few indifferent words passed, and a smile played on the countenance of Rich as he meditated his address to the unfortunate prisoner.

"Truly, Sir Thomas More," said he, after a silence of several minutes, "I marvel at you. I know you are a man both wise and learned ; you are a great lawyer, a profound logician. I pray you, sir, let me be so bold as to put a question to you. Suppose an act of parliament were made, that all the realm should take me for king, would not you take me for King also ? "

"Yes, truly," said More.

"Marry," said Rich, with an air of frankness, "I put the question further. Suppose there was an act of parliament to take me for Pope, would not you then take me for Pope ? "

"That is quite another thing," said More; "the parliament has power to meddle with the state of temporal princes. But before replying to your second question I ask you, supposing parliament should make a law that God should not be God, would you then, Mr. Rich, give it your assent ? "

"No, Sir Thomas," replied Rich indignantly ; " no parliament could make such a law." Rich added a sequel.

" No more could the parliament make the King supreme head of the Church," was the answer which Rich gave as the reply of More, and upon it he was afterwards indicted of high treason.

And his beloved books, the solace of the dreary hours of his captivity, were all removed ; then he closed his windows, saying with an irrepressible touch of his old humour, " When all the tools and wares are gone, the shop windows may be shut up."

Then he sharpened pieces of coal, which he found in the grate, and he wrote on the wall of his cell, the following sentences from the Psalms :—

"Who will give me wings like a dove, that I may fly away and take my rest."

"In peace, in the selfsame, I will sleep and I will rest."

"Taste, and see how sweet is the Lord."

There is something most pathetic in the fact that during his dreary imprisonment, which began in April, 1534, he, commencing his "Treatise on the Passion of Christ," continued it down to the words, "*And they layde hands upon Him, and held Him*," for says the old biographer, "Sir Thomas More wrote no more of this work, for when he had written thus farre, he was in prison kept so straighte, that all his bookes and pennes and ynke and paper were taken from him, and soon after was he put to death."

The following letter from Margaret to her father, alluding to his close imprisonment, shows that after the visit of Rich, he was now confined more rigorously than had previously been the case :—

"My own most entirely beloved Father,—I can never give you sufficient thanks for the inestimable comfort my poor heart received in the reading your most loving and godly letter, representing to me the dazzling brightness of your soul, that pure temple of the Holy Spirit of God, which I doubt not will perpetually dwell in you and you in Him. Father, if all the world had been given me, as I hope to be saved, it would have been a trifling pleasure in comparison of the joy I received at the treasure of your letter, which, though written with a coal, is worthy of being written in letters of gold. Father dear, what moved them to shut you up again, we can nothing hear. Truly, I conjecture that when they found your mind so well tempered, that you were contented to abide there all your life with *such* liberty as you already had, they thought it was never possible to bend you to their will, except it were by restraining you from the Church, and the society of my good mother, your dear wyfe, and your poor children, and bedesfolk.   But, father, this chance was not strange to you —for I need not remind you how you told us when we were with you in the garden, that these things were like enough to chance you later.   Father, I have often repeated to my own comfort, and that of others, your demeanour and the words you said to us when we were last with you, for which I trust, by God's grace, to be the better while I live, and when I am departed out of this perishable life, which I pray God I may pass, and end in true obedience and service to Him, after the wholesome counsel and faithful example of holy living I have had (good father) of you, which I pray God give me grace to follow, which I shall the better ensure through the aid of your devout prayers, as a special support to my frailty.

" Father, I am sorry I have just now no longer leisure to talk with you, the chief comfort of my life, I trust to have occasion to write again shortly.   I hope I have your daily prayers and blessing.

" Your most loving obedient daughter and bedeswoman, Margaret Roper, which daily and hourly is bounden to pray for you, for whom she prayeth in this wise, that Our Lord of His infinite mercy, give you of His heavenly comfort, and so to assist you with His special grace that ye never in anything decline from His blessed will, but live and die His true obedient servant.   Amen.

The reply to this letter is as follows :—

"A letter written by Sir Thomas, to his daughter, Mistress Roper, answerynge her letter here next before.

THE HOLY SPIRIT OF GOD BE WITH YOU.

"If I could with my writing, declare mine owne good daughter, how much pleasure and comfort, your daughterlye loving letter were unto me, a peck of coals would not suffice for pens. And other pens, dear Margaret, have I none here, and therefore can I write you no long letter, nor dare venture, good daughter, to write often. The cause of my close imprisonment again did likely grow out of my careless and very plain true words which you remember, and truly as my mind imagined, as I told you in the garden, that some such thing were likely to happen ; so doth my mind always warn me. Some folks weened that I was not so poor as appeared .in the search, and it may therefore happen that eftsoon, oftener than once, new and sudden searches may happe to be made in every house of ours, as narrowly as possible, which thing if ever it should so hap, can make but gaine to us who know the truth of my poverty, but suppose they find out my wyfe's gay girdle, and her golden beads ! However, I verily believe in good faith, that the King's grace of his benign pity, will take nothing from *her*. I thought, and yet think, that it may be I was shut up again, and some new cause suspected, grown perchance out of some secret sinister information, whereby some folks thought, there should be found out against me some other greater things. But, I thank the Lord, whenever this conjecture hath crossed my mind, the clearness of my conscience hath made my heart leap for joy. For one thing am I very sure of hitherto, and trust in God's mercy to be while I live, that as I have often said to you, I shall for anything regarding my prince never take great harm, though I take great wrong, in the sight of God, I say, however it shall seem in the eyes of men.

"To the world, wrong seems right, sometimes by wrong conjecturing, sometimes by false witnesses, as that good lord said unto you, who is, I dare say, *my* very good lord in his own mind, and said it of very good will. By the world, Margaret, my refusing of this oath is considered a heinous offence, and my religious fear of God is called obstinacy towards my King. But my lords of the council, before whom I refused the oath, might well perceive by the heaviness of my heart, appearing to them in more ways than one, that all sturdy stubborness whereof obstinacy groweth, was very far from my mind. For a clearer proof, which they seemed to take for an argument of obstinacy in me, that refusing the oath I would not state the cause why I opposed with a full and heavy heart, and albeit, that I would rather endure all the pain and peril of the statute than by declaring the cause give any exasperation to my sovereign, yet I would upon his gracious license as should discharge me of his displeasure and any peril of the statute, declare those points that made my poor conscience refuse what others had sworn to, and if I should, after disclosing the cause, find them answered in a way to satisfy my conscience, I would then swear the oath I now refused. To this Maister Secretary answered me, that though the King's grace gave me such leave, it could not discharge me against the statutes in saying anything prohibited by them under severe penalties. In this he showed himself my friend, and now you see clearly, Margaret, it is no obstinacy to leave the causes undeclared as I could not without danger declare them. But it is counted obstinacy that I refuse the oath for any cause whatever, considering that many wiser and better men have not stuck thereat, and Maister Secretary, out of the great zeal he hath for me, swore before them a great oath that on account of the displeasure he thought the King would bear me, and the suspicion he would have that the business of the nun was wholly devised by me, he had rather than that I should have refused the oath see his only son (a goodly youth of whom our Lord send him much joy) had had his head stricken off. This, Margaret, was a wondrous declaration of Master Secretary's great good mind and favor towards me, but was a sad hearing to me that the King's grace were likely to bear me such indignation for the thing which layeth not in my power to help. I have heard some say since that this obstinacy of mine may perchance force the King's grace to make a further law for me, but I am sure that if I die by such a law, I die innocent before God. Albeit, good daughter, I think our Lord, who hath the hearts of kings in His hands, will never in His goodness suffer so gracious a prince, and so many honourable and good men, as be in the parliament, to make such an unlawful law, yet left I not one point unthought on. I resolved and cast up in my mind before I came hither, both that peril and all others that might put me in danger of death by my refusal, on considering which, my own good daughter, although I found myself (I pray God be merciful to me) very sensual, and my flesh much more shrinking from pain and death, than a faithful christian man should do in such a case, as my conscience tells me that the saveing of my body will cause the loss of my soul, yet I thank God that in that conflict the Spirit had the mastery, for reason with the help of faith tells me that to be put to death wrongfully for doing well, as I am very sure I do in refusing to swear against my conscience, being not beholden to choose whether my death should come without law, or under color of a law, is a case in which a man may lose his head, and instead of taking harm have inestimable good at God's hands.

"I thank God, Megg, that since I came hither, I every day set less and less by life, for though a man lose of his years in this life, he is a hundredfold rewarded by coming nearer to heaven ; and though it be a pain to die while one is in health, yet see I very few that die with ease in sickness, and finally, very sure am I that whensoever the time shall come, that may be God wot how soon, in which I should lie sick unto death naturally, I should then think that God had done much for me if He had let me die before by the colour of such a law, and so my reason sheweth me, Margaret, that it were great folly in me to be sorry for that death which I would then wish that I had died, besides which a man may happen to die as violently and painfully by many other ways, as by the hands of enemies or thieves.

"And so, my owne good daughter, I assure you (thanks be to God) the thinking of such, albeit it hath grieved me ere this, at this day grieveth me not at all. Still I know my own frailty, and that S. Peter, who feared it much less than I, fell after in such fear that, at the word of a poor simple maid, he forsook and denied our Saviour. And so, Megg, I am not so mad as to warrant myself to stand, but I shall pray, and I beg thee, mine owne good daughter, to pray with me, that it may please God that hath given me this mind, to give me the grace to keep it.

"Thus have I, my dearest daughter, disclosed to you, the very bottom of my heart, referring the order thereof only to God, and that so entirely that I assure you, Margaret, on my faith, that I never have prayed to God to bring me hence, nor deliver me from death, but commit all things to His pleasure, to do with me as pleaseth Him, for never have I longed, since I came hither, to set foot again in my own house for any pleasure thereof, but gladly would I sometimes talk with my friends, especially my wife and you that belong to me, but sith God otherwise disposeth, I commend you all unto Him, and take daily comfort in perceiving you live together so charitably and quietly, and I pray our Lord to continue it thus. My owne good daughter, I bid you finally remember that I thank our Lord such quiet and comfort is in my heart this day, as I trust in God's goodness will continue till the end, yet, as I said before, I trust He will so inspire the Kyng's heart, that he will not requite my true and faithful service with such unlawful and hard dealing, only because I cannot think as others do. But his true subject will I live and die, and I will pray for him in this world and in the other too.

"And, my good daughter, remember me to my good wyfe and all my children, men and women both, and to all your maids and servants, kinsfolks and friends, I beseech our Lord to save and keep them. I pray you all to pray for me, as I shall pray for you, and take no thought of me whatsoever you shall hear, but be glad and rejoice in the Lord."

Another letter written by Sir Thomas to his daughter Margaret, answering a letter sent by her to him :—

THE HOLY SPIRIT OF GOD BE WITH YOU.

"Your filial loving letter, my dearly beloved child, was and is, I faithfully assure you, much more inward comfort to me than my pen can well express, for various matters that I noticed therein, but above all for that God of His great goodness giveth you the grace to consider the incomparable difference between the wretched estate of this present life, and the happy state of the life to come for them that die in God, and to pray to him in such a christian fashion that it may please Him. It doth me good here to repeat your own words, 'of his tender mercy so firmly to rest our love in Him, with small regard of this world, and so to flee from sin and embrace virtue that we may say with S. Paul, *Mihi vivere Christus est, et mori lucrum, est illud, cupio dissolvi et esse cum Christo.'* I beseech Our Lord, my dearly beloved daughter, that this wholesome prayer that He hath put into your mind, it may please Him to give your father daily grace to remember to pray as you yourself hath written it, and daily devoutly on your knees do pray it, and so good Margaret, when you pray this prayer, pray it for us both, and I shall do the like also, that as in this wretched world I have been very glad of your company, and you of mine, and still would, if it so might be (as natural charity bindeth the father and the child), so we may enjoy each other's company, with our kinsfolks and friends, everlastingly in the glorious bliss of heaven, helping each other thitherward; meantime, with good counsel and prayer. And whereas you write the following words of yourself, 'But, good father,

---

* For to me to live is Christ, and to die is gain; I desire to be dissolved, and be with Christ.

I, wretch that I am, am very far, farthest of all others from such a point of perfection, our Lord send me the grace to amend my life, and continually to think of my last end, without grudge (fear) of death, which to them that die in God is the gate of a happy life, to which may He of His infinite mercy bring us all.   Amen.'

" ' Dear father, strengthen my frailty with your devout prayers."

"Thy heavenly Father strengthen thy weakness, my good daughter, and that of thy frail father also, and let us not doubt but that He will, if we be not slow in calling on Him, of my poor prayers, such as they be you may indeed reckon; for christian charity, and natural love and your very filial conduct, both bind and oblige me thereto, and of yours in return I do not doubt.

"That you fear your own weakness, Margaret, nothing misliketh me, God give us both the grace to be diffident of ourselves, and to rely wholly on the strength of God.   The blessed apostle S. Paul, found such lack of strength in himself, that in his own temptation, he thrice called on God for help to take that temptation from him, and yet sped he not in his prayer in the way that he required.   For God in His wisdom, seeing that it was (as himself saith) needful for him to keep him from pride, that else he might perchance have fallen into, would not for his praying take it at once from him, but suffered him to bear the fear and pain, giving him at last this comfort against his fear of falling, *Sufficit tibi gratia mea.** By which words it seemeth that the temptation (whatever it was) was so great he was very fearful of falling through the feebleness of resistance which

* My grace is sufficient for thee.

he began to feel within himself, on which, for his comfort, God answered, *Sufficit tibi gratia mea*, reminding him, that were he of himself ever so weak and faint, or like to fall, yet the grace of God was sufficient to keep him up and make him stand, our Lord saying further, *Virtus mea in infirmitate perficitur*,* for the weaker that man is, the more the power of God is declared in his safety, and so S. Paul saith, *Omnia possum in co qui me confortat.*†

"Truly, Megg, a fainter heart than that of thy poor father thou canst not have, and yet I verily trust in the mercy of God, that He shall of His great goodness, so stay me up with His holy hand that He shall not suffer me wretchedly to fall from his favour. And the like trust in His goodness, dear daughter, have I for you, and so much the more as that both of us, if we call His benefits to mind, may find many reasons to make us hope, amidst all our manifold offences, that His great mercy will not be withheld from us. Truly, my good daughter, this is my great comfort, and though by nature I so shrink from pain that I fear even a stroke, yet in all the anxieties that I had before coming hither, and I have had neither small nor few, with heavy fearful heart, forecasting such painful deaths as might fall upon me, all night long awake whilst others slept, yet I thank the mercy of God I never was minded to consent, that I would for the enduring of the uttermost that might happen, do what should displease God. This is the least point that any man may come to, as far as I can see ; if he see danger, he is bound to examine his conscience by learning and good counsel, and be sure that his conscience be such as may

---

* For power is made perfect in infirmity.

† I can do all things in Him who strengtheneth me.

stand with his salvation or else reform it, then on which ever side he leaneth he is safe before God. Mine own may stand before Him I am very sure, I beseech our Lord bring all to His eternal bliss. It is now, my dear daughter, very late, and therefore I commend you to the Holy Trinity, to guide, direct, and console you with the holy spirit, you, and yours, my wife, children and friends,

"THOMAS MORE, Knight."

"Sir Thomas More, arraigned and condemned in the year of our Lord 1535, and in the 27th of the reign of Henry 8th, being shut up so close in prison in the Tower, that he had no pen nor ink, wrote with a coal an epistle in Latin to Maister Anthony Bonvyse, a merchant, then dwelling in London, his old and dear friend, and sent it unto him, the copy whereof here followeth :—

The translation into English of the Latin epistle next before.

"Good Maister Bonvyse,—Of all friends most friendliest, and to me worthily and dearly beloved, I heartily greet you. Sith my mind warns me (and yet perchance falsely), but so it doth, that I shall not long have liberty to write unto you, I resolve whilst I may, by this little epistle of mine, to say how much I am comforted by the sweetness of your friendship in this decay of my fortune, for, right worshipful sir, though I always delighted in this your love for me, yet when I reflect that I have been almost forty years, not merely a guest but as a child in Maister Bonvyse's house, and in the meantime have not requited you again, showing myself a barren lover only, my shamefacedness verily made that sincere sweetness which otherwise I received of the renewing of your friendship somewhat to wax sourish, by reason of a certain awkward shame as having neglected my duty to you. But I comfort myself with this, that I never had occasion to benefit you. For such was always your great wealth, that there was nothing in which I could in any way benefit you, and therefore knowing that I have not been unthankful to you but only for lack of opportunity, and seeing all hope of recompense taken away, you so persevering in love towards me, binding me more and more to you, you ever beforehand with me so that few men fawn upon their fortunate friends as you favour, love, foster, and honour me, now cast down, abject, and a prisoner, I throw away from myself my old awkwardness, and rest in the sweetness of this marvellous friendship of yours. And this faithful love of yours to me (I know not how) seemeth in a manner to counterpoise this unfortunate shipwreck of my fortunes, and saving the anger of my prince, concerning other matters almost more than outweighs it, for all these are to be reckoned amongst the mischances of fortune. But if I should reckon the possession of such constant friendship, which no storms of adversity hath taken away, but rather hath fortified and strengthened amongst the brittle gifts of fortune, then were I mad, for the happiness of such faithful friendship is rarely to be seen, and is a high and noble gift coming from a singular goodness of God. Indeed, as regards myself, I cannot otherwise esteem it, but that it was in God's mercy ordained, that you, Maister Bonvyse, so great a friend, and such a man as you are, should have been raised up, and by your consolation assuage and relieve a great portion of my troubles and griefs, which the storms of fortune hath hastily brought upon me.

"Therefore, my dear friend, of all mortal men to me most

dear, do I earnestly pray to Almighty God, that sith he hath given you such a debtor as shall never be able to pay you back, it may please Him to requite this bountifulness of yours, which you every day lavishly pour upon me, and that for His mercy's sake He will bring us from this wretched and stormy world into His rest, where there shall be no need of letters, where no walls shall separate us, no gaoler shall keep us from talking together, but that we may have the fruition of the eternal joys with God the Father, and with His only begotten Son, our Redeemer, Jesus Christ, together with the Holy Ghost. In the meantime, Almighty God grant both you and me good Master Bonvyse, and all mankind, to despise all the riches of this world, and all its glory for the love and desire of that love.

"Now of all friends most trusty and to me most dearly beloved, and as I was wont to call you the apple of mine eye, right heartily fare ye well. And may Jesus keep you and all your family, safe and sound, all of whom are of like affection towards me as is their master.

"Thomas More, I should in vain sign myself 'yours,' for thereof you cannot be ignorant, since you have bought it with so many benefits. Now, I am not such an one that it signifieth whose I am."

For the greater part, these letters bear no date. The following, as it was also written with a coal, may be classed amongst the later epistles of Sir Thomas More :—

" My good Daughter,—Our Lord be thanked, I am in good bodily health, and peace of mind, and of worldly wealth I desire no more than I possess. I beseech Him make you all rejoice in the hope of heaven, and of such things as I sometimes used to talk with you all concerning the world to come.   Our Lord put them all into your minds as I trust He doth by His Holy Spirit blessing and preserving you.

" Written with a coal by your tender, loving father, who in his poor prayers forgetteth none of you, nor your babes, nor your nurses, nor your good husbands, nor your good husband's wives, nor your father's shrewd wife, neither, nor our other friends, so thus fare you heartily well, for lack of paper.

" THOMAS MORE, Knight."

CHAPTER XXI.

ARRAIGNED AND CONDEMNED.

EMINENT as was the ex-chancellor for integrity, wisdom, and virtue, the King had ardently longed to win him over to espouse his interests, failing which he resolved to pursue him unto death. Henry was now showing his shuddering subjects that neither virtue nor talent, nor past favour, nor past services, could atone in his eyes for the great crime of doubting his supremacy.

On the seventh of May, having been in the Tower a little more than twelve months, for he was committed on the 17th of April the previous year, Sir Thomas was arraigned at the King's Bench. To make the greater impression on the people, perhaps to add to his shame and sufferings, More was led on foot in a coarse woollen gown, through the most frequented streets from the Tower to Westminster Hall. The colour of his hair, which was brown, had become quite grey, his face, though cheerful, was pale and emaciated, and the staff with which he supported his feeble steps, announced the rigour and duration of his confinement. At his appearance in this state at the bar of that court in which he had been wont to preside with so much dignity, a general feeling of horror and sympathy ran through the spectators. Henry dreaded the effect of his eloquence, and authority, and therefore, as if it were meant to distract his attention, and overpower his memory, the indictment had been framed of enormous length and unexampled exaggeration, multiplying the charges without measure, and clothing each charge with a load of words, beneath which it was difficult to discover the real meaning. As soon as it had been read, the chancellor, Lord Audley, who was assisted by the Duke of Norfolk, Fitzjames, the Chief Justice, and six other commissioners informed the prisoner that it was still in his power to close the proceedings, " The goodness of the King is so great," said Audley, " that he will yet pardon you, we trust, your great obstinacy, if you will even now change your opinion." These men, now his judges, had formerly been ranked amongst his friends, they had all partaken of his boundless hospitality in the day of his prosperity. To the left of the court sat Rich, the creature and tool of Cromwell. The principal charge against Sir Thomas was his refusal to take the oath respecting the spiritual supremacy of the King; allusion was also made in the indictment to the letters he had written to Bishop Fisher, his having compared the oath to a two-edged sword, killing both soul and body ; and his conversation with Rich in the Tower.

Calm and clear, as when himself in the high place of justice, did the prisoner's voice sound in the ears of the silent multitude, as he replied to the remark of Audley,—

" Noble Lords, I thank your honours for your kindness, but I pray the Almighty God I may continue in my present mind unto my death." Then he paused as if to collect his thoughts, and after a few moments, said he,

" When I think of the length of my accusation, and of the heinous matters brought to my charge, I am seized with fear lest my memory and my wit, which are both decayed with my bodily health through my long imprisonment, be not able suddenly to answer these things, as I otherwise could."

Here his voice failed, his limbs trembled, and the Lord Chief Justice ordered a chair to be brought to him ; and seating himself, he continued :

"If I am not mistaken, the indictment contains four principal heads, each of which I will answer in order. In the first I am accused of disapproving of the King's marriage with the Lady Anne Boleyn ; yes, truly, I always told the King my opinion therein as my conscience dictated, and you cannot find in my candour a crime of high treason, the King having commanded me on my oath of allegiance to give him my opinion on this matter ; if it can be an offence to tell one's mind plainly, when our prince asketh us, I suppose I have been already enough punished for this fault by the loss of all my goods, and imprisonment, having been shut up these fifteen months.

"The second charge is, that I have twice refused, in a spirit of malice, to answer the councillors of the crown this question, 'Is not the King the supreme head of the Church?' I answered them that this law belonged not to me, whether just or unjust. I protested I had never said nor done anything against it, that I desired henceforth to occupy myself only with the bitter passion of our blessed Saviour, and of my passage out of this world. In all this I have not rendered myself guilty of any crime of treason ; there is no law to punish silence, God only being judge of our secret thoughts."

Here the Attorney-general Hales interrupted him :

" We can impute to you no guilty word or action, but

we have your silence, which is a manifest sign of a malicious mind, for no faithful subject would refuse to answer when interrogated in the name of the law."

" My silence is no sign of a malicious mind," replied Sir Thomas, " which the King himself may know by many of my dealings, nor of any contempt of your law, for it is a maxim of civil as of canon law that *qui tacet consentire videtur*, 'he that holdeth his peace seemeth to consent.' You say that a faithful subject cannot refuse to answer; but the duty of a good subject is to obey God rather than man, to have more care of his conscience than of any other matter, especially that his conscience procure no scandal to the state or revolt to his prince. And mine, my Lords, is very tranquil. I protest, in the name of Heaven, that I have not revealed to any man living my interior thoughts.

" I come now to the third principal article in my indictment, by which I am accused of malicious attempts, traitorous endeavours, and perfidious practices against that statute, as the words therein allege, because I wrote while in the Tower divers packets of letters to Bishop Fisher, wherein I exhorted him to violate the same law, and encouraged him in the same obstinacy. I do insist that these letters be produced and read in court, by which I may be either acquitted or convinced of a lie! but because you say the Bishop burnt them all, I will here tell you the whole truth of the matter. Some of my letters related only to our private affairs, as about our old friendship and acquaintance, one of them was in answer to his, wherein he desired me to let him know what answers I made upon my examination concerning the oath of supremacy, and what I wrote to him upon it was this, that I had already settled my conscience,

and let him satisfy his according to his own mind. God is
my witness, and as I hope He will save my soul, I gave him
no other answer ! And this, I presume, is no breach of the
laws. As to the other principal crime objected against me
—that I should say upon my examination in the Tower,
that this law was like a two-edged sword, for in consenting
to it I should endanger my soul, and in rejecting it should
lose my life, it is evidently concluded, as you say, from
this answer, for Fisher made the like, that we conspired
together. To this I reply that my answer there was condi-
tional, if there were both danger either in allowing or
disallowing that act, and therefore like a two-edged sword,
it seemed a hard thing it should be put upon me, who had
never hitherto contradicted it either by word or deed.
These were my words. What the Bishop answered I know
not. If his answer was like mine, it did not proceed from
any conspiracy of ours, but from the similitude of our learning and understanding. To conclude, I do sincerely avouch
that I never spoke a word against this law to any man
living, though perhaps the King's majesty hath been told
the contrary."

There was little or no reply to this full answer by Mr.
Attorney, or any body else. The word *malice* was what was
principally insisted on, and in the mouths of the whole
court, though for proof it had, nobody could produce either
words or actions ; nevertheless to set the best gloss that
could be upon the matter, Mr. Rich was called to give
evidence in open court upon oath, which he immediately
did, affirming what we have already related concerning a
conference between him and Sir Thomas in the Tower.
To which Sir Thomas made answer, " If I were a man, my

Lords, that had no regard to my oath, I had had no occasion to be here at this time, as it is well known to everybody, as a criminal; and if this oath, Mr. Rich, which you have taken, be true, then I pray I may never see God's face, which were it otherwise is an imprecation I would not be guilty of to gain the whole world."

More having recited in the face of the Court all the discourse they had together in the Tower, as it truly and sincerely was, he added, "In good faith, Mr. Rich, I am more concerned for your perjury than my own danger; and I must tell you, that neither myself, nor any body else to my knowledge, ever took you to be a man of such reputation, that I or any other would have anything to do with you in a matter of importance. You know that I have been acquainted with your manner of life and conversation a long time, even from your youth to the present juncture, for we lived in the same parish; and you very well know, I am sorry I am forced to speak it, you always lay under the odium of a very lying tongue, of being a great dicer, and of no good name and character, either there or in the Temple, where you was educated. Can it therefore seem likely, your Lordships, that I should in so weighty an affair as this, act so unadvisedly, as to trust Mr. Rich, a man I had always so mean an opinion of, in reference to his truth and honesty, so very much before my sovereign Lord the King, to whom I am so deeply indebted for his manifold favours, or any of his noble and grave councillors, that I should only impart to Mr. Rich the secrets of my conscience, in respect to the King's supremacy, the particular subject, and only point so long sought for at my hands and which I never did nor never will reveal, when this act was made, either to the King himself or any of his privy councillors, as is well known to your honours, who have been sent upon no other account at several times by his Majesty to me in the Tower. I refer it to your judgments, my Lords, whether this can seem credible to any of your Lordships. But, supposing that what Mr. Rich has sworn should be true, seeing the words were spoken in familiar and private conversation, and affirming nothing, but only in putting of cases, said More, after a pause, it cannot in justice be said that they were spoken *maliciously*, and where there is no *malice*, there is no offence. Besides, my Lords, I cannot think so many good Bishops, so many honourable personages, and so many virtuous and learned men, of whom the Parliament consisted in the enacting of that law, ever meant to have any man punished with death, in whom no malice could be found, taking the word *malitia* for *malevolentia;* for if *malitia* be taken in a general signification for any crime, there is no man can be free : wherefore this word maliciously is so far significant in this statute, as the word forcible is in that of forcible entry ; for in that case if any enter peaceably, and puts his adversary out forcibly, it is no offence, but if he enters forcibly, he shall be punished by that statute. Besides all, the unspeakable goodness of his Majesty towards me, who has been so many ways my singular good and gracious lord, who has so dearly loved and trusted me, even from my first entrance into his royal service, vouchsafing to honour me with the dignity of being one of his privy council, and has most graciously promoted me to offices of great reputation and honour, and lastly to that of Lord High Chancellor, being the highest dignity in the kingdom, and then was pleased at my humble request, to allow me to lay aside that weighty dignity, all this is enough in my opinion to invalidate the scandalous accusation of that man."

The withering sarcasm with which Sir Thomas had spoken touched the reputation of the perjured witness, Rich, so sensibly, that with the hope of producing substantial witnesses to attest to the truth of what he had said, they called Sir Richard Southwell and Mr. Palmer, who were in the same room with Sir Thomas More and Mr. Rich when they conferred together, to be sworn as to the words that passed between them, but Palmer deposed "That he was so busy in thrusting Sir Thomas's books into a sack that he took no notice of their talk," and Sir R. Southwell likewise swore "That because his business was only to take care of conveying his books away, he gave no ear to his discourse with Rich." Rich, however, procured what he sought—his own advancement.

The speech of More, coupled with the evident falsehood of Rich, produced a visible effect on the bystanders, but neither his well-known innocence nor his eloquence, could avert his fate. His enemies were resolved to have his blood.

Audley, the presiding judge, then summed up. The moment had come, which he and they, the tools of their despotic master, had long desired, and he gallantly restored the fortunes of the day by an animated and sarcastic speech, in which he maintained that the silence of the prisoner at the bar was a sufficient proof of a malicious intention.

The jury then retired to the council hall, for a quarter of an hour, when they returned, the Chancellor turned towards the foreman, saying,

" Gentlemen of the jury, is the accused guilty."

"Guilty," replied the foreman, with his hand upon his heart.

Audley forgetting established customs in his eagerness to pronounce the sentence which was to crush the prisoner, arose to pronounce it, when More interrupted him, saying,

"My Lord, when I occupied the seat now used by you, my custom was always to ask the prisoner, before sentence, if he could give any reason why judgment should not proceed against him."

"What have you to say?" demanded the Chancellor, with somewhat of hesitation.

"My Lords," replied Sir Thomas, "the act of parliament in virtue of which I have been condemned is contrary to the laws of God and His Church, the supreme government of which no temporal prince may take upon him, as it rightfully belongeth to the see of Rome, to whom Christ has transmitted His authority in the person of St. Peter. No realm can make a particular law incompatible with the general laws of the Church. Your law is even contrary to the statutes of this our realm not yet repealed; as you may see by Magna Charta, where it was declared 'that the English Church, should be free, and have her rights and liberties untouched.'"

"But," said the Lord Chancellor, "do you not see the universities, bishops, and all the learned men in the realm have agreed to this act, and have taken the oath? I am much astonished, Sir Thomas, that you alone should so vehemently argue against it."

The prisoner arose, leaning for support on his stick, and his wan and emaciated countenance was lighted up as he exclaimed :

"And if the number of universities, bishops, and learned men were still greater, then do I, my Lord, see little cause why I should change my opinion. I do not doubt but of the learned and virtuous men that are yet alive (I speak not only of this realm, but of all Christendom about), there are ten to one that are of my mind in this matter ; and if I should speak of those learned doctors and virtuous fathers that are already dead, of whom many are saints in heaven, I am sure there are far more, who all the while they lived thought in this case, as I think now. And therefore, my Lord, I think myself not bound to conform my conscience to the council of one realm against the general consent of all Christendom."

Chancellor Audley paused, uncertain what reply to make. Then turning to the Lord Chief Justice, loath perhaps to have the burden of the condemnation to lie upon himself, he asked him openly to give him his advice whether this indictment were sufficient or no.

And Sir John Fitz James arose, and striking the table with his fist, he exclaimed :

"My lords all, by S. Julian, I must needs confess that if the act of parliament be not unlawful, then the indictment is not, in my conscience, insufficient." An answer like that of the Scribes and Pharisees to Pilate.

And my Lord Chancellor arose, and amidst the hush of the crowded assembly, said he :

"You have heard what my Lord Chief Justice hath said. What further need have we of witnesses, he is guilty of death." *Quid adhuc desideramus testimonium ? reus est mortis.* Audley was another Caiaphas.

And then he pronounced the sentence in a loud, firm

voice, delivering the usual barbarous formula : " that Sir Thomas should be brought back to the Tower of London by William Kingston, the sheriff, and from thence be drawn on a hurdle through the city of London to Tyburn, there to be hanged till *half* dead. After this, to be cut down, *yet alive*, and his four quarters to be set up over the four gates of the city ; his head upon London Bridge."

Whilst the sentence was being pronounced, the calmness of the poor prisoner's countenance remained the same, pallid it was indeed, but still unmoved. As the last words fell upon his ear, a slight smile was on his lips and his eyes beamed with joy.

"Well," said he, "seeing that I am condemned, God knows how justly, I will freely speak for the disburdening of my conscience. When I perceived that the King's pleasure was to sift out from *whence* the Pope's authority was derived, I confess I studied for seven years to find out the truth thereof, and I could not find in the writings of any one doctor of the Church that a layman was or could ever be the head of the Church ; it is contrary to the sacred oath the King took at his coronation."

"How ? " said Audley, in a scoffing tone, " do you make yourself out wiser than bishops, theologians, nobles, and all the people, great and small, of England ? "

" My Lord Chancellor, for one bishop opposed to me by you, I have a thousand on my side ; against this kingdom, the whole of Christendom in every age."

" Now, Sir Thomas," exclaimed his grace of Norfolk, "you show your spirit of hatred and malice, your obstinate and malicious mind."

" No, your grace," said the intrepid old man, "in me

there is neither hatred nor malice, it is my conscience which forces me to protest against your sentence; it is to God that I appeal."

"Have you anything more to say?" said one of the judges.

"More have I not to say, my lords, but that, like as the blessed apostle St. Paul was present and consented to the death of St. Stephen, keeping their clothes that stoned him to death, and yet they be now two holy saints in heaven, and there shall be friends together for ever, so I verily trust, and heartily, that though your lordships have been on earth my judges to condemnation, yet we may hereafter meet merrily together to our everlasting joy. May God be with you and with my sovereign lord the King, and grant him faithful councillors."

"A general feeling of sorrow and commiseration ran through the spectators; and after a lapse of more than three centuries, during which statesmen, prelates, and a king have been unjustly brought to trial under the same roof, considering the splendour of his talents, the greatness of his acquirements, and the innocence of his life, we must still regard his murder as the blackest crime that has ever been perpetrated in England under the form of law."*

The atrocious Audley, and we use not the word unadvisedly, "had the custody of the Seal for nearly twelve years; a period more disgraceful," says Lord Campbell, "in the annals of England than any of a similar extent. Within it were comprehended the King's divorce from one Queen after an union of two-and-twenty years, under pretence of a scruple of conscience; the repudiation of

* Campbell's Lives of the Chancellors.

another after a few days' intercourse, on the mere ground of personal antipathy ; the execution of two others, one of them sacrificed to obtain a new partner ; and innumerable judicial and remorseless murders. Those of Sir Thomas More and Bishop Fisher leading the dreadful array. The monasteries were dissolved, not for the professed purpose of purification, but for the sake of the riches they produced to the King's treasury, and to supply the means of rewarding the subservient minions of his power.

"Among these, Audley, who all along acted as a thorough tool to the King, and was a most zealous promoter of the suppression, secured no inconsiderable share of the confiscation, 'carving for himself in the feast of Abbey lands,' as Fuller humourously remarks, 'the first cut, and that a dainty morsel.' Thus was it with the fine Priory of the Holy Trinity or Christ Church, in Aldgate, London, founded in the reign of Henry I., which having been surrendered by the Prior, was granted to the Chancellor within a year after he attained that dignity. He pulled down the great church, and converted the Priory into a mansion for himself, in which he resided during the remainder of his life. It was subsequently called Duke's Place, from his son-in-law, the Duke of Norfolk. To this were next added many of the smaller Priories in the neighbourhood of Colchester, with which his former connexion with that town had made him acquainted. But he was not satisfied with even these extensive spoils, for having fixed his eye on the rich monastery of Walden, in the same county, in sueing for it, he not only lessened its value, but had the meanness to allege that he had in this world sustained great damage and infamy in his serving the King, which the grant of this abbey would recompense. He succeeded in his application, and took his title from the plunder when the King, on November 29, 1538, raised him to the Peerage, as Baron Audley of Walden. The Order of the Garter was soon after disgraced by his admission among its members."

Audley favoured Lutheranism; nevertheless, it was he who introduced the bloody bill of the Six Articles.

As to the equally infamous Rich, Lord Campbell observes, " It would be curious to discover by what means a character of this stamp pushed himself up so as to become a reader at the Middle Temple, which office he held in autumn, 1529. As his name is not to be discovered in the Year Books, or any other reports, it is difficult otherwise to attribute his advancement to the bench of that society than to the influence of opulent friends, and a mixture of that subtleness and insolence of his bearing which he exhibited in after life. By what patronage he acquired the office of Attorney-General of Wales, in 1532, is not told; that of Solicitor-General to the King soon followed. His patent for it, in which he is called " Gentleman," is dated October 10, 1533, and he held it till April, 1836, a period of two years and a half; during which, by his intrigues, his degrading subserviency and his bold-faced perjury, though he paved the way to worldly honours, he, at the same time, secured to his name the everlasting infamy that attaches to it. Cunning, much less than that of Rich's, would soon discover that his interest lay in gratifying the humours of the King; but it required a hardened conscience to pursue the perfidious course which he adopted to secure the Royal favour. The refusal of Sir Thomas More and Bishop Fisher to acknowledge the King's supremacy had irritated the monarch even beyond his usual ferocity, and every attempt had hitherto failed in bringing the two contumacious prisoners within the terms of the recent statute, which made it high treason to deny it. Either Rich was known to be considered a fitting instrument to make another trial, or he voluntarily undertook the degrading office. The manner in which he acted towards these good and pious men was exposed on their trials."

CHAPTER XXII.

FATHER AND DAUGHTER.

BRIGHT flashes of sunlight pierced through the windows of the old Hall on the morning of the first of July, 1535, shedding a brightness as of a halo of glory around the head of one who, crushed by unmerited suffering, the anger of the ferocious Henry, and the enmity of the sycophants who had tried him, was about to offer up his life as a testimony to the truth of the faith he professed.

He arose slowly, his wan and pallid countenance, even in this moment of direst anguish, was clothed with an expression of dignified composure ; his stern persecutors were before him still—Norfolk, Audley, Rich, the parasites of the King, his own false perjured friends, who had shared his hospitality in the days of his prosperity, and who now pursued him to the bitter end.

And yet would we recal that word, for truly, in the sight of God and His angels, it was not a bitter, but glorious, end ; for, was he not about to wear the never-fading crown of the martyr ? Was he not ready to shed his blood in defence of his faith ? Was not his name about to be enshrined in the hearts of Englishmen for generations yet unborn, who, whatever be their opinions, hold in reverent love the very memory of one who so unflinchingly stood true and firm to the last.

The King had determined to have his life-blood, as Lord Campbell has truly said, and when, pale and trembling, (for they had dragged him on foot all the way from the Tower, through the crowded streets,) he entered the hall at Westminster, the result of the trial was, doubtless, foreshadowed in his own prophetic mind, as it had been long since, when this terrible day was yet afar off. All, but himself and his judges, were moved to tears ; the court was crowded ; many had clung vainly to the hope that the life of so venerated a man would be spared, and along with the sorrow they felt, the sentence that had been passed struck terror into the hearts of all.

Thus was it, that when More raised his eyes as he was led from out the hall into the Palace yard, the executioner preceding him, with the edge of the axe turned towards him, on raising his eyes, he beheld the face of his kind friend and gaoler bathed in tears. The fresh air which blew from the river revived the poor prisoner, who, forgetful of his own suffering, strove to comfort him ; and Kingston, some time after, speaking of it to Roper, said—

" In good faith, Mr. Roper, I was ashamed of myself to be so weak, whilst *he* was so full of strength and courage, for he was fain to comfort me who should rather have been *his* comforter."

The mercy of a boat to the Tower was vouchsafed to the condemned man, and as he descended the steps, his only son John forced his way through the crowd, and kneeling at his feet, craved his blessing. He had left his home in Yorkshire, and wandered about all night to obtain this boon. More blessed and kissed him, and his pale face, for the first time that day, was bathed in tears.

Then John More, unwilling to prolong the scene, tore himself away, and the agonised prisoner, with Kingston and his guards, entered the boats and made their way to the Tower. During this short journey the grief he felt was pourtrayed on his countenance ; his cheerfulness for a time left him, for More was a father, and a very tender one. But the bright rays of sunlight danced on the surface of the waters, and as the boat neared the Tower wharf, it lighted up its time-worn walls, within which many who had ill deserved it had suffered so cruelly ; the foliage of the trees around the moat wore the gayest hues of summer ; the birds sang merrily ; all nature seemed so bright and beautiful this glorious summer day, as though to mock the misery of the captive and those who so dearly loved him.

One there was on the Tower wharf who had long awaited his coming—a pale and beautiful woman withal, clad in sombre garments, who, with eyes full of tears, had watched that boat which contained the prisoner from the time that it was but as a speck in the distance. As More landed, the crowd, of whom this matron was one of the foremost, gave way, for the guards and halberdiers pressed closely around him, so that he should not be seen by the people.

Of the females of his family on that terrible morning two had alone ventured to leave their homes, attended by an old maid-servant.

More's adopted child, Margaret Giggs, was there ; and out of her great love for her father, borne up by a superhuman courage, which defied every obstacle, Margaret Roper, his best-beloved child, had lingered to await the cortège at the Tower wharf.

" Mistress Roper, it is she," murmured those around, and

the hearts of all were full of sorrow and sympathy, as, bursting through the throng of guards and halberdiers who surrounded More, this child of his fondest affection, threw herself at his feet, embraced his knees, and with eyes streaming with tears, piteously besought his blessing. Then she arose, and flung her arms around his neck, exclaiming in accents of the deepest sorrow, "My father! oh, my father!"

For a few brief moments the cortège paused, and the hard-featured guards raised their hands to their eyes, as if to shade them from the burning heat of the July sun, but it was only done to brush away their tears, and hide their emotion from the bystanders.

An age of overwhelming agony must have been con-centrated in those short moments. Mutely, for he was unable at first to speak, so intense was his emotion, Sir Thomas raised his clasped hands and eyes to heaven, as though calling on God to help him, then he extended his hands over the head of his child. "My good daughter," at last broke forth in almost inaudible accents, "God bless thee. I am about to die, though innocent, it is the will of God. Submit, my dear one, to the decrees of Providence, and pray for them who have condemned me. Ye know (quoth he) the very bottom and secrets of my heart, and ye have rather cause to congratulate and to rejoice for me, that God hath advanced me to this high honour and vouch-safed me worthy to' lose my life for the defence and upholding of virtue, justice, and religion, than to be dis-mayed and so fall away."*

Like one bereft of reason, Margaret turned aside, whilst

* Harleian MSS.

her old servant and also More's adopted daughter came to utter their last adieus. " It was homely but lovingly done," said he afterwards, alluding to the simple way in which the old servant testified her sorrow.

The halberdiers moved on, and the procession resumed its way to the fortress, when of a sudden, Margaret, like one whom reason had for a space of time forsook, retraced her steps. She saw not halberdiers, or guards, or people, who pressed upon the martyr, as he bravely trod his thorny path ; but hastily she rushed back with streaming eyes and dishevelled locks, and the peerless Margaret, the jewel of British matrons, pushed her way through the crowd, endued with more than woman's strength, and again she stayed her father's steps, flinging her arms around his neck, still sobbing forth the words, as she pressed her lips to his pallid face, " My father ! oh, my father ! "

Speechless now was the unhappy parent, tears poured down his face, the very guards again turned aside to weep, their hearts wrung at the sight of grief so unutterable. And yet lingered she for one more kiss, and then—these two were severed, till they should meet in eternity. Margaret sank insensible at her father's feet.

A sign was then given, and the mournful cavalcade moved slowly on. One sad glance cast the unhappy More on the prostrate form of his beloved Margaret, and passed on his sorrowful way.

Then Sir William Kingston, a tall and comely knight, constable of the Tower, and his own friend, arrived at the Old Swan, near the fortress, and with a heavy heart, the tears running down by his cheeks, he bade him farewell.

" Good Mr. Kingston," said More, " trouble not thyself,

but be of good cheer, for I will pray for you and my good lady your wife, that we may meet in heaven together, where we shall be merry for ever."

As to death More feared it not, its bitterness was over now that he had parted with all he held most dear on earth. He was again composed, nay, cheerful.

He was not taken back to his old prison lodging in the Tower, but to one of its dismal dungeons, in which we ourselves have been privileged to stand, that so we might describe it to others.

Beneath the White Tower, are several darksome dungeons, two of which were used after their condemnation, for Sir Thomas More and Bishop Fisher. Come with us, in imagination, down the steep worn steps, leading to this dreary spot. It is a summer day, bright as was that first of July, on which good Sir Thomas was condemned to death, and our thoughts are full of him and his tragic end, as we follow one of the warders of the Tower to the most ancient part of the grim old fortress, the foundations of this portion of the Tower having been laid by our Saxon forefathers. A ponderous door is opened, and we pass down a flight of stone steps, so dark that it is only by degrees that our eyes become accustomed to the semi-twilight, till we reach a large vaulted space, from which open numerous recesses, once the dungeons of old. The walls are fifteen feet thick, the roof over our heads is grand and massive, and of Norman architecture. But it is not here we would linger, for we wish to stand ourselves in that awful spot in which those two great men were thrust, to abide the near approach of death, which must needs have been, to them, most welcome.

More and Fisher were very near together in the Bell Tower, their dungeons too were very near also. Six feet square may be rather beyond than otherwise as to extent of space. No light penetrated hither, no casement admitted one single ray, or breath of air, and the dense darkness of this living tomb, if light it had, must have proceeded only from the faint glimmer of a lantern suspended from the ceiling.

Pause with us, just one moment, while we linger here, and call to mind how two of the best and truest of Englishmen were left in these hideous dungeons, in coldness, darkness, and solitude, till they laid their heads upon the block, and let us contrast English rule three centuries back, and English rule as it *now* is, and heartily shall we thank God that the despotic age of the ferocious Henry VIII. has passed, and given place to Victoria's mild and gentle sway. Verily, the seed of the Church is the blood of the Martyrs.

Let us strive to imagine what the feelings of Sir Thomas *must* have been when he was thrust within this living tomb, in which he was destined to spend the intervening time between this and the day of his execution. "As the hart panteth for the water brooks," so must his soul have thirsted to be at rest.

Talk of the condemned cells such as our convicts have in our happier times, why they are like palaces compared with the dungeons of the Tower! In this dismal place, however, he abode even to the sixth of July.

For the space of an hour he was importuned by one of the courtiers, who was a personal friend, and who earnestly begged him to change his mind, to whom he replied at length, "I *have* changed my mind."

No time was lost in conveying the news to the King, and before the day was over messengers were sent to inquire the meaning of his words.

With a smile, replied More, "Good sirs, you are too quick in taking up my words. I had minded to have shaved my beard, but then I bethought me that my beard should fare no better than my head; that was the only change I alluded to."

Up to the very last the King must have felt no small anxiety respecting the course his own ferocious temper led him to pursue, for yet again, aware that by his recantation far more would be gained than by his death, persons were sent to More with fresh interrogations, which he answered with his usual prudence. In conclusion, they told him that out of the King's mercy and favour, the more revolting portions of his sentence would be commuted, and that he would be simply beheaded, to which, with something of his old humour, he replied, " I thank the King for his kindness, but I pray God to preserve my friends from the like favours."

His time was now passed in prayer, and in scratching on the dungeon walls, or writing with a coal on scraps of paper. The following sentences have been carefully preserved, and show how admirably his mind was engaged in these his last terrible and solemn days on earth.

" Who would save his life to displease God? If thou so saved thy life how would thou hate it on the morrow; and feel heavy at thy heart that thou hadst not died the day before! If thou hast been with Christ at the wine feast of Galilee shrink not to stand with Him at the judgment seat of Pilate. The moment draweth near when thou shalt rejoice with Him in the revelation of His glory !"

During his life this just man had chosen as his special patron, St. Thomas of Canterbury, his namesake, one who had filled the same office of Chancellor, and like himself had offered up his life in defence of the rights of the Church. It was by a singular coincidence that he suffered on the eve of the Translation of St. Thomas, also within the Octave of S. Peter, in behalf of whose supremacy he suffered Martyrdom.*

On the day before his execution he wrote his last letter to Margaret, in which he forgets none of his family, even naming Dorothy Colly, Margaret's old servant.

Now, too, he sent to his beloved Margaret the hair shirt and discipline. "Having finished his combat, he sent away his weapons," says his old biographer.

This letter to Margaret, with the heading thereof runs as follows,

"On the daye nexte before Sir Thomas was beheaded, bynge Moundaye, and the fyfte day of July, he wrote with a cole a letter to his daughter, Maystress Roper, and sente it to her (whiche was the last thinge that he ever wrote), the copy whereof here followeth :—

"Oure Lord blesse you, good daughter, and youre good husbande, and youre little boye, and all youre and all my chyldren, and all my godde-chyldren, and all my frendes. Recommende me when you maye to my goode daughter Cicely, whome I beseeche oure Lorde to comforte. And I sende her my blessyng and to all her chyldren, and praye her to praye for me. I sende her an handkercher, and God comforte my goode sonne her husbande.† My good daughter

---

* More.

† Giles Heron.

Dauncey hath the picture in parchemente that you delivered me from my Lady Coniers; her name is on the back. Shewe her that I heartelye praye her, that you may sende it in my name to her agayne, for a token from me to praye for me. I lyke special well Dorothy Colly; I pray you be good unto her. I marvel whether thys be she that you wrote me of; if not, yet I pray you be good to the t'other as you may in her affliction, and to my goode daughter Joane Alleyn* too. Give her, I pray you, some kynde answer, for she send hither to me this day to pray you be good unto her. I cumber you, good Margaret, much; but I would be sorry if it should be any longer than to-morrow, for it is St. Thomas' Even, and within the (octave) of St. Peter; and therefore to-morrow long I to go to God: it were a day verye mete and convenient for me. I never liked your maner toward me better than when you kissed me laste, for I love when daughterly love and deare charity hath no leysure to loke to worldlye curtesey. Farewell, my dere chylde, and pray for me, and I shall for you and all youre frendes, that we may surely mete in heaven. I thanke you for youre gret cost. I send now to my good daughter Clement, her algorisme† stone; and I send her and my good sonne and all hers God's blessing and myne. I pray you at time convenient recommend me to my good sonne John More; I liked well his natural fashion.‡ Our Lord blesse him and his good wyfe my loving daughter, to

---

* This was no kin to him, but one of Mistress Roper's maids.

† An Arabic word, used to imply the six operations of arithmetic in the science of numbers.

‡ On the Tower Wharf when he came from judgment, where his son asked his blessing.

whom I pray him to be good, as he hath gret cause ; and that if the land of myne come to his hande, he break not my will concerning his sister Dauncy.   And our Lord blesse Thomas and Austin, and all that they shall have."

More had been kept in ignorance as to the day on which the King had determined he should be divested of this mortal coil, and his heart must needs have exulted when early in the morning of the 6th July, his friend, Sir Thomas Pope, visited his dungeon.   He at once surmised what had brought him thither.

" My dear old friend," said Pope, " I bring a message to you from the King and the Council, and I would that I had not to deliver it ; you are to suffer death this day at nine o'clock.   Therefore it is meet you should prepare yourself."

" I heartily thank you for the tidings you have brought me," was the reply, " I have been much indebted to the King for his favours and benefit, but for none do I thank him more than for putting me here, where I have had much time to remember my last end and much am I beholden to him for ridding me of the miseries of this world."

" Moreover, it is the King's will that you speak not many words at your execution."

" You do well, Mr. Pope, to warn me of the King's desire. I *had* purposed to speak to the people, but on no matter at which his Grace might be offended, but I am ready to conform myself to his commands, and now I beseech you, good Mr. Pope, beg of his Majesty to allow my daughter Margaret to be present at my burial."

" The King is quite content that your wife and children should be present at it."

" Much then am I beholden to his Grace for such kind consideration respecting my poor burial."

Sir Thomas Pope then took his leave of More, who, on seeing the tears burst forth, for he could no longer restrain his emotion, exclaimed,

" Be calm, Pope, my kind friend. I trust we shall meet in heaven, where we shall live eternally and enjoy each other's company in everlasting bliss."

Then the friends parted, and Sir Thomas, as one invited to a great feast, arrayed himself in a silken gown, sent him by his kind friend, Bonvyse, and kneeling down he spent some time in earnest prayer.

Kingston was the first who entered the dungeon, and the silken garment at once attracted his attention, he begged him to take it off, exclaiming, " The fellow who will take it as his perquisite is but a javill."

" How say you, Mr. Lieutenant," was More's reply, "am I to reckon *him* a javill who will this day confer the greatest benefit on me. Nay, Kingston, were it made of cloth of gold he ought to have it. I mind me that St. Cyprian, the famous Bishop of Carthage, gave the executioner thirty pieces of gold, because he was going to do him so good a turn."

" Nevertheless," still urged the Lieutenant, " I cannot be of your mind."

For friendship's sake More would no longer deny him what he asked, so threw aside his silken garment, and put on a frieze gown instead, leaving for the executioner a single gold angel, as a sign that he bore him no ill will.

Just as the clock of the Church of S. Peter ad Vincula

struck the hour of nine, a melancholy procession issued from the dungeons of the Tower.

More walked beside the Lieutenant. His face was thin and pale, but his keen grey eyes were still clear and bright, his beard had become very long from neglect, and in his clasped hands he bore a red cross, and often raising his eyes to heaven, he showed that he was inwardly praying.

As the mournful procession passed by the house of a woman with whom More had dealt in former times, she came forth with a cup of wine, but he gently refused it, saying, "Christ at his passion drank no wine, but gall and vinegar."

Then followed the martyr a woman, who molested him in these his last solemn moments, when he would fain keep his thoughts fixed on eternity alone, concerning some books and papers she had placed with him when he was Chancellor, and turning towards her, said he, with unspeakable patience, "My good woman, have patience, but for one hour, and by that time the King will have rid me of the care of thy papers as of all other matters." Yet there followed another in the martyr's train, suborned by his enemies to cry out that he had done her grievous injustice when he was judge, to whom he replied,

"I remember you well, and if again I were to give sentence in your cause I would not alter what I have already done."

Then met him on his thorny way a citizen of Winchester, who was tempted to commit suicide, he threw himself at the martyr's feet, and begged his prayers,

"Go and pray for me," said More, "and   will pray

for you." And he went away comforted, and never after was he troubled with the like thoughts.*

Brightly shone the summer sun on the scaffold and its sad surroundings, and More for a moment paused and looked at it steadily, then said he, placing his hand on Kingston's shoulder,

"I pray you, sir, to see me safe up, and for my coming down let me shift for myself."

A numerous throng of persons had assembled, and More was about to address them, when the Sheriff interrupted him, so that he contented himself by merely asking the people to pray for him, and to bear witness that he died in the faith of the holy Catholic Church, and was a faithful servant of God and the King.

And then he reverently knelt, and in a firm loud voice he said the *Miserere* psalm, and when he had finished it, he arose, and the executioner asking him forgiveness, said he, kissing him,

"Thou wilt do me this day the greatest benefit one mortal man can confer upon another. Pluck up thy spirit, man, and fear not to perform thy office, but my neck is very short, so take heed that thou strike not awry to save thy credit."

The executioner would then have covered his eyes, but he stopped him, saying, "That will I do for myself," and he bound over them a cloth he had brought with him for that purpose, and kneeling down, he laid his head on the block, and bade the man stay till he had removed his beard, saying, "That at least hath done no treason."

One moment more, and amid the hush of a great

* More.

multitude, in the brightness of the early summer morning, one blow of the axe severed the martyr's head from his body, and his soul was carried up by angels to the foot-stool of the God whom he had ever faithfully served.

So passed he out of this world on the very day which he had himself so much desired.

And the head of this English Cicero was at once placed on London Bridge, as the head of a traitor.

His conduct on the scaffold has been censured as being too light for the occasion, but it was so natural to him, and the consciousness of his own integrity gave him such inward pleasure, that what was a mournful solemnity to the spectators was to him a subject of joy.*

Thus ended the life of the great Sir Thomas More, who for his judgment, humanity, devotion, sweetness of temper, and contempt of the world, was the ornament of his own, and may be an example to every age.†

* Campbell.
† Jortin.

CHAPTER XXIII.

MARGARET ROPER.

THE headless corpse lay in the Chapel on the Tower Green, awaiting the last sad duties, which were to be performed by the hands of Margaret. Vain would be the endeavour to express her sensations as she gazed on the mutilated and ghastly remains of one whom she had so dearly loved and reverenced.

During the confinement of More in the Tower, he had no means of support save such as were raised by his daughter from the charity of friends, or contributed from her own purse. When about to bury the body of her father, says the old biographer, she found she had forgotten to bring a sheet to wrap it in, and there was not a penny left amongst them, she having given the last as a dole to the poor. Her maid, Mrs. Harris, offered to try and get her out of her trouble, so going to the first draper's shop she bargained as to the price of some linen, and then taking her purse from her pocket she made as if she were going to look for the money before asking if they would give her credit, when to her amazement she found it contained the exact sum she had to pay, though she knew previously she had not one penny about her. This anecdote has been omitted in the modern accounts of More, possibly as savouring too much of the marvellous; those who read it will draw their own conclusions, we do not choose to let the narration pass unnoticed.

But great was the sorrow of Margaret and her family, while that venerated head remained on the bridge, and when the rumour reached the ears of William Roper that it was to be cast into the Thames, Margaret at once determined, at all hazards, to possess herself of it. *How* she got it in her keeping we know not, most probably she bribed heavily the person whose duty it was to remove the heads of those who had suffered for treason, when they had been exposed a sufficient time, and room was required for others. Any way, she possessed herself of the precious relic, and caused a leaden box to be made in which she placed the head of her martyred father, and left orders that after her own death it should be buried in her tomb.

Moreover, this celebrated woman did not rest till she had procured the remains of Fisher, Bishop of Rochester, they had been cast by soldiers into a grave in All Hallows Church-yard, Barking, but she is said to have obtained them and laid them beside those of her father in the Tower Church of S. Peter ad Vincula.

" A story current in the family was, that one day as one of his daughters was passing under London bridge, looking on her father's head, sayd she, that head has layde many a time in my lappe, would to God, would to God, it would fall into my arms as I passe under."

She was then summoned before the council, and this heroic and beautiful woman bravely maintained herself before the assembled lords. " You keep your father's head, esteeming it as a relic, Mistress Roper," said the Chancellor. " Moreover, you contemplate publishing his works ; remember, fair Mistress, he suffered death as a traitor." "I procured my father's head, my Lord, lest it should become food for fishes," retorted brave Margaret, and I have buried it where I thought it most fit; methinks, that I could scarce do less; it listeth me not, my Lords, to say *how* I obtained it. I glory in the deed, and if for such ye deem me worthy of punishment, I am in your hands; do with me as it pleaseth you. Moreover, I shall publish his works when opportunity shall serve." Margaret was then dismissed, while the Lords conferred together as to how they should punish her brave speech. Then they resolved to imprison this admirable woman; they dared not, however, detain her long, for the indignation of the people was excessive, and, after a short imprisonment, she was sent home to her husband.

. " Of all his children Margaret resembled her father most closely, as well in wit, wisdom, and learning, as also in pleasant and cheerful conversation. She was to her servants a mild and gentle Mistress, and to her brother and sisters most amiable and loving, to her friends very good, stedfast, and affectionate, and (a rare thing in woman) so grave and prudent, that when men of good calling were wont in difficult matters to counsel and deliberate with her, they found her advice so good, and profitable, that they doubted ever to have seen the like in woman; these were men of virtue, learning, and experience, who were held in great account."

" To her children she was doubly a mother, for, not content with bringing them into the world, she instructed them herself in virtue and learning. Once, when Roper had been imprisoned in the Tower, having incurred the King's displeasure, leave was given by the King to search the house, when suddenly coming on Margaret, his officer found her not bewailing and lamenting, but busily employed teaching her children, and beholding her evince no surprise, and admiring the wisdom and calmness of her speech, such as they little looked for, they were filled with astonishment, and left her full of admiration, nor ever afterwards could they speak too highly of her, as I myself heard from one of them. But above all things else, she was to her father, and her husband, such a daughter and such a wife as I suppose it would be hard to match in all England."

" But her filial love was notable not only in her conduct all his precious life, but after his trouble and imprisonment, as well for the pains she took to procure some relief and comfort for her father as for her wise and godly conversation; and for many other considerations she was his chief, and almost his only earthly comfort, to whom he at that time wrote amongst others, one letter answering two of hers, in which he says " that a peck of coals, if he had them, for he had no pens to write with, would not suffice to do her justice."

"On the other hand she was so good, and meek, and gentle a wife, that her husband esteemed himself a most happy man in the possession of such a treasure."

"A treasure I may well saie, for such a wife incomparably exceedeth (as Solomon saith) all worldly treasure, and he was on his parte so good, so sweet, so sober, so modest, so loving a husband, that as Erasmus long agoe writeth, if he had not been her husband he might have been her owne Germaine brother."

" And, Mr. Roper had her in such great estimation, or rather admiration, that he thought, and he hath also said, that she was more worthy, for her excellent qualities, to have binne a Prince's wife."

" And the said Erasmus for her exquisite learning, wisdom,

and virtue, made such an account of her, that he called
her the flower of all the learned matrones of England,
to whom as yet being very younge, but yet adorned with
a child, he dedicated his Commentaries made upon certain
Hymnes of Prudentius.   And so said he the truth, she was
a Sappho—Aspasia—Hypathia—Damiani—Cornelia."

"But why speak I of these, though learned, yet infidels.
Nay, rather, she was of Christian, Fabiola and Marcella,
Paula and Eustochium."

We will now, gentle reader, give thee a little taste of her
learning and of her pregnant wit.   St. Cyprian's works had
been in those days many times printed, and yet, after so
oft printing, there remained, among other defects and faults,
one notable one among all their printing uncorrected and
unreformed.   The words are these :—'*Absit enim ab
Ecclesiâ Romanâ rigorem suum tam prophanâ facilitate
dimittere et nisi vos servitatis eversâ fidei majestate dissolvere*,'*
which place, when Mistress Margaret had read without
the help of an ensample, or any other instruction, these
words (nisi vos), should be, quoth she, "I trow," wherein
she said a very truth, " nervos."†

* Far be it indeed from the Church of Rome to throw aside her
rigour with such profane facility, and to loosen the reins of subjection
by the majesty of the faith being overwhelmed.

† Harleian MSS.

CHAPTER XXIV.

THE KING.

THE account of Sir Thomas More's execution was brought to the King while he was playing at tables with Anne ; he cast his eyes reproachfully upon her, and said, "Thou art the cause of this man's death." Then rising up he left his unfinished game and shut himself up in his chamber in great perturbation of spirit.

We have omitted to mention a prophetic remark once made by More to Margaret, who clearly foresaw how the passion of Henry for his new Queen would end, and that at no distant date, said the captive,

"How goeth the outer world Margaret, and what news is there of the new Queen ?"

" In faith, father, never was it merrier," said she, "there is nothing at Court but sporting and dancing."

"Alas, Megg, is it even so, it pitieth me to think unto what extreme misery that poor soul will come, with these dances of hers. She will spurn off our heads like footballs, but it will not be long before her own head will dance the same dance as ours."

How very soon the event thus prophesied befel the unfortunate Queen Anne the reader well knows.

There can be no doubt that the brave old Chancellor's life was sacrificed to the licentious passion of Henry for Anne Boleyn.

For the time, hardened as was Henry's conscience, it was probably stung with remorse, but what we are about to say, will show that it could not have lasted long, else, he could not have borne that the head of his once honoured friend should remain upon the bridge as he passed it each day on his way from Whitehall to Greenwich.

Europe heard the tidings of More's execution with feelings of horror. The Emperor Charles the Fifth was one of the first to exhibit a burst of generous feeling, for when the intelligence came to him of the death of Sir Thomas he at once sent for Sir Thomas Elliot, the Ambassador. "We understand," said he, "that the King, your master, hath put his faithful servant and grave, wise, counsellor Sir Thomas More, to death." Sir Thomas Elliot affected ignorance, and replied that he had heard nothing of it. "Well," said the Emperor, "it is too true." And this we will say, that if *we* had been master of such a servant, of whose doings ourselves have had these many years no small experience, we would rather have lost the best city of our dominions than have lost such a worthy Chancellor."

The King visited with his vengeance nearly every one of More's family. All their land was taken away immediately after his death, for in spite of a conveyance, by which the property of More was settled on his son long before his committal to the Tower, even before any statute had been made about the Oath of Supremacy, an act of Parliament was passed, by which, against all right or justice, everything was forfeited to the Crown.

His son John was also committed to the Tower, and for bravely refusing to take the oath, was condemned to death; but after long imprisonment he was finally released, for, by the execution of the sentence, nothing was to be gained.

The story goes that poor John was not very clever, so that in his childhood Sir Thomas should once say, "Wife, you prayed a long while for a boy, now you have a son who will be a boy as long as he lives." John More, however, showed, when the hour of trial came, that he was not deficient in spirit and endurance.

Lady More was granted a pension of twenty pounds a year, out of the property, but she was stripped of all her goods, and turned out of her house at Chelsea.

By a conveyance made two days before the one that carried More's property to his son, the land which More allotted to Margaret and her husband, in lieu of a marriage portion, they were able to keep.

Of William Roper and the rest of this great man's family, we would say a few words. As the prayers and tears of Monica, his mother, won back to the Church the great S. Austin, so did the prayers of good Sir Thomas More, and the tears of Margaret, win back Roper, her husband. He became the helper and friend of all who suffered for their faith, especially relieving such as were imprisoned for it.

"Thus for relieving and aiding by his alms a learned man, one Master Birkenshaw, he suffered great trouble and imprisonment in the Tower. But his great alms did not stand within this list only, it reached far beyond to *all* poor and needy persons that (as I trow) in this kind, no one man of his degree and calling in all England was comparable unto him.

"So that a man may not without cause accommodate that

part of Holy Scripture unto him,—*He hath distributed, he hath given to the poor, his justice remaineth for ever and ever;* for with his great alms found upon the poor so liberally, I doubt nothing but, in the heavenly harvest, he shall plentifully reap mercy and grace, and the inestimable reward of eternal bliss.

" We will now speak of others that were of the family of this worthy man, Sir Thomas More. Among these were Dr. Clement, also his wife, a woman furnished with much virtue and wisdom, and with the knowledge of the Latin and Greek tongues, yea, and physic too, above many that seemed good and clever physicians, who were brought up in his house.

This Clement was taken by Sir Thomas More from Paul's School, in London. He proved a very excellent good Physician, and is singularly seen in the Greek tongue. And yet his virtue surmounteth his learning, and hath answered according to the expectation of Sir Thomas More, who writeth thus of him, being in an epistle to Erasmus :—

" My wife salutes thee and also Clement, who has also made such progress in Latin and Greek that I entertain great hopes of him that at some future day he will be an ornament to his country and to literature."*

Mistress Clement,† *neé* Giggs, after the death of Sir Thomas, devoted herself heart and soul to the succour of the Charter House monks and others, whom conscience

* Harleian MSS.

† For a beautiful and interesting account of Margaret Clement and her Family, see " Troubles of our Catholic Forefathers," by Rev. J. Morris, S.J.

forbade to take the oath, and were notable for their own constancy and banished themselves on account of the sufferings with which Catholics were visited, and retired to Belgium, in the reign of Edward the Sixth.

Peerless Margaret, the ornament of Britain, as Erasmus styled her, survived her father but nine years. She spent her time between the education of her children and works of piety, residing alternately at her husband's seat of Well Hall, Eltham, and at the Old Place House, St. Dunstan's Place, Canterbury. On each recurring anniversary of her father's death, it was kept by her in the strictest seclusion, fasting, and prayer. Margaret was the mother of two sons and three daughters. Her husband survived her 33 years. He succeeded his father in his office at Prothonotary of the King's Bench; the duties of which he discharged for 44 years, and then left it to his son Thomas. He died in 1577, aged 82.

Of Margaret's sisters, Elizabeth and Cicely, we find them only mentioned by name in the various lives of the great Chancellor, so we have not the slightest record of them after his execution.

"A tradition has been preserved in the Roper family," says Burke, in his Peerage, " that Queen Elizabeth offered a ducal coronet to Margaret Roper, but the high-minded daughter of Sir Thomas More refused the proffered honour, as being a compromise for what she considered the judicial murder of her father." Horace Walpole, in his correspondence, thus alludes to the subject. " It was like proposing to Margaret Roper to become a duchess in the court that cut off her father's head, and imagining it would please her."

It is astonishing how such a tradition can have been handed down, and gravely detailed to us by Burke. Margaret survived her father only nine years, and Elizabeth did not ascend the throne till 1558 ; Sir Thomas having been executed twenty-three years previous. If there be the slightest foundation for such a story, it must have been an offer made by Mary Tudor to Mistress Basset, one of Margaret's daughters, who was one of her ladies, and of whom she was extremely fond. Moreover, Henry VIII. gave much of the possessions of the unfortunate family of Sir Thomas More for the use of the then child Princess Elizabeth, none of which the lion-hearted Queen restored when she reached womanhood, as far as we have been able to see. Mr. Roper Curzon favoured us with a sight of his emblazoned pedigree, and there was the crest of Roper, a lion, rampant, Sa., holding between its paws a ducal coronet; but if there be any truth in the tradition it can only be in the way we have surmised.

CHAPTER XXV.

How Sir Thomas More was Mourned.

WE have already said that that the first outcry of generous indignation at the legalised murder of More proceeded from Charles the Fifth, and it was the key-note to a trumpet burst of indignant amazement, which resounded throughout all Europe, when the news reached the ears of the people.

Cardinal Pole, writing of him, says, " I loved him dearly, and yet I had not so many reasons to love him as others have, yet God is my witness, that my tears often blot out my letters, and hinder me from writing. Thou hast lost, O England, thy father, thine ornament, thy defence ; for he left his very life for thy sake, lest he should betray thy salvation. Thou hast slain the best Englishman living."

Erasmus writes, " Every man bewaileth the death of Thomas More, even they who are not of his faith, so great was his affability and courtesy to all mankind ; so excellent his nature. Whom did he ever send away from him without gifts, or to whom did he not seek to do a good turn? Many shew favour to their own countrymen only, but More's bounty to all has so engraven him in the hearts of men, that all lament his death as though he were their father or their brother. I have beheld tears flow for him from eyes that have *never* seen his face, or received any benefit from him, yea, while I write these lines, tears gush from mine

THE TOMB of SIR THOMAS MORE in CHELSEA CHURCH.

own eyes, whether I will or no. How many hearts hath that axe wounded which destroyed the life of Thomas More."

Jovius, bishop of Niceria, speaks of him as a "man *saintly in all virtues.*"

No letters passed between More and Erasmus for some time before the death of the former, who. knowing well, that he could write nothing but that which would afflict his friend, doubtless preferred rather to be silent.

In England, from motives of fear, the tidings of his death had indeed been received with silent sorrow, for it spread terror throughout the nation.

Erasmus, writing to his friend Latomus, says, "The English are living, at this time, under such a system of terror, that they dare not write to foreigners, nor receive letters from them."

The King of France spoke of these executions with great severity to the Ambassador, and advised that Henry should banish such offenders, rather than put them to death.

Henry was highly displeased. He replied, " That they had suffered by due course of law, and were well worthy, if they had a thousand lives, to have suffered ten times a more terrible death and execution than any of them did suffer."*

The names of Fisher and More had long been familiar to the learned, and no terms were thought too severe to brand the cruelty of the tyrant by whom they had been sacrificed.

Monsieur de St. Evremond is very particular in setting forth the courage and constancy of Petronius Arbiter, during his last moments, and thinks he discovers in them a

* Burnet.

greater firmness of mind and resolution than in the death of Seneca, Cato, or even Socrates.

Mr. Addison has observed upon this subject, "that if he was so much pleased with gaiety and humour in a dying man, he might have found a much nobler instance of it in Sir Thomas More, who died upon a point of religion, and is respected as a martyr by that side for which he suffered. The innocent mirth, so conspicuous in his lifetime, did not forsake him at the last. His death was of a piece with his life—there was nothing in it forced or affected. He did not look upon the severing of his head from his body as a circumstance which ought to produce any change in the disposition of his mind; and as he died in a firm and settled hope of immortality, he thought any unusual degree of sorrow or concern improper."*

"His character, both in public and private life, comes as near perfection as our nature will permit," writes Lord Campbell. "No good Catholic could declare that the King's first marriage had been absolutely void from the beginning. . . . . I own I feel little respect for those by whose instrumentality the Reformation was brought about, and, with all my Protestant zeal, I must feel a greater reverence for Sir Thomas More than for Cranmer or Cromwell."

It has remained for Lord Herbert and Mr. Froude alone to deteriorate from the character of this great man.

Sir Thomas More and the venerable John Fisher were the first to seal with their blood their adherence to the ancient faith, their loyal devotion to the Holy See. They were foremost in the rank of those noble souls who,

---

* Jortin's Erasmus.

encouraged by their example, laid down their lives in the same cause, and amongst them we must not forget to name the parish · priest of Chelsea, Dr. Larke, who suffered martyrdom shortly after Sir Thomas More.

More than three centuries of penal persecution were the small number of Catholics, who stood firm to the faith of their fathers, fated to undergo. Now we behold the Church, in these our happier times, rising like a Phœnix from its ashes, and not in vain has the blood of the English martyrs been shed, not in vain did they die in defence of the faith of their fathers, for truly the blood of the martyrs is the seed of the Church.

Inflexible, as is the faith for which he so nobly died, the character of Sir Thomas More is marked throughout by a firm and earnest straightforwardness of purpose. One and all alike, even those whose religious opinions were deeply imbued by the new teaching, bore unfaltering testimony to his sincerity.

Would that our humble pen could pourtray his character in the glowing terms it so well deserves; we are fain to say we can in no ways do it justice by any words of ours.

Sir Thomas More was an accomplished gentleman, a profound scholar, in the fullest acceptation of the term. He was an eloquent orator, a clever statesman, an equitable judge, and yet, it is amid the quiet scenes of his Chelsea home that we love best to contemplate his character. His playful, almost childlike simplicity, his tenderness as a father, his compassion to his servants, his earnest love of God and His Church, are strikingly pourtrayed in each and every action of his daily life.

Sir Thomas More lived the life of a saint, and he died the death of a martyr.

"The remembrance of him shall never be lost, and his name shall be in request from generation to generation.

"The nations shall proclaim his wisdom, and the church shall publish his praise."

CHAPTER XXVI.

CHELSEA, OR, *In Memoriam.*

AGAINST the south wall of the chancel in the old Parish Church at Chelsea, in which Sir Thomas More was wont daily to assist at Mass, is the monument erected by himself in the year 1532. The tablet on which the inscription is engraved is under a Tudor arch, the cornice of which is ornamented with foliage, and in the centre of it is his crest, viz., a Moor's head. The spandrils of the arch are ornamented with branches of the vine, and in the midst are his arms and those of his first wife, and on each side are the arms of himself and his two wives.

It may be observed that Sir Thomas More's tomb stands in the Rector's chancel, on the south side, near the communion table, once the altar; and, since he had a chancel of his own why did he not erect his monument there? I answer that Sir Thomas often officiated (served?)* at the altar, his intimate friend and parish priest, Dr. Larke, who suffered soon after him in the supremacy matter, and therefore it may be supposed he desired to lay his remains as near the altar as could conveniently be, and that was within the rails where he used to attend Mass.

* The above is evidently a mistake of the Protestant author. I quote from "Faulkner's History of Chelsea." It was the custom of Sir Thomas More to *serve* the Mass of his friend, Dr. Larke, in the Parish Church, at Chelsea. The word *officiate* can only be applied to the priest.

The following is the translation of the epitaph written by Sir Thomas himself, and engraven on his monument :—

"Thomas More, a Londoner born, of no noble family but of an honest stock, was yet well brought up in learning, who, after he had for some years, while still young, pleaded in the Courts, and acted as judge in the Sheriff's Court in the city, was summoned to Court by the invincible King Henry the Eighth, who alone, of all kings, worthily deserveth to be styled Defender of the Faith, which honour he merited by his sword and his pen ; he was chosen one of the Council, made Knight, and at first appointed Vice-Treasurer, after that Chancellor of the Duchy of Lancaster, and last of all, with great favor of his Prince, Lord Chancellor of England.   But in the meantime he was chosen Speaker of the Parliament, besides being in divers times and places the King's Ambassador, last of all at Cambray, being joined with Cuthbert Tunstal, chief of that Embassy, then Bishop of London, and awhile after Bishop of Durham, who so excelleth in wit, learning, and virtue, that the whole world hath none more learned, wise, and better; he both joyfully saw, and was present when the leagues between the chief princes of Christendom were renewed again, and peace so desired restored to Christendom; which peace may God confirm and make lasting.

"While he was thus employed in a course of honourable duties, so that neither his gracious prince could disapprove his doings, nor was he odious to the nobility nor unpleasant to the people, but yet he was to thieves, murderers, and ————, troublesome.

"At length, Sir John More, his father, knight, and chosen by the Prince to be one of the Justices of the King's

Bench, a man courteous, gentle, blameless, mild, merciful, just, and upright, in years aged, but in body hale and active above his years, having his life prolonged, and now seeing his son Chancellor of England, thinking himself now to have lived long enough on earth, gladly departed to his God. The son, after his death (to whom compared when alive he was called the young man, and seemed so to himself), missing his departed father, seeing four children of his own, and of their offspring eleven, began in his own conceit to wax old.

"And this opinion of his was increased by a certain infirmity of his chest, and a bad state of health succeeding, and he, therefore, sated with mortal affairs, and weary of worldly business, giving up his promotions, obtained by the incomparable goodness of his gracious Prince, a thing which from a child he had always desired, that in his latter days he might be at liberty, so that little by little withdrawing himself from the cares and business of this life, he might constantly remember the immortality of the life to come. And he hath caused this tomb to be made for himself, having brought hither the remains of his first wife, that it might every day admonish him of death that hourly creepeth on him. Good reader, I beseech thee, that thy pious prayers may attend him while living and follow him when dead, that this tomb may not have been made in vain, and that he may not fear the approach of death, but that he may willingly for Christ's sake, undergo it, that death to him may not be altogether death, but the gate of everlasting life.

"Here lieth Jane, the well-beloved wife of Sir Thomas More, who hath appointed this tomb for Alice, my wife, and for me also, the one being coupled with me in matrimony in my youth, brought me forth three daughters and one son; the other hath been so good to my children (which is a rare praise with step-mothers) as scarce any could be better to her own.

"The one did so live with me, and the other now so liveth, that it is doubtful whether this or the other were' dearer unto me. Oh, how well could we three have lived together in matrimony, if fortune and religion would have suffered it, but I beseech our Lord that this tomb and heaven may unite us together. So death shall give us that which life denied us."

The blank space in the epitaph after the word murderers [——] is understood by some to have been intended to be filled up with the word *heretics*. It is commonly represented as having been really engraved and afterwards *effaced*, but the surface of the marble is quite smooth and shows no marks of erasure.

That he was the sworn foe to heresy no one in his senses would attempt to deny, but the pen was his only weapon, or how was it that while he was Chancellor, Erasmus writes, no one was executed for heresy. This is said not to be strictly correct, but it is quite certain More did his best to soften the severity of the laws, and that if any suffered the capital punishment ordered by them the number of such was very small.

He wrote this epitaph soon after his retirement from public life, and chiefly that the report circulated by his enemies, that he had been *compelled* to retire, might by this means be publicly refuted.

"His mansion was granted to Sir William Paulet, being

taken from Lady More after the execution of Sir Thomas.
It stood at the north end of Beaufort Row, and fragments
of the wall, doors, and windows were, when Faulkner wrote
in 1829, still to be seen adjoining the burying ground
belonging to the Moravian Society. The King's Road
divided the Park from the Gardens. This Park seenis to
have belonged to More's house, as well as a large extent
of pleasure ground, and turning towards the river, ran a
little way down the west side of them.

" Till within some forty years the ground remained in a
state that might have enabled one to ascertain the exact
site of the house, but various buildings have since shut it
out from search, and nought remains but the name of
Beaufort Row, to tell how it was once honoured."*

* Faulkner's History of Chelsea.

CHAPTER XXVII.

CONCLUSION.

THIS volume would indeed be incomplete without an account of the works of the great man whose life we have here presented to the reader.

His first literary essay is supposed to have been the fragment which goes under his name, as " The History of Edward 5th and Richard 3rd," though some have ascribed it to Cardinal Morton, who probably furnished the materials for it to his precocious page, having been intimately mixed up with the transactions which it narrates. It has the merit of being the earliest historical composition in the English language ; and, with all its defects, a long while elapsed before there was much improvement upon it, this being a department of literature in which England did not at that time excel.

But the composition to which he attached no importance, which as a *jeu d'esprit* occupied a few of his idle hours when he retired from the bar, and before he was deeply immersed in the business of office, and which he was with great difficulty prevailed upon to publish, would of itself have made his name immortal. Since the time of Plato, there had been no composition given to the world, which, for imagination, for philosophical discrimination, for a familiarity with the principles of government, for a knowledge of the springs of human action, for a keen observation of men and manners, and for facility of expression, could be compared to the " Utopia."   Although the word invented by More has been introduced into the language, to describe what is supposed to be impracticable and visionary,—the work (with some extravagance and absurdities, introduced perhaps with the covert object of softening the offence which might have been given by his satire upon the abuses of his age and country) abounds with lessons of practical wisdom.*

Of his Latin works may be named his Epigrams, partly translated from the Greek, and in part his own composition. His Dialogues were written when he was Chancellor of the Duchy of Lancaster, and whilst a prisoner in the Tower; with other religious treatises, he composed his Answer to John Frith, and his Treatise on the Passion of Our Lord. That he was no poor poet may be gathered from the following elegy on Elizabeth of York :—

> " Yet was I lately promised otherwise,
> This year to live in weal and in delight,
> Lo! to what cometh all thy blandishing promise,
> O false astrology and divinitrie,
> Of God's secrets vaunting thyself so wise ;
> How true for this year is thy prophecy?
> The year yet lasteth, and lo ! here I lie.
>
> Adieu ! mine own dear spouse, my worthy lord,
> The faithful love that did us both combine
> In marriage and peaceable concord,
> Into your hands do I clean resign
> To bestowal on your children and mine,
> Erst were ye father, now must ye supply
> The mother's part likewise, for here I lie.

* Lord Campbell.

Where are our castles now? where are our towers?,
Goodly Richmond, soon art thou gone from me ;
At Westminster, that costly work of yours,*
Mine own dear lord, now shall I never see.
Almighty God ! vouchsafe to grant that ye,
For you and children well may edify,
My palace builded is, for lo ! now here I lie.

Farewell, my daughter, Lady Margarite,†
God wot full oft it grieved hath my mind,
That ye should go where we might seldom meet ;
Now I am gone and have left you behind,
O, mortal folk, but we be very blind,
What we least fear full oft it is most nigh,
From you depart I first, for lo ! now here I lie.

Farewell, madame, my lord's most worthy mother,
Comfort your son and be you of good cheer,
Take all at worth, for it will be no other,
Farewell, my daughter Katherine,‡ late the *phere,*
Unto Prince Arthur, late my child so dear,
It booteth not for me to wail and cry,
Pray for my soul, for lo ! now here I lie.

Adieu, Lord Henry,§ loving son, adieu,
One word, increase your honour and estate.
Adieu, my daughter Mary,¶ bright of hue,
God make you virtuous, wise, and fortunate.
Adieu, sweetheart, my little daughter Kate,
Thou shalt, sweet babe, such is thy destiny,
Thy mother never know, for lo ! now here I lie.

Lady Cicely, Lady Anne, and Lady Katherine,
Farewell, my well beloved sisters three ;
Oh ! Lady Bridget,‖ other sister mine,
Lo, here's the end of worldly vanity ;
Now are you well who earthly folly flee,
And heavenly things do praise and magnify,
Farewell, and pray for me, for lo ! now here I lie.

---

* Henry Seventh's Chapel.   † Margaret, Countess of Richmond.
‡ Katherine of Arragon.   § Afterwards Henry VIII.
¶ Princess Mary, her second daughter.
‖ The nun-Princess, Elizabeth's sister.

<blockquote>
Adieu, my lords, adieu, my ladies all !
Adieu, my faithful servants every one !
Adieu, my commons, whom I never shall
See in this world, wherefore to Thee alone,
Immortal God, verily Three in One,
I me commend.   Thy infinite mercy
Show to thy servant, for lo ! now here I lie.
</blockquote>

In conclusion, we must not omit to say that John More's only son married Anne, daughter and heiress of Edward Cresacre, of Barnborough, in Yorkshire.   His grandson, Cresacre More, has been proved by Mr. Hunter's investigations to be the author of the life of his celebrated ancestor, which had been previously attributed to his brother Thomas. The last descendant of the Chancellor in the male line was a Jesuit.   He died at Bath, as recently as the year 1795.

FINIS.